The Bells of Moses Henry

Lavila

The Bells of Moses Henry

a novel by
Peter Skinner

with love,

BIRCH
BROOK
PRESS

First edition
Library of Congress Control Number: 2008927005
ISBN: 9780978997441 (hardcover)
*   9780978997458 (paperback)*

Cover photo by Rufus W. Holsinger (1866-1930), Copyright © 1997, University of Virginia, Courtesy of Special Collections, University of Virginia Library

Author's photo by Mary Motley Kalergis

Printed and published in the United States

>*Birch Brook Press*
>*PO Box 81*
>*Delhi, NY 13753*
>
>*birchbrook@copper.net*
>*(607) 746-7453*

To view a complete catalog of books and letterpress art published by Birch Brook Press, you are invited to visit:
www.birchbrookpress.info

for Saana, Kayla, Max, and Jay

CHAPTER ONE

The road was caked with dust on warm midsummer days such as these. The boy walked head down, his bare feet eliciting low, fluffy clouds with each step. He paced himself, understanding that the journey was long, his crew cut already damp from the midday sun. He knew the weeks ahead would be hot.

He'd considered it all morning. It didn't bother him anymore, what people thought. There wasn't much to be done one way or the other. Except for the occasional shimmer from the sun hitting the eyelets of his fishing pole, or maybe the dust he was kicking up, he figured he could walk all day before they'd notice he was gone.

He'd had just enough time to grab his pole and run. The dust settled lightly in the distance just ahead of the last curve he had taken. He'd walked for hours. His jaw ached from where his father had hit him. His forearms smelled of bourbon and his belly growled with hunger.

As he walked, the wind circled high above, sending quiet shivers of warm air overhead. Maybe he'd catch a ride? Maybe he'd hide somewhere? Or call for Jesus? But he wasn't scared. It was more like he'd swallowed himself, himself and everything he'd ever known.

As the day progressed, trees appeared more frequently, providing undulating canopies of tepid shade. By early evening their trunks resembled the legs of colossal giants from fairy tales. At sunset the boy wandered up a steep logging road to a plateau. Lying against a large chestnut oak, he rested the bamboo rod across his chest. His feet were swollen from walking and the back of his neck burned with sun against the rough bark. Before closing his eyes, he looked east through a corridor of branches toward the lights of Charlottesville in the far distance.

"'Let your tender mercies come to me, that I may live . . .'" he recited to himself.

As his head dropped and sleep set in, the skies over Albemarle County, Virginia, turned mauve, casting a faint and ominous sheen upon the earth below.

He slept deeply throughout the night, as if he had let go of a great and horrible burden.

At sunrise, long, radiant shafts of light fanned out across the Shenandoah Valley before ascending majestically over the Blue Ridge Mountains directly behind him. As the forest awoke, he rolled to one side, still clutching the bamboo rod with both hands. Facedown on a pillow of moss, between the voluptuous roots of the oak, he did not hear the black bear that circled in the distance, nor recognize the haunting call of the whippoorwill, nor sense the palpable stillness of his heart.

When he opened his eyes the bear was standing over him. As it shifted its weight from side to side, the bear's eyes met his, and his heart pounded fiercely as he smelled its warm, noxious breath. A senate of ravens gathered in the far distance, their cries momentarily distracting the bear. Ferns rocked gently around them as the breeze swept down the mountain slope. The bear reconsidered the boy by sniffing his shoes. Cocking its head slightly to one side, it gazed coldly into the frightened boy's eyes, grunting softly, until the boy passed out.

CHAPTER TWO

Stick Watson rode the train every summer. After forty years it was in his bones. In August he'd slide down the darkened tracks of Richmond and wait patiently for the right one. He'd done the hot shots and dog locals from the Bay of Fundy to the Gulf of Mexico. He'd ridden the B&O until his balls were blue. He'd heard the roar of the Chesapeake, the Mikados, the Sharks, and seen the Hiawatha. But that was history. This was Tuesday and Stick had a rail to ride.

He hated getting old. He hated everything about it, every ache and memory too heavy to carry and every piss-poor imitation along the way. What sustained him was the sound of the empty car under his legs—with a door wide open and the world shooting by. What revived him was the spirit of the iron road, the noisy collaboration of steel and steam. Hopping a car at twenty miles an hour. The risk, the kitchen lights at night, and the endless darkness above.

As the train gathered speed, Buster Kitchen reached down between swigs and caught Stick by the wrist.

"Well, shit, Stick, I thought that was you."

With one foot on the edge and a strong pull from Buster, Stick's body lifted up into the empty freight car. "Goddammit!" Stick replied, smacking his knees against the dusty floor.

"You okay, Stick?"

"I'm good," he said, catching his breath and rubbing his right knee.

"I thought that was you," Buster repeated as he sat down against the wall and took a hard hit from his Kentucky bourbon. "Now there I go again," he said, offering the bottle to Stick. "Forgetting my manners, for heaven's sake! You old sonovabitch, Stick! You look pretty decent. Monty Harris saw you outside Tuscaloosa last spring. Said you been down to Mobile, or something like that. Said you been churchin'."

As he took the bottle, Stick rolled over to a seated position and surveyed the empty boxcar. Flashes of light whipped across the back walls as the train sped up. "Churchin'?" he asked, sounding pissed.

"What he said, Stick. Says you got religion."

Stick pressed the bottle up to his lips. He thought about Buster's question and sensed the weight of the bottle to determine how much to leave when he was done.

"Says your wife died."

Without drinking, Stick put the bottle down, leaving a quickly fading blue circle around the middle of his lips. Feeling the floor shift from side to side, he focused on circles of murky booze trembling inside the bottle. Noticing a slash mark halfway up the edge of the label, he remembered his wife's long, slender fingers. "Thanks for the hand, Buster," he replied, passing the bottle back.

The two men sat across from each other in silence. As they listened to the rails, the boxcar continued to hop from side to side. Today was different, Stick thought, looking out the open door to get his bearings. Like finding a word he'd never heard of in the dictionary he carried, or finding a train you'd never ridden—a train you'd heard about before, but had never been close enough to catch. As ditch banks of clay filled with an amber light, Stick touched the bell jar of ashes in his knapsack and imagined the presence of angels overhead, their long and opulent wings brushing past him to Appomattox, to Bedford, and further north towards the Peaks of Otter.

CHAPTER THREE

Drenched in sweat, the boy's legs began to twitch. He had no way of knowing if he was awake or dreaming, whether the bear was standing over him or had walked away.

"Boy?" his mother seemed to call from a great distance. "What you done, boy?" she asked. "What on earth you done?"

In his dreams, perched in the Lucky Bean tree, he could see them leaving church. Lefty Vest called it the Lucky Bean the day he won at craps, before Fayette Jones killed him in Lee Park on the Fourth of July, and before they said his Lucky Bean was a black gum. Thirty feet up, the boy could see from the Midway School on Vinegar Hill to the rooftop of Albemarle Power along the Rivanna and hear the wires in the wind whistle like a distant train between the three Charlottesville Ice Company stacks.

"Higher 'n cotton!" they'd shout from below the great tree. "King a the roost!"

On Main Street, ladies in hats strolled with boys in fancy wool pants, and with young girls wearing tiny white gloves. On Pantops there were rocketing balls from baseball games, the sullen Woolen Mills on East Market, lumber wagons, C&A Streetcars, and teeming crowds on the West Main Street bridge over the tracks of the Southern Railway. Charlottesville's world was too far away to be his. A world of moving air and clouds as soft as cotton, with sparrow hawks and fish crow, purple martins and scarlet tanagers, catbirds, chickadees, and ruby-throated hummingbirds. In The Bottom it was like you were deaf or missing an eye, or walked with a wooden leg.

In winter you could see a long way in the tree. In summer the world was fuzzy with leaves, and it was hot, but the heat was much worse in the house. In the family's shotgun shack next to Matt Abel's white clapboard on Garrett Street, it was so awfully hot, whichever way you cut it; things weren't right.

One night at dinner his mother was so drunk she'd had a hard time keeping her head from falling forward. His father had passed out an hour earlier on the bathroom floor. He'd been drunk since breakfast. When he passed out, the house was much quieter. His mother would light the candle and the beautiful lady on the glass would reach her arms out towards him. When his father passed out, the boy would place the candle on the kitchen table for his mother to light when she got home; he would listen for her footsteps from the house next door where she worked. Sometimes he would stare for hours at the linoleum floor until it became a marble sea of swirling pink veins, like lava, consuming everything that got too close.

When the boy awoke on the morning of August 11 one mile north of Angel Knob, the rancid smell of the bear was gone. The ferns had stopped moving and the crows had dispersed, leaving a distant sound of falling water. Clearing his eyes of sleep, he raised his head off the oak root and looked about in a dazed fashion. He measured the height of the sun as beams of sunlight bled across the Shenandoah Valley behind him towards the Appalachian Mountains beyond. Cool air passed across the back of his neck and stirred the canopy of trees overhead. Sitting up, surrounded by goat's beard and fairy candles, the boy figured that if this was the beginning of his new life, he'd better stand up and start walking.

CHAPTER FOUR

Moses Henry had rung the University of Virginia bell for as long as anyone could remember. From the Rotunda's musty South Portico, the dark-skinned Negro rang for peace, for war, for death, and from habit. He said ringing bells was "like fallin' off a log, or prayin'." He was as true to his bell as he was to his God. "Befo' the Surrender," he said, "ever'body knew what I was ringin' 'bout, 'cause back den, it meant somethin' for a man to ring a bell." People learned a lot from Moses Henry's bell. Like, "When it eases your mind to do a thing, it's right. And when it don't, you better slow down."

One June afternoon when the boy was away, Moses Henry had stopped under the Lucky Bean for lunch and read the sign.

Baseball Tonight — Colored Jefferson vs. T.S.T. — Horse Show Grounds

"I dun walked all mornin'," he told Ange Dye, dropping gently to the ground and offering him a handful of boiled peanuts. "I ring duh bell end a Rugby an' I be lookin' for a woman lives 'round here," he said softly. But by the time Ange could size him up a crowd had gathered.

"So, you the bell man, Mr. Henry?" Ange boasted, checking out the curious faces. "Heavens to Betsy, you famous 'round here, I bet, if you be ringin' dat bell long time."

"Name's Moses," the old man replied humbly. "Bin ringin' fifty-one years."

With an incredulous look, Big Lee Hutton stepped in closer.

"You kinda old an' puny to be ringin' a big bell like dat, mista."

Moses swung around into the sun from his seated position against the tree to see where the question was coming from and removed a tattered Panama hat. Cupping his battered hands over his head for protection from the glare, he searched for the man's voice. But the voice emanated from a closely packed group of men.

"Bell ringin' don' mount t' much. Dey go right on wit'out no bell jus' fine," he confessed, looking down and fumbling with his hat.

"You with the University?" someone asked.

"Yes, sir."

"Rotunda bell?"

"Be duh one, sir."

"How old are you, Moses?" Nellie Bishop asked, pushing through the gathering with her twins in each arm to get a better look.

"I be one hundred Fo'th July—day Mr. Jefferson die."

"Lordy!" a voice gasped from the back.

Moses looked around to get his bearings. There were too many people watching today. It was a long walk home. Next time he'd take the trolley.

"My momma belong to Mr. Jefferson. Married his body servant. She git my name from outta duh Book," Moses continued.

"You knew Thomas Jefferson?" Ange Dye joked, winking at Nellie Bishop.

"No sir, he be long gone." Moses rose shakily to his feet and placed the Panama hat back on his shiny head. "But," he announced, leaning back against the tree for balance, "I remember my momma and she was a good woman."

Straightening himself against the tree, he looked up at the faces, hoping that the boy might be among them. He felt a certain victory for having traveled so far. As he shuffled through the dirt to Garrett Street, he knew it would be two miles to his room. The small crowds watched silently as Moses Henry left The Bottom, knowing that they had witnessed a momentous event. It was as if they had looked time in the eye and recognized themselves.

CHAPTER FIVE

Sadie Graves tried to eat ice cream when all she really wanted was a drink. And, because doing what she wanted was what she was good at, she finally gave up altogether and went to the sink. He'd heard her fixing drinks in the middle of the day, and figured if she needed bourbon that bad, it must be good for her, like the apple juice from Buck Mountain when he was sick. He figured she'd eat when she wasn't so tired from working all night at Mr. Abel's place.

"Momma?" he inquired cautiously as she emptied the glass. "Momma?" he asked again, not sure if she was listening.

"Well, I'm here, boy, now ain't I?"

"Yes, ma'am. Well . . . " It wasn't as if he couldn't ask, but he was scared what she might do to him if he did. He'd started counting the money inside a box in the top drawer of her dresser one day when he knew she'd be gone, but he'd had to stop at nine hundred and thirty-seven dollars—mostly in fives and singles—when he'd heard her shoes on the front porch steps. His hands had shaken when he put the box back.

Refortified with liquor, his momma returned to her place at the end of the table and gave him a look. He knew that if he said it wrong, her eyes would freeze and her heart would stop.

"You know Mr. Matt long time, Momma?" he began in a tiny voice.

"Mr. Matt? Who you talkin' 'bout, boy? What you sayin'?"

"I mean . . . "

"Abel? Talkin' 'bout Mr. Matt Abel?" she sputtered. "Is dat . . . ?"

"Mr. Abel, Momma, I mean . . . " He chose his words with care. "What he do really? I mean, what he do when he ain't talkin' to me like he do?"

"What in the name of God you talkin' 'bout, boy?! I swear, talkin' to you gonna fry my brain if I listen long 'nough. Absolutely turn me inside out." Looking through the kitchen window, she took a long, distracted sip from her glass of bourbon.

The boy heard a bell.

"What you do for him, Momma?"

"You know what I do for Mr. Abel," she answered coldly, still looking out the window at nothing. "How many times I told you?"

"Yeah, I know, but Mr. Matt told me different. He don't say nothin' 'bout no books."

"Oh, he don't?!" she protested, pushing her chair back from the table and crossing her legs.

"No, ma'am," the boy confirmed.

"He don't say nothin' 'bout no books?!" his mother mimicked, looking directly at him.

"No, ma'am, he don't," the boy persisted. From over the hill at the top of Garrett Street, he heard the bell again. "I ask him sometimes when we talkin', you know, but he just kinda change the subject on me like he don't want to talk 'bout it."

"He don't wanna talk 'bout it?"

"No, ma'am."

"What that mean?"

"What you mean?"

"He don't wanna talk 'bout it? What you mean by that, boy?" His mother gave him a faraway look like she was gazing at a stranger from across a room. "Mr. Abel don't tell you what you wanna hear, but you keep askin'?"

"Ain't exactly like that, Momma," the boy answered cautiously.

"Ain't?" she burst back.

"No, ma'am."

"Well, then, ring-me-out-and-set-me-up-to-dry, Willie, 'cuz *I'm all yours, honey!"* she shouted, holding her arms straight up in the air.

The last bell looped through him like a ghost. He felt bad asking his momma all these questions, but all his life he figured she'd had secrets. He could see it in her eyes, when she combed her hair in the mirror. When she drank. He could tell by the way she watched the beautiful lady when they lit the candle. His momma had things inside her waiting to come out. Things she would tell him someday when he was big enough. Things he just had to know so he wouldn't spend his whole life in an empty dark hole like The Bottom. On that particular Sunday, with his father passed out in the bathroom and the bell ringing up and down the streets of Charlottesville, young Willie Graves figured it was time to take a deep breath and pull the trigger.

"You a whore, Momma?"

The window was quieter, suddenly. When she heard the word, a wave of silence enveloped her, and she felt herself lapse into sadness. He looked small and unfamiliar to her.

"Momma?" Willie asked softly.

Emptying her whiskey glass, Sadie Graves left the kitchen. Halfway down the hallway she turned left into a long, windowless bathroom. Stepping over her husband's body, she opened the faucets and watched as a milky gray liquid gushed down into the porcelain whiteness below. Her body felt smooth and seductive. Passing the palms of her hands delicately over her breasts in front of the mirror, she closed her eyes and let her head fall back upon her shoulders as the water faded into pale pink and her silver slip fell silently to the floor.

Standing outside the bathroom doorway as his mother got into the tub, he felt a sudden sense of panic. The water stopped. The house became still. His head throbbed from the pounding of his heart and his mind raced uncontrollably through a series of hallucinations. Lipstick and railroad tracks, Moon Pies, and the smell of the ice stacks. Walking away, he heard the sound of water surging through the walls of the house. As his mother lowered her delicate brown shoulders further down into the tub, her dark, erect nipples rose up through the water into a dwindling expanse of misty blue air.

Willie Graves had been born in the whorehouse next door on a Full Beaver Moon in 1939 to a mulatto from Louisiana who loved sex and opium. As he grew, they watched his skin change color. In the summer of 1940 it turned pink. By autumn it was caramel. On Easter morning of the following year he was the color of Tuscarora sandstone.

"Look at that!" his father announced on his fifth birthday. "See what I'm sayin'? And his eyes! What kinda blue is that? Crazier than shit, this one—little fish-eyed fool!"

Willie was a patient boy. He could tow the line or cut bait. On a bad day, he imagined until his fantasies were real, and his fears were swallowed up by the machinations in his head. Sometimes, as he sat in the Lucky Bean, the sound of the bell rained down like molten lava onto the unsuspecting town below, melting streets into pools of glowing magma, until the final note. Sliding carefully down the trunk, tumbling through the blackened sky, he would follow the sound, racing home across the muddy creek, touching the doorknob for luck, before saving the world forever.

When Sadie woke, her knees were curled to one side and the walls of the tub were bathed in candlelight. Her neck was stiff and the water was cold. She listened for sounds. The evening had arrived and she would tell him. He would listen. And in his silence she would know that he could understand. And in the light of the Beautiful Lady they would feel their love for one another and they would watch the ceiling dance.

Willie was up the Lucky Bean, floating in a sea of cicadas and katydids. The night appeared muggy and moonless as his mother reached the tree. Cinching the belt more tightly around her robe, she sank down against the trunk and waited. Her body was empty and calm. Tiny crystal stars appeared between the branches as she looked up, as she considered the night world. In The Bottom, lights had scattered and houses looked like dark monuments, or lost cities without the prejudice of man. And in that darkness dreams could be revived, could be drunk, without repercussions, without memory, or regret.

"Remember when we saw the train that day ridin' back from Virginia Beach with Mr. Matt?" she said, looking up at her son. "You remember what you said to me? We rode along with it for a while and you was so excited. I never seen you so worked up about a thing. Eyes big like the moon! And you watched that ole train racin' by with them cars all full a stuff and you looked like you was 'bout to pop!" Pulling her knees up, she cupped her hands around her ankles and rocked gently. As Willie sighed, she felt his heart upon hers. "Remember what you said to me when it pulled away and we was so close you could just reach out and grab it? You remember, Willie?"

"No," he said in a small voice.

Sadie Graves smiled, remembering. "'*Is it goin' to our house, Momma?*' you shouted through the window. I never seen you so happy. Like you *knew* somethin', 'cuz you was so excited and when you get like that . . . " she paused.

"What, Momma?" he asked, suppressing a smile. "When I get like what?"

"Like you was! . . . Like it was suppose to be! . . . Like . . . " she stopped rocking.

"Like what, Momma?" he pleaded.

"Like . . . we . . . was loved!" Sadie closed her eyes and bowed her head. "Like we was finally loved."

He gripped the tree and cocked his head slightly to see if he could hear her crying. He wanted to climb down, but he was afraid. He didn't know what he was afraid of in particular, but thinking about it made him shiver. He longed to hear the bell. The sound made him feel good, like it was coming from a place that would take care of him, the kind of place where people stopped what they were doing and listened to what a boy had to say.

"Momma?" he called down.

"I'm here, Willie," she reassured him. With her palms she wiped the tears off her cheekbones.

"You a whore?"

Leaning back against the trunk, she remembered standing in the mudflats outside Pilottown where the Mississippi shook itself free and drifted away, leaving a thick line of gray-blue mud over her ankles. Her dirty white skirt rolled up over her knees, she'd scanned the vast expanse of silky-smooth distance and listened for her sisters. Where are they now? she wondered. Glistening wet faces with bellies full of cane. "Dead like all them days," she whispered to herself. "Come down. Come on down now!" she shouted, leaning forward.

He didn't like the sound of her voice. It reminded him of his father. It pulled the air out of him and made his head spin.

"Why, Momma?"

"Show you somethin'."

"Show me what?"

"You ain't gonna find out sittin' way up there now, are you?" She rose to her feet.

By the time Willie reached the ground his mother had returned to the house. He wasn't afraid to be standing alone under the tree in the dead of night. He figured he'd follow her to the moon if he had to, because he was old enough to know the truth. It would be like looking for bodies under the wheels of the Southern Railway wreck one rainy morning last December.

CHAPTER SIX

Along the Maury River five miles past Lexington, Stick Watson gave Buster Kitchen a nod and jumped. It was getting dark and Buster thought Stick was nuts.

"Where you gonna sleep?" he asked, slurring his words.

"What difference does it make?" Stick replied.

"You need somethin' before you go?"

"Got what I want."

"Well, okay then. Good to see you, Stick. And like I said, I'm sorry about Crystal-Ann. She was a looker."

As Buster's train disappeared, Stick dusted himself off and adjusted his knapsack. He wasn't far now. He heard the falls. It would be dark soon, but he'd know the way.

Before she died, Stick had sworn to his wife that he'd never ride another train. "It's in your blood, honey." She laughed. "And it beats walkin'."

One summer they'd ridden a boxcar to Milwaukee together, and she'd liked it. Five years later, she'd liked it even more. And then there were the covered bridges. She talked to them like they were people, like they had souls. When the Buffalo Creek Bridge came down in 1945, she felt a lump in her neck. When the Otter Creek Bridge washed out a year later, they removed both of her breasts. The week she died, the Little Reed Island Bridge of Carroll County burned in a fire and collapsed.

They would not speak of her death. They knew when they touched each other. They tasted it when they kissed. They talked about bridges instead, they talked about plants, they coined phrases, they got stoned and jumped trains.

As Stick steadied his pace up the shale path, he saw a faded shard of orange as he passed a group of wood lilies in the dwindling light. Was it a bluebeard? *Not in the summer, you stupid sonovabitch,* he remembered. Flat stones rattled under his boots and the sound of the falls intensified. He wasn't in a hurry. At the top of a hill, the breeze stirred as he lifted himself over a low stone wall onto Route 39. He recognized the cool air moving down from Little North Mountain. It cleared his lungs. When he saw the bridge, he could taste her. They'd slept beside it exactly two years earlier and stood in the falls, his wet flannel shirt over her knees as she took him in. Pressing her up against the smooth rocks, she'd arched her hips and the river had raced between them.

CHAPTER SEVEN

By August 13 the boy had walked along sixty-seven miles of abandoned road cuts from the Blue Ridge Mountain Railroad. As his swollen mind drifted in and out of consciousness, he gazed down upon himself as if, with each step, he might rise up gently into the cool air and never return. Or up the Lucky Bean into the arms of his mother. Without knowing it, Willie Graves had reached the end of one life and the beginning of another.

Tumbling down an embankment to Goshen Pass at dawn, his head hit a ledge of quartzite before he dropped into the churning water. As he fell, he opened his arms, hoping that she would forgive him for what he had done. Slicing through the spine of Little Mountain towards Lexington, a revolving sun flashed between the clouds like the flame of the beautiful lady. Rolling under a jackknifed sycamore at Swinging Bridge, he felt his body touch the silt of the shallows as his parched throat filled with water. Caressing his forehead gently, Sadie Graves blew the candle out. In the shimmering rapids of Devils Kitchen, Willie felt her tenderness touch down upon him, with a sudden and irrevocable sense of peace.

CHAPTER EIGHT

Stick was stiff as toast when he got off the ground. Hungover and half-asleep, he felt tiny black-and-white mollusks stuck to the side of his face. For a moment he'd forgotten that she was dead and looked for her in the falls. As water rolled over the edge, his head was numb and he was sore. He'd never gotten sore before. The river slid by as he swatted at the shells. The river didn't give a shit about him, he knew that much. His hands shook. He cleared his throat and tried to spit. No purpose could be found in this river or the next. Whichever train he jumped, it would be the same wherever he landed. Looking downriver, Stick understood that, except for Crystal-Ann, everything in his life had passed over him like piss on slate.

Rolling up his pants legs, he retrieved the glass jar from his knapsack before stumbling towards the river over patches of grass and finely powdered sand. Sliding his bare feet into the water, he moved carefully over a series of flat stones towards the falls. Infinitesimal clouds of river mist swirled around him as sunlight fell across his shoulders. Raising the jar, he felt a certain sense of resignation. He'd forgotten how she'd looked at him when she died, the way she'd gasped for air when there was no air to be found, like she was drowning in herself. Standing in the river with her ashes, he closed his eyes and listened to the falls.

When his eyes opened, the world was filled with color and as he lowered the jar, flashes of sparkling green light raced across the falls. Upriver the sun's reflection shimmered off the metal roof of the covered bridge, transforming the water below it into the color of malachite. Turning downriver, he cradled the jar in both hands and considered its contents. The dust that had been her bones came halfway up the sides. Not much to it, he thought. No bells, no fucking fanfare. No wedding ring. Unscrewing the lid, he thought about all that she had meant to him, to this day that he was spending alone, and about everything that they had touched together. Having killed a man, he understood the senselessness of death. But he'd never loved something so much, he thought, pouring her ashes into the river. Before this moment he'd never said goodbye.

While the ashes flowed from the jar, a car passed through the covered bridge. As Stick listened to the tires work their way over the wooden planks, the murky cloud slid reluctantly towards the falls. It didn't hurt half as much as he had thought it would. In fact, as her remains cleared the edge and dropped over, it made perfect sense to him suddenly. She didn't belong to him anymore. She never did.

Her ashes drifted away towards the James River, bending east at Glasgow past the crashing stairs of Balcony Falls before slicing seven hundred meters deep into the Blue Ridge Mountains. Free of the mountains at Big Island, she headed south to Lynchburg before turning with purpose northeast across the rolling plains of the Piedmont to the eastern side of Richmond. During the night a cavalcade of muskie, bass and catfish joined her at Hopewell, as the lazy Appomattox spilled alongside and the land went flat.

Off Old Point Comfort past the forbidding shadows of Fort Wool, Crystal-Ann Watson left Hampton Roads Harbor in the Chesapeake Bay for the Atlantic Ocean. It was a brilliant late summer day as the ebb tide took her out. And with a hint of grace, the buoy off Cape Henry began to sway.

Stick grabbed his bottle and took a long hit. His head felt good enough to drink again. If he stayed drunk for the rest of his life, it wouldn't matter one way or the other. Sitting on a large boulder in the sun, he saw her in the falls again and his dick swelled as he gazed across the river. She'd loved sex more than any woman he'd ever been with. She'd loved it like it was a part of her. You could see it in her eyes. They sparkled like stars when she came.

Because Crystal-Ann's body was ripe at an early age, she'd walked like a woman from the time she was thirteen. And because she walked like a woman, men watched her ass as if their souls were connected to it. For many men in Goochland County, Crystal-Ann's ass was the center of the universe. The first man she'd loved was twice her age. He'd sold pianos. They'd met on Tuesdays in his truck behind a Baptist church—until the night he stopped showing up. When she gave him a lock of her reddish-brown hair he said it smelled like South Dakota.

Crystal-Ann had loved a lot of men before she met Stick and he knew that from the start. But she'd never known the men she loved. She'd loved only their bodies. When she first met Stick, she knew. In the middle of their first kiss she stopped and looked at him without speaking. He could tell by the way her lips moved. He could tell by the way her head fell back and the tips of her hair danced off his thighs. It was like she understood him. It was like they'd been inside each other for a long time.

Stick looked across the water towards a hedge of arrowwood to get his bearings. It rocked from side to side as the water flew by. The river sounded like a smooth fast-moving train and it made him sleepy. As he slid from the rock, a slender brown skink shot out behind him over the boulder and down into a soggy blanket of alder leaves. Curling up alongside the river and closing his eyes, he rested his head against a smooth, flat stone as tiny sparks of rushing water splashed onto the side of his face.

As he fell asleep he levitated over a sea of wet, sunlit palm trees, and a devilish wind swirled around him as fluffy white eddies of stratocumulus clouds called out to him. He caught a glimpse of Crystal-Ann gazing down at him. Her eyes gleamed like distant lights. She wanted to tell him something. He reached up to her with one arm as if she might, as if she could touch him. He wanted to bury himself in her hair and feel her breath on him. Stretching his hand up between two clouds, her soft fingers slid gently into his, as they had done a million times before. But it was difficult to see her in the rushing wind. Or was it the water?

Suddenly, he felt something cold to one side of his body. The sound of the river was in his head now, but as the clouds moved it was difficult to find her in the sky, or feel her hand in his. When her face came into focus, he was staring into the open eyes of a lifeless young boy.

When Stick saw the puffy white hand in his and a stream of bubbling clear vomit cascading from the boy's mouth, he screamed, careening backwards out of the water. On a bank of wet clay his bare feet sent him crashing down upon the rocks, as his shrieks were carried quickly downriver. Righting himself, he stared at the body, his head pounding with fear, as his legs pumped against the water until he scattered stones in all directions, reaching a ledge of grass. Crawling backwards past the boulder, he landed safely in a thicket of buttonbush and steadied himself, tucking his knees up against his chest. The cloudless sky spun around as his heart pounded against his knees. It slowed a bit when he heard the river. His eyes on the boy, he thought about his dream and wondered how he had fallen in the river.

Dropping his knees, he sat up. The ground was covered with creamy round flowers. As he raked the earth with his wet hand, small blossoms stuck to his palm. *Buttonbush,* he thought to himself as he sniffed. *No smell. Too late in August.*

He squinted, studying the boy. The river had pushed him into an eddy at the base of a ledge, as the current gently worked his legs. Or was that him moving? Crystal-Ann would have stayed, he knew. She would have grabbed him by the belt and sunk her lips upon his and sucked death out of his little mouth. She would have warmed him with her breasts and cradled his lifeless arms in hers until he could breathe on his own, until he became a real boy again.

Time was running out. As Stick leapt to his feet, his forehead caught the broken branch of a redbud overhead. Wiping the sting away, he raced across the grass and dove over the bank into a shallow pool of water.

A cool breeze skipped across the falls. Standing slightly upriver, he could see that the boy's head rested on a stone above the water. Bubbles escaped periodically from the corners of his mouth, and it gave him the creeps.

Stepping closer, Stick saw a bare foot through the water. He'd heard cars on the bridge. He would call for help and leave the boy alone until someone came. Crouching down to get a better look, he noticed how small the boy was. His hands were open and his hair was short. His pants, ripped down the side, exposed a milky gray leg underwater. He was too dark to be white, white enough to be something else. Despite the vomit and bruises it was a pretty face, but it unsettled him. He heard Crystal-Ann's voice singing a song he couldn't make out. She'd liked singing to herself sometimes for no reason. Whatever it took to save the boy, he would do it. He'd taken a life once. Now it was time to give one back.

Stick grabbed the back of the boy's pants with one hand and pulled. As he dangled over the river, water poured off the boy's head and feet as they reached the bank. He was careful not to slip on the clay, or bang his head on the rocks. Reaching the grass, he lowered the boy to the ground and caught his breath, remembering he'd seen a man drown in Biloxi once, but had been too drunk to save him.

He slapped the boy's back and waited. It didn't matter one way or the other how it all worked out. What mattered was that he'd tried in good faith. If the boy was dead he was dead. He slapped him again.

"Wake up, boy!" he shouted. He slapped him twice as hard with the edge of his palm. "Come on, goddammit!" he shouted, straightening up.

Sunlight flashed off the metal roof of the covered bridge and blinded him momentarily. The wind had kicked up and it felt like rain. Downriver a cap cloud was forming over Sugarloaf Mountain. His eyes on it, he dropped to his knees.

"If you can read a cloud, you can read a human heart," Crystal-Ann had said from the edge of a flatcar.

"Bullshit!" he'd protested. "What the fuck does a cloud have to do with me?"

"Oxygen," she answered.

"That's it?"

"In the breath," she explained as they hit a tunnel.

When the train emerged east of Pocatello, his mouth was deep inside her. Pressing her bare feet against the bouncing floor, she dug her fingernails into his hair as the sun sliced through an open cloud.

Rolling the boy over on his back, Stick placed his palms over his small chest and pushed down, before releasing his weight slowly.

"Breathe, boy. Breathe for me," he coaxed as he pushed and released, his mind suddenly calm. He knew you could take a life a lot faster than you could save one.

When the boy's eyes opened, a rush of water and mucus exploded from his mouth, covering both of Stick's arms.

"Shit!" Stick bellowed triumphantly as the boy's stomach began to purge.

"Breathe, son! That's it! Breathe! Breathe! Breathe!" he repeated, not knowing what to do next.

When the boy's body began to shake, Stick stopped pumping and cleared his mouth of liquid using his fingers. His face to the river, the boy vomited repeatedly, until Stick was convinced he was turning inside out. As the vomit changed from clear to green to brown, the cap cloud over Sugarloaf Mountain lifted up and warm drops of rain began to fall.

When the heaving stopped, the boy opened his eyes and felt the rain. The first drop bounced off his cheek as he looked around. Another drop landed next to his ear and trickled across the bridge of his nose. Stick rolled him over on his back. There was color in his face now. He checked his exposed leg for cuts, but found none. The boy's eyes were glassy and opaque as he looked up at Stick. He wanted to speak, but as the drops of rain fell with greater urgency, he let go and closed his eyes, and the sound of the river and the sound of the rain became indistinguishable.

CHAPTER NINE

Descending the tree, Willie followed the path his mother had taken back to the house and found her at the sink fixing a drink. Closing the screen door carefully, he remembered the time the wooden door had smashed his finger as he'd dashed out after a white cat named Cotton. He'd shrieked and cried, and after he'd stopped, the cat was gone. From behind the door he listened to the frogs outside, while his mother sat at the kitchen table. The night was screaming hot and it was past his bedtime. She tapped the table with her hand as an invitation for him to join her, but he did not budge. She had that faraway look again and he figured he would stand there all night until she told him the truth. He figured even if he was only a kid, he had a right to know, and she would still be his momma.

Sadie Graves leaned back against her chair and felt the bourbon. It calmed her down, and helped her see straight. She knew he'd ask someday. She didn't think it would be tonight, but if it was going to be tonight, so be it. She took a long sip from her glass as she stared out the window. The night was hazy and gray. She didn't want to hurt him or make him hate her for what she was. Mostly, she wanted him to understand that it wasn't what a person did that mattered as much as how he did it.

"Hand me my Bible," she ordered, draining her glass of bourbon. The boy did not move. "Come on, Willie, don't be stubborn with me. I'll tell you what you want to know, but right now, I want the goddamn Psalm of David!" she demanded.

"'If it had not been the Lord, who was on our side?'" he asked softly.

"The very one, baby doll, the very one!" she marveled. "Good God, your head is like a camera, I swear. Like it just sucks it all up and puts it somewhere in case you need it later. Swear to God, Willie Graves," she said, looking him over, "you best be careful what you do in this life, boy, 'cuz someday somebody gonna come along and scoop you right up, 'cuz you got one big-ass brain inside that little ole head a yours."

The boy stood still while he listened. He could see the bourbon kicking in and it upset him. He'd stand there all night until she told him the truth. He'd find out once and for all if what Junko Pinkowski said was true.

"You a whore, Momma?" he asked.

"Hand me my Bible," she replied dismissively.

"You sleep with men for money, Momma?" he repeated defiantly.

"Psalm 124:18," she answered, slapping the table angrily with both hands. "'Then they had swallowed us up quick!'" she began to rant. "'When their wrath was kindled against us . . .'"

"Momma?" he interrupted warily.

"A song for the ascent of Jerusalem, Willie!" she pleaded, opening her arms up into the air. "Say it for me and then I'll tell you what you wanna hear. But say it to me, honey, please, 'cuz I just love it when you read the Bible to me like you do." She swung around in her chair and her eyes pierced his with something that he did not understand. He looked at her slumped forward in the chair. She was his momma, but some days she was just like somebody you'd see on the street, when you look out the window and you wonder who it is and where he's going. She looked old tonight, as if she'd given up.

"'If it had not been the Lord who was on our side . . .'" he recited finally,

". . . when men rose up against us . . ." he watched her as he spoke, ". . . then they had swallowed us up quick . . . '" When she started crying, he looked down at his feet. "'When their wrath was kindled against us.'"

As her eyes closed, her face throbbed and large tears dropped over the open robe onto her thighs.

"'Then the waters had overwhelmed us.'"

"Then," she murmured, raising her head.

"'Then the proud waters had gone over our soul,'" he spoke dispassionately.

"'Blessed,'" she whispered, gathering up her robe and readjusting the belt.

"'Blessed be the Lord, who hath not given us as a . . . '" he continued.

"'Prey to their teeth!'" she chimed in, her eyes popping open.

He wanted to stop, but she raised her index finger, gesturing for him to go on.

"'Our soul is escaped as a bird out of the snare of the fowler. The snare is broken, and we are escaped!'"

"Pleasant words," she said softly, without him. "Come on, baby, keep going . . . 'Pleasant words . . . '"

"No, Momma. I'm tired," he said flatly.

"No, you ain't! 'Pleasant words . . . ' you know it—keep goin'!" she insisted.

"But I am, Momma."

"No, you ain't, goddammit! Now say it with me!" she demanded, slamming her fists violently down upon the table. "Say it!"

"'Pleasant words are as an honeycomb,'" the boy spoke in a small voice, "'sweet to the soul . . . and health to the bones.'"

"' . . . to the *bones!*'" his mother repeated emphatically, clapping her hands in the air. "You hear that, Willie?" she implored. "'Cause the *body* is a *holy* place. A *pleasant* place . . . "

The boy was not listening to her, because she was not listening to him. Because she was drunk and he did not understand her anymore.

" . . . and we are *free*, child!" she concluded, folding her arms together. "You understand, Willie?" she mumbled, bobbing her head from side to side spastically.

"Yes, Momma, I understand."

"Good . . ." she said, dropping her head and closing her eyes, " . . . all I'm trying to say."

"I ain't leavin' till you tell me," the boy insisted.

His mother did not respond.

"Stand here all night till you answer me, Momma."

She appeared to be almost asleep.

"Wake up!" the boy shouted, stamping his foot.

Sadie shot up from her chair. "Yes, please!" she spat, sounding confused.

"Answer my question once and for all!" he demanded.

Clearing her head, she sat down and pretended to listen to sounds coming through the screen door.

"Told you already."

"Million times, Momma, but it ain't true, is it? You ain't no bookkeeper?" he pressed.

"That a question, Willie?"

"No—well, yes, ma'am. You ain't no bookkeeper, are you? You're a whore, Momma, that's what you are. You get all that money sleeping with men. You get it working at Mr. Matt's. I seen the men, Momma. I see 'em every night goin' in the place. Daytime too, I see 'em. They go in and they ain't there for no bookkeeping, are they? They go for somethin' else. Somethin' you do for them, Momma? Junko told me stuff the other day when we was fishin'. Said his daddy goes—"

"Paul Pinkowski's a Red!" she protested. "And tight as a tick's ass!"

"But he goes in there and Junko says—"

"I don't wanna hear what Junko says, 'cuz whatever you think I'm doin' in there is nothin' other than what I told you I'm doin', which is takin' care of the business side, Willie. I ain't sleepin' with nobody in there, honey. I told you what I do. I told you a bunch a times. I'm Mr. Matt's bookkeeper and that's it. I count the cash, I take it to the bank, I keep track a things. I add it all up and then I write it down. That's all. That's all I do, honey. Take care of the business side."

"Side a what, Momma?" he interrupted.

"Side a what they do in there," his mother answered bitterly. "Add it all up."

"But what they do? Come on, Momma, you can tell me. I seen stuff, come on, don't lie to me no more."

She looked at him with a blank expression.

"What business you addin' up in there? He ain't sellin' no ice."

"Ice?" She laughed. "No, baby. It ain't ice he be sellin', now is it?"

"Well, I don't know, but . . . seems . . ." The boy stopped.

"Seems like you need to know so bad you wanna spit," she said wearily, giving him an exasperated look. "Seems like you can't go on until you know."

"I ain't stupid, Momma. Just want the truth, that's all. So I know what it is." He spoke quietly, but firmly.

His mother took her empty glass from the table and shuffled to the sink.

"You wanna grow up so bad." She shook her head, staring through the dirty dishes.

"I wanna know," he said.

She took a bottle of bourbon from under the sink, gazing deeply into the glass as she filled it, as if it contained something precious.

"Well, like they say . . . " Her hands shook slightly. " . . . what we learn

. . ." She downed the glass before turning to look at him. ". . . is how we learn."

Sadie Graves took her son by the hand and led him out of the house through the screen door. Willie knew from her voice that she was going to show him something. Once she cleared the backyard, he fell behind. It was dark and he wasn't sure exactly where she was headed until they reached the back of an old outhouse next door. Passing a pile of empty bottles, they turned towards the Abel house. There was a light above the back porch and he heard music somewhere. Looking up at the red bulb, he stopped.

"Well, come on," his mother ordered. He looked at her, but did not move.

"You want to know . . . or not?"

"Yes, ma'am," he murmured.

"Well, I'm about to show you," she replied, moving up the steps.

He'd been on the porch with Matt Abel eating Carter Mountain apples once. They'd been hard and sweet and when he got to the core, Mr. Abel wiped his puffy white hands on the front of his overalls and spit the seeds out across the backyard.

"You a gambling man, Willie?" he'd asked, throwing his core over the rail and giving him a cagey smile.

"Sir?"

"Gambling man. Like to wager some?"

"Well . . . " The boy looked quickly away. " . . . not exactly, Mr. Abel."

"I understand. Well, let's see here." He snatched an apple from a basket by the door and surveyed the backyard. "See that outhouse back there next to all those bottles?"

"Yes, sir."

"Bet you a buck I can hit it with this ole apple. Better yet, bet you I can

The Bells of Moses Henry / 45

hit that little door right in front. What do you say, Willie? Bet you one dollar!"

"Don't have no dollar, Mr. Abel," the boy said despondently.

"You don't, huh?" Mr. Abel said, tossing him another apple from the basket.

From his shirt pocket, he pulled out a dollar and gave it to the boy. "So how about if I hit the door, you give it back, and if you hit it, you get to keep it? That seem fair?"

Willie looked at the dollar and he looked at the apple. He peered out across the yard towards the outhouse. He figured he could get it there, but hitting the door would be more difficult. "I got to hit the door to win?"

"No, sir, just part of the house," Mr. Abel decided, looking it over. "Any part you like, Willie. What about it? Think you can do it?" He glanced sideways at the boy.

Willie's chin dropped to his chest as he thought about it.

"Well . . . " he drawled, scrutinizing the outhouse again, " . . . I'll give it a shot."

"'Atta boy!" Mr. Abel shouted, slapping his free hand against the railing. "What the hell, Willie! Give it a shot . . . Ladies!" he crowed, turning towards the house, "We got ourselves a wager!"

Willie's face turned red. "You go first, Mr. Abel."

"Want me to go first?" he replied, spinning around and cocking an eyebrow. "Very good! Put some pressure on the ole coot!"

"If you don't mind, a course," the boy added politely.

"None at all! *Let the apples fly!*" he called out, as the porch filled with exotic-looking women.

By 1949 Matt Abel's house had become a prosperous place for sex with women of all ages. They came from Richmond, from Dinwiddie, and the Bronx. He had soft-skinned mulattos and mysterious Creoles, a Swede, a tall, red-haired Russian, and a pair of Brazilian twins. They were fast, slow, rough, or gentle. They sang, they moaned, they whispered, they cooed. It was a willing group in the house of a good-natured and reliable man on the streets of a small and prosperous college town. At the abattoir two blocks over they slaughtered pigs. Across the street they made chitlins. Next door they sold ice.

From the back porch, Matt Abel tossed his apple in the air and studied the outhouse while his ladies settled in around him. There were only five of them at this early hour of the day. At 11:00 A.M. they were mostly in good spirits except for Carla Salo. She was still drunk from the night before. He'd warned her more than once. At twenty-six she was looking hard and had one foot out the door.

By the summer of his first year in business, Sadie was running Matt Abel's house. He'd found her a four-room shack next door where she and her man could raise Willie. It was small, but it had a good stove and running water and it was free. He'd won the house in a crap game under the Lucky Bean tree late one night from a man who swore he'd kill him. But Matt Abel was a lumberjack from Buckingham County, and by the end of the week, the deal was done.

Sadie was a caramel-colored woman from the Mississippi Delta with a smooth and sensual body that men loved to touch, if she let them. And for money, she did. She reveled in sex, they could tell. And sometimes, she touched them back, if they made her feel good. For ten years they'd come from all around to be with her, to watch her writhe across the sheets, to drink her up.

"Boy's going to whip your ass," Carla declared, adjusting her robe. "Ain't that right, peanut?" She winked at Willie from across the porch.

"Name's Willie, ma'am." He tried to sound grown-up. Leaning against a post at the farthest end of the porch with a long leg hanging over the rail, Carla sized the boy up. He could see her thighs where the robe had fallen away.

"I know, I know, darling. You remember? I sang you to sleep when you was a baby."

"Come on, Carla. Boy's got some work to do here," Mr. Abel interrupted.

"Work?" she spat, crossing her arms.

"That's enough a your bullshit for one morning! Now pack it up!" he commanded.

Carla Salo pierced Matt Abel with her frozen eyes before pushing away from the railing towards the screen door. No one spoke as her pink satin slippers slapped against the floor and a pale nipple slipped provocatively out from under the loosely tied robe.

"Going to whip your ass," she muttered to herself, opening the door and retreating into the dark house.

When Matt Abel's apple missed the outhouse and hit the pile of empty bottles at the end of a fence six feet to the left, the porch erupted into catcalls and laughter. Trying to remain calm, the boy stood still as the cackling died down.

"Well, well, well . . . " Mr. Abel sighed. "Guess it's not my day, Willie."

Peachie Price rolled her eyes as the girls doubled up with laughter. "After dat, ain't yo' week, honey!"

The boy waited for things to quiet down. He figured hitting the outhouse was like memorizing a book. If you wanted something, you just put it inside you like it was a part of you and the rest would take care of itself.

"Five bucks says he can hit da house," Miss Price wagered.

"Five?" Farcy Grover contested. "Ain't nothin' to it with a boy like him, you little cheapskate!" she chided. "Ten bucks even!"

"Whoa, whoa, whoa! Ain't you the riverboat queen!" Peachie Price proclaimed. "Been holdin' out on us all dis time, but nows I can see yo' true nature, girl."

"What you talkin' 'bout, Peach?" Miss Grover put her hand on her hip.

"You ain't no mouse, Farcy Grover!" Miss Price said, swiveling around and strutting over. "You ain't just a-watchin' no more. No, ma'am, today Miss Farcy be puttin' her ass on the line for one itty bitty apple. God bless you, child!" she bellowed, opening her arms to the woman. "Ten bucks it is, darlin'!" she said, placing her hands to either side of Miss Grover's face and kissing her forehead.

Willie took a deep breath and approached the railing from where Mr. Abel had thrown his apple. He didn't like everyone looking at him. It made him think too much. "You can do it, Willie," someone called out softly from an upstairs window. He thought maybe it was the girl he'd passed once on the street out front. She'd had long blond hair all tied up on her head and pretty blue eyes. He'd remembered the sound of her voice from that day.

With her voice in his head, he rotated sideways like he'd seen a colored baseball player do at the Show Grounds. The porch was still when he drew up his left leg, swung his shoulders, and cocked his right arm back. When Willie Graves's apple struck the outhouse door dead center, Matt Abel's back porch roared in jubilation.

"*What you done, child!?*" Peachie Price screamed, stamping her feet against the floorboards; the other women joined in.

"*Holy Mackerel!*" Mr. Abel exclaimed as the porch began to shudder and sway.

"*Hit dat door dead center, Mr. Matt!*" Ms. Price howled.

"*On the money, Peachie! Fifty yards smack dab on the money!*" Mr. Abel shouted, astonished.

While they celebrated with jokes and laughter, the boy stepped down into the yard to get a better look at the apple's wet impression on the door. Basking in glory, he glanced at the open window. As the curtains moved slightly, he imagined the blond girl there like the Beautiful Lady, and as they surrounded him and picked him up into the air he made a wish and blew her out.

Sadie held the screen door open. "You comin', or not?" she asked impatiently.

"Yes, ma'am." Clearing his head, Willie moved quickly up the steps.

"One thing . . . " She raised a finger and pointed it at him. " . . . you listen to what I have to say and den we go."

"Yes, ma'am," he said.

"Period."

"Yes, ma'am."

" 'Cuz this a business place, Willie, you understand me?"

"Yes, ma'am."

"Ain't no place for a child!"

"Yes, Momma."

"Doin' this for you," she reminded him, holding the door.

"Evenin', Sadie," a man's voice whispered from behind the stairs.

His mother nodded to the voice before turning to Willie. "Ain't doin' this for me," she clarified, indicating with her head for him to follow.

When he cleared the doorway, the place was dim and smelled of cigars. Passing a tall, narrow staircase, he figured the voice had gone the other way. He felt clumsy on the carpet. It was red like at the Paramount Theater, when he'd walked inside and a man had chased him out with a broom.

He followed his mother down the hallway past a narrow table with a large red dish full of keys. The keys had names. One of the names was "Sapphire," but he didn't have time to look. He knew that she was watching him, and she didn't seem drunk anymore. At the end of the hallway she waited with a guarded smile for him to catch up.

"Now turn around."

Anxiously, the boy did as instructed, but he could tell by her tone of voice that she wasn't angry anymore and was watching out for him.

"You see them doors?" she whispered.

"Yes, ma'am," he lied. He hadn't noticed a series of doors to one side of the hallway.

"Every door represents a room that is used in the business of bringing together a man and a woman," his mother declared, as if she were reading from the Bible. "Be Sunday night, so the place is quiet, but some nights you got every room filled, and people waitin' their turn upstairs," she explained.

"Waitin' their turn for lovin'?" the boy asked.

His mother relaxed when she heard the word. She looked like herself now, or more like the part of her that loved him and would always love him no matter what.

"Yes, honey. They waitin' for some lovin'."

Sadie crouched down so they could be face to face. She stroked the back of his head softly as she spoke.

"Lotta hurt in this world, Willie," she murmured.

"Yes, ma'am."

"Ton a bad."

"Yes, ma'am."

He thought he heard footsteps upstairs and glanced back towards the hallway.

"Look at me, Willie." With her palm, she turned his face towards her.

"Yes, ma'am."

She looked at him sweetly and took her time. "You got to get your love from those who give it and then you got to pass it on."

"Yes, ma'am."

"Send it out into the world," she said.

Before he could think of what to say to her, she had taken his hand and led him around the corner and through a small wooden door on the opposite side of the staircase. The door was so small she had to bend down in order to get through it.

"It's in the cellar," she whispered, flipping a light switch at the top of a tiny staircase.

"What is?" he whispered back.

"What I wanna show you," he barely heard as she descended the stairs, and he followed.

On the last step, it was hard to see.

"Wait here," she instructed.

In the darkness he felt a wall of cool, damp air. It smelled alive like the ground around the Lucky Bean. He wasn't afraid to be standing in such a strange quiet in the dark. It sounded like after the snowstorm on Christmas Eve.

"This the cellar?"

"Someone done moved my lamp."

"Oil lamp, Momma?"

"Yeah, how you know that?"

"One next to me," he answered, seeing it off to the side of the last step. "Just make it out."

She picked up the lamp and examined it. "In the wrong place," his mother complained, checking her robe pocket. She was annoyed about something again.

"You wanna show me another time, Momma?" the boy asked.

"Wanna show you now. Just sayin' it ain't in the right place, that's all."

A match struck as his mother lit the lamp, flooding the cellar with warm, soft light. Looking around, he could see that it was small. Four posts held up the ceiling with a square brick column in the middle. There were no windows, or other rooms, and the dirt floor stretched out to the walls.

"This a lovin' place?" he asked timidly.

"Come on," she ordered, holding the lamp up. Stepping off the last step, he followed closely as their shadows floated against the wall. The figures of the shadows were upright, but the heads bent forward.

"All right now." She stopped in front of the brick column. "Want you to hold the lamp."

"Yes, Momma." The handle was warm.

"Hold it up so I can see."

Steadying his feet, he lifted the lamp up over his shoulders.

"Good there," she said. "Get my pick."

"What you need a pick for, Momma?" She crouched down at the column. "Need more light?"

"No, I'm fine, Willie. Be quiet now. Got to open it up first."

The boy was mystified. He couldn't figure out what he was doing standing in a cellar to find out if his momma was a whore. He thought maybe she was looking for more bourbon or maybe she was going to lock him up and keep him there until she felt like letting him out after he promised not to tell. Or maybe they'd go somewhere secret and this was how you got there. When she stood up, his mother was holding a shallow rubber bucket with a tin canister, a trowel, and a small rock pick.

"That your pick, Momma?"

"Hold the light up, Willie."

He did as he was told. She took out the pick and placed the bucket on the ground.

"That good?" A circle of light trembled against the column over their heads.

"Fine, right there." She held the pick in her left hand, caressing the middle of the wall with the fingers of her right hand. "There," she announced, her fingers on a particular brick. She tapped the brick lightly with the wooden handle of the pick and, cocking her head to one side, listened. He didn't know what she was listening for until she hit the brick below. It had a different sound.

"*Voilà!*" His mother turned the pick around in her hand. The air was suddenly warm and still and he was tired of holding the lamp. Slicing at the mortar around the brick with her pick, she looked back at him and smiled as the mortar came apart easily. "Made it soft so I can get it," she boasted.

"Get what, Momma?"

With the point of the pick at one end of the brick, she pulled it gently from the wall and placed it in the bucket.

"Hold the light up, Willie."

"Ma'am."

"Part a the chimney," she whispered, reaching into the hole with her slender arm and lifting something out.

In the lamplight, the boy could see that it was a box like the one he'd seen in the drawer of her dresser. It said "RED CLOUD" over an Indian on his horse.

"There," she said proudly, handing it to him, dusting off her hands.

"What is it?"

"Go ahead an' open it," she urged. "Give me the lamp."

Passing the lamp to her, he took the box.

"Go on."

"This an old box? Says 1910 right here at the bottom."

She held the lantern up to get a better look. The boy was right. It did say 1910 next to "HIGH GRADE HAND MADE." She'd never noticed. She'd found it one day on the floor of a closet in the attic. She'd liked the Indian on his horse. She'd liked his name and the tranquil expression on his face. From the edge of a vast plain he stared out towards a range of distant mountains, as if he and the place he lived in were indistinguishable from one another.

Willie opened the cigar box gingerly. He expected a snake to jump out and scare him half to death. She watched his eyes as the lid lifted.

"Full a money!" he whispered.

"Lotta money, Willie!" she whispered back. "Lotta nights in there, baby."

Wide-eyed, he peered in. "All this your money, Momma?"

"Every lick."

Cradling the box against his chest, he hesitated. "From the lovin'?" he asked softly.

She thought about her answer. She'd never told him and she'd promised herself that she never would until he was old enough, but she was aching for a shot and dead-ass tired. She'd lied to him about so many things. He needed to get on with his life, so she could sleep better. Maybe someday, he'd find a way in this life and see the world for what it was.

"You a whore, Momma?" He closed the lid.

"Yes, baby."

Sadie Graves sealed the brick with mortar mixed in her bucket. When the mortar dried, it would be difficult to find the brick unless you knew where to tap, but soft enough to open easily. Her father was a mason from Louisiana. When she was ten, he'd shown her how to get into a flue and make a ledge, to mix soft mortar, and to use a trowel. The day he'd died she'd opened their kitchen chimney under the floorboards and retrieved his bag of coins to buy a coffin. Two coins were black—one had teeth marks, and one was dated before the Civil War.

When the lamp went out, they climbed the stairs. He wanted to look back, but she was behind him moving quickly. He could tell that she was tired by the way she bent over the steps. He wanted to see where she had hidden her bucket, but when she disappeared around the corner of the chimney, he looked away. He wanted to ask her how much money was in the box and about the men, but she looked as though there was nothing left to say. At the top of the stairs he looked back for her.

"Comin'," she whispered, out of breath, raising herself up and placing her hand on the wall for balance.

"Thanks, Momma," he said gratefully. When she looked at him, her face relaxed. Maybe she was feeling good, because she'd shown him the box, or maybe it was just that she didn't feel so alone now. Lit by a bright bulb, his mother stroked the back of his head tenderly, and for the first time in as long as he could remember, her eyes were full of love.

The hallway still smelled of cigars. He wanted to take a key with him, but his momma would've skinned him alive if he'd done that, or if he'd asked about the blond woman with the pretty blue eyes.

"Can I see your room, Momma?"

"No."

Willie's shoulders slumped with disappointment. He wanted to see inside the rooms. He didn't so much care if it was her room. He only wanted to know what a room for lovin' would look like. He figured it wouldn't be a normal kind of room. A room for lovin' would be different somehow and you could tell just by looking at it.

"Willie!" His mother slapped her hand against the open door.

The boy came immediately, knowing she was about to lose her temper. "I thought maybe you could show me some more? I won't get in the way, Momma. I just want to see—"

With her long, red-nailed fingertips, Sadie Graves took her son by the left ear and steered him through the door, across the porch, and down the steps. She was in no mood to show him a room or anything else. He had been inside and seen the box and that was enough. She had told him the truth about who she was and where the money was and now it was morning.

Outside, the air smelled cool and fresh. Pieces of broken bottles sparkled in the sunlight. Taking his hand, Sadie Graves stared into the shimmering pile and closed her eyes. Her mouth was dry and her shoulders ached. It had been a long night, but they were still a part of each other. In spite of herself, she hadn't lost him after all.

It comforted him to feel her pulse in his hand. It didn't matter who she'd loved, or why she'd done it, so long as she'd told him the truth. It didn't change the way he felt about her, or make him love her any less. As the sunlight intensified against his face, he closed his eyes. It wouldn't always be like this. There'd be bad days and more nights alone. But occasionally there'd be times when everything made sense, when all the pieces fit like a puzzle and, for a moment, you'd feel just like that ole Indian on his horse.

CHAPTER TEN

When the rain stopped, the covered bridge appeared to Stick in the distance like a great ship, as thick silver clouds lifted off the river. He thought about Sister Mo in Goshen. He'd carried the boy inside the bridge and placed him on his bedroll between the side posts. In his own wet pockets, he found two soggy fives. Mo would know what to give the boy. She'd feed him and hang a bottle on the tree and do the mumbo jumbo like she'd done for him after the fight.

While the boy slept, Stick waited outside the bridge for a ride and drank bourbon. During the night the sound of the river intensified and pink bats danced over his head.

When the truck approached, it was barely dawn. From the engine's sound he judged it was a logger, or some asshole with the C&O. He'd been on his feet all night and the bottle was empty. As the truck slowed, he recognized the timber company. He'd been on their green chain one summer moving four-by-eights off the belt once they'd cleared the saw. He'd worked his ass off for a prick named Frank, until he got a job for more money nailing slate to the roof of the Alleghany Hotel in Goshen. The front end of the truck was hot when it stopped and the engine rattled like a timber snake. As Stick gazed up into the dark cab, a small round face popped out the window.

"You all right, mister?" the driver yelled down.

Stick had a hard time hearing him over the engine.

"Appreciate it!" he shouted, trying to sound sober. "Got a boy here who needs some help. Came down the river yesterday and got all turned around. Need to get him to Goshen." The driver's cap had the bill pulled straight up.

"Where is he?"

"Put him in the bridge. Just take a minute to get him. Much obliged if you could help. Just take me a minute," Stick pleaded, holding his palms out.

"What's wrong with him?" The driver leaned further out the window to get a better look.

"Took on lotta water, I 'magine. Don't know. Thought I'd take him to Sister Mo at the Alleghany an' see what she can do."

"Ole nigger in the shack?" The man eyed Stick suspiciously.

"Yep."

"You know her?" The driver raised his eyebrows.

"I do."

Straightening up and shifting back in the seat, the man looked through the windshield toward the bridge. A dead dragonfly stuck out from under the windshield wiper.

"Give you a five spot for the gas?" Stick proposed, holding up a bill.

While the boy slept in the back seat, they rode in silence through stands of rhododendron and laurel. As the truck picked up speed, lazy green eddies faded away and the river intensified. Past Wilson Springs the rapids flashed white before the roar of Devil's Kitchen consumed the cab. *The boy must be one lucky sonovabitch,* Stick thought, watching a roller double back over a logjammed pine.

"Came through the Kitchen?" the driver asked, glancing out at a thirty-foot drop.

"Mighta," Stick mumbled.

The gravel road was still damp enough to keep the dust down, and the pine trunks were black with rain. Up ahead a young red fox trotted across the road and disappeared into a thicket of spicebush. In a month the thicket would be the color of the fox. Above Undercut Rock, water slid into translucent ripples of gray and blue. In a few weeks sumac and chokeberry would turn its banks the color of blood, stinkpots would hatch, and the surrounding hills of oak and maple would lighten.

Stick had ten dollars to his name. Coasting across the bridge at Goshen, he looked down through the girders and remembered Crystal-Ann's ashes melting into the falls. He would miss her all his life, but come hell or high water, he would learn to be without her.

For now, he would take the boy to Sister Mo and find a man in Clifton Forge. He was glad the boy's eyes were closed. It wouldn't be long now, he knew, watching the river. It was indifferent, like a glassy-hard photograph. It was silent and still.

Sister Mo's bottle tree was out front. Her laundry was hanging off to the side. Stick hadn't been back since the fight, when she'd laid him out in a shack behind the burned-out hotel. Some goons had jumped him on a Friday night when he was drunk and left him in a pile of soot. His eyes were swollen shut and his left shoulder had been dislodged. She'd wrapped it in comfrey leaves, soaked his eyes in goldenseal, and, as the bottles moaned in the wind outside, rubbed him down with arnica. For days she'd called out to the spirits. She'd fed him pony's foot and prickly ash. When he finally came to, she'd taken his hand in hers and closed her eyes.

"Dose dat luv pleasure come fo'," she'd said, gently stroking the top of his hand. "Tec him frum dese lions. Tec him from o' shabala." When her eyes

opened, she'd managed a lazy, sweet smile. "You'ze free," she'd declared, letting go of his hand. "You'ze awright now, skinny man."

Sister Mo stood in the doorway of her two-room shack with a broom in her hand. Her eyes still crackled with light. In ten years she had not aged. Stick emerged from behind the truck in a cloud of dust, the boy in his arms. He was relieved to see her.

Sister Mo was scowling. "So, was *you* lass night, skinny man?" she declared, stepping outside the doorway and sniffing the air.

"Ma'am?" Stick's voice was weary.

"Was you bring me duh *water boy!*" She raised her voice like he was slow. Stick had no idea what Sister Mo was talking about.

"Need your help, Mo," Stick said, dragging the boy's legs through the dirt.

"See dat." Her face was hard.

"Think he's been through the Kitchen. Doesn't look like anything's broke, but he spit up a bunch a water and . . . " the boy was getting heavy. " . . . seems like he ain't all there."

"Bin wit de Devil," Sister Mo announced, leaning her broom against the front of the shack. "Hard t' say."

Stick caught his breath. "Hard to say what, Mo?" He noticed the boy's complexion.

"Hard t' say," she repeated, walking into the shack.

He followed her in. It was cool and dark and smelled of smoke. Tables were piled with dried plants and beams of dusty sunlight streaked across the room as she opened a large shutter. When the light hit her profile, her skin glowed like shiny tar.

"Lemme get a look a' him," she said, pointing to a tiny daybed under the open window. Exhausted, Stick leaned his shoulder against the headboard and gently laid the boy down.

"Now git me dat broom 'fo' they steal it."

"Yes, ma'am." He backed away.

Sister Mo sat down next to the boy and watched his breathing for a few moments, then placed the palm of her left hand across his forehead. Closing her eyes, she saw flames under his eyes. She smelled candle wax and nicotine and felt the river inside him.

"Dair," she said with her eyes closed, as Stick appeared in the doorway with her broom.

The shack was deathly still. Stick leaned against the doorframe and let his head drop. The sun felt warm on his back. He needed to sleep more than he needed to eat. His mouth was dry from the liquor and his neck ached as he thought about the boy. His hands were small and pale. The boy looked like shit. Stick believed in the spirits more than in churches. He believed in bourbon and he believed in Sister Mo.

Sister Mo was born with the touch in Durham, North Carolina. When she was little, she'd resisted the idea at first.

"Makes you free," her momma had said. "Makes sense a things, child. Like you'ze a part a somptin'."

People came from all around to see the little black girl born with a fetal sac around her neck. They brought bottles for the bottle tree and she turned their bitter blood to sweet. They bought herbs and she made hoodoo.

When her husband died at twenty, she placed broken bottles, shards of pottery, and old bricks around his grave. In time his spirit would become white bakulu and live underwater. In 1889 she left for Virginia. The Negro is "a sort a seventh son," her mother would say as she bid her farewell at the side of the road. "We born wit duh veil an' we born with duh sight."

The Alleghany Hotel gave Sister Mo work and a room in the basement with no windows. For five years she ironed napkins and chopped wood. For the next ten she tended to the ladies' room at the swimming pool. At age fifty she moved upstairs to a room with a view of Bratton Cemetery. As she sat at the window, lost souls would visit her and ask for help. "I'ze just a poor Negro," she would tell the dead ones as they danced around the candlelight before she set them free. Sister Mo lived between this world and the next. For Bratton Cemetery and most of Rockbridge County the black lady behind the Alleghany was the final sacrament. When it burned down, they let her stay. She was black as the fallen floor beams. Her shack was small, but the soil was rich, and there she remained.

Willie stirred as she pressed the warm mud against his chest. It smelled of hawkweed and fish. His hands grasping at air, he felt the poultice press against him. He tasted cramp bark as the soapwort dried his skin and his dusty white body trembled in the firelight. His legs twitched from time to time as she hovered over him, rocking her head from side to side. Soon he would be taken outside and covered with sticks.

"Wake up, skinny man!"

Stick had fallen asleep on the floor hours ago. She had washed his bottle in rosemary and salt water for her tree. Her bottles shined like ice.

"Git branches!" she instructed, taking the boy's hand.

Stick had forgotten where he was. The side of his face was stuck to the wooden floor.

"Long as yo' arm. Thick as yo' finga," she said.

Swallowing, he cleared his sore throat. "Branches?" he croaked, rolling over on his back and lifting up his knees.

"Hear me, man?" she barked, closing her eyes to concentrate.

"What kinda branches?" he asked, looking around the room.

"Kind I just say. Long as yo' arm, thick as yo' finga. Now git, 'cuz dis be duh time."

Stick pushed himself up. "He gonna make it?"

Releasing her hand from the boy's belly, her face smeared with mud from the poultice, she stood up. She'd closed the shutters earlier, tying the handles with a strip of burlap when the wind had kicked up. It would be morning soon, and the boy would die. She felt sure of it.

"Got till sunrise," she said, looking through the slats.

Stick did as he was told, collecting branches from a large sycamore near the river and piling them up in front of her shack. As the light grew, she had him dig a shallow pit. She'd taken the bourbon, but it didn't matter. He'd do whatever she asked of him. He owed her that much. As he carried the boy out and placed him in the pit, he felt his ribs. He looked like a ghost and his face was the color of milk.

Sister Mo stuck a branch into the ground. "No, man!" she scolded when he tried to help, pulling a small knife from her apron pocket and stabbing the earth. She carefully placed six branches evenly spaced from one another around the pit. *"Vodu vodu . . . "* she chanted. *"Woto Nuba Bele. Vodu Vodu Woto . . . "* Sister Mo continued, looked up as she measured the sky. Watching with her, Stick saw nothing but dark gray mist.

"Nuba!" she called out, her eyes on the bottle tree. Stick recognized his bourbon bottle on a branch.

As Sister Mo balanced the branches over the pit, the wind strengthened.

"Hooch," she instructed, placing the final branch, "in duh sink. An' duh match."

Racing into the shack, he located a jar of moonshine in the sink. He'd left the matches on the chimney.

"Poah duh hooch furst," she muttered to herself, taking the bottle.

A few dry poplar leaves lifted off the ground around his feet as she poured the hooch around the base of each branch and bent over. Stick figured the boy was nearly dead. As the leaves around them scattered, he peered down into the pit.

"*Bing duh fire!*" she shouted over the wind.

More than anything, he wanted something to do. The air made a strange sound, like it was hurt. He shielded his eyes. Mo would set fire to the boy. His legs shook through the branches.

"Hear dat? Bottle tree talkin'," she said, lighting the first stick.

"No," Stick lied.

As each branch burned, the basket of flames crackled over the boy's body. Backing away from the heat, she took the ends of Stick's long fingers in hers.

"Ten steps back, skinny man . . . " She closed her eyes. " . . . den three steps fo'wad."

Clasping her hand for balance, he had trouble backing up straight. After the tenth step, they stopped, watching the flames arch over the pit. Stick saw the boy's face through the sparks. His eyes were glazed over and his arms were wet with sweat, but his body wasn't burning.

"Hear dat?" she asked, her eyes snapping open.

Stick listened.

"One," she said, stepping forward.

While sparks of sap jettisoned from the burning branches, he heard the crown of poplar above them swaying in the wind.

"Two." Sister Mo paused, cocking her head and closing her eyes again. She let go of his hand and they stepped together as glowing cinders fell around the pit. "Lissen," she urged, quietly coming to a stop.

As the fire died down, Stick heard it from a great distance, rolling towards them through the morning sky. Sister Mo watched the boy and grinned from ear to ear. The wind had stopped. The boy looked up at them and blinked.

"Dat be a bell," she said.

CHAPTER ELEVEN

Moses Henry sat in his old cane chair at the top of Cabell Hall and listened to the lecture entitled "Animal Behavior of Oceania." The window behind him was open.

"In a study of two hundred thousand ostriches over a period of eighty years, no one has reported a single case where an ostrich buried its head in the sand," the professor concluded to a smattering of applause.

The heads below him moved like pigeons. He called time in Cabell Hall "God time" and said that "learnin' is like prayin'." He loved his old chair. The school had given it to him on his one hundredth birthday with a letter that he could not read. "Greatest day ma life," he'd said to Willie. "Like puttin' a window in ma head lettin' me see out."

As was his habit, he waited in his chair for what he called "dat note in ma head" before climbing the stairs and ringing his bell. Gazing out on the portico to catch his breath, it would come to him—the sound of animals, the sound of young men, or sometimes, the sound of war. He'd seen hundreds of Confederate soldiers lying injured on the Rotunda grass. "Make no difference how much dey was sufferin'; didn't make no noise," he remembered. "Not a peep."

After the lecture on animals, Moses thought about what the boy had done and how it had torn his momma up. Pulling hard on the rope, his bell began to swing. *Can't bring duh mornin' back,* he thought to himself. A fresh breeze crossed through the portico as he counted to three. He pulled again and listened, before gently letting go.

CHAPTER TWELVE

When the branches stopped burning, the boy looked around in the pit. He was confused and disoriented, his body streaked with soapwort and sweat. As his eyes filled with tears, Sister Mo spoke.

"Man here pull you out duh river an' ole Mo fix you up."

The boy's faced relaxed. The black lady had been a comfort. Her skin was shiny and she had kind eyes.

"Tink you was dead. Man here save yo' life." Sister Mo pointed to Stick.

Stick couldn't meet the boy's eyes. He'd leave tonight and Sister Mo could figure out what to do with him.

"Git him sum hoecake," she mumbled, walking away.

The boy's head spun around as he sat up. Stick lifted him out and placed him carefully against a tree trunk.

"Lost my pole," the boy said faintly, his fingertips grazing a large bruise over his eye.

"Brought you here yesterday. Found you at the falls," Stick explained, looking anxiously towards the shack for Sister Mo.

By her fireplace, Sister Mo dragged the hoe over the coals. Yellow batter splattered first on the hoe, then sizzled into the embers, sending fuzzy brown smoke up the flue. She was tired and the cake was done as her thoughts turned back to the boy. Crossing to the kitchen, she remembered his milk. *Where you send a child who done what he done?*

Sister Mo and Stick sat under the poplar and watched the boy inhale his hoecake.

"Like that pone, huh?" Stick asked.

The boy nodded with a dazed expression. He had some color in his face, but you could see that he was a million miles away.

"What's your name, boy?" Stick broke the silence.

"Willie," the boy answered. He wiped milk off his mouth. His lap was covered with soot.

"Stick Watson. Where you from?"

Pressing his lips tight, the boy's eyes filled with tears.

"Naw, child," Sister Mo cooed, sliding over to him and wrapping an arm around his shoulders. "Nothin' but love. Nothin' but love," she murmured, placing her free hand on top of his. As she spoke, he fell into her lap. "Done it good, done it good," she whispered, looking at Stick coldly. "No mo' to say." She stroked the side of his head. "No mo' to say."

As Stick walked away, the boy closed his eyes and felt her rough hands passing through his hair. Her lap was greasy and smelled of cornmeal. Suddenly, he remembered his trip to Virginia Beach in the back seat of Mr. Abel's white Studebaker. He'd never seen a place so wide open, so full of light and with so much water. As her fingertips touched his ear, he remembered what he'd done and how flames had shot out the back of the house before he'd touched the Lucky Bean and run. The smoke was everywhere.

A moment later, the boy was fast asleep as sunlight spliced the open water in his dreams, and a long blue wave collapsed across the sand before sliding back to sea.

As the boy slept in Sister Mo's lap, Stick made his way through the Alleghany. Except for the foundation, there wasn't much left. A large turret sat on its side halfway down the hill, swallowed by honeysuckle, its roof stripped of slate and its eaves singed with silver and black. From a broken slab of concrete, he heard mourning doves in the distance and watched the sun dip behind Rough Mountain, while nettles lifted up through the tennis court and catalpa rose from where the pool had been. He thought about his job on the hotel roof. Except for Crystal-Ann, he'd forgotten most of it. He remembered places better than people and he remembered faces better than names. The boy would be all right. Whatever he was running from he'd forget about sooner or later, and as the days rolled by, he'd remember something else.

A yellow moon rose over the Maury. Sister Mo saw it through the door when Stick came in. She could smell the mill in Goshen. The bottle tree was quiet and the dawn would be red. Summer was over. Pouring Stick another glass of hooch, she waited by the fire for his answer.

Stick stared at his glass. "Don't know," he finally said.

Shuffling over to her chair, she doubled up her shawl and dropped down backwards. "Take 'em to duh sheriff?" she asked, looking into the fire.

"Don't matter to me, Mo. On my way to Humpback Bridge," he answered, draining his glass.

"Big ole somptin', dis one. No good jes' leave 'im on duh road. Jes' a child. Bes' I can tell, he got a momma, das it." Mo heard Willie breathing in the daybed. His lungs were still congested, but the cowslip had helped. His blood was sweet now. Stick was perched next to her on an old wooden apple crate, stoking the fire with her hoe. He was a good man, she thought, watching him. "Lost yo' flame," she said, feeling the moonlight through the open door.

"Excuse me?"

"You like a dead man," she stated, closing her eyes.

He stared at the old black woman as hooch buzzed through his veins and milky moonlight washed her back. A part of him understood what she was saying. Standing up, he faced the mantel stuffed with dried roses, jasmine, peonies, and gardenia. Dead flowers. Maybe she'd saved the boy or maybe she hadn't. It was all a bunch of monkey shit, when you got right down to it. He'd leave before sunup. What happened to the boy was of no importance to him. He wanted nothing. He felt nothing. She was a good ole witch, but the jig was done and the C&O was down the hill.

At 7:00 A.M., Sister Mo's eyes opened a crack. She watched the sunlight through the top of a partially boarded-up window at the foot of her bed. At dawn, the shadow of a cross stretched across the floor from a piece of pine nailed vertically to a patch of broken board. She took comfort in it. She never called it anything. She never prayed. For Sister Mo, faith was about something you felt, not something you did to prove it.

Her head still on the pillow, she considered the boy. She'd sewed up his pants and given him some old shoes. Now he would be hungry. She'd fix him eggs and scrapple before the two of them headed out, and give him apples for later. Then she'd run him to the sheriff. She didn't want trouble. He might drive him home once he figured out where home was, or he might not. She knew one thing. The boy had been flush with sour blood, devil drunk, and nowhere in this world before she'd set him straight. It surprised her, the way he'd burned. She thought he was white bakulu, but she was wrong. He was quick in the eyes, and you could hang the moon on that. Slipping into a clean white smock, she shuffled over to a frameless mirror nailed to the wall. Her hair was streaked with dried poultice where she'd run her fingers and one of her cheekbones was smudged with charcoal.

"You all there, child," she giggled, gazing into her yellow eyes, "but you ain't right."

Outside the bedroom she heard a wood thrush and saw that the daybed was empty. The bird called again, but she would not listen. Sometimes she had to push it all out, when she was tired. She needed time alone without interruption.

"Ain't no difference," she muttered, shutting the door. "One way or duh other, you'ze hear it all duh same." Sister Mo had lived between this world and the next long enough to know it didn't take a little bird to tell her that the boy was gone.

CHAPTER THIRTEEN

At dawn, an empty C&O stack and coal train backed up half a mile from the mill to the embankment below Mo's shack. Hearing two men, Stick crouched in the bushes before jumping onto a hopper as the train pulled out. Small towns were tricky and security bulls were pricks—pricks in white trucks. He preferred a hump yard where he had time to choose a car.

Crouching down against the wall of the empty car, he waited for the train to pick up speed. As he lay still, two voices passed alongside. One complained about the engine of his truck, while the other agreed. As their conversation faded, he sat up against the wall and drew a deep breath. A bull had shot at him once outside Spokane. The first shot had hit a water tank, but the second had hit the back of his leg. Removing the bullet with a pair of pliers, he'd thrown it off the Grand Coulee Dam and made a wish.

As the train gathered momentum, the floor swayed, and Stick fingered the scar behind his knee. Before he'd stitched it with canvas thread he'd washed it out with rubbing alcohol.

"Don't drink it, Stick! Make you queer as pink ink," Wink Nixon had shouted over the noise of the train.

Stick had met Farleigh Nixon on oil platform No. 24 in the Bay of Mexico in 1947, three hundred miles south of Galveston. It was a rough crowd made up of ex-cons and drifters like Stick. After a fight over hookers in Corpus Christi, Farleigh's left eye glassed over and quit. A week later they called him "Wink."

Wink took a shine to Stick when he'd heard he was from Richmond.

"Got family there," he said one night, staring at the stars with his good eye. From the top of the rig on a clear night you could see the lights of Galveston and, if the wind was right, smell the pulp from Port Lavaca.

"Where?" Stick asked with some ambivalence.

"Clifton Forge," Wink answered, looking down at the platform below.

"What's that star, Wink?" Stick asked. "That red one there." He pointed up, changing the subject. "See it? Big ole thing—see?" Wink closed his bad eye and forced the other one wide open. He was a funny little guy, dark and brooding, but he knew some things. Small things, mostly. Things most people would discard as junk.

"Red one there next to the Belt, you mean?"

"That a star?" Stick wondered aloud.

Gazing out across the dark and musty waters of the Bay of Mexico, Wink Nixon left before answering his question. It was a flat and humid night, drained of pretense or mystery. Stick heard his boots down the ladder and watched him cross under the drill light towards the bunk room door. The red star had lost its intensity and the air stirred around him for a moment. Whatever you called it, the thing in the sky was beautiful. He figured it would go on forever whether he knew its name or not.

Next morning a drill bit caught Wink's jacket and ripped his arm off at the shoulder. Stick was below deck when it happened. By the time he reached his friend, they'd tied off the stump and shot him up.

"I'm right here, Wink," was all Stick could say when he finally reached him. The separated arm rested in a puddle of blood. The blood was dark with deck oil and he took a mental picture. Time was money on a rig and money wasn't red. Twenty minutes later the drill on platform No. 24 began to spin and Wink's arm was tossed out to sea. Before they lowered him into a boat to the mainland hospital, Stick crouched down over the stretcher and took his friend's remaining hand.

"Mars," Wink managed, squeezing his fingers lightly before passing out.

The main line to Clifton Forge pulled north to Panther Gap before swinging south past Millboro into Rough Mountain. As the train gathered speed, Stick's legs bounced with the rails. He loved the motion of trains. It quieted every part of him. Crystal-Ann understood that about him, that he belonged to her and to something else. She'd loved him for it, but it tore her up sometimes.

The wooden footbridge was still over Sharvers Run, with churning walls of shale in the distance. It was a fine morning and he was hungry, but it was a good hunger because the booze was gone. It had been a while. When she died, he drank until it didn't matter anymore. Or until he couldn't tell the difference.

Past Rainbow Gap, the Old Iron Furnace was bathed in yellow sunlight. Years ago, late winter, he'd climbed it on his way to Humpback Bridge outside Covington. At the top, he'd straddled the tapered stones to get a better look. He liked the way the hillsides rolled and buckled with shale, and how, to the west, limestone cliffs rose capriciously, shadowing swirls of dark gray currents below.

As the train slowed, he checked for the trucks. Late summer was busy. He'd be careful getting out. Best to ditch shy of a stop, just after the switch shack.

The town of Clifton Forge stood between the Jackson River and Virginia Central line. After the iron had dried up and the last coal car departed, the Panic of 1893 cleared the streets for good. Wink must have been a fish out of water here, Stick thought, walking into town—with or without an arm. His death surprised him less than the way it had happened. People could fool you. Even a guy like Wink. The telegram was two years old, but the message was clear.

At Main Street he turned down Ridgeway Avenue and followed the numbers to a narrow, squat building with three buzzers at the entrance:

J. GLOVER ATTORNEY AT LAW

D. WEBSTER

NIXON BOOKKEEPING

CHAPTER FOURTEEN

Except for being suspicious, Rudy Nixon didn't seem much like his brother. For one thing, he was tall. Watching him read the telegram, Stick apologized for dropping in out of the blue. "Been on the road."

"Watson?" The man's look was gruff.

"I am," Stick answered, sizing up Nixon.

"Been two years," he admonished, handing the telegram back to Stick. "No other address to find you with 'cept what he gave me."

"I know." Stick folded the telegram and slid it into his back pocket.

"First name 'Stick,' right?" He put his hands on his hips.

"I am."

"Outta Richmond?"

"Look, Mr. Nixon, you want to forget this, I'll just mosey on . . . "

"No, no, no, I'm sorry, Mr. Watson . . . "

"Stick."

"I mean, Stick, I just . . . want to make sure I've got the right fella, you know? I'm sure you're the one . . . but, I mean, it's been a while and my brother ran with a rough crowd sometimes, you know? Just doing my job like he wanted. Want to make sure that his money goes where it's supposed to go."

"I understand. Your brother and me had some good times together, Mr.

Nixon. Sorry it worked out the way it did. You're a patient man. Most folks woulda said 'Screw it.'"

"Well, thank you." He perked up. "I'm retired now, so . . . " He stole a quick glimpse of the sky before backing up and gesturing for Stick to enter the building. " . . . I got all the time in the world."

Stick had heard about Wink on a train from Memphis. The trip had been a mistake. Crystal-Ann was sick and he was mostly drunk, but they'd promised each other one last ride to Memphis. She threw up going down and slept coming back. They walked Beale Street looking for music, and heard Muddy Waters at The Orpheum before he took her home. Everybody's different, he thought, while her head rocked against his chest. Some people throw in the towel and some people go down swinging. When Wink's liver quit, he shoved the barrel of a shotgun into his mouth and finished the job. When they found him, the room smelled of feces and gunpowder.

"Got the letter here, Stick." Wink's brother pulled out a desk drawer. "Don't come in much anymore. Usually at the house."

Stick took a survey of Rudy Nixon's office. It was simple enough to figure out. Two diplomas behind a desk with two chairs. Filing cabinets against the wall. Two cups and a hot plate under a map.

"Like my map?" he boasted, offering the envelope.

"Pretty old, ain't it?"

"1854," he said proudly.

"Different place back then, I imagine?" Stick took the envelope.

Rudy Nixon stood transfixed by the map of Alleghany County on his office wall. Gazing at the swamps, the mountain peaks, and vast rolling spaces of possibilities, he remembered the history of his family. As a bookkeeper, he was not prepared for moments such as these. Staring at the territorial lines and ambling creeks, he felt uneasy.

Stick sensed his discomfort. "Been here a long time, Mr. Nixon?"

"All my life." He was still staring at the map.

"Well," Stick replied, admiring the map with him, "imagine you seen the best a this place."

Wink Nixon's letter was written to his brother on Kodak stationery with a return address in Rochester, New York. There was no date.

Dear Rudy,

Please hold this letter for my friend Stick Watson. The only address I have for him is a Post Box in Richmond, Virginia. On account he moves around so much, please keep this until you find him.

Your brother,

Farleigh

"Have a seat." Rudy Nixon gestured to a plush leather chair. "Want some coffee?"

"I'm fine, sir, thank you," he answered, opening the letter as he sat down.

"Stick?"

"What?"

"Call me Rudy."

Dear Stick,

I am in Rochester pretty much full time now on account of my health is not what it used to be. I got a good job with Kodak as a watchman. They treat me real good and gave me a room over one of the maintenance shops. You should see the size of this place. I get to use the cafeteria for meals and got a fridge full of giveaways from the kitchen. I have been following things down at the library. Do not care much like I used to for history as such, but have been interested in geography and learning more about how things work. Sure do wish you and I could have seen Mexico together but I guess things got all spread out and we just lost track of one another.

I hope you are good. Marty Kessler wrote me and said you and Crystal-Ann were in Richmond sometimes. He said someone saw you near Chattanooga and that you had asked about me. They said you were fighting fires somewhere.

You remember the kitchen fire on 24 and how we all ran in and pissed on it till the thing went out? That was quite something. There is a lot of piss on a platform I guess. Good thing we could put it to good use. Here is the $100.00 I owe you. Kodak gave me some money when I stopped working and I pretty much spent what I was making up here on doctor bills. My liver shut down last year so I have been on one of those dialysis machines ever since. They cost an arm and a leg, which is pretty steep for a fella with only one arm. I have been feeling bad lately. You remember me talking about my brother in Clifton Forge? His name is Rudy Nixon and he runs an accounting office on Ridgeway Avenue. I will have him telegram about the money. He will hang on to it until you get there. Or maybe he can send it Western Union? I am leaving you some books. You can do whatever you want with them. Some of them deal with things you and I talked about. There's one on astronomy you might like. The big one about machines and engines I gave to the boys in the shop here. There is a book about rocks you might like. It is the one I was reading in Galveston when you came to see me in the hospital. You remember that red-haired nurse? I wanted a piece of her real bad. I think her name was Betty.

If you do not want the books just pass them on to someone who does. I always wanted a place where I could keep them together. I been real lucky up here with everything, I guess. It has been good to stop long enough to settle into a place. Before I got sick I never could sit still. You remember how we used to be? Like there was no tomorrow, you used to say. Well, tomorrow is just around the corner now and I got one more rail to ride. I hope you been making out. See you later, Stick.

Your friend,
Farleigh Nixon

Stick said goodbye at the bottom of the stairs. It was bright outside. Rudy looked away when they shook hands. Stick figured whatever was bothering him had nothing to do with Wink. When the door shut, he heard him slowly climb the stairs.

The knapsack was light. He would need some supplies from the A&P before he hopped a train. He was dying for fresh apples and remembered the liquor store around the corner. They had a special on vodka last time. Crystal-Ann said it made him harder. He liked tequila better than vodka, but as Wink would say, "You can't fly on one wing."

The librarian was grateful for the books. In a small town, books were hard to come by.

"From around here?" she asked, handing him a slip of paper.

"No, ma'am." Stick squinted at the tiny print.

"It's a receipt for the books in case you want to take a deduction," she explained.

"What kinda deduction?"

"For your income taxes," she whispered, leaning towards him over the counter.

Stick realized an opportunity when he saw one. The place was deathly still. The idea of sex with a decent-looking girl between the shelves made his blood race. Her eyes were the shape of large almonds. He considered the wide circumference of a nipple through her thin cashmere sweater. It looked as hard as a stone.

"Thank you kindly, but," he said, dropping the receipt on the counter and backing slowly away, "be a waste a paper."

Dunlap Creek was almost dry. Halfway across Stick looked up and saw the bridge. The heavy knapsack made it hard for him to stay balanced. He tasted the tequila in his mouth. Stepping over a long chain at the bridge entrance, he crossed into the musty light and listened to the swallows nesting overhead.

Crystal-Ann had never seen Humpback Bridge. They were close one day on a hot shot to Norfolk, but she was too sick to jump. He'd lifted her up to see through the cargo door, but it was raining and the bridge looked beat-up. *"Only curved-span covered bridge in America,"* he shouted as it raced through the trees. *"Middle's four feet higher than the ends."*

"'Bout how I feel, darlin'," she said when he put her down.

At night the skies over Alleghany County filled with crystal blue stars. His body felt radiant and warm underneath the blanket as the tequila revived him. Looking up into the universe, he remembered the evening skies over Platform 24. He didn't care if it had been a red star or a pink planet, ole Wink was up there somewhere. Maybe his arm came back. Or maybe you don't need arms when you're dead. Maybe you just get lucky and live on all the good dreams you ever had that never came true.

Over the fire in the morning, Stick stood as bacon smoke swirled around him and the wind shifted. His face was smooth from having shaved in the creek, and he was hungry. The bacon wouldn't last long and the tequila was gone, but he'd wrapped some eggs in a pair of wool socks and his new knife was sharp as a razor. Lifting the cooked bacon with his fork, he placed each strip on a flat slab of shale before throwing the eggs into the pan they curdled in, then sprinkling broken strands of wild chives on top.

As he ate from the pan, his legs dangled over a sandstone ledge at the base of the foundation under the bridge. The stones were still damp with dew. He was tired of the heat. The creek flowed under his boots like dark velvet. Two clouds of black flies hovered side by side in the sunlight direectly upstream. It would rain today. Smallmouth would be under him somewhere if he looked hard enough—slicing the dark water with flashes of bronze. A gravel bar rose up downstream where they'd driven ripe females to spawn.

Stick heard footsteps on the bridge overhead. Leaning back against the wall, he put his empty pan down and considered the reflection of the bridge in the water below. He was out in the world again. It would take some time, but the truth was, he was still living. Everybody passes through something, he thought, nodding off, and one way or another, they all get to where they're going.

When he opened his eyes, his legs were bathed in sunlight. Underneath the bridge, he saw abandoned swallow nests. Cliff swallows, he figured, by the muddy, bulblike shape—must be halfway to Savannah by now.

Across the creek, walnut trees yellowed slightly and the sky deepened with the color of rain. When a shape under the span caught his eye, for a moment he thought he'd seen a ghost. But as a rush of cool air lifted from the water below, he sensed that he was not alone. Like a dog, he had licked his wounds and tracked him down.

"Hello, mister."

"Hello, Willie."

CHAPTER FIFTEEN

As Captain Snyder read from *The Daily Progress,* Moses understood that he would never see Willie again. There was a picture of the burned house, but it didn't say anything about Sadie. Mostly it talked about the body and the boy. He had come to think of the boy as his own and it saddened him to realize that Willie might be thought badly of by others or be ashamed of himself. A one-hundred-year-old black man understood these things, but for a kid it was different. The boy was like a possum up a tree, but he'd be coming down eventually.

That Sadie, she 'uz a pretty woman, Moses thought as the bell's rope ran through his fingers later in the day. Sometimes she was a bunch of women all rolled into one, but she was good to him and he cared for her because of that. Moses rarely counted anymore when he rang. After so many years, he didn't have to. *Like dem clouds . . .* he thought, looking out over Alderman Library, *dem clouds goin' by.*

In Charlottesville, the death of any man was a story of great importance, and this time, because a child had run from the burning house, people sat up and took notice. The streets were buzzing now that the boy's photograph had hit the state's largest newspapers and the desks of police commissioners. *Where was he now?* old Moses wondered as a warm rain fell and students ran for cover. The bell could not protect the boy, he understood that. But, still, he rang as if it could.

When she heard the bell, Sadie Graves opened her eyes. It had been a long but profitable night. Her last client was eighteen. His hands were rough from square baling, but his body was smooth, sunburned and taut. They had lain together for over an hour. She didn't mind. She coaxed his head into her neck and caressed his back. His blond hair was long, and curly at the ends. After a while, her hand slid quietly down between his soft, strong shoulders and down further to the top of his ass. She stopped there. He was asleep. She remembered Willie would be fourteen in November. Across the room the candle was nearly out. Closing her eyes, she felt his presence. She knew why he'd run away. The old man's bell would comfort him, lifting her baby up into the arms of Jesus, into a new life, where he would learn to love again, to laugh, and to forgive.

Because Sadie Graves ran a whorehouse, word got out quickly. She didn't expect a miracle, but when you loved men, they were good for something sometimes. Or then not. She'd been knifed by a drunken Puerto Rican and abused by her husband more than a time or two. That's just the way it was. Her sisters had died of typhoid, her daddy had died of syphilis, and now her child was gone. Asleep in her room next door when the fire broke out, she'd been too stoned to hear the sirens and too confused to understand. When Matt Abel woke her to explain what had happened, she'd asked him to leave and locked the door. At the open window, she smelled the smoke and felt her head go numb, as if all the switches in her brain had been turned off. Then she'd passed out from the shot of smack.

At dusk, she rose like a ghost from her bed and followed the sound of a brown thrasher calling from the bushes below. At the window, a breeze lifted the thin lace curtains across her face. She was thirsty. Everything in her was dry. "Ain't what been done," her momma used to say, "but what you done with it."

The boy had left an old black woman in Goshen. When Sheriff Sheffield got a call, he called Matt Abel. They went back a ways together. The sheriff had slept with the ladies from time to time. "Keeps me sharp," he confessed one night on his way out.

"Keeps you hard," Matt had replied, handing him a cigar.

Matt Abel would find the right time to tell Sadie. God was protecting her boy, she would tell him, like the knife that had missed her heart.

"Ain't right," old Moses told her, standing in the burned-out kitchen. "Just a boy." He looked down at his shoes.

Sadie was sober. Taking his hand in hers, she led him next door to fix him some tea in her room, and before he rode the streetcar home, he gave her a wrinkled envelope full of single dollar bills.

"For dat box in duh celluh when he come," Moses said, sitting on the edge of her bed. "Don't 'spect ta be 'round fo 'evah.'"

Sadie considered the envelope.

"From duh weddin's, mostly," he explained. "Give me a lil' extra when I do it 'tween duh hour. Not all duh time, 'course, but . . . sometime people real nice."

"I can't take this, Moses," she said tenderly. "Besides, I got plenty saved up as is."

"Ain't fo' you, Miss Sadie." He shook his head from side to side. "Fo' ma Willie."

CHAPTER SIXTEEN

When he saw Stick, Willie could see that something was wrong. He looked like his father when his momma told him things he didn't want to hear.

"What you doin' here, boy?" Stick said sullenly, washing his pan before pouring water on the fire, the steam hissing around his legs and into his face.

"I jumped the local at Dunlap Reach." Willie shuffled his feet, looking away. Stick's expression did not change. "First time I done it, but it went pretty good. Hard part was climbin' in." Riding in the empty car, he remembered what Matt Abel had said about hopping a train to Poughkeepsie. "Piece a cake!" he'd explained from the front seat of his convertible. "You catch the right one and the world's your oyster!"

"How'd you find me here?" Stick tossed his knife into his knapsack.

"Heard you talk'in."

"'Bout the bridge, I 'magine."

"Yes, sir." Willie noticed two strips of cooked bacon on a rock by the fire.

Stick was impressed that the boy had hopped a train. He wasn't all that big and the platform of most cars came up to his own chest. "Well, I'm movin' on and you can't be comin' with me."

Willie's face deflated. His feet were sore from the shoes that Sister Mo had given him, but he'd need to keep walking. She might tell someone, and by sundown they'd be up and down the creek looking for him.

As he packed the final items into his knapsack, Stick watched the boy from the corner of his eye. He was pissed. With everything else on his mind, he'd done what he had to do getting him to Sister Mo. The kid could jump back in the river for all he cared. He must have run from the old lady before she'd been able to tell the sheriff. They'd be after him if he'd done something.

The bacon Stick had given him took the edge off, but Willie knew his stomach would be growling again in an hour or two. He'd taken Sister Mo's last pone and eaten it on the train. Curling his knees up, he lay down against the ledge, his head resting on his arm. Closing one eye, he watched Stick fold a bright red poncho, the shimmering green water refracting against his face. Stick looked like a clown with a red balloon.

Half a mile upriver, Stick collected wild onions along the railroad grade and looked down. The dam was about where he'd remembered it. Some of it had broken out, allowing a confluence of creek to escape to one side, but what remained flowed easily over the edge, forming a foamy gray chute on the embankment closest to him. He looked for the old cedar, but it was gone. Maybe he was turned around and it was farther upstream?

A catbird watched him from the other side of the river. It had wandered too far west the spring before. Within a day or so it would fly south over Springs Mountain.

Along the far ledge, wind snaked through a shallow line of juniper. In October, rain would run the creek up against the roots, loosening their hold upon the limestone and travertine. He thought about the boy for a moment before turning back towards his campsite. He had familiar eyes. They made him uneasy. Crystal-Ann would have figured it out by now. Her voice was gone lately, probably because it hurt too much to hear it. Dry leaves crunched under his boots as he walked, before an oak branch snapped in half.

Under a silent cloud of diving crows, Dunlap Creek drifted away, past the broken limbs, past the giant Deodar cedar, past the sleeping boy under Humpback Bridge, skirting the tracks below Callaghan and the bloodhounds that had gathered there to find him.

The lead hound was a tawny bitch named June. The Albemarle men didn't think much of her or her owner, but she'd famously cornered a man in Gum Spring, an ex-con on the run from New York City who'd killed his wife and dumped the body off a road near Albany.

"Saw it in her eyes," the dog's owner had explained, watching his dog sniff the edges of Sister Mo's blue blanket. "Got all quiet, 'cept for the tail. Went back and forth real deliberate before she took off."

Jasper Willis was halfway down a mine shaft when they pulled him out. He was headed to Lynchburg to find a girl. "Shoulda killed duh dog," he muttered when they took him away.

Clearing the tracks east of Callaghan, June led them south towards Humpback Bridge along a trail above Dunlap Creek.

"*On it!*" Sheriff Sheffield shouted to his deputies racing behind the barking pack. "*Call his momma, Johnny, and tell her we're closin' in!*"

Across the creek from his campsite, Stick heard the dogs and felt a sudden sympathy for the boy. He'd done some things he wasn't proud of. Crystal-Ann would've hidden the boy somewhere until it was safe, and it wouldn't have mattered what he was running from.

"Get right down to it, honey, we're all running from something," she would say.

Collecting his knapsack, Stick followed the gravel bar downstream under the bridge before hopping across the water on the tops of rocks to a slope of broken gneiss on the opposite side. Stepping quickly, he heard the dogs approaching and measured the distance. Half a mile, he figured, maybe less. If the boy was upwind, that was good. Most people run the wrong way.

The bitch had two smells in her head. One was an old cider bottle from her house and the other was Sister Mo's blue blanket. She missed her spot in the corner of the porch under the swing. She missed her trout and biscuit in the morning. And she missed the old cat.

When she smelled it again, she froze. The blue blanket was just below the big tree straight ahead. Pulling with all his might, Lawson Brady lost circulation in his right hand as the leash tightened. The bloodhound stopped dead in her tracks as the remaining eight dogs flew past her.

"*Whoa!*" he shouted, fumbling through a shirt pocket with his left hand. "*Bring it up!*" he bellowed as the sheriff and his men drew alongside.

When Lawson Brady blew his whistle, the dogs lifted their noses into the air and turned back. Dropping her head, June walked forward to join the other dogs as they leapt about with great excitement and barked uncontrollably.

"*Load 'em up!*" the sheriff shouted.

One by one a deputy leashed the dogs in groups of three and led them away. Some of the males resisted, but within minutes June stood alone, pointing forward, her eyes riveted on a man standing in the distance under an enormous pale blue cedar.

Stick smelled the tree before he saw the boy's shoes. Crystal-Ann kept a blue vial of cedar oil over the sink in Richmond for his shoulder. Fumbling through the cabinet one day, he'd called her a witch.

"What kinda witch would be dyin' a cancer?" she'd asked.

"A shitty one," he replied.

Stick had passed the tree on his way to Humpback Bridge the day before. Forgetting where things were made him feel old. It was snowing the first time he'd seen the tree. He'd been logging some land nearby for a family in Moss Run and its yellow-green crown glistened in a sudden burst of sunlight as he passed from the opposite side of the creek. Given its height, he figured it was a couple hundred years old.

The boy was halfway up the backside of the tree. It was a good place to hide unless the dog picked him up. The bloodhound's nose dropped down over the ground, and as she slowly approached Stick, he slid the knapsack off his shoulders and opened the top flap.

"Afternoon!" Sheriff Sheffield called out from behind the hound.

Stick had a poker face as he stood.

"Mind if we talk to you?" the sheriff asked, walking towards him.

"Already have."

"I'm sorry?" The sheriff cupped his hand behind his ear.

"Come on." Stick motioned with his hand for the group to advance.

Including the sheriff, four men—one too skinny to be a cop and one drunk—moved forward cautiously. Stick noticed the hound had stopped. That would help the boy, unless somebody got a notion to look up.

No one spoke at first.

"Lookin' for someone?" Stick asked.

"You from around here?" The sheriff could size up a person quickly enough.

"Sometimes," Stick answered.

"How 'bout now?" the sheriff replied, understanding the game.

"Spent the night at Humpback. Figure on workin' apples next week."

"Which outfit?" He grinned.

"Springdale south a Winchester, if they're lookin'."

"Howie Pettit's place."

"That be it," Stick confirmed.

"Well . . . " The sheriff took his hat off and wiped his sleeve across his forehead. There was more hair on his head than Stick would have thought. "Tell him I said hi. We're cousins," he said, looking away. "At least that's what they tell me."

Stick nodded, saying nothing.

The men laughed nervously and shuffled their feet from side to side. They preferred the chase to standing around, but the sheriff was as smart as they come.

"Stick Watson." Stick put his hand out.

"Dave Sheffield outta Charlottesville." The Sheriff's grip was firm. "We've got a missing boy."

"Kid about twelve with short brown hair?"

"Be the one, Stick. You seen him?"

"Said his name was Willie."

"Willie Graves. When you see him?" His face had turned serious.

"Goshen two days back."

"The Sister's place?"

The drunk's eyes wandered about as they spoke.

"Yep. Fished him out of the Maury day before, figured she could help." Stick wasn't sure how much to tell them. "What's he done?"

"Don't know yet. Need to talk to him, though. Tell you anything?"

"Said he lost his fishin' pole."

"That's it?" said the sheriff.

Stumbling closer to the cedar, the drunk stared up directly at the boy. The bottom tip of his shoe stuck out over the branch.

"All he said. He was pretty shook. Think he washed through the Kitchen."

"That's what they said in Goshen. How the hell you do that?" The sheriff shook his head.

"Fallin' in, I guess. Tell you one thing, somebody's lookin' out for him.

Least they was." Stick bent over his knapsack. "Got some bacon for your dog, if you want it."

"No, it's okay, Stick. Thank you all the same. We better be movin' before we run outta light."

"Cooked it this morning. Make her happy till she finds the boy." Stick unwrapped a small piece of butcher paper from inside his drinking cup and held up the bacon.

"*Dog like bacon, Mr. Brady?*" the sheriff shouted.

"*If she don't, I do,*" Brady shouted back, releasing her leash.

June panted, eyeing Stick, then walked cautiously towards him. She'd forgotten the smell of the blanket and Brady had forgotten the rules of the game.

"Come here, girl," Stick encouraged her. "It's okay." Still edging forward, the dog watched Stick. There was something about him that she liked, and his voice was gentle.

Stick let the bacon fall to the ground as she reached him, tempted to pet her soft, dusky coat. He'd always wanted a dog, but they had no place on trains. He'd seen one roll under a hot shot one night under the lights in Roanoke and it cured him once and for all.

"Where you headed, Sheriff?" He closed the knapsack and stood up.

"Oh . . . " The sheriff slid his hat on and gazed across Dunlap Creek. " . . . suppose we'll head back to the trucks and make a few calls. He's somewhere, and we're gonna find him. Just a matter of time." He twisted the heel of his boot into the ground.

Stick swung into his knapsack and tightened the straps. He'd heard enough of their crap.

"Yep. Just a matter of time," the sheriff repeated.

When the dog sneezed, the drunk looked away, startled. The boy had felt his eyes upon him. He'd reminded him of his father. For courage he imagined being in the branches of the Lucky Bean as the sound of bells spilled through the creek.

When the drunk stumbled toward June, she growled.

"June!" her master snapped. The men laughed when the dog sneezed again.

"Sorry boys," Stick apologized, "musta been the pepper."

Trotting back to her master, the hound dog sneezed three more times until the smell of the blue blanket was gone completely, replaced by the flavor of bacon and cayenne pepper.

The drunk walked unsteadily past Stick. His bottle was under the front seat and, as the day had progressed, his mind had become increasingly unreliable. River stones resembled the smooth hips of naked women, monkeys called out from across the water, and the kid they were after was hanging upside down from the top of a tree.

CHAPTER SEVENTEEN

On Garrett Street, surrounded by a swelling crowd of onlookers, firemen had worked the house clean. People had spent their whole lives avoiding The Bottom until that day, until curiosity finally got the better of them. From all walks of life they came. While children stole blackened detritus, vendors sold peanuts and lemonade. The autopsy was simple enough—death undetermined. The electrical lines were clean. The bedroom fan was off and the hot water tank was new. Since the fire had originated in the kitchen, the arson squad from Richmond paid particular attention to the appliances. When the final report reached Junior Lessor's desk, he closed his office door and, between sips of Nehi Grape, studied the envelope. As Charlottesville's fire chief, he was aware of two things before he opened it up. The victim's son had run away and his momma was a hooker.

Mopsey Graves hadn't fooled anyone—especially his story about being from Texas. If he had anything going for him, it was a good imagination. But as the stories changed, and things became more desperate, he took to calling his wife a worthless whore.

The birth of Henry Graves was complicated by opium. At five pounds he was the color of slate, and when the drug wore off, his body shook like "a dog shittin' shoe tacks." As his lungs labored, Doc Wilkerson stood over him like the Angel of Death. "Boy's slippin' away," he told the room. "Best let the Good Lord take over from here on out."

A pallor came over the faces at Matt Abel's house that night as the women gathered outside Sadie's door. They prayed for the baby and for Sadie's luck to change. They prayed for salvation and they asked the Lord to turn things around. That night in The Bottom it was quiet and, as the Good Lord listened, men limped home unfulfilled and dissatisfied.

At first Willie had loved his father deeply—most especially when he smelled of Lucky Strikes and Brylcreem and sliced the air with wild enthusiasm. But being young is not the same as being stupid and falling from a tabletop was not the same as being pushed. By the time he understood the difference, it was too late.

When Mopsey looked at Willie, he saw the all of it. The boy was black and he was white. He saw it in the faces uptown and in Sadie's eyes sometimes before she rolled over. Willie touched his father's rage like a child touches fire—without understanding the attraction completely and only half meaning to. At first his anger seemed almost magnetic, but as he felt its force time and time again, eventually, it scared him half to death.

His mother had met Mopsey at the Dogwood Festival one warm April night. He ran the Loop d' Loop and, just because he was handsome, she'd fucked him for a week. They were married by a white judge from Alexandria. She slept with both men that day, but her new husband was never the wiser.

Mopsey was wild and made Sadie laugh. He'd done some time, but she never asked why. It wasn't so much about knowing a man as about having one around. And so, at first, she gave him time to be who he was. He cooked a bit and, because of the hours she kept, he called her "Sunrise." But in the house next door their life changed quickly. She could tell one night by the way he came. It tore him up watching men pass at night—hearing their catcalls. Mopsey Graves had married a whore, and even worse, a whore with a child in her belly. She'd told him the child was his, but eventually he'd figured it out. And that was that. Habitually drunk, he became a sideshow in her eyes. A trick gone bad on an empty ride going around and around.

Mopsey Graves had been burned beyond recognition, and when they swept him up, half his bones were gone.

CHAPTER EIGHTEEN

When Willie reached the ground the moon was up and Stick was gone. He figured he had until morning before they'd start looking again. Where Stick had been standing, he found a red bandana with something wrapped up inside. Undoing the knots, he wondered why the drunk man had not seen him. His eyes were like the eyes of a pirate and it scared him to think what he would've done to him. If his daddy weren't dead, they wouldn't be after him so hard. But no one would believe him. They might look like they wanted to when they caught him. They might feed him something good or buy him a root beer, but soon enough, they'd change their tune. He might only be thirteen, but he wasn't stupid—the Bible said, "an eye for an eye."

Within the folds of the bandana he unrolled a box of matches, some jerky, and a five-dollar bill. He was grateful to Stick for what he'd left him and especially for having sidetracked the dogs. Maybe the Beautiful Lady had sent him. Or maybe he was just a hobo. Through the shadows of the forest, the creek sounded closer than it had during the day. He wanted to make a fire, but it wasn't cold enough to take a chance and it wouldn't be long before the sun was up. He'd spend the night following the creek back to Dunlap Reach, the same way he'd come.

As the sounds of the woods rose up inside him, he listened until he became more confident that the dogs were gone. Since the morning of the fire, he'd done a lot of walking, and as long as he did, he felt safe. As he walked, he prayed for forgiveness and for the strength to understand what he had done. He prayed for his mother and for all she meant to him. He prayed for old Moses and his bell and for God to look out for him and protect him on his journey. He prayed for Stick Watson and thanked him for saving his life and he prayed for his dead father, only because his mother would've wanted him to.

The sound of Dunlap Creek intensified as shadows of cool, milky moonlight swirled around him. He was hungry for the jerky, but resisted the temptation to eat it. The important thing was to keep on while the dogs were gone. Finding the Main Line at Route 660 under a C&O track light, he would wait for morning and, if he was lucky, hop an eastbound local to Winchester.

Under the Covington yard worklights, bulls held their rifles up and milled about. They'd combed the tracks all night while the dogs slept in a motel near Callaghan. Stick watched them from behind a thicket of quince. They were after the boy, all right, but some were heading out. He'd need to be careful on his way down the line. A flatcar wouldn't make it this time. Unless the doors were closed, even a boxcar was out of the question. They'd use a mirror as the train passed and catch him pushed up against the back corner.

As the trucks pulled out, Stick rose to his feet, cradling his knapsack over one shoulder. He'd have about an hour to catch out during their breakfast. A hot shot would do the trick, or a gondola. The kid was damaged goods. Whatever had happened back in Charlottesville, he was in some sticky shit.

CHAPTER NINETEEN

The morning skies over Albemarle County were suede blue. As the last ring faded, Moses put his coat on and shuffled over to the open window. It would be hot today. In another hour the sky would lose its color and the students would arrive. Most would be first-year men. They were fresh-faced, more vulnerable than the others. He liked the first-years most of all. They were still under the influence of something innocent. Still cordial, still connected to their families. The older students were different, their eyes touched by alcohol and greed, as if they'd stopped caring for one another. From the bell tower, Moses smelled the stillness where summer met autumn. The university had done him right all these years and it was a pretty place Mr. Jefferson had made—even to a black man. Peering down to the Corner, he located the pool hall and imagined his tiny room below. For fifty years it had been a place to hang his hat for the night, but nothing more. In truth, Mr. Jefferson's tower was where he found what he was after in this world and where he found the wantin' to.

Ten miles south of Winchester, Stick Watson slid cautiously down the rusty ladder of a slow-moving C&O gondola before jumping onto Cedar Creek Bridge. The orchard was two miles upstream and he needed a walk. As the sound of the train faded, his spirits lifted. With nine hundred acres, the Pettits had been in the fruit business for forty-five years. Howie Pettit was a regular guy with a big heart. The money was decent and Stick liked the family. In late August, near the West Virginia line at Frederick County, the heat was down and the nights were fresh. If he stayed long enough, they'd ask him for dinner and he and Howie Pettit would sit together on the porch while the women did dishes. The Pettits were curious about the world and Stick had seen some of it. They'd watch him carefully when he spoke, measuring his words, and in the same way, he would listen to them. Certain people stayed in his head. And in the darkess of a boxcar or rocking on a porch, if he trusted someone, he'd open up.

Through the open window of the Pettit bunkhouse, stars flickered between the branches—dispersed occasionally by an errant cloud. Hearing the roll of a distant hot shot, Stick rubbed his aching shoulder. He was glad to be off the line. Pulling the horse blanket up to his chin, he gave in to the mattress and closed his eyes. Crystal-Ann was gone and he'd be boxing Ginger Golds in the morning. Drifting off to sleep, he imagined his hands to either side of her slender, pale belly as he pulled her hips gently into his and smelled her hair. By the window in the corner of Howie Pettit's bunkhouse, the air was ripe with apples, with sleeping men, and their desires.

As the night called out, Willie walked towards what would prove to be his only escape. They hadn't found him yet. His mother was drunk tonight, he knew that much. He didn't miss that part of her. He didn't miss the part of her that wanted to forget. He missed the part that wanted to remember. She'd told him once how she'd lost her way until he was born from the light of a Full Beaver Moon.

Before morning, Howie Pettit's men were in the branches working the last fifty trees of Ginger Golds. It had been a good two weeks. The men were quiet and worked well together. They kept their drinking to Saturday nights. Some had been together for a while and a few were new. There were ten Mexicans, one Guatemalan, and three white brothers from West Virginia. There were no women.

Stick kept to himself as he worked the tree. The apple twisted off the branch easily and was hard in his hand. Taking a bite, he understood Howie Pettit's expression the day before in the barn. It would be a bumper crop. By mid-August the Golds would be ready and his fifty-year-old grader would be thumping away in the packing shed behind the main barn. He'd bought it used in Covesville for eight thousand dollars ten years earlier. At the season's peak, eighty bushels an hour would be dusted, shined, and moved hydraulically from a wooden bin to a hamper and then onto the conveyor belt of an L-shaped table where wife and daughter would strip them of stems, grade their size and quality, and direct them into boxes. The jumbos and peewees went to fruit stands and the rest went for cider, sauce, and butter. There were faster machines and it sucked up oil, but "she's a beauty," he told Stick one night over a beer. "And besides," he added, "you can't shoot your grandmother."

The apple was crisp and sweet. Repositioning his feet on the ladder, he wiped juice off his chin with the back of his hand and watched the sun hit North Mountain. It would be a fine day. In a few hours Howie Pettit's wife, Rachel, would call the men to lunch. First they'd wash their hands in the outdoor sink at the back of the barn, then gather around the long table under a big beech. She would ask them for silence before they began and they would look up as if she were an angel of some kind. Most of the men would close their eyes and pray, but some would look away. Still, each face expressed a certain pleasure, a willingness, as if for that one moment at least, their differences didn't matter.

After lunch Stick went to the kitchen door to thank the women. He wasn't shy in their company and some of them looked down as he spoke. But Pettit's young daughter rushed over to Stick right away.

"You the hobo man?" she asked boldly.

"Rebecca!" her mother scolded. "That's no way to talk to Mr. Watson."

"It's fine, Mrs. Pettit," Stick assured her. "Been called a whole lot worse."

"You ride them trains?" her daughter persisted.

Stick looked down at the girl. She had her mother's red hair and the shape of her father's head. She was a good five years younger than Willie.

"Yes, ma'am, been 'round." He grinned.

"Been to China?" she blurted.

"China?!" her mother marveled. The other women giggled nervously.

"Never been to China," Stick answered.

"Been down the Mississippi?"

"I have."

"Seen an alligator?"

"Now that's enough, child! Mr. Watson has work to do," her mother declared, reaching down and taking her hand. The girl was now directly in front of Stick. He could see her eyes more clearly. They were dark like agate.

"Down in the 'Glades, seen a croc the size a your daddy's square bailer eat a man in one bite."

The girl gripped her mother's skirt as her face turned white.

"Then you know what happened, Miss Rebecca?" Stick asked the terrified child turning her face to her mother's sweater.

"What?" she almost whispered.

"He smiled and swam away."

As the day drew west, the eastern slopes of North Mountain dissolved into a sudden charcoal darkness, sending the final group of men down their ladders. Stick had enjoyed the day. Hoisting the last box of Ginger Golds onto the tailgate of the truck, he turned back to admire the row of fifty trees they had worked together, their branches still stooped from the weight of the apples. For a moment it all made sense to him, standing there in a dark orchard surrounded by strangers. He was glad to be alive, even if it meant he was alone. He could miss her and still get around, still put in an honest day's work. But it wouldn't last forever. By Thanksgiving the trees would be bare with empty wooden crates stacked inside the barn and men scattered to the wind.

The following day before sunrise, the Mexicans left for a stud farm in Albemarle County. Stick remembered the area east of Charlottesville where the farms sat along Route 22 with white fences running in all directions. The houses looked like God had put them there Himself. If there was money in the world, it ended up in houses like that, with fields full of horses instead of dandelions. He'd heard there was work from time to time, but never asked. It would be barn work mostly and haying in the summer, which was all right. But places like that belonged in fairy tales. Like a pretty woman, the less you knew about her, the better.

Red stripes over specks of yellow glimmered in the sun as they approached the lower east section of the orchard. The soil was still damp from an overnight shower and mud stuck to their boots. They'd spend most of the morning moving crates and getting ready for the Jonathans. It would take all week and new men were expected by the middle of the day, but with so many apples, they'd need more hands.

The Jonathans were smaller than the Golds, easier to twist, and tart. Sometimes Stick could get two in each hand. The skin was beautiful to him with its red lines against a thick yellow skin. Bees hovered overhead as he filled the sack around his waist. He'd keep his eyes out for hornets. They were easy to miss working apples, and he'd been stung once building bridges in Maine. Reaching under a dock in the darkness, his hand had entered the opening of a nest. He'd felt five stings before calling for help.

"Señor Stick, vamos!" the Guatemalan shouted from below.

The others had left. Squinting through the branches, he saw the man's cheery square head and smiled. Pepe was a hard worker. It was his third year at the orchard and he'd be leaving after lunch. He mailed his money home and snored like a pig.

"Thanks, amigo," Stick called down.

"De nada," the man replied, walking away.

Stick washed his face and hands with a bar of soap before dragging his wet bandana across the back of his neck. The water was colder than yesterday. He'd shower tonight before they ran to town. He'd forgotten it was Saturday until he'd heard the men talking. There was a bar he remembered from when Crystal-Ann was with him, and they'd had a good time. The West Virginia boys had a truck and it was time for liquor. He'd taken a nip from the bottle in his knapsack a few times, but this was a good job and he didn't want to lose it.

While Rachel Pettit stood at the table end and prayed silently, locks of golden red hair tumbled across the shoulders of her simple blue dress. Stick closed his eyes and imagined her naked shoulders writhing through soft, cascading curls. She would be tender against his rough hands. She would give herself to him if he asked. As he opened his eyes, Willie Graves dropped to the bench, looking like a mongrel dog. Watching him closely, it was hard to believe that he'd found his way again. He'd call the cops this time—that was it. He'd had enough of this shit. It was payday and, come hell or high water, he'd stay drunk until the kid was out of his fucking hair.

Except for the West Virginia boys, the table was quiet. Heading for town later, they'd be keeping their eyes out for one another. One liked to whistle, one was shy and laughed too much, and one had a chip on his shoulder.

Stick picked at his food. The sliced ham smelled good, but he was too upset by the boy's presence to eat. Finishing his iced tea, he rose from the table with an uneaten plate and watched the boy inhale a second helping of grits. Heading towards the kitchen, he heard Howie Pettit following behind.

"Stick?" Howie called quietly.

"Yes, sir," Stick replied, halting.

"You all right?"

"Yes, sir," he said flatly.

Howie Pettit looked him over for a moment before glancing back towards the table.

"Got a new man today," he said after a moment.

"More like a boy, ain't he?" Stick shot back, giving the table a dirty look.

"That bother you?"

Stick took a deep breath. It wasn't Howie Pettit's fault that the kid was here. He had apples to bring in and it didn't matter who did the work. He needed hands and it sure as hell didn't matter how big they were. The kid was a way to get it done.

"Well, I'm here for the work, make no difference to me. Seems kinda young, though, don't he?"

"Says he's thirteen," Howie replied, turning to Stick. "I get 'em all sizes 'bout this time a year, you know? Few years back half the bunks were kids. And some of them were a lot younger than this one. Wife said it was wrong, but after a while she gave up. We figured it was better they was working with us than out on their own. Kinda rough out there, ain't it?"

"Can be," Stick agreed, scratching the back of his neck.

Howie Pettit handed him a small manila envelope of money before taking his plate.

"I'll run this in. You need a ride to town?"

"I'm good, thank you," Stick said, putting the envelope in his back pocket.

"You up for supper tomorrow? Just family and some fried chicken."

He wanted to say no because he knew that he'd be six sheets to the wind by Sunday, or sooner than that. He wanted to tell him to call the sheriff so that he could lose the kid once and for all, but he knew that Crystal-Ann wouldn't have stood for it. He missed the sound of a house and he missed the smell of a woman.

Howie Pettit smiled. " 'Bout five?"

The truck cruised down National Avenue alongside the cemetery. It looked the same to Stick. Surrounded by the graves of Union and Confederate soldiers, he'd passed out one night under a marble cross and in the morning a nicely dressed family had walked by on their way to church. Noticing his presence, they didn't seem particularly frightened or alarmed. Winchester was good that way. The doors swung both ways. Passing Handley Library on West Piccadilly Street, he remembered how someone had helped him to his feet and offered him a meal.

By late afternoon the Red Wolf was full of smoke. They found a spot at the end of the bar before the brothers wandered off towards a table in the back full of women. Stick could see that the place had changed. It didn't surprise him particularly, but it made him feel old. The crowd was mostly Mexican. That would have turned her on. She would have wanted to dance and his body would have been stiff as a horse until the booze kicked in. Crystal-Ann made her own magic. Like there was nothing she wanted more than what she had.

Because Stick preferred drinking alone, the truck had stopped at an ABC store on its way to town. He'd left a bottle under the seat, and told them that if he wasn't back by midnight to head on home. The brothers wanted whores that night. They'd asked him if he knew of any. He'd heard about a trailer behind the airport, but that was long before he'd met Crystal-Ann and chances were it was long gone. But in a town the size of Winchester, sex wasn't hard to find. All you needed was ten bucks and a dick.

After his fifth shot of Virginia Gentleman, he headed out. Some of the Mexicans were getting rough and you could tell by the way they put their drinks down it was only a matter of time before the shit would fly. The brothers were being set up—he could see that at the door. One girl was all over the older one. He looked pretty far gone. The other two were eyeballing two Mexican girls at the next table and laughing like donkeys. Stick had advised them to leave most of their pay in the bunkhouse in case they got rolled. You could always tell when a man had money.

After the dishes were dried and put away, Rachel Pettit and her daughter, Rebecca, walked Willie to the bunkhouse. The boy was dirty and tired. On their walk together they asked him where he was from.

"Been west, ma'am," was all he said.

The little girl offered to carry his bag, and while he wanted to say yes, he didn't want to give her the impression that he couldn't take care of himself. He was grateful that her father had taken him in. He had Stick's five dollars and was halfway through his last Moon Pie when he'd jumped off the train. He'd had no idea where the Pettits lived until a C&O linesman had steered him in the right direction. It was five miles away.

For an old chicken coop, the bunkhouse looked pretty good. They gave him a bed by a window with a trunk to store his things.

"May be chilly in the morning," Mrs. Pettit warned, handing him a blanket from the trunk. "Outhouse is through the back door. Don't forget the sawdust and lime when you use it."

"Yes, ma'am," the boy answered politely.

"More men will be comin' tomorrow, so enjoy the quiet while you can."

"Yes, ma'am," he repeated.

From the foot of his bed, Rachel and Rebecca Pettit regarded Willie with some curiosity. Boys of various ages had been through the orchard before. The Pettits didn't know them well. Some were tough and some were broken, but when you looked into their eyes, when you saw them at the table, they all looked pretty much the same.

"How come you're not in school?" the girl asked out of the blue.

"That is none of your business, Miss Rebecca!" her mother scolded, folding down Willie's top blanket. "This young man needs to rest up and gather his strength for the morning."

"But it's Sunday tomorrow, Momma. There's no work on Sunday," her daughter protested.

"Well, then, child, unlike yourself, Mr. Graves will have a day to do as he pleases," she replied firmly.

The girl looked at Willie as if he were an exotic creature. Something about him made her curious, but she didn't know what. His eyes were sad, but not like he'd quit on himself. It was more like he had something to say and no one to say it to.

"Shower's in the barn and there's plenty of hot water. Soap's on the wall. Just hit the light when you go," Rachel Pettit recited, turning to leave. "Oh," she remembered suddenly, "since the Johnson boys are leaving, why don't you have dinner with us tomorrow? About five o'clock, if that suits?"

"Suits just fine, ma'am, thank you." He was glad for the food. He was stuffed, but he'd be hungry soon enough. Her husband had said the kitchen was closed on Sunday. Maybe they felt sorry for him, or maybe it was a trick. He hoped they hadn't called the sheriff on him. He hoped Stick hadn't spilled the beans. But he was too tired to care one way or the other and the only thing in the world he really wanted was to lie down on his new bed.

"Well, then." Rachel Pettit dusted off her hands at the door, satisfied that all was in order. "Rebecca?"

Rebecca slid off the trunk with a pouty look. She was excited about the new boy and wanted to ask him a million questions. Maybe she could speak with him after her chores were done in the morning. Maybe he would push her on the swing and tell her everything about himself and his secrets.

"Good night, Willie." She shuffled off to her mother.

"Good night, Miss Rebecca," Willie sighed, watching them go.

He didn't mind being alone in the bunkhouse. He had his own window and a trunk. He didn't have anything to put in it, but it felt good to know that it was his in case he ever did. Maybe they'd want him to stay on after the work was done. It was quiet and he liked the Pettits. It seemed like they belonged together. In the shower he wanted to sing a song that he'd heard in church, but he couldn't remember the words, as if he'd learned the song in another lifetime. Walking back to the bunkhouse, he saw a faint star overhead. It was good to be clean again. He wondered if after a while you could forget everything you'd ever done and be somebody else.

As his head hit the pillow, he sighed contentedly and smelled the room. His window was open. His momma would have scolded him for not drying his hair. When she was sober, she was afraid for Willie. When she was drunk, she didn't care. Closing his eyes, he thought about the sound the glass candle had made when it hit his father's head. He heard a truck in the distance, rumbling in the dark. It was too early for the men to come back and too late to change what he had done.

As Stick left, the Red Wolf was cranking into fifth gear. Whatever came down, he'd hear about it in the morning, if the boys were still in one piece. Retrieving his bottle from under the truck seat, he thought about pulling them out before they did something stupid. They could hold their own with the ladies, but when it came to fighting, the Mexicans would slice them to pieces.

As he took a hit from his bottle, he remembered it was rum. Under the broken streetlight it had looked like bourbon. Over the sound of mariachis, the younger brother laughed hysterically from inside. They were too worked up to stop now. As Stick swallowed, the crowd roared like a caged animal. It was good to be drunk again. You pick your fights or you walk away. Simple as that. With the flask of Jamaican rum in his back pocket, Stick Watson had it all worked out. His cheeks were flushed and the sidewalks sparkled. As he turned down Braddock Street and saw the National Cemetery sign overhead, he remembered how they'd moved the buried Union soldiers back North to their homes in Harper's Ferry, Martinsburg, and Romney. So much fighting, he thought, swallowing more rum. All that blood and you're right back where you started.

When Willie opened his eyes, he had no idea how long he'd been asleep. A light outside the front door was on. He needed to pee, but the bunkhouse was cold. Sliding out from under the blanket, he tiptoed to the back door. Maybe he'd go in the bushes, he thought, pushing against the door. No one would see him.

Behind a wild quince he felt slippery rough grass under his bare feet. He recognized two stars that he'd seen from the Lucky Bean. Orion's Belt, he remembered, as he pulled his underwear down and took aim at the bushes. That's what it said in the star book his momma had found in the box of books. "They all belong to you, darlin'," she'd told him. He never felt like he owned the stars, but it was easy to remember what they were. They seemed more like places than names.

When a door slammed shut, Willie peed on his right foot. Dropping behind the bush, his face flushed. He'd heard a rooster crow from behind the barn. It was almost morning. Raising himself, his heart pounding, he looked up toward the farmhouse light off the kitchen, but no one was there. It was too quiet to be the brothers. It must be Stick, he thought, squinting at the back door. In his underwear and T-shirt, Willie stood trembling behind the bush. It had to be Stick, he decided, as the rooster crowed again.

Rubbing his hands on his arms for warmth, Willie stepped gingerly around the bush before hot-footing it towards the bunkhouse. Past the outhouse his feet hit soft clay. If he was quiet, he could slide into bed.

Through the screen door he saw Stick facedown in the bed next to his with his clothes and boots still on. He was drunk as a skunk and must have walked home ahead of the others. Willie smiled, knowing it was Stick and not the sheriff. Maybe he'd found a good place to hide after all. Maybe the hound dog had sneezed her brains out and gone home.

From under the warm blanket, Willie listened. Moses would be climbing to his bell right about now. When you rang the bell, Sundays were busy. He wondered how long it would be before he could go home again. Before falling asleep, he remembered when Moses let him ring his first bell, how long it lasted. As if the sound had a place to go and would keep right on until it got there.

Waking up a few hours later, Willie heard wheels approaching the bunkhouse. *The brothers will be full of liquor,* he thought. He'd pretend to be asleep like when his momma came home drunk. After they passed out, he'd go see if the little girl wanted some help with her chores, or a push on the swing.

When a car door closed, he knew something was wrong. Squeezing his eyes tight, he inched the blanket up over his head as the front door opened and closed.

"That him?" a deep voice asked.

"Be the one," Howie Pettit replied as the two men walked down the bunkhouse towards his bed. One of them was wearing boots.

"Got more comin' today?" the voice asked.

"What they said," answered Mr. Pettit.

"How many you figure?"

"Six or seven. Need ten, but we'll be all right."

"Want me to ask around?"

"No, Sheriff, I'm good, thank you. Appreciate it."

Willie's face flushed and the balls of his feet started sweating. He wanted to scream.

"What time he roll in?" the sheriff asked.

"Don't know. 'Magine it was late. Got up 'bout six-thirty when you called," Mr. Pettit said.

"All right, well, let's get him up and see what he knows. Smells like rum, don't he?"

As sheriff of Winchester, Spanky Weist had revived a good many drunks in his thirty-seven years, and his methods were painful and effective.

"Stick?" Howie Pettit called.

"Think he's in la-la land, this one." Sheriff Weist took a pen from his shirt pocket. "You say his name's Stick?" he asked, by the bed.

"Stick Watson outta Richmond. Well, outta lotta places now, I guess. Wife died while back—third or fourth season here. He's a good man. Likes his liquor on the weekends, though. Been a while since I seen him like this."

"*Mr. Watson!*" the sheriff bellowed. "*Want you to wake up, buddy. Need to ask you some questions!*"

From under the blanket Willie could hear Stick snoring. Bending down, the sheriff took one of Stick's hands in his.

"Last call, Stick!" the sheriff shouted casually.

Placing his blue ballpoint pen between the knuckles of Stick's index and middle fingers, the sheriff squeezed the fingers together with all his might.

The sound was more animal than human. Frightened as he was, Willie had to take a peek.

". . . kiing chrrrrrrrraaaooooowaaat the fuck!!" Stick screamed. *"Jesus!!!"* he shrieked again, jolting upright, his legs flying over the edge of the bed. *"What the fuck you doin' to me?!"* He winced, adjusting his eyes and whipping his fingers back and forth.

"That you, Howie?" Stick looked behind the sheriff, rubbing his sore fingers. "What's goin' on here?"

"Sorry, Stick, I know. You were passed out and the sheriff here needs to talk to you 'bout the brothers. Been some trouble in town, Stick. Thought you might know somethin', that's all."

"Shit, Howie," he said. "Break your pen, Sheriff?" He dropped his head down and rubbed the back of his neck with his good hand.

"Sorry, Stick. Not a lot of time to pussyfoot around. Got three dead people on my hands."

Stick stopped rubbing his neck as his eyes rested briefly on the sheriff, then shifted around the room.

"On the side of a road next to a '57 Dodge pickup. Found 'em three hours ago after a fight at the Red Wolf."

"Jesus," Stick mumbled, looking down between his legs and shaking his head.

"Bartender said you came in with 'em 'bout six P.M."

"Tell you I left about eight?" Stick said, sounding more sober.

"Somethin' like that. Said you were on your way out just before the fight broke out."

Stick looked at Howie and rubbed his dirty face. "Catch some trouble growin' apples, huh."

"Terrible thing, Stick," Howie Pettit confessed, looking bewildered. "They were good boys, you know. What happened down there?"

"Pissed off a bunch a Mexicans," Stick said flatly.

"Mexicans, you think?" the sheriff prodded.

"They were over their heads with some whores. And too drunk to figure out they had boyfriends."

"Mexicans?" the sheriff repeated.

"Hispanics," Stick said sarcastically.

"But Mexican-looking," the sheriff clarified.

"What's the difference? Couple big guys with little shits next to 'em watchin' the boys all night. Didn't like their money. Just a bad situation, I guess."

"You want some water, Stick?" Howie Pettit asked.

"Thanks, Howie," Stick said weakly, looking around for the boy. "Mouth's a little dry."

"How 'bout some coffee, Howie, if you don't mind. Might help. Been a long night," the sheriff said.

When Howie Pettit left the bunkhouse, Willie's eyes were the size of two silver dollars. He felt better hearing that the sheriff wasn't after him, but the brothers had been murdered by Mexicans on the side of the road while he'd been sleeping, which was a terrible thing to imagine.

"So, Stick, tell me what happened while you were there? You hear anything, some names, stuff like that?" Sheriff Weist questioned.

"One of the girls was Rosa, one was Conchita . . . or Chita. Somethin' like that. The big guy was Rick. I remember, 'cause it seemed like a funny name for a Mexican. Had a big-ass ring on his right hand. Seemed like the main event until the little guy showed up," he remembered.

"Little guy?" The sheriff moved over to the bed across from Stick's and sat down.

"Guy named Polly," Stick told him. "Never said nothin', but you could tell by the way they moved around him. Bartender, too. Got all funny when he came in."

"What you mean, 'funny'?"

He needed water more than coffee. His mouth felt stuffed with cotton.

"Preoccupied," Stick answered more thoughtfully, rising to his feet. He felt shaky all over. In twelve hours he'd had five shots of bourbon and a bottle of rum.

"Sink's over there if you need it," the sheriff said, pointing towards the back of the bunkhouse past the boy's head.

"Know where the sink is, Sheriff!" he barked, shifting his weight around the bed corner, his legs unsteady.

"What else about the little guy?" the sheriff continued as Stick limped away.

"That's 'bout it."

"Say anything to the bartender?"

At the sink tap Stick bent down and swallowed soft, warm water. He preferred the cold water of a stream.

"Didn't say nothin'." He turned and saw the boy's blanket move. "Didn't have to," he said, remembering, "if you'd seen his eyes." Limping back to his bed, he could tell the sheriff was waiting for him to finish.

"Bartender gave him a whiskey straight up," he finally said, sitting down on his bed.

The water had helped, but his fingers hurt. Swinging around and leaning back against his pillow, he considered the situation. He remembered falling off the curb in front of the Old Stone Church on East Piccadilly, drunk as a coot.

His last memory before that was of Polly and Rick laughing when the whore slipped under the table.

"How'd you get home?" the sheriff asked.

"Walked."

"It's eight miles to Howie's road, Stick," the sheriff pointed out.

"And a bottle of rum."

As the sheriff shook hands with Howie at the door, Stick lay back on his bed and felt his mouth buzz with caffeine. He felt sorry for the three brothers. He'd been cut a time or two. But it wasn't his deal, it was theirs. He'd warned them to watch their backs. As he heard Willie's bed shift, he wondered why the sheriff hadn't asked about the boy. Howie Pettit must have told him he'd taken the boy on.

"Anything else you can think of, give me a holler, Stick," the sheriff called back at the door. "Anything at all."

"There is one thing, Sheriff." Stick rubbed his swollen knuckles.

"What's that?" The sheriff shifted around.

Willie could tell from his voice that Stick was pissed. His eyes tightly closed, he prayed for him to keep their secret as he imagined the light of the Beautiful Lady flickering before him. He prayed for the bell's sound to circle Stick's heart and lift it up into the clouds the way old Moses had done it for him, sometimes, when he needed it most. He prayed for his momma to forgive him and to know why he'd done what he did. And he prayed for a way to make something good with the life he'd been given.

"Thanks for the coffee."

Several minutes later, Willie emerged from under the blanket and took stock of where he was. His hair was damp with perspiration. From his own bed, he watched Stick sleep. He wanted to thank him for what he'd done. A lot of people had been good to him here. In The Bottom he'd always taken care of himself. He'd never been scared or gotten himself into situations he couldn't get out of. But the fire had changed all that; it had burned through him— consuming the only world he'd ever known.

CHAPTER TWENTY

Rebecca Pettit's long red hair sailed into the air before circling back against her freckled cheeks with each descent. He didn't want to frighten her, but with each push of the swing, he could tell she wanted more.

"Higher, Willie, higher!" she screamed, falling back to earth. *"Never been so upside down!"*

Grabbing the scratchy ropes, she straightened her thin arms and leaned back, happy to be pushed by a strange boy. Closing her eyes, she imagined herself atop the mast of a great ship heading through the open sea, a great ship on which to discover everything there was to learn about the world. She didn't belong to apples or churches or boring summer days. She would have secrets like Willie Graves and stories to tell like all the workers, and a trunk full of mysterious objects from her adventures.

Rachel Pettit snapped peas and watched from the kitchen window as the swing came to a stop under darkening skies. If she could make time stand still, she would in a hearbeat. This would be everything she needed—a happy child, fresh-cut grass, a worn-down wedding ring, and the sound of rain.

As Rebecca and Willie ran for the barn, the sky collapsed. Midway down the center aisle they came to a raucous stop and looked back towards the house, which had disappeared under the storm. Willie thought of the murdered brothers lying on the roadside, the rain mixing with their blood. No, they wouldn't be there; they would've been taken off somewhere, and maybe he didn't want to know where.

"*Let's watch the storm!*" the little girl shouted, racing towards a ladder to the hayloft.

Maybe she had a Lucky Bean too, he thought, watching her climb from under the ladder.

"*C'mon, Willie, gonna be lightninin', quick!*" At the top, she disappeared.

He climbed quickly as her footsteps echoed above him. She was a pistol, all right, and pretty fearless on a swing for a girl. Maybe it was the rain, or the fact that Stick hadn't turned him in, but flying up the ladder, Willie felt like himself again. Instead of running away from everything, he was running towards something. When he reached her at the edge of an open door, the barn flashed with light.

"One thousand one, one thousand two, one thousand . . . " she was out of breath before it struck.

Dropping to the floor, they grabbed each other as thunder coldcocked the roof.

"One thousand one, one thousand—" she repeated calmly.

Again it hit, exploding up through the posts and rattling the timbers. There was no need to count to determine the distance of the storm. It had found them. Holding her gaze, he could see that she was not afraid.

"One thousand one, one thousand two, one thousand three, one thousand four . . . " she counted, hoping for more. "It's moving away," she whispered.

Releasing her arm, Willie looked out through the open door. He was the one who had been afraid and had latched on to her. Under an expanse of low, diaphanous clouds, twisting rivulets of water snaked across the ground. He smelled fried chicken.

"It hit the roof, Willie. Musta been right over us," she said, awestricken.

"It was close," he agreed. He felt like a coward.

"Ever been that close before?"

"Nope. Been 'round my house," he said, picturing the red cowboy blanket on his bed, "but never like this."

As Howie Pettit called up to them from the kitchen door, a brilliant patch of aquamarine pierced the western sky. Climbing down the ladder, she did not ask about his secrets, but they were on her mind all the same. If secrets were the things you never talked about, how was she ever going to get to his?

A lone cicada called out from under the picnic table. Summer was almost gone. Trudging across the soggy yard to dinner, they saw the wet swing.

"Push me tomorrow?" she asked.

"Better hold on tight."

At five o'clock Stick appeared at the front porch with a fist full of purple asters.

"You bringin' me flowers?" Howie Pettit chuckled from his rocking chair.

"Not exactly. Found 'em up a ways outside that ole cave," he said, looking down and polishing the top of his right boot against the back of his pants.

"One off Poorhouse?"

"That's it. Don't remember seeing it before."

"Some people livin' here never seen it. Daddy used to run me up there. Said he found arrowheads inside when he was a kid, but I never did. Went up fishin' with Rebecca not too long ago and showed her. She loves the place—got some red sandstone inside and fool's gold. Bunch of tunnels, too. Some of 'em run a ways, but it's pretty dark. You need a good light. You ever work a mine?" he asked.

"Did some outside Charleston in the thirties, but can't say I took to it. Pretty crappy way to spend the day, if you ask me," he added, holding the flowers awkwardly. "Rather be pickin' flowers."

"Very kind of you, Stick. She'll like 'em a lot," he declared, standing up and stretching. "Get you a Schlitz?"

"Wouldn't hurt, thanks." Stick adjusted the flowers in his fist.

"She's in the kitchen, come on." He motioned to the screen door. "I'll get the beer."

The Pettit home was built of white oak in 1834 by a Baptist preacher from New Jersey named John Leslie Huston, whose diocese had bought Winchester's Old Stone Church. Eventually John Huston became a part of things, but it took a while for some members of the congregation to believe there were Baptists in New Jersey.

The clapboard farmhouse Huston erected was a two-story four-over-four with a staircase down the middle. The interior walls were hand-plastered and the studs were oak. Stick could tell the place was solid by the way his boots felt against the door.

"Old pine," Howie Pettit said, noticing his interest.

"Solid," Stick marveled.

"Eight-by-eights over Massanutten limestone. Same stone they got down at the railroad station. Not goin' anywhere soon, I imagine," Howie added.

"Nice lookin' wood, too."

"Outta Norfolk, some lumberman said. Big ole trees by the water, they figured. Wide grains. Must cost a pretty penny even back then."

"This him here?" Stick asked, pointing his asters towards an old photograph on the wall.

"That's the man. Rachel found him in the attic. Seems like a nice enough fella."

"Don't look much like a priest, though," Stick observed.

"You're right." Howie Pettit smiled. "Looks pretty happy, don't he?"

Rachel Pettit blushed when she looked up from rolling pie dough and saw Stick in the kitchen doorway with flowers.

"Got a man who walked up to Poorhouse to get you flowers, Rache," her husband announced.

With her flour-dusted hands, she pushed spindles of red hair from her face, and stopped to admire the arrangement.

"Very kind of you, sir. And my favorite, purple asters. Rebecca, honey, get me Momma's white vase from the living room and we can put them on the table for dinner."

"Yes, ma'am." Her daughter walked briskly towards the door.

"Honey . . . stop!"

"What?" she protested.

"Wash up first."

Earlier she'd helped Willie with the apple pie crust, and her cheeks and hands were covered with flour. "The best part," she'd explained to him while they worked, "is pressin' your thumbs around the edge."

"And, Stick, you've met our new young man Willie, I understand?" Rachel gestured towards the sink where the boy was cleaning up.

"I have, thank you," Stick acknowledged with a curt nod.

"He was helping with the pie before you came just now. He's got a nice way with dough, this one."

"Born to bake," Stick joked sarcastically.

As Willie laughed, his shoulders relaxed. Drying his hands with a dish towel, he turned around. "Hey, Mr. Watson," he said gently.

While Rachel and her daughter made final preparations for dinner, Willie joined Stick and Howie on the porch. He appreciated being asked. He hadn't seen Stick since the sheriff left. He'd never seen him so cleaned up or without a beard of some kind. But the best thing was he didn't look so pissed off.

"Got some nice chicken for you tonight, Willie." Howie Pettit leaned back in his rocker.

"Thank you, sir." Willie listened to the sound of dishes in the kitchen and wondered if it was time to eat. Except for a couple of apples, he hadn't eaten all day. There was a dark cloud to the right of the house in the distance. It looked like an alligator.

"Got you bakin', does she?" Howie Pettit interrupted his thoughts.

"No, sir, not really. Just the dough part. Me and Rebecca was helpin' with the pie top," he explained.

"Thanks for spendin' time with Rebecca. She's a handful sometimes," he confessed.

"Not really, sir. Just . . . well . . . "

"Kinda pushy for seven!" Howie Pettit laughed, admiring his bottle of Schlitz.

"A little, but . . . " Willie looked away from the cloud and collected his thoughts. "Mostly just kinda . . . excited, I guess." He wanted to tell him how brave she'd been during the storm and how high she'd gone on the swing.

"Good way to put it, son, there you go! Quick outta the gate, that one. Not like her brother," he said, finishing his beer.

"How's Jake doin'?" Stick asked, bringing his rocker to a stop.

"Doing fine, thanks. Gotta good job with John Deere last year in Waynesboro through a friend a mine. Drove down and got hired on the spot. Like it was meant to be, is all I can figure. And the job he always wanted."

"Fixed my radio last time I was here," Stick said. "Said he used somethin' from the barn."

"Piece a copper," Howie Pettit replied.

"That's it! Damnedest thing I ever saw. Worked like a dream after that."

"That's my Jake, all right. Mr. Fix It." He stared off, looking suddenly tired.

"He married?" Stick asked.

"Nope." Howie Pettit checked the bottom of his bottle.

"Gotta girl?"

"Name's Sally. Nice-looking. Quiet like Jake, a course. I don't know . . ." he spoke abstractedly, glancing at Willie. "Just wish he hadn't wandered off's all."

Willie briefly caught Mr. Pettit's eye. He looked sad all of a sudden. He wanted to tell him about his momma and how he missed her too, but it wasn't the right time.

"Dinner's on!" Rachel Pettit called from the hallway.

"Comin', Rache!" her husband called back, halting his rocker.

Willie watched Stick as he stood up. He was hungry, but he wanted to tell them before they walked away that he could pitch in and learn things to help. He could stay friends with Rebecca and no one would have to know what he'd done.

Moving towards the door, Stick saw something in the boy's expression that he'd seen before—something desperate. He'd seen kids in the thirties like Willie. He'd seen a lot of them. Their lives were over before they began.

As they walked through the hallway's warm golden light to the dining room and took their seats, the house fell silent. Howie Pettit said a prayer for the boys from West Virginia. "It was a hard thing to imagine," he spoke solemnly, "but they were good men and good men go to heaven."

He would stay forever, Willie thought to himself, placing the napkin neatly on his lap and noticing the white vase of purple asters. He would work the orchard and learn how to fix things. He would top the pies with dough and thumbprints and thank his lucky stars.

CHAPTER TWENTY-ONE

It was known throughout Franklin County that Rachel Pettit's fried chicken was to die for. She claimed it was nothing special. "Just buttermilk and cornmeal," she would say. But people knew better. Like her husband, she gave more than she took, and when you left her table, you were full.

In The Bottom, Willie had never seen such a table spread—not even on Christmas day. Snap beans, onions, and red bell peppers drizzled with raspberry, sugar, and mint. Collard greens bathed in cider vinegar and honey, and sprinkled with pumpkin seeds; fluffy garlic mashed potatoes; cream-simmered hominy grits; buttered sweet potato biscuits; and succotash were in porcelain bowls all along the table. And, of course, the chicken on a platter.

Biting into a crispy thigh, Willie's eyes watered. It was beyond any fried chicken he had ever tasted. Potatoes, collards, and honey swirled together on his fork and he sighed between bites. Who would have thought a white woman's chicken could taste this good?

"There's plenty when you're ready for more, Willie," Mrs. Pettit offered. "Don't be shy."

"Thank you, ma'am," he stammered with some embarrassment, wiping his mouth with the corner of his napkin. "Sure is good."

Stick looked around the table. It was good to be with a family again, good to be cared for. It reminded him of Crystal-Ann, though they'd never had children or much of a house. The Pettits belonged to one another and to a place they'd made their own. Some people do well for themselves and some people miss the boat. The important thing wasn't what you had, but what you did with it.

Rebecca took her last bite of potatoes. "Tell a train story, Mr. Stick?"

Her father gave her a strong look. "Let the man eat, Rebecca."

"No, it's fine," Stick replied, wiping his hands on his napkin. "Let's see." Raising his glass of water, he glanced at the girl and took a sip.

"Another beer, Stick?" Howie Pettit pushed his chair back from the table and crossed his legs.

"I'm good, Howie, thanks. Don't need a thing after that. You know your way to a man's heart, Mrs. Pettit. I'm very grateful for this meal. It's kind of you to ask me over."

Rachel Pettit smiled at Stick. He was a mixed bag but she liked him all the same. She always had. Howie Pettit was proud of his wife for giving an orchard hand a place at her table. Most of his friends would not have understood, but you could count it in the apples at the end of every season.

"A pleasure having you here, Stick. Just wish we'd see more of you."

Rebecca could see that her mom liked Stick by the way she looked younger all of a sudden and more interested in everything that was going on. "Let him tell the story, Momma." She wiggled around in her chair to get comfortable.

Stick leaned back in his chair. "How old are you, Rebecca?" he asked.

"Seven," she answered matter-of-factly.

"And how old are you, Willie?"

Willie looked up, surprised. "Thirteen," he answered without thinking.

"Well, I was a tad younger than Willie here when I took my first ride. It was after school in early June when me and another guy caught our first train outta Richmond. There were about twenty guys in the boxcar and they had to help us up, 'cause I couldn't even reach the floor."

"You run away from home, Mr. Stick?" Rebecca interjected.

"Three different times. Yes, I did." He glanced briefly at Mrs. Pettit. "Not proud of it, but . . . well, there it is. Left a note the first time on my dad's workbench in the garage telling him not to worry."

The table was dead silent.

"My dad was a car mechanic, jack-of-all-trades kinda guy. He did pretty good for himself until the Great Depression, but then everything came unglued and he flat-out lost it . . . so one day I just took off. He got to drinkin', so I figured I'd sow some oats and see what I could find. Pretty crazy idea when I think about it now, but when you're that age, you're not always thinkin' straight."

Willie and Rebecca exchanged glances.

"Can't usually catch a freight train in the yard 'less it's real late at night. So bein' kids, we had to sit outside and wait for one to go by. Which means you're catchin' it on the run . . . and, a course, you're runnin' along and you're trying to keep up with the train to get your hands onto somethin' and try to lift your foot up." Stick looked around the table and nodded. "Pretty tricky the first couple times, and I was kinda scrawny, so somebody grabbed me by the seat of my pants and tossed me in."

He chuckled to himself. "But it was a good feelin', once I dusted myself off, you know, 'cuz you hear them wheels hit the joints and . . . " he paused, "that whistle kicks in and you're zippin' along. And it sure beats walkin'," he quipped.

Quiet laughter danced off the walls.

"You ride a freight train one time and you're hooked," Stick declared, folding his napkin into a square.

"Ever had an accident?" Rebecca blurted.

Stick caught her eye. She was full of piss and vinegar, but he couldn't help but like her.

"First ride outta Richmond we picked up speed, and the plank I was on started to bounce up and down. The thing tossed me on my keister. . . . So, I'm bouncing around, and all I'm thinkin' is: I shouldn't a taken off, an' if I let go, I'm gonna bounce on out the door and kill myself and never see my momma."

"You had a momma?"

Stick grinned at Rebecca.

"We all got a momma, darlin'. And they're usually right." Stick took a sip of water and felt their eyes on him. "I'm headin' towards the door and my shins are slammin' against the floorboards and someone grabs me by the leg before the train spits me out and I'm hangin' on to this guy for dear life and I'm thinkin': It's a whole lot harder than it looks!

"Takes a while to learn the ropes—especially ridin' on top and doin' sixty or seventy miles an hour. You best watch your curves if you're standin' up. Little tiny curve'll throw you off. I saw it once. Guy turned his head to look at something, he was gone."

"Dead?" the little girl whispered.

Stick glanced at Mrs. Pettit before deciding to give it to her straight.

"Yep. Not a pretty sight, but there you have it."

"You seen others get killed?" She was wide-eyed.

"Rebecca, honey," her mother cautioned.

"No, I don't mind, Mrs. Pettit. I mean, you jump a train, you better have a plan, 'cuz it ain't no movie show." His eyes took in both Willie and the girl. "I was on one that pulled up for water outside a tunnel and we was all stuck inside a boxcar breathin' in the smoke."

"What'd you do?" Rebecca leaned over her plate.

"Got the door open and dropped to the ground for air 'fore I passed out.

Two boys didn't make it. Found 'em at the passenger station in Parkersburg."

"West Virginia?" Howie Pettit asked.

"Yes, sir. Ann Street Station. Place was crawlin' with bulls—they're like cops for the train people . . . so I dropped off before we got there and, man, I'm tellin' you, I was coughin' for a week. Still taste it sometimes. Like them miners, I guess, it gets a hold a you and don't let go."

"Your daddy come after you?" the little girl asked.

"No," Stick said, his expression wistful.

"How come?"

"Well, first off, he didn't know where I was, and second, he was a drinkin' man. And then the Depression kicked in," Stick said, looking at her sadly. "In '38 he lost his shop and pretty soon after that he couldn't keep the house goin', so . . . somebody near Carps Corner put us up while he was lookin' for work, but . . . never happened. Went from livin' pretty decent to havin' nothin', just like that. So, I just kept rollin' on freights and did some fruit trampin' to help out. But it was rough . . . I sure wanted to come home sometimes."

Willie knew what it felt like to miss a place. He felt tears pooling in his eyes.

"But I wasn't no sand lapper. I had it good compared to a lotta folks. I mean, I didn't go west like some of 'em, but I saw a lotta places and met a buncha fine people along the way. Never had to bum much," he admitted, looking around the table.

"What's a sand lapper?" Rebecca asked.

"Eats sand to put something in his belly."

"What's a bum?" she pestered.

"Somethin' they give you in a sack to take when you went to the back door. They also called it a 'lump.' "

" 'Cause you were hungry?" she asked softly.

"Hungry all the time, honey. Sometimes goin' on three or four days with nothin' to eat. Nothin', you know. . . . So you'd sit down by a house somewhere and maybe if you were lucky they'd bring a sandwich or soup or somethin'. This was called a 'knee-shaker.' Or you could work a restaurant by goin' in and askin' for work—doin' anything for somethin' to eat. If they said no, then somebody beside you might feel sorry for you and pay for some breakfast or a cup of coffee. And then you felt good for a while. Truth is, it's pretty hard to watch another man go hungry. If you got a job, of course, you felt real good. But they were hard to come by and, mostly, you were pretty much hungry all the time."

"You travel alone, usually?" Willie asked quietly.

Stick glanced his way. The boy had a sweet face once you forgot about what a pain in the ass he'd been.

"Just my wife, really. Got close to a couple guys. Met a ton a people, you know. But things don't stick, movin' round so much. Just the way it is, I guess."

"Like pirates!" Rebecca exclaimed.

"No, I ain't no pirate, Miss Rebecca. What I got in this life I earned. And what I lost wasn't worth much in the first place," he said, his face clouding with emotion.

"Except for your wife?" she asked cautiously.

The house was quiet, but for the clock behind him. Stick stared at the table.

" 'Cept for her."

Rachel Pettit pushed back her chair.

"Sorry I went on so long." Stick half smiled with embarrassment.

"Heavens to Betsy, Stick, we love hearing you talk—you know that," she assured him as she stood and walked over. "Always learning about the world when you come around. Howie and I were talking just yesterday about how much we look forward to it. Breath a fresh air for all of us." She collected his place. "Come on, missy." She nodded to her daughter. "Let's get that pie out here, see how you and Willie did today."

"Yes, ma'am!" Rebecca jumped out of her seat. "Then can we ask him more questions?"

The secret to Rachel Pettit's apple pie was a tablespoon of rosewater, a quarter cup of cornstarch, and fresh churned butter. Her husband chose the apples and, except for the cinnamon, she made the rest.

"Didn't have time for ice cream, I'm afraid. So help yourself to milk," she apologized to the table.

Willie ate his pie in four bites and washed it down with two large glasses of cold milk.

"Best pie I ever ate, I'll tell you that, Mrs. Pettit," Stick confessed, wiping milk off his upper lip with his napkin. "Hands down," he added.

"It's good to see a man with an appetite. Got more if you want," she offered.

"Oh, no. You topped me off tonight, I'm tellin' ya. But thank you both for letting the boy and me sit down with your family. It's an honor. Everything was mighty fine. If I die tonight, I'll be a happy man."

"Killing you wasn't what we had in mind, Stick." Howie Pettit tossed his napkin on the table. "But let me ask you something."

"Yes, sir?"

"I read somewhere there were four million people on the road back then."

"In '38?"

"Was it '38? That sounds about right with the Dust Bowl and all . . . just a buncha people out there on their own. Musta been a couple hundred thousand kids too, don't you think?"

"Least that," Stick agreed. "Mighta been more, 'specially in them New

Deal camps."

"The 'Triple C' camps?" Howie Pettit remembered.

"Yep," Stick confirmed. "Was a buncha them, maybe twelve or thirteen hundred."

"What's a 'Triple C'?" Rebecca interjected.

"Civilian Conservation Corps," her father explained. "President Roosevelt got some jobs goin' and fed people because everyone was outta work. It was called the 'New Deal.' Built a lotta parks and stuff like that."

"Built the Skyline Drive," Stick added.

"And paid the workers?" Rebecca asked.

"Half a year room and board, as I remember, yep," her father declared, looking at Stick for confirmation. "My Uncle Earl did it for a spell. Sent money home to help out, my daddy told me. You remember him telling us that, Rache?" He was glancing across the table at his wife. "Made a big difference back then, 'cause you could rent a decent place for fifty cents a day. Told me 'bout this time he worked for a man around here wanted him to unload a lumber truck. So he threw wood down all day and at the end of the job, the guy gave him an apple." Willie and Rebecca looked at each other with their mouths open.

"And that was a good day," Stick added. "I worked wheat all day one summer in this field south a Emporia, and at the end of it, they give me a dime."

"What'd you do?" Willie asked, dumbfounded.

"Gave it back. But that was pretty foolish. Truth is, we were all hurtin'."

"Tell 'em 'bout the jungle, Stick, if you don't mind," Howie Pettit suggested.

Stick figured the story was meant for Willie and Rebecca, but Rachel seemed curious, too. He took a moment to collect his thoughts.

"Back then, bein' homeless was against the law. Probably is now as well, but back then they called it 'vagrancy' and it was a crime an' you went to prison. And when you showed up in front of a judge lookin' bad and smellin' worse, it was hard to avoid the charge. Unless you had some kinda business in town, you had to pretty much stay on the outskirts and away from people who might notice you. So when we weren't waitin' for a train, we all slept outside a town in these camps called 'jungles.' A jungle was nothin' more than some trees or bushes where we could make a fire and settle down. Those who were real lucky maybe had a bedroll."

Rebecca's brow knitted. "How come they called them 'jungles'?"

"Suppose it had to do with how we all looked, more than likely. I don't really know. There was shavin' mirrors hangin' from the trees and we probably all looked like a buncha monkeys," Stick joked.

Rebecca and Willie laughed happily before seeing the sadness in Stick's eyes.

"You do what you have to do and that's where you end up sometimes. We didn't have a whole lotta choices in those days. That's just the way it worked."

Stick took a sip of water as Rebecca and Willie leaned forward in their chairs waiting for him to say more.

"We called the people livin' there 'jungle buzzards,' 'cuz they lived there sometimes for weeks or months and pretty much called the shots. Sometimes, if you wanted somethin', you had to get their permission."

"Somethin' like what?" Willie asked.

"Like a branch to hang somethin' on, or water from the creek—stuff like that. Or if you wanted to wash your clothes, the jungle buzzards would say, 'Well, yeah, go into town and bring us somethin' back to eat and you can have some a what we got.' That's how it worked."

"What they have?" the little girl asked.

"Usually some kinda soup made with whatever you could find," Stick answered. "I usually got the job bringin' in the money, so I'd have to go and offer to work at a Piggly Wiggly or some place like that. The store had to be big enough to need somebody extra and I'd offer to work and the boss would say, 'You clean all that up and I'll see what I can do.' And after I was done I'd ask him for somethin' like a can of coffee. Wasn't like beggin', but felt like it sometimes. I'd come back to the buzzards with the coffee and maybe somethin' else if I got the guy on a good day. And you just kinda hung in a jungle for a while if you had to, but you had to watch yourself 'cuz it got hairy sometimes—'specially for the young people. They got tricked into doin' stuff and knocked 'round a bit."

"You too, Stick?" Willie asked.

"Yeah, me too, I guess. Wasn't much I could do 'bout it. The way it works. One time, these three fellas started workin' a con game, so I told 'em to leave me alone. I mean . . . a man could get killed for a cigarette, but they thought I had money—so one of 'em came after me, and then they took off."

"Good Lord. What happened?" Rachel asked.

"Cut me up a bit—but I was real lucky. Sometimes you got the next train outta there, wherever it was rollin', 'cuz it was tough and the weather beat you up."

Stick stretched his arms over his head. His head still hurt from the booze.

"Bein' on the road was rough. Kinda humblin' sometimes, when you get right down to it. Good thing I was young and a lotta things just rolled off me. It was harder on the old folks, though. Some of 'em hadn't worked for a year or so and hadn't seen their families in a while. But it hit us all pretty hard and you didn't make a lotta friends."

"You miss your momma and daddy?" Rebecca's eyes were wide.

Stick was thoughtful as he smoothed his napkin. He'd missed talking to people. He'd missed being around people who cared enough to listen.

"I was sittin' in a cotton field once feelin' sorry for myself and a black man gave me a piece of his cake."

"Was it your birthday?" Willie interrupted.

"No. Just somethin' he did, I guess. So I walked a ways and plopped down between the rows a cotton, I still remember . . . " He paused, inspecting his swollen fingers. " . . . and I held the cake out in my hand and it was kinda squashed from holdin' it."

Willie's eyes lit up as he listened.

"The frostin' was all messed up . . . but it still tasted good. . . . And when I was done . . . " Stick smiled slightly and winced. " . . . I cried like a baby."

Leaning forward, Rachel Pettit clasped her hands together.

"You never went back?" she asked softly.

Stick sat back in his chair. He felt uncomfortable being the center of attention but he had only himself to blame.

"No, ma'am. By '41 the Depression was over and the war came 'round. I went back. But when I did, they was gone."

When Willie's tear hit the pie plate, he slid back in his chair before anyone could notice.

"You still a hobo, Stick?" Rebecca inquired in a loud voice. Her mother closed her eyes and shook her head from side to side. "What, Momma? I don't mean nothin' by it."

Stick smiled. "It's okay, Rebecca. Let me ask you somethin'. You know what a hobo is?"

She thought about it as he pushed his chair back and crossed his legs.

"Not really, sir." She bit her upper lip, watching his reaction.

"Well, it's nothin' to be ashamed of, so don't you worry 'bout it. Ain't any way to know somethin' unless you ask."

"Yes, sir," she said, sneaking a look at her mother.

"We all traveled with hoes in case there was fieldwork," he explained.

"You were hoe boys!" she cried triumphantly.

With a tender look, Stick put his napkin on the table and recited the lyrics of a song:

"As I was walkin' in the rain
I heard the whistle of a train
And a voice down deep inside
Says one more ride's your middle name."

While Rebecca and her mother did the dishes in the kitchen, Howie walked Stick and Willie back to the bunkhouse. It had been a good night for everyone.

"You catch that storm today?" Howie asked, his eyes on the stars over the barn.

"I did. Got to Poorhouse 'bout the time I was comin' down. Went right over your place," Stick said.

"Hit the barn when me and Rebecca was in there." Willie pointed to the hayloft door where they'd stood.

"Came down pretty good." Stick checked the sky.

"Be a good day tomorrow. Gettin' colder, though," Howie remarked.

"Seems early, don't it?" Stick put his hands in his pockets.

"Yep." Howie Pettit came to a stop. "Not like it used to be."

It was a moonless night and the orchards were dark.

"Well, y'all get some sleep. Gonna need it tomorrow. Not sure where the new boys are—shoulda been here by now. I need to call and see what's goin' on." Howie Pettit sounded tired. He'd almost forgotten about the three workers he'd lost. Dead over hookers.

"The hirin' must be a pain in the ass," Stick said.

"Not the best part a this job, that's for sure, but what the hell. Beats punchin' a clock."

"Well . . . I'm grateful for a nice evenin', Mr. Pettit. That wife a yours is somethin' special."

"Sure is. Thank you, sir," Willie added.

"Well, just glad she has nights like this. All these people comin' and goin' all the time—she's got more food to make than time to enjoy it. So, I appreciate you bein' here—both of you." He put his hand on Willie's shoulder. "Where you from, Willie?"

Willie tensed. Where he was from wasn't a place anymore so much as a bad feeling.

"Lexington," he replied, but regretted it as soon as he'd said it.

"I've got a cousin down there. What's your family's name?"

As his face flushed, Willie's eyes briefly met Stick's. "Maury," he lied, looking at his shoes.

"Maury? Well, I'll be!" Howie Pettit's head tilted toward him.

"Know his folks?" Stick asked cautiously.

"No, sir, but they named a river after 'em!"

His eyes still on his shoes, Willie smelled the wet grass and listened to frogs croaking in the distance.

Stick snored softly as Willie gazed at the three empty beds in the bunkhouse. The men were gone for good. It was one thing to run away from a place, but the place wasn't dead—you could always go back. He wanted to tell the truth about where he was from. The sheriff would be back asking more questions about the murders. He couldn't stay here forever, he knew that. The bed was lumpy but warm. His breathing slowed down. Closing his eyes, he tried to remember everything Stick had said at the table and how he had looked when he'd said it. How he'd admitted to being ashamed of the way he looked sometimes, and especially the part about the cake and the messed-up frosting.

By morning, three men were in the empty beds. When Willie raised his head from the pillow, it startled him to think that they had come in while he'd been sleeping. It was close to 7:00 A.M. He figured Rebecca would be leaving for school soon and there were tons of apples to pick. He liked standing on the ladders. It reminded him of his Lucky Bean. He hoped the new men would be all right. They were asleep, so he couldn't tell. One guy looked big.

Sitting up, he slipped on the gray sweatshirt that Mrs. Pettit had found for him the day before and a pair of her son's pants from when he was small. He figured she missed him and that was why she hadn't given them up.

"We don't throw much away around here, Willie," she'd explained. "So if you need something, more than likely we've got it."

"Thank you, ma'am."

She gave the boy a tender look. "What happened to your clothes?"

"A bear took 'em."

"A bear?"

"Came into this camp where I'd been livin' and ran off with my knapsack."

Mrs. Pettit looked alarmed. "Oh, my! Were you all right?"

Willie's face was serious. "Yes, ma'am, he let me be. Probably just smelled the bacon I'd been saving. I threw him a piece and that was pretty much it."

The tap water was ice-cold against his face. He'd taken a small towel from the barn shower to polish his teeth in a hand mirror nailed to the wall. The towel was rough and smelled of Clorox. He'd buy a toothbrush in town as soon as he got paid. He was too embarrassed to tell Stick he'd lost his five dollars. Being poor and being broke weren't the same, his momma had said.

In the mirror he saw the large man sit up in his bed and look around. He had deep dark circles around his eyes and scruffy black hair.

"You the kid from Lexington?"

"Yes, sir," Willie answered, half turning around.

"Cold in here," he muttered, swinging his legs off the edge of the bed, the blanket still on his shoulders.

"Yes, sir." Willie watched cautiously.

"Name's Jim Falcon," he said pleasantly. His weather-beaten face softened, and Willie figured he was a nice guy.

"That's Stick Watson." Willie pointed. "Him an' me been here a couple days. You get in last night?"

" 'Bout three in the mornin'. Broke down in Carolina yesterday. Been South workin' goobers last couple weeks. Hot as hell down there," he said wearily, with a yawn. "Don't miss that part."

"What's a goober?" Willie crossed to his bed.

"Peanuts," the man answered, rolling his head in a circle. "We was early this year on account a the weather. Ground's too hard. I run the digger, but we was a bit thin this time 'round. They pay you by the pound." He yawned again.

Willie watched his big head come to a stop directly over his shoulders and his eyes refocus. "You work here before?" he asked, sitting down on the trunk at the foot of his bed.

"Goin' on five years—all three of us. That's my cousin, Vasco," he said, pointing to the bed closest to the front door. "And that little guy there is Petie." He nodded to the bed next to him. "We call him Spud."

Willie reached for his mud-stained sneakers, a hole where the big toe was.

"It's a nice operation," the man said, checking out the bunkhouse. "Always treat you right. Buncha apples in the headlights last night, so we may be here awhile."

"Where you live when you ain't workin'?" Willie slipped his shoes on.

"Pittsburgh," he answered, " 'cept for Spud."

"Where's he from?" Willie asked, nodding at the last bunk.

"Pocatello, Idaho," he said, throwing back the blanket and standing up.

By seven o'clock, Howie Pettit had loaded the tractor wagon with one hundred empty crates, some paper cups, two bags of doughnuts, and a large thermos of coffee. Despite being tired, he was relieved to be starting the week with enough hands to do the job.

"Mornin', Mr. Pettit!" Jim Falcon yelled from the barn doorway.

"Hey, Big Jim. You get some sleep?" Howie Pettit climbed up into the tractor and pressed the starter button.

"I'll be all right *once we get rollin'!*" he shouted over the engine noise.

"You all meet each other?" Howie Pettit shouted back.

The men nodded one by one, except for Willie. He felt self-conscious standing next to them. Working for real money was exciting, but he figured the men knew a lot more about apples than he did.

"Climb up here and ride with me, Willie!" Mr. Pettit bellowed, sensing the boy's discomfort. *"Y'all jump in the wagon! We're down by the creek this mornin'! Got coffee and doughnuts when we get there!"*

"Get on the bus, Spud!" Jim shouted, jumping onto the wagon. *"Goin' on a picnic!"*

Dropping down into the orchard's lower east section, the tractor was swallowed by fog. As it stopped between rows of tree trunks, the men looked around as if they had entered another world. From the front, it was difficult for Willie to see them at the back of the wagon.

"Pretty thick, ain't it?" Howie Pettit remarked.

"Sure is, sir," Willie agreed.

"Well," he joked, turning the engine off, "you can't get lost pickin' apples."

In the silence, Jim Falcon listened to the creek. He was grateful for the fresh air.

"Man overboard!" he shouted, leaping to the ground.

After unloading the crates, they ate doughnuts and drank coffee. Vasco and Spud were still wasted from their trip. Willie could see that Stick wasn't much interested in small talk. Sometimes he felt grown-up and other times he felt small and useless. "You feels dat way till you does somethin' good for somebody," he remembered Moses telling him one day. "Den you knows what you wurth."

"You good to go?" Mr. Pettit asked Willie, holding his ladder.

"Yes, sir." Willie started to climb.

By the time he was halfway up the ladder, the ground was lost between thick leaves and branches, and the tree trembled. Yellow stripes flickered in the branches, and he appreciated the fruit being small and manageable in his hand. At the top he'd find the sweetest one to eat. Probably the other men would do the same. It would be like taking water from a stream.

When the sun touched his head, he realized how low the fog had dropped. Pressing his damp shoes against the ladder rung, he grabbed a slender branch for balance and looked down. He'd climbed too high for most of the apples. He heard a cowbell in the distance as the fog returned, and fumbled for his sack. The bell reminded him of Moses, and he wondered if he thought about him as he rang his bell at the top of the tower, if the sound of his bell still went on forever. With each passing day, the bells seemed farther away. As he heard the cowbell again, closer this time through the fog, his left foot slipped on the rung. He couldn't afford to daydream. Stepping carefully down several rungs, he scanned the tree for his first apple. He wouldn't eat it. He'd work hard to fill his sack, however long it took. And when no one was looking, he'd cry like a baby.

At noon, finishing the lower branch of his third tree, Willie heard Rachel Pettit's triangle clang.

"You've done ten boxes this morning, Willie," Howie Pettit marveled, penciling figures into a small spiral notebook. "Ready to eat?"

"Yes, sir," Willie said, still caught up in his work.

Howie Pettit asked each of the men to give a box count, which he then entered into his notebook.

"You stay on that ladder, boy?" Jim Falcon kidded, messing up Willie's hair.

"Yes, sir," Willie said shyly.

"Did ten boxes, Big Jim," Howie Pettit proudly declared.

"*Ten?!* Man, don't that beat the band! I only done six." Jim Falcon made two boxing fists, smiling at the boy. "It's always the little guy!"

Stick was glad to see Willie coming along. Maybe it would all work out. He'd done some stupid things himself and maybe what worked for him might work for the boy.

At the lunch table, Willie could see that Stick's face had softened a little. They hadn't much in common, but he seemed more tolerant of him.

"More iced tea, Willie? Gonna get hot today." He topped off the boy's glass.

After lunch, Vasco, Spud, and Jim went into the bunkhouse for a brief nap before starting work again. Rachel Pettit, seeing they were run-down, passed out extra sandwiches and hoped that what her food couldn't do, a good night's sleep would. Men could be babies sometimes, and she'd learned years ago that running an orchard wasn't all about the apples.

Willie and Stick worked next to each other all afternoon. Whenever one moved to a new tree, the other followed. Stick was surprised by the boy's speed and determination. Maybe when it came to Jonathans, it was easier being little. And he could keep quiet. He guessed the boy had a lot on his mind.

Together they would move his ladder, which was too tall and heavy for Willie. They worked together out of necessity, with increasing familiarity. As the afternoon wore on, an agreeable silence developed between them. Willie had never worked for real money before, it had always been for coins. He felt sad knowing his momma had to sleep with men instead of picking apples. From the last tree, he watched the sun disappear behind North Mountain. He didn't miss her as much as before, but his arms had goose bumps when he thought about never seeing her again.

Stick watched the boy disappear down the ladder. He was still tired from the rum. If he'd had more he would have finished it.

They walked in the direction of the bunkhouse several minutes behind Howie Pettit and the others. Rachel had left a plate of leftovers in the barn refrigerator for the men to nibble on with cookies and milk. As darkness surrounded the bunkhouse, the apple trees disappeared.

After a round of matchstick poker, Jim Falcon and his men went to sleep.

"Here." Stick offered the boy a red toothbrush and small tube of paste at the sink. "Works better than your finger."

Willie had a guilty look when he took it. "I lost my money, Stick."

"No big deal. I always carry an extra," Stick replied, heading to his bed. He wanted to ask about the situation in Charlottesville, but he was too tired to get into it and this wasn't the place.

Willie brushed his teeth over the sink for several minutes until they felt smooth against his tongue. He'd forgotten to take a towel from the barn. His face was red from the sun and his fingernails were dirty.

"When you're done, hit the light, Willie," Stick called out from bed, his eyes half-closed.

Willie looked at Stick's reflection in the mirror over the sink. Since Sunday supper, things had changed between them.

"See you in the mornin', Stick," he called quietly.

Throughout the week, the men worked hard, and towards the end, most of the orchard's eastern section had been picked. Jim had done most of the talking. Vasco and Spud didn't say much, but when they did, people took notice.

"Coca-Cola was originally green," Spud muttered willy-nilly one morning, staring into his coffee.

"And honey's the only food that don't spoil," Vasco added.

Willie liked their company.

"Nice work today, Willie," Jim shouted from the back of the wagon at the day's end. "You was born to pick apples, boy."

Stick watched Willie from a distance. For a thirteen-year-old he was a hard worker and mixed in well. It would be a shame to think he'd done something so bad it would fix him for good, or that he'd spend the rest of his life looking over his shoulder. You could see he was a good boy. Whatever he'd done, he must've had a reason.

Howie Pettit grinned with satisfaction when the eastern orchard's last box came off the trailer before lunch. Five hundred boxes of Jonathans would make it to town that week, and God willing, five hundred more would follow. Unless they had a freeze. And then there were the West Virginia brothers. He was expecting the sheriff to drop by for lunch and ask Stick some more questions. It still turned his stomach when he thought about it. He'd sent their shares home to their parents. Whoever killed them had been quick about it. Their throats had been sliced in one deep cut from ear to ear and each had been stabbed in the heart.

Excited, Willie stared at his envelope for a moment. The orchard paid one dollar an hour, twenty-five cents more than minimum wage.

"You good?" Jim asked, counting his own money.

"Yes, sir!" Willie was surprised by how much there was in the envelope. The only time he'd seen serious cash was in his momma's cigar box. He had exactly forty-five dollars.

At 12:15, the patrol car pulled up.

"Y'all kinda quiet for a Saturday, boys," Howie Pettit chided. "Ain't nothin' but the sheriff droppin' by for lunch—unless you boys robbed a bank or something?"

"I was gonna kill my wife . . . " Spud confessed, heading towards the door, "but I figured the next guy would do it for me." Everyone laughed.

Rachel introduced all the men to Sheriff Weist one by one. When she got to Willie, she ruffled his hair.

"And this one is Willie, Sheriff," she beamed. "From Lexington, Virginia."

"Hey there, Willie." The sheriff extended his hand. "Howie tells me you're the cream of the crop."

Willie's cheeks flushed. He couldn't imagine why the sheriff had come back unless he'd found something out. He badly wanted to run, but he knew he was stuck.

"You servin' the coffee today, Sheriff?" Stick asked pointedly.

"No, man, I'm just here to have some lunch with y'all and ask a few more questions about last weekened," the sheriff replied. "Your fingers okay?"

Stick knew the interrogation would be no skin off his back, but he was worried for Willie and glad the sheriff didn't seem interested in the boy.

"Long way from my heart," he said with a slight grin.

During lunch Willie sat at the corner of the table next to Spud. Rebecca had gone to a friend's house for the day. He'd seen her the evening before, but she was busy with her chores. He could tell she'd wanted to talk and he felt the same way. Being with the men made him miss her more. But he was too hungry to think on it further. Rachel had made New Brunswick stew and cornbread.

"Mighty good stew," Rachel," the sheriff declared, dragging his cornbread around the bottom of his bowl. "I might get a job here," he joked.

"Better hours than what you've got, I imagine," she replied.

"I'll put it this way, there're times I'd rather be in one of your trees than doin' what I'm doin'," he confessed wearily, glancing at his patrol car. "Not to mention your ice cream," he added, looking at her with a big smile.

Stick figured the sheriff was probably a decent guy. He'd been around enough cops to know it wasn't all stew and ice cream. "You find out who done it?" he asked flatly.

"Well . . . let's say we're gettin' there," the sheriff pushed his plate back and rubbed his forehead with his hands.

"They take off?" Stick folded his napkin.

"They did."

"In a black '52 Chevy," Stick said.

"How'd you know that?"

Stick sighed, looking at the sheriff as if he were a child.

"They're Mexicans, sheriff. They're headed home."

"But how'd you know about the Chevy?"

"Was out front that night when I left."

"But how'd you know it was theirs?"

Stick enjoyed having people by the balls sometimes, especially cops. "Texas plates," he said, filling his bowl with ice cream.

While the sheriff spoke with Stick, Willie and the rest of the men helped clear the table. With each load of dishes Willie strained to listen in on the conversation as best he could. The sheriff was asking Stick about someone, but he couldn't catch who it was. You could tell that Stick was calling the shots.

"Hey, Willie!" Sheriff Weist called from the picnic table as Willie headed toward the kitchen door. "Bring me a glass of water when you come, will you?"

He wasn't sure why the sheriff had picked him to bring the water, but it gave him a bad feeling. While Rachel filled the sheriff's glass, Willie thought about slipping back to the bunkhouse and getting under the covers, telling Rachel he didn't feel good.

"Rebecca's all worked up about me making her go today," Mrs. Pettit explained, interrupting his thoughts.

"Yes, ma'am."

"She's kinda taken to you, Willie." She handed him the glass.

Willie had heard only part of what she'd said. "Yes, ma'am." He took the glass, smiling politely.

Rachel Pettit watched him cross the yard through the kitchen window. She'd seen a lot of boys pass through over the years like this one, but she'd never asked why, because when the apples were in, they were long gone.

Willie put the water glass down and started back towards the barn.

"Hang on, Willie," the sheriff said. "Come over here and talk to me."

Willie froze.

"Ain't gonna bite you, son—get over here!" He laughed.

"Yes, sir." Willie walked over a little stiffly.

"Stick here says you're from Lexington?"

"Yes, sir," the boy said, taking his seat.

"Well?" The sheriff waited.

Willie had no idea what he was after. He felt the blood rushing to his head.

"What you doin' here?"

Stick gave Willie a hard look.

"We need the money, Sheriff. My dad ain't around and my mom's sick.

Figured I could make me somethin' and then get on back," he explained.

The sheriff looked sympathetic. He'd heard the story a million times from kids passing through Winchester.

"You doin' all right, then?" he asked kindly.

"Yes, sir. Thank you," he added, not knowing what else to say.

"Well, you're a good boy for tryin' to help your momma. I'm sorry you got so much goin' against you right now, but sounds like you're gonna be just fine, and you found the right family to work for. They've got a good thing goin' here," he said warmly. "Stick needs to sign some papers 'bout last week. You wanna come with us?"

"No, I'm okay," Willie said unhesitatingly.

"Get you some clothes or somethin'?" Stick suggested.

"No, I'm good, Stick. Thanks for asking." He rose to leave.

"You sure you don't want anything?" Stick asked again.

"Can I have some Bazooka?" With an embarrassed half-smile, Willie reached into his pocket and took out five dollars.

"That's a mouthful." Stick took the money and gave him a wink.

Rachel Pettit stood alone in the kitchen window, drying the last glass and listening to her father's clock. The departing men had paid their respects and her daughter would be home soon. She felt like a cat stealing time. As sunlight caressed her face, she undid the band around her hair and gently pressed her hips against the sink.

Stick sat up front with the sheriff as they drove to town. It was good to be out on the road, even in a cop's car. Through the window, he saw that Cedar Creek was high for October. He understood creeks and rivers better than he understood people. "Mind if I roll the window down?" he asked the sheriff.

"This would be the day," the sheriff said agreeably.

As warm fresh air filled the car, Stick rested his elbow outside the door. He'd never owned a car, but there were times when the idea appealed to him.

"What's goin' on in Richmond these days?" the sheriff asked, crossing over a small creek.

"Not much." Stick watched the bridge disappear in the side mirror.

"Tough gettin' work down there, ain't it?"

"Not a lot goin' on since the war."

"Which one?" the sheriff asked.

"Only one they care about." Stick looked at him.

Sheriff Weist had spent his whole life in Winchester. In five years he'd retire and hit the road.

"You think them Mexicans did it?" he asked, after a pause.

"I do," Stick answered.

"You see anyone that night that mighta helped 'em?"

Stick recognized a building. After the station he'd head to the ABC store for liquor. It was the same old story. "One way or the other we all helped," he said flatly.

The station was quiet, but things would pick up by the evening as every orchard had men on the loose. An officer named Frank was on the phone when they arrived and nodded to the sheriff as if he'd seen too much of him lately.

"Only take a minute, Stick." The sheriff pointed to a chair.

The room was in complete chaos, with papers and empty soda bottles everywhere.

"Been a mess here since the murders; I apologize. Don't have much help, since they cut our budget. Tell those boys in Richmond when you get home," he joked, pulling out a drawer behind his desk. "Now where'd I put that thing?" He closed the drawer and opened a smaller one to the right. "Here it is!" With a sheet of paper, he sat down behind his desk.

On the floor beside the desk were several paper stacks, and Stick noticed a picture of Willie on top of one next to his chair leg.

"So let's see . . . " the sheriff started, puzzling over the form, "this . . . um . . . this is gonna be your statement to us about what you, uh . . . what you saw last Saturday night and . . . some of the things you said that you think mighta happened before you left."

"Fire away."

"Right," he said to himself, distracted. "Oh . . . and also the part about the car and everything. That should be in there, too," he added.

"And that part about my fingers?" Stick raised his eyebrows.

"Your fingers?" the sheriff shifted uneasily in his chair. "Oh . . . yeah . . . well, hell, Stick. I thought you was just a drunk."

Stick could tell by the sheriff's questions that they didn't have a case. The Mexicans had long since dumped the car somewhere and jumped a train to El Paso, or somewhere with enough going on so they could slip, unnoticed, across the border. Winchester was a one-cop town, and bad as he felt for the three men, he was glad he'd kept his mouth shut that night. If he hadn't, they'd have cut his balls off.

"Well, Stick, my man, I appreciate your cooperation. Let me give you this carbon here for your records."

When the sheriff turned his back, Stick reached down and took Willie's picture. "That's all right. I don't keep no records. But a lift to Western Union would help, if you don't mind."

When he realized the place was empty, Willie took a shower. Rebecca would be looking for him after her birthday party so he'd make it quick. Stick was right about him needing some clothes. Except for Rachel's sweatshirt and pants he was in bad shape. Even the sole of his right sneaker flopped when he walked. He was worried about Sheriff Weist. He figured it was only a matter of time before the sheriff in Charlottesville gave him a call, or sent him a picture.

In the bunkhouse he made a mental note to buy a towel and some soap. He'd watch Stick carefully to see what he had. He'd need a knife, matches, and a bunch of other things, and it would help if he could make more money before he left. He wondered if Stick's moving around made him miss people, or if every place was pretty much the same.

He took a roll of black electrical tape Mr. Pettit had given him before lunch and wrapped some around his shoe. He didn't care so much about the way he looked as long as he didn't stand out. His momma was usually too drunk to look after him that way. He'd dress himself in the morning and fix something to eat. On days when she was out of it he'd climb the Lucky Bean, or fish the creek, or walk uptown to see Moses.

Willie had met Moses crossing Rugby Road one day. The wind had blown the old man's hat into the path of an oncoming car, and without thinking, Willie had rushed out into traffic to retrieve it. A fat woman behind the wheel of an Oldsmobile had hit the horn, but she'd braked in time for Willie to grab the hat, which he breathlessly handed back to Moses.

"I thank you kindly, sir," he said with a small bow. "Been on ma head a long time." He dusted it off affectionately. To Willie, the old man was ancient.

"Ain't nothin', mister." The boy was a little embarrassed.

"I beg ta differ. 'Tis somethin' when a man helps 'nother like you done. Name's Moses—Moses Henry. I ring da bell."

Willie had no idea what kind of a bell he was talking about. Moses was so old and skinny, Willie didn't think he could've had a job doing much of anything, and while he didn't seem to be drunk, he could've been a little crazy. He'd met a lot of crazy people in The Bottom, especially at night around the

Lucky Bean. His momma would explain to him that most of them "weren't in their right minds," but he'd seen some of them the next day and they seemed okay to him. But old Moses wasn't muttering and yelling and stumbling around the way most of those men were. His eyes were clear and seemed kind, but his body was frail.

"What they call you?" Moses put his hat back on.

"Willie Graves, sir," he said politely.

"Willie Graves," the old man repeated, as if he were listening to the sound it made in his head. "Where you live?"

"In The Bottom." Willie noticed Moses' long dark gray topcoat worn over a pair of faded pin-striped pants. The coat looked too big. "Where you live, sir?" he asked shyly.

"Got me a room on duh Cornah," Moses answered proudly. "Keep me close ma bell."

Willie wanted to ask what bell, but didn't want to appear to be stupid. "Well, nice to meet you. I best be gettin' home."

"Well, den. T'ank you for ma hat." Offering his smooth hand to the boy, he gave a strange childlike smile.

"You welcome, Mr. Henry." He let go of his hand and headed off down the street.

Heading down University Avenue himself, Moses called after him.

"Excuse me?" the boy answered back.

"Duh Bottom, you say?" Moses remembered.

"Yes, sir," Willie replied, surprised.

"Nice folks down dere." Moses nodded, walking away.

Rebecca stood outside the screen door while Willie taped his right shoe. She wasn't sure what he was doing and her mother had always told her to stay away from the bunkhouse unless she or Howie was with her, but since the men were all in town, she decided it would be all right.

"Hey, Willie," she called in quietly.

Startled, Willie sat up. "Hey, Rebecca! You back from your party?" He'd missed her company. Even at seven, she was closer to his age than the rest of them.

The little girl opened the screen door and walked into the bunkhouse before checking to make sure they were alone.

"My momma made me go. I wanted to stay, but she made me go."

"You have fun?" Willie asked, checking the tape on his right shoe before standing up. He didn't plan on telling her he'd never been to a birthday party before.

"Guess so. They had that thing you bust up—a pin-somethin'-or-other. Looked like a big sock, but they put some ears on it and we hit it with a baseball bat till the candy came out. Brought you some taffy!" She threw him a piece, and smiled when he caught it. "It's orange," she said, as he unwrapped it.

He bit down into it. "Mmmm . . . it's real good."

"Got lots in my pocket. Wanna fish? Poles are in the barn."

Willie remembered his bamboo pole lost in the river. It didn't matter so much anymore where it was, but it made him sad to think that he'd lost the one thing he'd taken with him. Maybe the old black lady had it.

"What kinda fish you got here?" He was excited about the fishing trip.

"I caught a bullhead last time. This big!" she boasted, spreading her hands apart about eighteen inches. "Couldn't get him in the bucket!"

"What's a bullhead?"

"Catfish, I guess you call 'em. Had ugly whiskers and all."

"You got crappies?"

"Daddy got a black one down in some deep water somewhere, but I never saw it."

"I got me a white one once," Willie bragged.

"They have bones like Daddy's?"

"Pretty much. Fight real good, though."

He took a step forward to test his shoe.

"Is your shoe broken?"

"Naw, good to go. Do we need crawlers or somethin'?"

"Got jigs in the box." She opened the door.

"Well, let's hit it, girl."

By the time they reached the creek, it was midafternoon. Locating a mound of brush at the creek bank, Rebecca put her pole and metal buckets beside a small redbud and squinted at the water.

"Daddy says it's good here 'cuz the crappies can hide," she said, putting the tackle box on the ground and popping it open. Willie held his pole and crouched down to examine the contents of the box. For a girl, Rebecca was good company. Any girl who liked to fish was all right in his book.

"Got lots a jigs," he marveled.

"Yeah. Flies too, see!" She lifted the box shelf up to show him another layer of tackle below.

"Man, look at all them flies!" Willie gasped. "Must be hundreds!"

"Daddy makes them from birds and stuff. Got a whole drawer full."

"Look at this one," Willie said, taking one between his index finger and thumb from a tiny compartment and holding it up in a shaft of brilliant sun. "Like it's on fire or somethin'. Must be a cardinal."

"Or one a those woodpeckers," Rebecca guessed, putting her head next to his so she could look too.

"Bet that makes 'em nuts when they see it," Willie speculated.

"Daddy catches lots a fish," she said proudly as he carefully deposited the fly back into the box.

"Look at all these! Like snowflakes!" Willie exclaimed.

"He's got lots of owl stuff. Sometimes people bring 'em over after they go hunting or if they find one dead somewhere. We had a big ole hooter out back once that left a bunch a feathers and fur on the ground. He must have torn something up one night because he sure made a mess. But Daddy was real happy."

Willie watched as Rebecca attached a new jig to his pole. He felt funny letting a girl dress his line, but it was her lure and he could tell she knew what she was doing. He'd never fished with such fancy 'tackin,' as he called it.

"Might be crappies 'bout there." Rebecca nodded towards the bush, handing him the pole. "Kinda shallow, so don't go down deep. I'll be down a ways in case you chase 'em out."

CHAPTER TWENTY-TWO

Standing on the Cedar Creek bridge, Stick took a hit of rum and thought about the boy facedown in the river. He felt light-headed from the booze. Some people turned to mush when they drank, but Stick went the other way. Or so he thought. He figured the sheriff hadn't seen Willie's picture yet. But when he did, the shit would fly. Just for the hell of it, he imagined jumping. He'd done foundation work on girder bridges in Maine one summer the year before he'd met Crystal-Ann. He'd have jumped back then. His hands had been rough with granite when he first touched her. "Like a wild animal," she'd said.

Stick opened two Cokes and poured them into the bottle of rum. This time he'd bought enough to last the week. Watching the two liquids swirl together, he felt a binge coming on. The boy would get what was coming and there wasn't anything to be done about it. At least they wouldn't cut his throat.

Putting the empty Coke bottles back in his knapsack, his hand found the paper.

MISSING PERSON OF INTEREST

August 31, 1953
Albemarle County, Virginia

WILLIE GRAVES

Date of Birth: November 30, 1939   Place of Birth: Charlottesville, Virginia

Sex: Male   Hair: Brown

Height: 5'4"   Eyes: Hazel

Weight: 110 lbs.   Race: Mixed

DETAILS

August 10, 1953, in the Garrett Street section of Charlottesville, Virginia, Willie Graves was seen running from a domestic fire. On August 30, 1953, the First Judicial District Court, Albemarle County, Virginia, issued an arrest warrant for Graves FOR QUESTIONING ONLY. Future charges TBD.

REMARKS

Last seen in Goshen, Virginia. Limited funds. May be train hopping. Individuals with information on his whereabouts who are in the Charlottesville/Albemarle jurisdiction should contact Sheriff David Sheffield of Charlottesville, Virginia. Under no circumstances should civilians take action themselves, and if outside said jurisdiction, are instructed to contact their nearest law enforcement agency.

In the photograph Willie was smiling as if he had only good things on his mind. As Stick read, a familiar weariness, tinged with sadness, came over him. He'd seen it a million times—lives out of luck—and it pissed him off. When he looked down the creek, the water appeared darker than before and it made him want to drink.

Willie felt the cool air around him as he reeled in. He'd need a longer branch for all the crappies.

"You done?" Rebecca called out.

"Gettin' dark," he said, looking downstream.

"Got a ton in the bucket, Willie!"

Willie bent over to see. "There's a bunch, all right. Ten, maybe."

"Ten?!" Rebecca clapped.

"You got more down there?"

"No, I put 'em all in the bucket."

"Need a stick or somethin'," Willie said, peering in the bushes.

"Just string 'em with this." She pulled a long blue ribbon from the front pocket of her jeans. "My mom likes me to wear it, but I never do." She made a face.

"Your momma gonna mind if we mess it all up?"

"Don't think she'll mind, not with all a this! Look at all these crappies she can fry!" Rebecca jumped up and down.

"We could use a stick and save your ribbon," he suggested.

"You think?"

Using the tackle box knife, Willie strung the gills through a slender limb of mountain laurel.

"Good knife you got. Lotta things on it," he said, folding it up.

"Got a toothpick on it, see? It was Grendaddy's. Gave it to me when I was five."

He liked the way she spoke about her grandfather.

"Momma made me wait till I was seven to use it. It has a can opener too, but it's broken. My brother said he'd fix it."

"One a them Swiss Army knives, ain't it?" Willie handed it back.

"It's kinda dirty on top, but you can see it right here." She showed him a faded white cross on the side. "Got that cross thing, see."

"Oh, yeah. I seen one like that before, but I never had one. Does a lot a stuff for you, I bet."

"'Everything 'cept the dishes,' Grendaddy used to say," she said dreamily, closing the tackle box. "We can look at jigs tomorrow—come on!"

As dusk set in, Willie and Rebecca walked through the lower east orchard. Willie was exhausted from his first week of work.

"You tired?" she asked after a few minutes.

"Kinda."

"It's a lotta up and down on those ladders. My legs hurt sometimes." Her look was trusting and friendly.

"You help out?"

"Every once in a while," she said. "Daddy pays me, too—that's the best part. But I don't like climbing all day."

"You born here?" Willie noticed the sky over North Mountain straight ahead.

"Yep," she answered, checking the fish. "Where you from, Willie?"

He'd tell her the truth. "Keep a secret?"

"Promise. I won't tell anybody." She looked at him straight on.

"Charlottesville," he said.

"You're not from Lexington?"

"No."

"So how come you said you were from Lexington?"

Willie looked off. He wasn't ready to tell her everything.

" 'Cuz I ran away," he confessed.

Rebecca's heart began to pound, but she didn't want him to know. "How come you ran away?" she whispered.

A flock of catbirds passed directly overhead and veered away. When she and Willie got to a lilac hedge, Rebecca could see her parents sitting on the back porch. The lilacs would bloom a deep purple come May, but weren't much to look at the rest of the year.

"Pretty sky," Willie said, repositioning the stick on his shoulder while he walked. He couldn't tell her. She would have to figure it out on her own someday.

"I won't tell anyone, Willie, I promise, cross my heart and hope to die." She pursed her lips.

From behind North Mountain a confluence of lime and gold melted into the darkening skies above. Catching sight of her daughter, Rachel Pettit raised her hand in the air and waved.

"Here, Momma! Got tons a fish!" Rebecca shouted.

As the colors in the sky vanished, Willie felt sad to be so far from his own momma, and his own home. Tightening his grip on the stick of dangling crappies, he lowered his head without speaking and ran towards the farmhouse.

Around midnight a figure appeared in the headlights of Jim's truck as it climbed the last hill below Pettit's orchard. Stick was leaning forward and weaving from left to right while he walked. Slowing down, Jim followed him for a minute or two before stopping the truck.

"That you, Stick?" he called through the window.

Stick squinted into the lights with a dazed expression. "Thought you was the law!" He rubbed his forehead with an open hand.

"Been called a lotta things, but that ain't one of 'em." Jim swiveled around to check the truck bed.

"Boys fall out?" Stick chided.

"Slept the whole way. Musta been the hooch." Vasco and Spud were still asleep in the truck bed. "Come on, get in," he offered, opening the passenger door. "Been a long night."

Looking dirty and drunk, Stick approached the driver's side with a defiant expression on his face.

"You look pretty fucked up, Stick. Let me give you a ride."

Grabbing the side mirror with one hand for balance, Stick looked east down the road where the truck had come from. "Dark down there, ain't it?" he mumbled.

"No moon and tons a trees, buddy." Jim eyed him. He looked lost. "You all right?"

"Fair to middlin', I guess." Stick let go of the side mirror and adjusted his knapsack.

"Sure you don't want a ride?"

"I'm good," Stick said. He blinked and backed away from the truck.

When the truck's dust had settled, Stick started walking again. Crystal-Ann would have called him a chicken shit, but he'd lived too long and knew better than to plant his nose in other people's bullshit. If the boy was cooked, he was cooked, whether he deserved it or not. Nothing to be done except get out of the way. Maybe he'd cut down on the booze and get himself a place to grow flowers, or ride the Northern Pacific. Wink was right about one thing—there was a reason he never got a dog.

"Fuck it," he said, staring into the blackness.

In the early morning, Willie found Stick curled up on his bunkhouse bed with his clothes on. He smelled like rum and the side of his face had grass stains on it. The boy figured he'd fallen down drunk in the yard. He wanted to take his boots off for him.

"Let him sleep, Willie," Jim said, from his own bed.

"He's drunk again, ain't he?" Willie sighed.

"Got him again, my boy," he murmured.

Willie passed Stick's bed on his way to the door, but couldn't look at him. Except for Moses, all the people he'd ever gotten close to were drunks. When Moses rang the bell, he made Willie stand by the window until the rope went slack and he was done. Afterward they'd stand together and look at the sky or watch the grounds below. One day, sitting on the floor, they closed their eyes and listened to the bell. When Willie's eyes opened, Moses was smiling.

"How long it go on ringin', Moses?" Willie asked.

"Don't know." The old man shook his head slowly, his eyes still closed. "Till it git where it goin', I 'magine."

Willie left the bunkhouse and sat alone on the swing. The Pettits had left for church and the men were all asleep. Stick made him think of all he had lost. His behavior didn't surprise him, so much as it reminded him of his own situation. If his parents hadn't been drunk, the fire wouldn't have happened and he'd be high up in the branches of the Lucky Bean right about now watching people file into Mt. Zion Baptist Church, or counting cars on Carter Mountain. His momma would be rolling in late morning. Saturday night was a long night for liquor and a longer one for lovin'. Willie was glad he didn't drink. He had enough problems of his own. Any day now the sheriff could come back, and he was tired of running. The Pettits had been good to him, they were different that way, but he knew he'd have to leave and he was scared. He'd have to think hard about where to go. He'd be alone.

"Got a minute?" Stick startled him. He looked pretty awful.

"Boys said you was out here when I woke up. Was gonna talk to you last night when I got in, but . . . " He stopped talking and leaned against the poplar trunk, lowering himself slowly to the ground as he leaned against the tree.

"Slipped on the grass last night. Near broke my neck," he said, his chin practically to his chest.

"Good thing you was drunk or you would've," Willie said sarcastically.

"Suppose you're right about that." Stick took a deep breath. "Drunks and fools, Willie. I'm a bit a both sometimes," he confessed, stretching his legs out and crossing them.

The boy was surprised to hear Stick say something so personal about himself. It was almost like an apology. He could tell that he had something on his mind.

"Found this in the sheriff's office yesterday," he said, pulling a folded piece of paper from his shirt pocket and tossing it on the grass next to Willie's feet. Stick could see by the boy's expression that he'd already guessed what it was. Willie's mouth tightened as he opened the page and saw his picture. His momma must have given the photo to the police from the box under her bed. The notice seemed more about someone else than about him—until he saw his father's name.

"Oh, God!" he gasped, dropping his head. The swing's ropes rocked from side to side as the balls of his feet lifted off the ground. There wasn't much he could do for the boy. Willie tried to collect himself, breathing hard through his nostrils, looking wild-eyed and desperate.

"Don't say nothin' else," Willie sputtered, dragging the top of his hand under his nose. "Didn't have no choice." He'd be finished picking apples. They'd be here today to take him back.

"Choice 'bout what?"

He'd forgotten Stick was there.

" 'Bout nothin'," Willie barely whispered.

Uncrossing his legs, Stick sat back against the tree trunk. He needed some water and his hands were shaking. "You're gonna need some help, boy," Stick said, rubbing the side of his head as he stared at the dirt, as if to get his mind around the situation.

The swing's rope in his grip, Willie tilted his face to the sky and listened. Stick's voice seemed to come from far away. "Ain't nobody can help you 'cept yourself, son. If you did somethin', then you got to go back. And if they got it wrong, you better go anyhow 'cuz there ain't nowhere to hide, if they want you bad enough." Stick felt the tree bark against the back of his head. "I done some things I ain't too proud of, but when you're right 'bout somethin' . . . you got to do somethin' 'bout it. What they want you for?"

Willie let go of the rope and rubbed his heels into the dirt. "Killin' my daddy, I 'magine," he choked out.

"You *'magine?*"

"Was a fire," the boy admitted dumbly.

"You start it?"

"Sorta, I guess."

"What do you mean, 'sorta'?"

"I think I hit him . . . with a candle."

"You think a candle," Stick repeated.

Willie let his chin drop to his chest.

"It had glass all around it."

"Where'd you hit him?"

"In the kitchen."

"I mean, where'd you hit him on his body?"

"His head. I hit him in the head and the glass broke and he fell down on the floor with his bottle and there was blood all over him so I juz . . . dropped the candle . . . and ran to get my momma, but she was drunk somewhere so

I run back to the kitchen," Willie gushed, choking back tears, "and his head, oh, man, he was lyin' in blood and his head was on fire and his hands, so I juz . . . " Willie sobbed and started shaking as Stick stood and came over to him.

"Why'd you hit him?"

Willie looked up at Stick. He wiped his face with both hands and tried to stop crying. "Why'd I hit him?" he choked, his eyes wide with shock and disbelief.

"What'd he do to make you want to hit him?"

Willie sat up in the swing and took a deep breath. Not even Moses knew. "What he always did when he was drunk," he spoke quietly, wiping his face. The tears were gone. When he looked at Stick again, his eyes were dead. Stick was waiting for him to speak.

There was a moment of silence. The only sound was the phone ringing in the Pettits' kitchen.

"You want some help?" Stick nodded towards the bunkhouse.

Willie nodded back, dazed. His shoes were still damp with dew and his feet were cold. He'd never thought much about the weather before, but everything had changed now. His body felt heavy and he'd had a hard time going to sleep, like he'd had the weight of the world on his shoulders and was a million years old. The sheriff would show up soon and he'd have to run. He'd go as far and as long as he had to. But he had no place to go . . . he'd need a knapsack with food, a knife, and something to sleep on. And he'd be alone. The leaves had started to fall and not long from now there'd be snow. He'd head south where it was warm. He had an aunt in Louisiana, but that was too far, and if he showed up out of the blue, she might turn him in. No matter how far he went he'd be alone. The swing's rope in his hands, he leaned back, his face toward the sky, until his mind became so completely empty he stopped thinking.

Sheriff Weist's cruiser stopped at the house. No one had answered the phone when he'd called from his office, so he figured they'd left for church. It didn't matter unless they'd taken the boy with them. Either way, he'd be here when they got home and, except for an empty swing moving, the place was still. As he opened the car door, he smelled a cigarette. At eight o'clock on a Sunday, most of the men were probably sleeping it off.

Sleepy and hungover, Spud sat on an old apple crate, smoking by the front door of the bunkhouse when the sheriff approached.

"Mornin', Sheriff," Spud mumbled.

"Mornin', Spud," the sheriff said cheerily. "Boys around?"

Spud noticed his holster clip was unsnapped. "Sleepin'," he said, taking a hit of his cigarette and crossing a leg. Sheriff Weist had gotten the scoop on Spud from Howie Pettit. His real name was Russell Paley. One season with the Pettits he'd carved a duck out of wood for Rebecca. "Be lots a snow this year, Sheriff," he said, blowing smoke.

Sheriff Weist grinned. "How you know that, Spud?"

Spud looked over at the swing. It had stopped moving. "Spicebush got no berries," he said, pointing.

The sheriff turned to the bush. "That mean somethin'?"

"Can't take two loads in a year, what my granddaddy said."

"Well, what d'ya know! Never heard that before, but if you think about it, makes sense, don't it?" the sheriff agreed.

"What he said." Spud sounded pleased. "So what you doin' here so early?"

"Like to talk to the boy." He nodded towards the screen door.

"What you want with him? Kinda young to be a suspect, ain't he?" Spud dropped his cigarette into a large brown glass bottle by the door.

"Ain't a suspect I'm after, Spud," the sheriff said, pushing open the bunkhouse door.

When the door slammed, Vasco and Jim sat up in their beds.

"Sorry, boys!" the sheriff announced.

Stick's and Willie's beds were empty.

" 'Scuse me, Sheriff." Spud shuffled in, heading for the sink.

"Thought you said everyone was here, Spud." The sheriff sounded edgy.

Spud stopped to look at the beds. "Thought they was, Sheriff." He yawned. "Just woke up."

Swinging out from under the blanket, Jim sat up in his bed. Willie's bed was made.

"Stick here last night, Jim?" the sheriff inquired. Rubbing his eyes, Jim looked over at Stick's bed to get his bearings.

"Got in 'round three in the mornin', I think, Sheriff. Passed him in the truck 'round midnight by the gate a ways. He was pretty messed up."

"You alone?"

"Just me and the boys."

"Been drinkin'?"

Jim ran his hands over his beard with a wicked smile. He needed a shave. "Don't drink, Sheriff. Never have. But the boys here . . . they make up for it," he said, looking over at Vasco.

Vasco dropped his head back against the pillow. "Moonshine legal 'round here, Sheriff?"

"It is not," the sheriff said flatly. "You drink it?"

"Pinetop Perkins was playin' some juke joint off Route 15. 'Bout tore my head off."

"The music or the shine?" asked the sheriff.

"Had that Howlin' Wolf band with him. Man, them boys can rip it up!" he declared, getting a bead on the sheriff.

"Where'd Stick go?" Jim wondered aloud, as Spud cleaned his fingernails with a pocketknife over the sink.

"You tell me," the sheriff said. No one spoke. The only noise was the faucet water as Spud washed his hands.

"Boys?" the sheriff insisted.

Vasco rolled over on his side. "Saw him couple hours ago when I went to pee."

"Might be in the shower, or maybe at church or somethin'," Jim added.

"Church?!" the sheriff barked in disbelief.

"Mighta gone with 'em to church, yeah. What's wrong with that? We're not all heathens here, Sheriff. There are some believers among us." Jim pushed his blanket aside and stood up.

"And the boy?"

"Hell, I don't know, Sheriff," Jim said with irritation. "Maybe he went with him."

Crossing to the end of Willie's bed, Sheriff Weist caught a glimpse of Spud's face in the mirror.

"You sleep through all this, Spud?" he asked, taking stock of the trunk at the foot of Willie's bed.

"All what?" Spud said through the mirror.

"Well, seems like with everybody comin' and goin', you mighta heard or seen somethin'."

"It's like I said, Sheriff . . . " Spud stared back, his face deadpan.

" . . . you just woke up," the sheriff finished. An uncomfortable silence set in as the sheriff leaned down and cracked Willie's trunk.

"The boy in trouble for somethin'?" Jim asked, sounding more awake. Sheriff Weist closed the trunk lid. Something about the men's demeanor wasn't right. Moving next to the end of Stick's bed, Weist reached down and opened his trunk. Jim could see that it was full.

"Got a call this morning from Charlottesville about a missing boy. Seems he may know somethin' 'bout a fire. Been a while since he was home. Name's

Willie Graves and as it turns out, he ain't from Lexington."

"Damn!" Vasco exclaimed, propping his pillow up and leaning against it. As Spud spun around, his eyes met Jim's.

"Well, what do you know?" Vasco added, shaking his head. The sheriff took a telegram from his shirt pocket and unfolded it.

"Looks like they found a body, boys. Willie Graves was seen runnin' from the house. Haven't seen him since."

Jim sat back down. "He a murder suspect?"

"He's officially, as it stands right now, a 'Person of Interest.' " Something next to Stick's bed caught the sheriff's eye. "That a Bible?" He pointed to the chair. Spud looked at the floor and smiled.

"Dictionary," Jim said agreeably. "Said it helps him sleep."

The sheriff rolled back his shirt cuff and glanced at his watch. "I'll be here till they get back from church. And then we'll see. I realize it's Sunday, boys, but I want you all here for the time being, if that's all right. At least until I can figure things out." He was all business when he looked at Spud. "And get your shovels ready, boys. Spud here says we're in for snow this winter."

From her bedroom window Rebecca Pettit looked west over the roof of the barn. In a few weeks it would be Christmas. It had been a good year. Her father had said so the night before. A good year for apples and a bad year for help. She sighed. It didn't feel much like Sunday. Willie was gone for good and she didn't think he'd ever be back. She missed their fishing trips, and felt bad about what he'd told her, the fire and all, and she hoped they'd be zillions of miles away from anywhere they might get caught. She imagined him with Stick sailing on a huge white schooner. Her Swiss Army knife would open the crocks or mend the ropes. She'd keep Willie's secrets, cross her heart and hope to die. And someday they'd see each other again.

She wanted to cry when she thought about him living in that cave. She'd showed it to him one day when they'd gone exploring together and he was smart enough to run there with the sheriff on his heels. It was a good place to hide, but it wasn't the kind of place a person could live in. And being a half hour from the house, she worried about her father finding out.

"Tell your mother I appreciate what she's done." Willie's eyes were wet.

When she gave him the Swiss Army knife, they hugged each other for a long time.

"And save me some crappies for when I come back, okay?"

When Rebecca left, tears streamed down Willie's face. After a week in the cave alone, it was finally time to go. If he stayed too long her father or the sheriff would find him, and in a few weeks it would be snowing. But all was not lost. He'd gotten this far and been all right. And, most important, Stick had a plan.

CHAPTER TWENTY-THREE

After the noon bell, Moses stood with the barbers Charlie and William Lloyd on the Corner and listened to Captain Snyder read the news from behind his newsstand. They couldn't read and the captain was good about reading whatever people wanted to hear. When a passerby stopped to listen, he said, it helped him sell papers.

"Somet'in 'bout duh Graves?" Moses interrupted. " 'Cuz, mos' time, seem like duh same news all o'er again."

Captain Snyder laid the paper down and lit his pipe. "Think you're hearin' somethin' new, but half the time, it juz dressed up to look new." He gave Moses a sheepish grin, pointing at the open paper with his pipe. "Facts er left out, or else dey chop up a story so it come out different. A good newspaper boy make you wonder what day it is." His eyes lit up suddenly. "But here's your story, man. Right here." Captain Snyder put his pipe down. As he read, Moses cocked his head and listened carefully to every word.

The story was mostly about Mopsey Graves and how he'd worked in a carnival with gypsies. Moses wasn't sure what that had to do with the fire, but he listened all the same, hoping they'd say something about the boy. It seemed they knew more about the dead than about the living. For some reason, Mopsey Graves's death was more about his wife's being a prostitute than about what Willie might have done. Or at least that's what Moses got out of it. They talked about a church service for the deceased. Even for a man of God, he understood that Charlottesville loved its whorehouse as much as it loved its churches and that you couldn't have one without the other.

"Here we go." Captain Snyder held the paper up to get a better look.

"'The woman described the young man she met as a twelve- or thirteen-year-old boy fitting the description of Willie Graves, to whom she attended after a miraculous escape through the Devil's Kitchen section of the Maury River near Lexington. According to the woman, he'd been found near death by another individual, who delivered the boy to her for help. When asked for a description of that individual, Sheriff Sheffield had no comment.'"

As the captain read the last paragraph, Moses stared across the street towards the Rotunda.

"'Having eluded police officers with dogs near Dunlap Creek, Willie Graves is presumed to be traveling on foot. Whether he has remained somewhere in the Lexington vicinity is not known at this time, but he is regarded as a Missing Person of Interest. Citizens having any contact with him should notify their local police department immediately.'"

When Captain Snyder was finished reading, Moses thanked him and shuffled off to his room to lie down. When he woke up, he'd send the two o'clock bell to Willie. If the boy was as far away as the paper said, he didn't know what good it would do. But that wouldn't stop Moses from trying. Even on Rugby Road, the only people who heard his bell were the ones who listened.

Sadie Graves stood outside her room waiting and listened to the girls below. The house had been full of men. She'd put money in the cellar twice last month and still had enough for a fix or two each day. The sheriff had called when he had news about Willie, but she was usually too messed up to call back. Once the boy was home she'd clean up, but smack took the edge off. Matt Abel had kept the reporters away. He'd told them that if they wanted her, they'd better have cash.

One *Progress* reporter had been around before. When she saw him on the stairs, she smiled and untied her robe. He was not unattractive. It was their second time together. She wouldn't go as quickly as before, and this time, she'd remember his name. As the drugs kicked in, their kiss would be harder, and when he came, she'd close her eyes and dream about their life together.

Sheriff Sheffield dropped a pinch of Rooster between his cheek and gum and knocked. He'd been there enough times to walk in, but for the sake of people passing by, this was business. The boy had been gone long enough to make any mother afraid. Afraid he was gone for good, or dead. When no one answered, he opened the door and walked in.

"Hello? Sadie?"

"Out here, Sheriff," she spoke through a screen door at the end of the hall.

Passing the dish of room keys, he saw the name "Rose." It had been a while since he'd needed a visit, but when he did, she'd always found the right girl. Sadie had a reputation, but the sheriff was glad she'd never been his lady. Under the circumstances, it made things a lot easier. It'd be hard telling her, but it was unavoidable. The law was the law. "There you are! Thought you were here." He moved through the door.

Wearing a knitted pink shawl around her shoulders, Sadie looked over with bloodshot eyes from a white wicker rocker. Despite a chill in the air, her knees were curled up under a red skirt and her bare brown legs stuck out over the edge of the seat. They'd spoken on the phone several times, but he hadn't seen her in a while. He smiled and checked her eyes. They'd been pretty eyes once, eyes you couldn't easily forget. But not today.

"Pretty as a picture, darlin'," he lied, closing the door and taking off his hat. Sadie watched him like a child.

"Still got all that beautiful hair, don't you, David Sheffield. 'Swhat the girls always said 'bout you." She was stoned. "They'd go on and on 'bout it sometimes." Her eyes wandered, out to the backyard. "But . . . that was a long time ago and now we got somethin' else to talk about." The sheriff stood awkwardly, shifting his feet as he held his hat over his crotch. "Come on," she said, smiling and tapping the arm of the rocker next to her, "I won't bite." He could see the needle marks on the inside of her arm. Some were infected. "Got a spitter by that door, or you can do it on the roses there. Be good for them aphids." She nodded, looking out over the rail.

"You wanna pinch, Miss Sadie?" He sat down next to her.

"Look like I need a pinch?"

"No, ma'am, it don't." He tucked the tin in his shirt pocket as she scratched her arm under the shawl. Whatever she was on, it seemed to be working.

"Need a drink?" She dropped her feet to the floor and slid them into a pair of soft leather slippers.

"Another time, Miss Sadie. Thank you." He wondered if she was even listening. They sat together for a moment before she spoke.

"He dead?" she asked flatly, staring straight ahead.

"Not that we know of."

"So, he's alive?"

"Well, if he ain't showin' up . . . that way you might think . . . then we figure he's got to be somewhere." He smoothed the edge of his hat brim.

"So . . . you don't know?" Her eyes narrowed.

"We have a pretty good idea."

"But you don't know for sure?" She began to rock.

"Got a lotta things goin' on that make it hard to verify," he explained.

"Thought I had him near Lexington, but he popped up in Winchester. Seems to be runnin' with an older fella."

"You after him too?"

"No, ma'am, we hadn't been . . . until now. The problem is, we may be on to somethin', an', you know, he ain't exactly around to prove me wrong."

Sadie pushed her shawl off her shoulders onto the rocker. Her arm was starting to burn from the junk.

"You all right?" he asked, seeing her discomfort.

"Fine," she mumbled. "Just want my boy back 'sall I want." Her eyes started to tear. "Or alive somewhere." She took a short breath. "Never see him again an' I suppose I got it comin', but . . . " she trailed off, lapsing into a daze. It had been a while since he'd seen a junkie. Matt Abel had warned him she was on the needle. He stood up.

"Listen to me, darlin'." He moved to the rail directly in front of her. Sadie stared at him. He was a big man. She liked big men. They were usually gentler than the little ones. "Lotta work to do yet, but . . . the Richmond boys may be on to somethin'." He leaned back against the rail.

"What you mean, 'somethin'?"

"Somethin' that ties him to it."

"Like what?" she asked defensively.

"Fingerprint on the glass."

Sadie glanced in the direction of her former house. Willie hadn't been her whole life, but he had been the best thing in it. Her glassy eyes took in the burned-out foundation. "Mopsey wasn't the boy's father." The sheriff winced. It didn't matter who his father was.

"Appreciate you telling me, Sadie, but it still don't change the situation. Bottom line is, we got a piece a glass taken from Mopsey's skull with a partial print on it. Too small to be anything but a child's, they're thinkin'. Now, maybe, Mopsey'd been drinkin' and passes out and the booze fires up. Nothin' your boy meant to do . . . candle flame lights the booze, maybe your boy panics and takes off . . . at least that's what it's lookin' more and more like every day." Sheriff Sheffield paused to let it sink in. "That's what we got to go on till he tells me otherwise. And he ain't here to do that."

"I was in my room upstairs that night. Lyin' on the bed," she said vaguely, blinking several times. "Why'd he run like this 'less he know somethin'?" she asked, rubbing her arm. Some belligerence had crept back into her voice. The sheriff kneeled down in front of her on one knee and took her two limp hands into his.

"Don't know why, Miss Sadie, until he tells me. But people I work for want answers and they want 'em quick, and I need Willie to get 'em."

" 'Cept he ain't here." Her eyes pleaded. Her anger had burned out.

"No, he ain't," he finished sadly, reaching for his hat next to her chair and standing up. "I issued an arrest warrant for Willie this morning and if I hear anything at all, I'll call you, but chances are, if the boy wants to stay gone . . . that's what he'll be. You need to prepare yourself for that, Miss Sadie, so it don't eat you up . . . this waitin'. You . . . "

Sadie had passed out, her head on the rocker. Disheartened, the sheriff covered her arms and shoulders with the shawl. He remembered how pretty she'd looked the first time he'd seen her at the front door. Now spittle ran down the edge of her mouth and her lips were dry and cracked. He'd seen plenty of misfortunes in his time, and this was just one more. When a person falls apart, it never amounts to one thing so much as a whole bunch of unfortunate events. He suspected in Sadie's case it wasn't the boy leaving that tore her up so much as why he'd left.

On his way out, the hallway was quiet. It was Sunday morning and the girls were sleeping. He let himself out as he put his hat on. His back was sore. In a few hours the Virginia students would show up still drunk from Saturday night. After a whole night of drinking, they'd have their courage up and there'd be fire in their eyes.

On that same afternoon Moses rode the trolley back from The Bottom. He was tired from the long walk down and sad when the girls told him that Sadie was indisposed. It was the third week in a row. Every Sunday since the fire he'd tried to look in on her, but recently, she'd taken a turn for the worse. Mr. Matt had told him about the drugs. He'd understood how hard her life had been, especially with the men. But she'd always been nice to him and she was Willie's momma.

Matt Abel's girls were sweet to him. In a small town you didn't have to ask. Things got around. It didn't change the way he felt about her. It only made him miss their visits more. Sometimes they'd sit on the porch if the weather was right, or she'd serve him iced tea in her room. She always had a box of gingersnaps and he was particularly fond of those. When the girls had told him about the sheriff's visit, and that the boy had been spotted alive not long ago, a world of worry had lifted from his shoulders. Moses would keep on about his business as he had done his whole life. It didn't matter so much where Willie had gone. What remained to be seen was where he'd end up.

CHAPTER TWENTY-FOUR

Riding in the back of Jim's truck from the cave to a grade crossing south of Winchester, Stick had started to educate Willie on hopping trains.

"Now don't go goofy on me up there, Willie. Ain't no joke when we do this thing, 'cuz the train ain't stoppin' when you get scared and change your mind—don't work that way. You gotta understand that, son. The wind'll pull your sack back when you jump on, and I guarantee you that when the car rocks, your hands'll be slippin'. You fall off and you're gonna feel it in the morning. And if it's a shot, we don't have time to dink around."

"What's a shot?" Willie's face was losing color fast.

"Hot shot. Watch yourself, boy!" Seeing a car, he ducked fast, his head between his knees, as Willie did the same.

"So what is it?" he asked anxiously.

"Train that's got priority over everybody."

"Oh," Willie said, breathing out. "Like a special?"

Stick smiled. "Sorta like that. How you know 'bout a special?"

" 'Cuz I seen one once when I was ridin' in a car. It was real fast."

"They can scoot, all right. Makes it hard when you catch out, though," he added.

"Catch what?"

"Catch out."

"What's that?"

Stick grinned at the boy's enthusiasm. "Since you started talkin', you been askin' a lotta questions!"

" 'Cuz I wanna know things. So I don't mess up." Willie looked at him earnestly.

Holding on to the side of the truck bed, Stick felt the wind racing over the top of his hands. Helping the boy made him feel good. Crystal-Ann would have liked what he'd done so far. She'd always said that, after you got past the bullshit, Stick's heart was in the right place.

"Just hold on to the ladder," he said as they hit a bump.

Stick hated coal cars, but they were his best shot. Bulls had a hard time looking in, especially when the train was moving. They'd gotten lucky, though. Judging by its length, the train was more than likely a southbound out of Martinsburg. If he was right, they'd ditch near D.C. or Fredericksburg and catch a truck to the Chesapeake before morning. Sunday was a good day to hop, he remembered, as he started running for the ladder.

"Climb!" Stick shouted, lifting Willie up to grab a ladder, and he jumped on another one at the end of the car a split second later. The train was moving fast and the boy's heart pounded as they climbed to the top, then down inside the car. "We can move up to another car later," Stick said, catching his breath.

When the train stopped, Stick jumped up to take a look. It got harder on his body with each passing year. Sitting in an empty coal car was all he needed. "Come on," he whispered down to Willie. Willie's head was woozy when he stood up. He'd kept his knapsack over his shoulder to cushion his body against the wall, but his neck was stiff. "Follow me out!" Stick disappeared over the top.

When Willie reached the top, Stick was on the ground below the ladder, motioning hurriedly for him to come down. "Hug the cars as we run up the tracks."

It was easier going down when the train was stopped than it had been climbing up when it was moving. Grabbing the rungs, his hands were slippery and black with coal dust. He didn't care if he was dirty, he just didn't want to fall. When Willie was three rungs from the bottom Stick grabbed him around his waist and lowered him to the ground.

"Now, listen," he said, dusting off the boy's arms, "they're losin' a line a coal cars, so we don't have much time. Stay close and when we find one with a ladder, get on it," Stick directed, taking off.

Putting his head down to offset the weight of his knapsack, Willie ran with all his might. He was surprised to see Stick move so fast. As he ran, Willie tried to figure as best he could where they were. The landscape had changed. It wasn't as hilly and the trees were all the same. Counting the cars as they passed, Willie guessed Stick had a plan, but he wasn't sure if it was the bulls or the sheriff they were running from at this point.

When Stick came to a dead halt, Willie's knapsack nearly fell off his shoulders, as he stopped too. They were both out of breath, but Stick wasted no time. "Climb," he stammered, lifting the boy up by the waist. As his hands gripped the rungs, Stick pushed his feet up. "Go!" he ordered, stealing a look towards the front of the train and jumping up himself. When Willie had climbed to the top, he was afraid to look down. He felt the vibration from Stick's boots below on the ladder. "There's a ladder on the inside," Stick said, out of breath. As the car jolted forward, Willie's hands slipped, sending him backwards over Stick's head. *Shit, boy!* Stick shouted as his hand flew up to break his fall.

Past the Shenandoah River north of Front Royal Junction, empty coal cars were waylaid for the trip north. The coal was back in Martinsburg and the hot shot was full of lumber bound for Fredericksburg before heading west. If there were a perfect train, Stick thought, they were on it. The gondola was empty, so the ride would be quick, and best of all, it wasn't raining. After some jerky and the last of Rebecca's taffy, Willie settled into his corner and watched the sky. They'd be back from church by now. She'd be fishing for crappies with her father, or swinging by herself. Maybe someone might come along and push her high the way she liked. He missed his bunkhouse bed and the warmth of Mrs. Pettit's face.

Willie's head bobbled with the movement of the train. He wanted to sleep, but there was too much to think about. Watching Stick curled up against his canvas sack; it wasn't clear in his mind how it had happened. Maybe the old black lady had put a spell on him, or maybe it was Moses ringing his bell that saved him. Leaning against his knapsack, he felt himself ease into sleep. He'd never depended on so many people before. He'd never had to. Before closing his eyes, he noticed long scratch marks on the walls as the sun raced through a row of puffy clouds, flickering with shadow and light.

CHAPTER TWENTY-FIVE

Potomac Creek was smooth as glass when Zach Park's boat pulled into the small dock at Belle Plains east of Fredericksburg. Once he'd tied off, he'd go below to get some sleep. With only a knot of current heading north from Tangier, he'd worked the slack flood perfectly and made good time. If the truck was there by six o'clock he'd catch the ebb off Smith Point and be home for dinner. As with most trips, he expected the worst. When the weather changed, he'd watch for thunderheads up the Potomac and dark gray smoke from whipped-up water on the horizon. He had to be vigilant at this time of the year because the bay could turn in a heartbeat.

Running liquor for Hilda Scarburgh's inn was no picnic, but over time he and his wife had gotten used to the money. And because Tangier was a dry island, his work was of no small consequence. Six runs a year to six drops kept the customers satisfied and Hilda happy. Half the load was hard stuff and beer. The rest of it was cigarettes. Like blue crabbing, the trick was being in the right place at the right time and having a dependable boat like the *May Jane*.

She was built by a yard in Maine during the winter of 1950 for seaworthiness and speed. For a thirty-four-foot flat-stern lobster boat, thirty knots was flat-out fast. With two one-hundred-and-twenty-gallon fuel tanks and a 2'9" draft, she could put in to shallow waters and reach home quickly from most locations within five hundred nautical miles without a stop. With two storage compartments under the cockpit floor and no galley or berths below, her cargo, except for the crab pots, could not be determined by the naked eye.

Twenty-year-old Zachariah Parks of Camden, Maine, met eighteen-year-old May Jane Pruitt, the daughter of Tangier's only Methodist minister, at the gas dock one muggy summer morning in 1935 as he was filling the tank of her father's skiff. They'd seen each other before, but this time his shirt was off. Perched in navy blue bloomers at the bow, she could not resist herself.

"I saw you fixin' peeler pots at the Scarburgh shack," she flirted, taking in her father's grave expression. He disliked it when she made eyes at boys. "We were down a ways jumping off a pier."

"Thank you, young man," the Reverend Thomas Pruitt interrupted as the pump clicked to a stop. "How much do we owe you today?"

Closing the gas tank tightly, the boy remembered the girl's long brown legs pushing off the tall black piling. "Pump says $1.73, sir." He wiped the cap with a rag.

"You goin' to the dance?" May Jane asked quickly.

"May Jane Pruitt!" her mother admonished from the middle seat of the skiff while her younger sister gigled.

"That's quite enough, young lady!" her father cautioned. "On our account, son, if you would be so kind," he said, reaching for the gas tank.

The night of the dance it took only two songs before they kissed. Zach smelled of Aqua Velva and told her his plans for the future. He said he worked hard. He wanted a lobster boat and children. And he wasn't raised on church. "If a way can be found to doubt the truth of any statement, look to a Methodist," his father warned in a letter from Maine a few weeks later, before

Zach proposed. "But she sounds terrific, son. When the sap runs, grab the bucket."

Zach and May Jane Parks had a baby girl named Emily the following September. The baby was delivered in a house owned by Esther Scarburgh—the island's oldest matriarch. She liked May Jane, but didn't think much of Methodists either. The house came with a job at the inn, a good salary, and all the blue crabs you could eat. On an island the size of Tangier, people belonged together whether they liked it or not, and it had been that way for as long as anyone could remember. A hint of Elizabethan English set them apart, and when they expired, they were buried above ground. The day Esther Scarburgh died in 1940, her estate was left in its entirety to her only child, Hilda, with instructions to see that Zach and May Jane Parks were given funds for Emily's college education, the title to the house they'd been living in, and enough money to build a decent lobster boat from a yard of Zach's choosing. There was no funeral or memorial service. Two days after her death, she was buried above ground in the backyard of the inn, next to the island's largest Loblolly pine. Not a penny was left to the Methodist church.

At 6:15 A.M. the truck from Fredericksburg pulled up with twenty cases of gin, fifteen cases of bourbon, ten cases of vodka, twelve cases of whiskey, six kegs of beer, one hundred cartons of assorted cigarettes, and two people needing a lift to Tangier. Zach didn't mind having company. If they were friends of Hilda's, his job was to get them to Tangier in one piece.

When Willie read Hilda Scarburgh's telegram to Stick, he thought he'd bust a hubcap. "You gotta take a boat?"

"That's how you get there," Stick said.

"How come she's helpin' us?"

Stick tightened his knapsack. Jim had done a fine job at Western Union that day. " 'Swhat good people do," he said.

Hilda's telegram had instructed them to jump at Dahlgreen Junction north of Fredericksburg and wait at State Route 212. When the truck pulled up, they hopped in back behind a canvas drop and settled between cases of liquor for the drive to Belle Plains, where a boat would be waiting for a load to Tangier. Except for a passing police car, there hadn't been much to get excited about. It had all gone smoothly. Hilda could find them a shack on Tangier and there was always plenty of crabbing to go around. He'd teach the boy some tricks about scapping crabs, and after a while, they'd shake hands and go their separate ways, once he was sure the boy could handle himself.

Leaping off the truck, Willie saw the *May Jane* and his heart jumped. Its hull was white with baby-blue trim on the cabin and it had a proud, high bow with two diamond-shaped windows to either side of the house. "Is that it?" he asked breathlessly.

"Must be," Stick said, walking towards it.

Zach Parks waited at the dock wearing a Greek captain's hat. He looked sleepy.

"Hey, Cappy!" the driver shouted, raising the canvas drop at the back of the truck.

"Buzzman!" Zach shouted back warmly. "Thought you was back in Camden."

"And leave Miss Hilda high and dry?" he joked. Like the captain, John "Buzzy" Osbourne was a lobster head out of Maine who'd driven trucks for most of his life.

"Thought you'd had it with the limelight!" Zach joked back, walking towards them.

"Well . . . this'll be my last one too many." He pulled out a Lucky Strike and lit it.

"Zach Parks," he said, shaking Stick's hand.

"Stick Watson. Appreciate the ride."

"My pleasure. This must be Willie," he said, letting go of Stick's hand and taking the boy's.

"Yes, sir. Mighty fine boat you got there," Willie stammered.

"She'll get you where you want to go. You been around boats?" he asked, grinning at the boy.

"No, sir." Willie straightened his shoulders.

"Well, today's your lucky day, Willie, 'cuz I'm making you my first mate!" He winked. Willie looked at Stick as if he would burst. "So get on board and walk around while we load her up and then we'll head out."

Willie's face flushed. "Only seen the water once, sir."

Zach smiled. "It's all right," he said, pushing the brim of his hat up. "I got your back."

"Can I help you load?" Willie asked.

Zach liked his eager face. "Be a real help, Willie. Why don't you handle the smokes and me and Stick will get the rest."

By twelve o'clock the *May Jane* had cleared Marlboro Point and swung east into the Potomac. Willie sat with Stick on the back of the stern and gazed north across the river towards a shore Stick said was part of Maryland. As the boat accelerated and the bow rose slowly up over the water, Willie grinned.

"Goes real good, don't it, Stick!" he shouted over the engine, his eyes wild.

Stick inhaled as spray kicked up off the transom. It'd been a while since he'd worked the bay, but it still smelled rich with life.

"Got a good engine, I 'magine!" he shouted back. *"Said we'd be there by five if it all goes right!"*

Zach swiveled around. *"Willie!"* he called, signaling for him to join him at the wheel. Willie nudged Stick in the ankle. All his life he'd wanted to see a place like the Potomac River, to be a part of something and not just be hearing about everything from a book. Spreading his feet apart over the cockpit floor for balance, he stepped cautiously forward. The past month had been rough, but if running away felt this good, he might as well keep going.

As Willie steered, Zach explained their direction.

"The Potomac River meets the Chesapeake Bay at Smith Point. The area's called the Kettle and gets a little rough. When the current flows downriver and the bay meets the wind coming up from the south, all hell can break loose."

"Am I steerin' good?" Willie asked nervously, gripping the wheel tighter.

"Watch the compass when you start to swing," Zach put his hand on his shoulder and gave it a reassuring squeeze as Willie corrected the wheel. "That's it . . . just like we said . . . south-southeast . . . there you go, right down the middle . . . good boy!" Willie concentrated with all his might on the compass. "When it's calm like this you can always find yourself a landmark somewhere just to make it easy on yourself."

"Like that big dock there?" Willie pointed out over the bow.

"Bingo! As long as it's half between south-southeast without pullin' you too far off, you're in the money."

Willie smiled at Zach before his eyes shifted back to the dock.

"That's Stratford Hall to the right a your dock there," Zach indicated with his head.

"What's that?" Willie asked.

Zach took an immediate shine to Willie. Now that his daughter was grown, he missed their days together when she was the boy's age. "You heard of Robert E. Lee?"

"I think so. Wasn't he a president or something?"

"He was a general," Zach said kindly.

"Oh, yeah. That's right. The Civil War. I read about that," Willie said, assessing the bow's position against the targeted dock. "I know a man who rang a bell back then."

Zach raised his eyebrows. "How old is he?"

"He's really old. His momma was a slave and she worked for Thomas Jefferson when he was the president or somethin' like that. He's a good friend a mine."

"Rings a bell, your friend?"

"Yep."

"What kinda bell?" Zach's interest was keen.

Willie checked the compass. He was right where he was supposed to be. "The big Virginia bell." Willie felt proud of Moses. "The one in the tower."

"At the University?"

"In Charlottesville." Willie regretted this as soon as he'd said it. His face paled. Zach saw immediately that something was wrong. "Is that where you're from, Willie?" he asked quietly.

Willie exhaled, momentarily confused. He'd slipped up. Stick had told him what would happen if he went off at the mouth. Maybe he could let his guard down a little with Zach and the lady on Tangier. She was as good as it gets, Stick said. But he still felt stupid. It didn't matter if people liked him or not. If they caught him, they'd send him back.

"Not anymore," he said, returning his attention to the compass.

By midafternoon off Smith Point, the *May Jane* caught the flood perfectly and swung southeast into the Chesapeake Bay towards Tangier Island. There were no on- or offshore breezes to contend with, no gray smoke ahead. Except when hurricanes blew in, late fall was a good time to run. The summer boats were long gone and the Coast Guard had more or less packed it in.

Three years ago, Zach's engine had quit in Kedges Straight between Tangier Sound and the Chesapeake with a load of champagne and bourbon. Without power it had been a rough ride, and the bilge was taking water. Using a small Mercury outboard, he'd worked his way against the wind to Solomons Lump Light and tied up. Over the radio his wife had pleaded with him to call the Coast Guard. "It isn't worth it, honey!" she'd cried as the transmission broke up and the bow line snapped. At sunset two days later, a lone crabber from Smith Island spotted the reflection of a cabin window on the horizon fifty nautical miles south of Tangier. The May Jane was out of gas and taking on water. During the tow home, they split a bag of squirrel nuts and a bottle of Hilda's finest French champagne.

Willie watched a line of white-winged scooters flying single-file off the water towards the mainland. The air smelled of pine trees and the temperature had dropped slightly. Watching the Maryland shore melt away, he wondered if the birds would make it home before they had to rest.

"Look, Willie!" Zach shouted, pointing towards the bow. Through the windshield, mottled with dried seawater, Willie saw something. "Big ole osprey up there! You see him?"

One hundred feet above the water's surface, a large dark bird with flashes of white on its undercarriage made wide elliptical circles. Stick bent down next to the boy to get a better look.

"See him?" Zach pointed again, slowing down.

"He's a big bird, ain't he, Stick?" Willie gasped, his eyes riveted on the osprey.

"He is," Stick agreed. "Lookin' for somethin' to eat, don't you think, Zach?"

When the bow dropped, Zach leaned back onto his heels and cut the engine, as Willie grabbed Stick's arm for balance.

"Go to the stern!" Zach instructed, swinging the boat around.

Stick could see that the boy was anxious. "Come on, Willie," he said moving aft.

The Chesapeake quieted around the *May Jane* as it stopped. His eye on the circling osprey, Willie felt small and inconsequential.

"He's fishin', Willie," Zach said, taking a bottle of RC Cola and two beers from a hatch door under the floorboards. Catching a warm updraft, the osprey rose higher into the sky, while Zach opened the cola against his belt buckle and handed the bottle to Willie.

"How's he gonna catch one way up there?" Willie took the bottle, his eyes following the osprey.

Zach and Stick exchanged glances and smiled.

"Watch him, Willie," Zach replied, opening Stick's beer.

Leaning against the gunnels, Willie sipped his drink. He'd seen some red-tail hawks before from the Lucky Bean, but the osprey was a lot bigger. As it drifted closer, he could see under its wings. It looked like his momma's white lace curtains. He didn't know what to think exactly. He'd never heard of a bird that could fish. Suddenly the osprey drew its wings into its body and paused in midair.

"Look!" Zach whispered to Willie as it arched its wings and dropped. Clutching his bottle, Willie felt the stillness of the bay as the bird fell, hitting the water with deadly precision. Surfacing instantly, it lifted off the water with a large fish in its talons and banked slowly around the *May Jane* before heading off.

"Got a shad! Watch him flip it!" Zach said, squinting into the sun. "Better flyin' with the head forward!" As the osprey turned the fish in his claws, Willie's mouth dropped open.

"He's goin' home, boys," Zach said, throwing his dead soldier into an empty bucket and heading towards the wheel.

"Where's that?" Willie was awestruck, watching the bird disappear.

Zach had a whimsical look as he turned the key. It had been a good run and he'd enjoyed showing Willie a bit of the world. His daughter at the boy's age had always brought out the best in him. Sometimes when he needed it most. *"Tangier!"* Zach shouted over the roar.

After ten years the island still looked the same to Stick. For Willie it was a new world. His empty stomach growled from the cola as the shoreline expanded. The place was still flat as a pancake and Stick was in no mood to talk it up. The boy would learn soon enough. Tangier was a one-by-three-mile island with no cops, no newspaper, and plenty of monkey business.

As the boat squeezed through Oyster Creek, the shoreline was strictly marsh. Erosion had eaten away at its edges, reducing the island over time. As they slowed, eelgrass and sea lettuce came into view through the shallow gray water to either side of the boat and a white heron stood frozen in a nearby ditch, waiting to skim its dinner up the creek before nightfall. Stick knew well the soft light washing over the spartina. The Canton Creek Bridge would be just around the bend. During its construction the pilings had given them trouble, but they'd managed to get it done. As sunset streaked across the bow, Stick took a deep breath of salty, cool air. Riding a boat full of booze with a runaway kid made him feel alive again. You had to take chances in life, he thought, glancing down at Willie. On a disappearing island in the middle of nowhere there was still magic in the world.

In the dwindling light, a line of darkened crab shacks and moored workboats appeared to either side of the *May Jane* as Zach navigated closer to shore. As he swung the bow against a strong current, a silhouette of rooftops and tall cedar trees appeared off the stern from the center of town.

"Handle the bow line, Stick?"

"I'm on it," Stick said, grabbing the cabin's top rail and moving forward.

"Should be someone there to toss it to."

Zach glanced back at the boy. "And, Willie?"

"Yes, sir." Zach had his full attention.

"There'll be a spring line on the dock when I back up. See if you can grab it and hand it to me."

"What side's it on?"

"Dockside. Side you're standing on."

"Yes, sir, I'll try."

"Hey! You're my copilot!" Zach corrected the wheel and closed in on the slip.

At the edge of the dock, a dim figure held a mooring line. Stick spread his feet apart as the boat moved closer and tried to get a better look. Whatever lights the *May Jane* had were off, but Zach could land her with his eyes closed if he had to. As the engine kicked into neutral, the figure appeared more clearly.

"Hello, Stick," Hilda Scarburgh said, throwing the line towards him. Stick caught it with his right hand as Zach put the boat in reverse.

"Give me some slack, Stick!" Zach shouted over the engine noise. When the boat lurched, Stick avoided falling off the bow by dropping to his knees. Swinging the stern into the dock, Zach put the gears into neutral and moved quickly aft.

"Got your rope, Zach." Willie handed him the spring line.

"Good work, Willie!" He took the line and secured it to the stern cleat. Pushing off the dock with his feet, Zach grabbed a long pike pole from the cabin top and crossed over to the opposite side of the stern. "You good, Stick?" he shouted forward.

"I'm good!" he replied, looking at Hilda. To help control the bow from falling away in the current, Stick had run his line through the chock and under the bow cleat. Using the end of his pole, Zach snagged the aft mooring line off a nearby piling and brought it onboard. He'd leave it slack while they unloaded and tighten it up when they left.

"Want me to put the pole back, Zach?" Willie was proud of his new responsibility.

"Goes right there on the cabin top, Willie, thanks. Kinda long, though, so be careful," he warned, tying off the stern line. Stick remained on the bow waiting for instructions. Hilda looked older, but her eyes were still wide and inviting. Crystal-Ann would never age, he suddenly realized.

"She's good! Tie her down, Stick!" Zach instructed, heading towards the wheel.

When the engine stopped, Stick eyed Hilda as a cloud of diesel fumes passed between them.

"Prettiest girl on the island," Stick flirted unabashedly.

"How would you know?" she replied, grinning and shaking her head.

"Bridge's still there."

"So's the girl," she said, moving away.

Since the 1920s, Esther Scarburgh's Tangier Inn had been the only show in town. The rooms were clean, the food was pure comfort, and from May to October the liquor flowed. In the off-season Hilda closed her doors and read books until the last week of April. Then, amidst a cascade of daffodils and white hyacinth, she'd start up again. In season, the inn dished out a collective conscience, without reproach, without fanfare, straight up or on the rocks. And if something needed doing, Hilda Scarburgh was the girl to get it done. Like her mother, she was fair, good-looking, and adventuresome. Her heart, however, was a different story.

Bobbie Taylor was a waterman from a waterman's family. He'd met Hilda after the war, and they'd gotten together when, as Hilda put it, the moon was right. When they met at her place, the sex was good, the walks were long, and it seemed as if they belonged together. But, in the end, Hilda was not accustomed to such domesticity, and when she'd had enough, she'd walk him home with a bag full of fish heads for his cats.

On the first morning of February 1942, after picking up his gray tabby, Spike, from a veterinarian on the mainland, Bobbie Tyler watched the barometric pressure over the Chesapeake Bay drop like a stone. By noon, waves rocked his forty-foot workboat off the dock in Reedsville, Virginia, as the temperature fell twenty-three degrees in under an hour. When he radioed Hilda, a frozen gale sailed high overhead from the northwest. *"Got that book you ordered!"* his voice careened through the speaker, five miles east of Reedsville. *"And a cat with no balls—over!"*

She had told him to stay put, but he wouldn't listen.

"Pretty rough—over!" he'd shouted through the static. *"Pretty goddamn rough out here!"* He couldn't hear Hilda's response.

Standing on her top porch step, a snowflake burned her cheek. His old box stern had an oyster dredge and the bilge pump needed work. It wasn't the first time she'd worried about him. Her mother had warned her about watermen, but this was Bobbie and she'd let her guard down.

When the dredge broke off, ten-foot swells crashed over his port bow and the boat began to tilt. With each wave the wheel swung wildly, and at three o'clock, a lighthouse on Tangier clocked winds at sixty-two miles per hour.

Seven days later, a marsh hawk circled over the Tangier Inn and the life ring from his cabin was found in a streak of oil one mile southwest of the island. She didn't believe the news at first. A man and his boat were not the same thing, she kept repeating to herself.

Another grave was nothing new, but it hit the island hard just the same. Hilda skipped the funeral and, for weeks, waited stubbornly for his bow to appear in Mailboat Harbor. Bobbie had never asked for her hand because he'd known she wouldn't give it. "Somedays when I'm not fishin', I feel like I'm only here to care for cats," he'd told her the week before he disappeared.

When his sister offered Hilda his life ring, she refused it. "You can't hold on to something that isn't there," she'd said.

The summer of the next year, Stick Watson appeared with a crew of bridge builders from Richmond. They'd been given a house half a mile east on Upper Ridge. To Hilda, he'd seemed nice enough. They'd appreciated her food and drank whatever liquor she had. She knew what working men were good for and she wasn't shy. She liked the way Stick stood and the way he chose his words and his voice was enough to make her almost forget about Bobbie.

A ten-foot skiff with oars was waiting for Stick and Willie on the opposite side of the slip.

"Blew in from Morattico and nobody claimed her." Zach pointed out into the bay. "See that crab shack halfway up on the left with the light on?"

Stick located the light. "Got the porch out front?"

"That's it. You're all squared away inside. Best place to be till this blows over."

Willie was embarrassed to hear Zach mention his situation so openly. "So, where's the motor?" Willie asked, admiring the skiff.

Except for a new sign, the inn looked the same. After twenty years the streets had grown some houses and the cedar out front was bigger, but the rest of it was just the way Stick remembered.

"Same red shutters," he remarked, peering over the white picket fence out front.

One autumn night, a month after Stick's arrival, he'd appeared at Hilda's door and knocked. At the bar, the bridge crew had whistled when they'd guessed his intentions. "She'll eat you alive," a sodden foreman had predicted before he'd walked out.

But Hilda was gracious about it. She'd had her eye on him from the start. The bridge was half done—and so was he, she figured. "You here to ask me out, Stick?"

"I am," he answered.

She thought about Bobbie and all the times she'd missed him. "Kinda late, isn't it?"

"Late for what?"

"What'd you have in mind?" she asked simply.

Stick leaned back on his heels and looked down. It was her island, but it was his bridge. "We're gonna walk on water," he said, looking up.

Even if he'd been drinking, she liked the way he put it together. Hilda leaned against the doorway and smiled. If anyone believed he could walk on water, this would be the one. "You a Methodist?" she asked, feeling a chill.

"No, ma'am."

Hilda bit her lip. Crepe myrtle leaves littered the steps. "Let me get my coat."

Willie followed Stick and Zach through the screen door of the inn and onto the porch with four rockers. Zach's comment on the dock had worried him.

"Hungry, Willie?" Zach put his hand on the boy's shoulder.

"Yes, sir."

"Well, you came to the right place." He lifted the door knocker.

Hilda Scarburgh stood in the doorway smiling warmly, and looking supremely confident. "You must be Willie?"

"Yes, ma'am," Willie said cautiously. She had pretty eyes like his momma, but not as sad. With the hallway light behind her it was hard to see the exact color of her hair, but it was short and wavy. She seemed taller now than when he'd seen her on the dock.

"Welcome to Tangier, Willie. I'm Hilda." She took his hand.

As Willie and Zach entered the house, Stick lingered long enough to remember their first date. Two weeks into the bridgework he'd discovered an old submerged ferry dock. On a windless slack tide the sawed-off pilings were level with the bay, allowing him to step on their tops without getting wet. Following him down to the shore that night, she'd had no idea what he was up to. "Follow me," he'd whispered, stepping out onto the water.

Willie's eyes watered when he saw the food on a large round dining room table. At the end of the season the cook prepared dishes for Hilda. What couldn't be canned was eaten and what was left was passed around so that, by October's end, her kitchen was a treasure trove. "Gladys and I thought you all might be hungry. Iced tea's on the table, beer's in the icebox," Hilda announced, pulling a chair out for Willie. "Sit next to me, Willie."

"Get you a beer, Hilda?" Zach was on his way to the kitchen.

"Be fine, Zach, thanks." She checked out Stick. "Look who's back!" Her eyes twinkled.

Willie understood her expression to be something more than just friendship. He'd seen it sometimes when his momma passed a man she'd known and her eyes did all the talking. He wondered if most every woman would remind him of his momma. He'd had the same feeling with Mrs. Pettit and it made him sad. But he could see why Stick had wanted to stay here. Sometimes, you needed people for more than just the day-to-day things.

Zach handed a cold Budweiser to Hilda and sat down across the table.

"Come on, Willie! Grab a plate and pass it around," Hilda proposed merrily. "Let's see, you got the crab cakes right there. That's it," she said, watching him take a platter off the lazy Susan. "Gladys is the queen a cakes 'round here."

Willie eyeballed the crab cakes, hesitating.

"Ever had one?" Hilda asked, noticing his reluctance.

"No, Miss Hilda, I ain't." He was a little embarrassed.

"Well, throw one on your plate. If you don't like it, I'm sure the boys will polish it off."

Watching Hilda, Stick smiled. Her auburn hair was shorter with flecks of gray, but her spirit was still something. He'd forgotten how beautiful and independent she was. "Thanks, Hilda." He raised his bottle in her direction.

"For what?" She helped herself to a plate of corn pudding.

"For the crab cakes." Stick winked at Willie.

After a round of cakes, Virginia ham, clam fritters, potato salad, coleslaw, pickled beets, apple sauce, green beans, corn pudding, and dinner rolls, there wasn't much talk. And Willie had listened only partly to what was discussed. Except for the fritters, each bite was too delicious for him to care one way or the other.

"You ready for some pound cake, Willie?"

"No, ma'am, I got no room. It was all real good. Sorry 'bout the clams."

"Got a cat for that. I'll wrap up the cake and you can eat it later," she said, glancing at Stick. "Did Zach show you where you'll be?"

"He did," Stick answered, polishing off his fourth beer.

"They'll be all right in the skiff, Zach?"

"Willie wants to know where the motor is," Zach chuckled. As Hilda and Stick laughed, their eyes connected for a moment. Willie didn't know whether he should be embarrassed or laugh along with them.

Watching Hilda and Stick, he couldn't imagine being old or not seeing someone for ten years. They'd have to be deep inside you somewhere so you wouldn't forget. Maybe that's where his momma lived now. He thought about Moses and wondered if he'd ever see him again. Moses was so old he never seemed to live in the real world.

The air was warm and the bay was quiet. As Stick rowed, Willie watched a light in the crab shack grow brighter. He'd never smelled air so full of so many different things. Even the stars seemed closer. He couldn't imagine what was in a shack with water all around it. "You seen the shack before?" he asked quietly.

"Not this one," Stick said.

"They catch crabs in there?" A line of dark shacks passed by in the distance.

"Use 'em when they molt and for fixin' pots. Like your cakes?"

"Yep. I ate four," Willie said happily, but Stick could see that he was tired. It'd been a long day for both of them. As the skiff rocked, Willie's eyelids closed a little, reminding him of how Crystal-Ann would fall asleep against his shoulder just before they jumped from the train. As he looked back, the roof of Hilda's inn appeared against the streetlights between some trees. You don't spend your life loving one person only. Tangier looked the same today as it had the day he'd left. The only difference was the time it took him to return.

CHAPTER TWENTY-SIX

At the 8:00 A.M. bell, U.V. students raced through the leaves to their morning classes. His cold was better, but Moses still didn't feel quite right and it hurt his head to look down. Lately, he'd had a hard time breathing when he rang, like there wasn't enough air to fill him up. As he leaned out of the bell tower, a group of young men caught his eye. Watching them pass behind an old magnolia, he could tell the difference in their ages. Fourth-year students were always late for class and the most poorly dressed. A cardinal called out from a branch near the top of the magnolia. He couldn't see it very well, but he heard it. It hadn't flown away for the winter. A cardinal meant rain.

A month or so after they'd met, Moses taught Willie how to read the clouds.

"Tell you 'bout duh future."

Willie shook his head. "Don't know, Moses. Sounds kinda strange."

Standing at the portico window, Moses smiled and put his hand on the boy's shoulder. "Ain't nothin' to it once you git it in yo' head," he said, quietly. "Momma taught me long time 'go."

The boy looked suspicious.

"Trick is ta feel what you lookin' at and don' tink so much 'bout what s'pose ta be." He pointed to the sky over Cabell Hall. "See dat one wit duh big ole bump?"

It took a moment for Willie to see it.

"It be ole down duh bottom and den duh top all new." Moses lowered his hand from the boy's shoulder and placed it on the window ledge.

"How you know that?" Willie asked, doubtful.

"Juz do. Duh dark dere on duh bottom mean it be from somewhere else and den duh top dere all white mean it be made afta dat—like dey joined up dere, kind a t'ing."

As a blast of sunlight lit up the cloud, Willie could see what Moses was talking about.

"How come they're different?" Willie scrunched up his nose and squinted to get a better look.

" 'Cuz dat duh change cloud," Moses answered, admiring the vivid light. "Bring duh new way, when you seez it," he explained.

"What new way, Moses?" Willie asked quietly. Moses' expression became suddenly hard, as if he'd seen something that frightened him. Willie watched him collect his thoughts.

"Pretty in the light, huh?" Moses' face relaxed a bit. "Change be good, but sometime it be hard." He stopped and turned to Willie. "Yo' daddy a mean man," he said, gazing abstractedly into the boy's eyes. Willie was stunned by his words. "Cloud say he go 'way," Moses said, returning his attention to the sky.

Chapter Twenty-seven

Stick smiled when he saw the jar of hooch she'd left in the refrigerator. Depositing the pound cake next to a bottle of milk, he made note of the bacon and eggs for the morning.

They'd need some sleep after the past few days. He knew the drill. Pots needed mending, oyster boats would dredge, and there was always scapping. He'd done it early mornings on his days off from the bridge work, with the crew's skiff. As he drifted over eelgrass, the crabs were easy to get in the net. The trick was finding them.

Willie slept with his mouth open and his shoes on. He'd almost fallen into the bay trying to get off the boat. Stick had caught him by the arm just in time. Tangier would be good for the boy, Stick thought. It would give him some confidence and time to think straight. Hilda ran a tight ship and their crab shack could only be reached by water. As long as the locals kept their mouths shut, the place was no-man's-land, even for a sheriff.

Unpacking his knapsack, Stick put his dictionary and knife on the floor next to the bed. He'd promised Crystal-Ann he'd work on his words every day, but he hadn't. Pushing down on his mattress, he was surprised to discover that it was soft and comfortable. The shack was insulated, with two windows to one side, a door up front, and a potbelly stove in the middle. Hilda had run a waterline off the gas dock for a kitchen sink, a bathtub in the back corner, and a marine toilet outside. With the lights off, the shack fell in with the others. If you were running from something, this would be as good a spot as any—at least in the state of Virginia.

As he stood on the front porch, the hooch burned his throat and rushed to his head. They'd need a chair, but an old jimmy pot would suit just fine. As cool, moist air caressed his face, he heard the first few raindrops. He'd spent his whole life hopping trains and, except for one snowy night, it had been a pretty smooth ride.

In 1937, Stick had killed a man from Omaha in a liquor store parking lot outside Bangor. The man had rushed him from behind with a hunting knife while he was climbing into the passenger's side of a pickup. Stick's hand landed on a crowbar stored under the seat as the blade entered his shoulder. In the final report the police had called it self-defense, one drunk against another. The dead man's name was Richard Priest and he'd run out of money. The report made no mention of the Penobscot woman they'd both screwed. Priest's head split open when Stick swung the crowbar. A witness walking by said it sounded like a deer hitting the front of a car doing fifty miles an hour.

Over time, he couldn't drink it pretty, so he gave up trying. What bothered him the most was the sound of the crowbar. For years the cracking skull played over and over in his head. When he told Crystal-Ann the story, she touched his scar with her fingertips and said he'd had no choice. She said the only one he'd fucked was himself and that he'd hear it until he understood. When she died, the sound went away. He couldn't have saved her, he realized. It wasn't up to him, and the man from Omaha was no different.

Barely sober, flipping through his dictionary, Stick found the word:

Hil-de-garde [G. <Gmc. *hild-, battle (cf.
HILT + *gard-, to protect (see yard): hence, lit., battle protector]
A feminine name: see HILDA.

In the early morning, a low ceiling of rain worked its way north over the island. Their Indian summer was gone and the ground was hard and brittle. Willie stood on the porch in his underwear and watched the skiff fill with water. It was cold enough for a sweatshirt, but he was too excited about his new surroundings to put one on. Leaning out over the railing, he saw his head reflected upside down in the water above a wavy line of jet-black pilings. His face was thin and his hair needed cutting.

As the rain intensified, Willie's reflection dissolved into blurry elliptical circles before a gush of water poured over the rail from the metal roof overhead and washed the image away. The sound of rain had become deafening now, and as his view of the bay washed away, he remembered the previous night's conversation after dinner. There were big storms from time to time, Hilda had said. The last one had been in August east of the Outer Banks. They'd dodged a bullet. On The Upards, Tangier was only seven feet above sea level at its highest point. It was an easy call to make—anything over seventy miles per hour sent you packing.

At noon Salty Crockett knocked on the front door holding a cardboard box. Willie had gone back to sleep, and when woken by the knock, he'd momentarily forgotten where he was.

"Got your net an' pole. One you got don't look good," he said as soon as Willie opened the door. "Put 'em in the skiff with a basket and two sticks," he added. Willie looked back to see if Stick was still asleep. He had no idea what the old man was talking about. "Name's Salty." He squeezed the bill of his cap with his thumb and forefinger. "You the boy?"

"Yes, sir." The man looked pretty fierce.

Salty was seventy-five years old and short. His face looked like leather and his long hair was the color of salt. "Got some food here for you boys," he said, passing a heavy cardboard box to Willie. "You got an open in there?"

"Excuse me?"

"Can open?!" Salty shouted, as if the boy were deaf.

"Got one on my knife," he said quickly.

"Swiss Army?"

"Yes, sir."

"Can't go wrong with one a them, son! He 'round?"

"Excuse me?" Willie adjusted his arms under the box.

"Stick Watson! Where is he?!"

"Hey, Salt," Stick said, appearing over the boy's shoulder, looking sleepy. "Here, Willie, let me take that."

"You old sonovabitch! We thought you was *dead!*" Salty shouted, leaning back on his high-tops. Willie handed the box to Stick and went inside.

"Not yet, Salt. You still got the ponytail," he observed with admiration.

"Hasn't scalped me yet," the old man chuckled.

"She all right?"

"Eighty years young this year. Or that's what she says."

"She's somethin'. Still sore from that night we arm-wrestled."

"You remember? Dang! Her sister's the same. Built like a truck. Must be the crabs!" He slapped Stick's shoulder. "Well, good to see you, Stick, been a while."

"Likewise. I'll stop in on Peggy."

"She'd like that. Got all goofy when she heard you was here. So, stow your gear, I got your outboard in my shop. The old one wasn't worth a shit," he muttered, backing away from the door. "Buy you a drink later?"

"Drink's on me, Salt. Appreciate the help." Stick opened the box.

"Cans mostly, stuff like that. Thought you might need things for scappin', so I put 'em in the skiff. Be back with the motor and a pair of gloves—forgot 'bout 'em." Salty leaned forward. "Boy in trouble?"

From inside, Willie caught the old man's whisper.

Stick admired Salty. If crabbers had faces, his would be it. "Heads up," Stick replied with a wink.

The next morning, the sky was solid sunshine. After breakfast Stick and Willie bailed the skiff with an empty tomato can and motored out towards East Point Ridge to try their luck at scapping. The name of the outboard had worn away on both sides, but it was clear by the way it ran that when it came to motors, Salty was the man. Stick and Salty had gotten to know each other on Stick's days off, during which time Salty had taught him what he could about motors, the Chesapeake, and crabs. "Know why blues mate for life?" he'd yelled at Stick, motoring home after their first day scapping. "Only live a couple years!"

Facing forward, Willie felt the warm wind blast his face and arms. As his hair peeled back, he recognized Oyster Creek off the port side from the day before. Following the flight of a gull, he caught Stick's eye and smiled.

It was a fine morning for November and Stick could see that Willie was happy. Looking out towards the middle of East Point for a place to put in, it had taken him a while to get his bearings, but it was coming back. He'd slide in and work the grass north. Hilda'd said the crab and oysters were down over the years, and on the way out, he'd noticed that some of the shacks had looked pretty beat-up. If he could teach the boy a thing or two and grab some dinner along the way, it'd be a perfect day.

As the engine died, a line of faint white smoke trailed behind them before drifting sideways into a thick line of spartina. When the skiff stopped, Stick spied a brown blanket of gently waving eelgrass. "Need you here, Willie," he said, standing at the stern. Willie's face tightened with concentration. Except for Miss Scarburgh's cakes, he'd never seen a blue crab. He wondered if they were blue or if it was just an expression. "I'll move us with one end of the pole and net the crabs with the other end from the bow, you with me?"

"Yes, sir."

"Not real complicated, but I'll need you with the basket once I get one in the net." Without speaking, Willie stood up carefully and waited for Stick to move. "All right, let's do it," Stick commanded, moving around the boy.

Ten yards from shore, Stick poled the skiff quietly north as Willie sat at the stern, his knees around the wooden basket. "You ready?"

"Good luck, Stick." Willie drummed his fingers nervously.

Stepping up onto a small triangular platform over the bow, Stick positioned his feet carefully before peering down into the water. The skiff rocked from side to side slightly as he adjusted his feet, drawing the bow down with his weight. It would take a while, but eventually the crabs would show. In ten years, he figured, crabbing couldn't have changed much.

For the first few minutes his balance would be off; he expected that. But what surprised him was the look of the eelgrass. "Lot thinner than I remember," Stick thought aloud.

"The crabs?" Willie asked, looking, his eyes on the water.

"Eelgrass." Stick looked at a small island off the southwest side of East Point to get his bearings. "Same place Salty showed me. Sooks run south 'bout now and again in the spring. They like to hide in the grass." Stick poled the skiff forward.

"Who they hidin' from?"

"Ducks, turtles, certain kinds a fish, raccoons sometimes. And each other."

"They eat each other?" Willie was horrified.

"Yep. 'Specially the old ones—'cuz they're sick or missin' claws an' stuff. Or molting." Stick stopped poling and flipped the net around.

"What's that?"

"Molting?"

"Yeah."

"They lose their shells." Stick had spotted something in the grass just above the shore.

"How come they do that?"

Stick flipped the pole around and stuck it on the bottom directly over the bow. "You see that, Willie?" he said, motioning his head towards a clearing on the land near where they'd stopped. Surrounded by spartina, two large crabs sat in mud puddles facing each other.

"Don't see it. Is it a crab?" Willie whispered, tightening his grip on the basket rim.

"Two of 'em. Good size, too. Right up there in the marsh. They're makin' holes before the tide goes out. They sit in 'em like a bathtub," he said, polling the bow into shore. "Hand me your basket," he whispered as the bow rose up against the bottom. Stepping down, Stick moved towards the middle seat as Willie raised himself and offered him the basket. As Stick jumped, the stern swung around into open water before he pulled the bow further into shore. Moving to the middle seat, Willie watched him hop the short embankment holding the basket upside down in both hands. Hilda had shown Stick how to do it one day on the south end near Sund Spit. If he was lucky, the crabs would be looking at each other when he dropped the basket. "They're like men," she'd told Stick. "They get cocky in a crowd."

When the basket fell, Stick slapped his hand over the bottom and shouted down to Willie. *"Gottem!"*

"You did?!" Willie shouted back, greatly excited. *"Can I look?!"*

"Pull the bow in some more and bring the net!"

The boat was heavy, but in his enthusiasm, Willie managed to get it farther in to shore. His pants were wet and covered with mud by the time he appeared, gingerly, at Stick's side. They were surrounded by foot-wide crab holes full of muddy water.

"Under the basket?"

"Yep! Didn't know what hit 'em."

Spartina shifted as Willie took a deep breath and tried to calm down. The stems sounded dry in the wind.

"Here's the deal," Stick explained. "When you're ready, put your hand where my hand is here and, when I tell you, lift one edge of the basket up enough for me to slide the net in. When the net's all the way under I'll count to three and we'll flip it over together, okay? You with me?"

"Ain't gonna bite me or nothin', are they, Stick?"

Stick resisted smiling. "Do it right they won't." Putting the pole down, Willie took a deep breath and stood over the basket, beside Stick. Bending over, he placed his hand next to Stick's, and heard the crabs scuttling beneath. "Push down! They're not going anywhere. You're a lot bigger than they are," Stick reminded him. His hand off of the basket, Stick grabbed the pole and stood up. "You see?" he said, positioning the front of the net carefully against the wicker basket. "Nothin' to it. . . . Ready?"

Willie placed his free hand on the basket's side and stared at the net as if his life depended on it. "Ready," he said, before holding his breath.

"Go!" Stick whispered. As the basket rose off the ground, Stick shoved the net quickly underneath. Adjusting his grip on the pole, he spoke softly. "Now flip it on three. One . . . two . . . three!"

When Willie saw the two crabs through the net, he dropped the basket and jumped back. *"Gottem!"* He clapped, bouncing up and down. *"Is it a blue crab?"*

Raising the empty net, Stick set the pole on the ground. The two crabs were beauties. The boy got lucky on his first day. "Two big boys, Willie." Lifting the basket, he tipped it over for him to see.

Willie had circles of brown mud around his knees, and eyes the size of silver dollars.

"You know they was up here?"

"Yep." Stick bent over to retrieve the pole.

"Thought they was always in the bay." Willie inched towards the basket to take a peek.

Stick looked at the boy affectionately. He remembered being full of questions once. "Not when you're mud larkin'," he said, checking the skiff to see if it had moved.

"That what this is?"

"Yep. Pretty simple. Catch 'em in the tub. Here . . . " Stick handed him the basket. "Gotta take a leak."

Willie held the basket at arms' length and stared apprehensively at the crabs. "Ain't gonna climb out, are they?" Stick had disappeared into a wall of tall grass.

"Can't climb the sides," Stick shouted back.

Huddled together, the crabs faced each other. Their heads were scary, and their bodies more mechanical than real. When a front claw opened wide, Willie almost dropped the basket and took off.

"Stick?"

Amidst trembling waves of rust-colored spartina, Stick felt tall and sober. The air had something to do with it. Life was bullshit, mostly, but for a few moments when it all came together.

Back in the skiff they switched places and Willie tried his luck with the long pole. It was hard to get his balance. "Spread your hands a bit and lean back," Stick instructed as they floated north. Willie scanned for crabs through the blurry eelgrass. The crab pole wasn't heavy, but it was awkward. He didn't want to tell Stick he was afraid of falling. "You okay?" Stick asked. Willie nodded absently. He should have told Stick, but it was never the right time.

"There you go!" Stick pointed, stopping the skiff with his oar and swinging the bow around. "Right there! See it? Between the grass there . . . right in front of you!"

Willie's face flushed when he saw it. "There's two of 'em!" he whispered loudly.

Smiling, Stick held the skiff in place with his oar. "Get the one in back."

"Somethin' wrong with the other one?" Willie checked his feet, adjusting his balance.

"Nothin' but shell. Want the one behind it."

"Okay," Willie said, taking a deep breath.

"Just like we said. Quicker the better."

"One behind?"

"Yep."

Leaning back, Willie rotated the pole so the net would enter the water sideways. He was worried the crab would run away before he had time to scoop it up.

"That's it, now turn the pole and scoop," Stick said, his eye on the net as it dropped. "Gotta do it quick!"

The net became heavier and more cumbersome underwater. Twisting the pole, he pushed down with all his might to position it near the second crab.

"Now scoop!" Stick commanded.

Pushing the pole forward, Willie felt something hard hit the net's rim before he lifted it up.

"Get it?" Stick tried to make out the net through a cloud of mud.

Willie had no idea whether he had the crab or not, but the pole was easier to bring up than it was to push down. He'd completely forgotten about falling. As the net cleared the water, Stick was about to burst. "Shit, Willie, you got 'em both! The heir and the spare!" Resting easily in the dripping net were the two crabs, one moving and one still. "Now swing it to me and we'll put 'em in the basket. Watch your feet."

As Willie slid his feet around towards the stern, the net floated up and into the boat. His heart pounded as the crabs dropped into the basket. Stepping back, he released his breath and felt the boat drop out from under him.

As the pole slammed across the seat, Stick, startled, looked up. The boy was gone. Except for the splash of his body against the water, Willie didn't make a sound. Stick acted fast. Hopping out of the skiff, he felt the cold water from his thighs to his toes. Gathering the boy in his arms, he was reminded of the river where they'd first met.

Willie gasped for air before he spoke. The water stung his eyes as he squinted at Stick.

"My foot slipped," he stammered.

"I saw that." Stick suppressed a smile. "Somethin' you forgot to tell me, Willie?"

"What you mean?" he answered, not understanding.

"We're in three feet of water."

"So?"

Stick righted Willie and lowered his feet. Willie felt slippery soft mud under his sneakers as he stood up on his own.

Stick waded out to the skiff and swung the stern around next to Willie.

"So?" Stick's eyebrows were raised.

"What?" Willie asked, averting his eyes, his face flushed.

"You can't swim."

Willie suppressed his tears. Again, Stick had saved him from the water, and he'd been unable to save himself.

Surrounded by cloudy water, Stick remembered Crystal-Ann's ashes in the river, how they'd lingered above the falls before speeding away. Willie could disappear just as quickly if he wasn't careful. Noticing his eyes, he saw for the first time what had been so disturbing. He was surprised it had taken him so long to figure out.

"What color are your eyes?"

Standing there unable to swim, Willie had no idea what Stick was after. He was pretty sure he hadn't been drinking. "Momma says they're hazel." He looked confused.

Stick leaned back against the motor and held the corner of the stern. "So are mine."

The boy's body shook as he stared up at Stick. Most people would have left him back in Winchester.

"You cold?"

"Sorta," Willie chattered.

"So, let's get in the boat." Stick extended a hand to lift him up.

From the top-floor window Hilda watched one last time for their skiff. On her way out she stopped at the hallway mirror and laughed at herself. There was no question about it. She felt like a schoolgirl.

A table was set for four. Salty had left oysters on the back porch and would be back in time for dinner. And Stick and the boy had promised her some blues. Hilda liked cooking in the off-season, when the rooms were empty and she could take her time. Pouring herself a drink, she dusted the oysters with cornmeal and lowered them carefully into a hot pot of her cousin's fresh peanut oil, then added a pretty striped bass from a boat out of Smith Island. Hilda wasn't hard to figure out. She liked port and smooth bourbon and trashy novels. She liked men who weren't afraid to touch her and women who laughed. Like her mother, Hilda had most of what she needed, and when she didn't, she found a way to get it. A man was inside her head now. On an island in the middle of the Chesapeake you didn't fight it. Things happened for a reason, however long it took.

Wrapped in a blanket, Willie stared into the molting tray outside on the porch. He was afraid to touch the crabs, but he wanted to. The three crabs hadn't moved much, but when they did, it was clear that they were looking for a way out. At dinner Salty had said they could lose a leg if they had to and grow a new one to replace it. He wondered how long that would take. The empty shell was on the kitchen table. Stick had dropped him off in the skiff earlier and gone back to Hilda's. He felt safe in the shack by himself; it reminded him of the Pettits' bunkhouse. When a boat passed, he felt the waves against the pilings underneath and it made him sleepy. The mail boat came once a week and the Tangier Inn was closed until April. Stick had found the right place, out in the middle of nowhere. He'd said they were so far away you couldn't hear a train whistle.

Maybe he'd go back to school. Hilda said they had one. He wanted someone his own age to be with. He'd get a pole and fish off the porch for a big one like the osprey had. He could help Stick that way, and he'd start by learning how to swim. He'd have to forget how afraid he'd been when he fell and how cold the water was, but it would be all right. He'd learn.

Willie's head sank deep into the pillow. Tomorrow was another day and Salty would be expecting him at noon. Before breakfast he'd write to Rebecca, but he wouldn't tell her where he was. Hilda said she'd get someone on the mainland to mail the letter. He'd explain that he was okay and that he was taking good care of her knife and he'd tell her he hoped the apples were all sold and that he missed her momma's cooking and pushing her on the swing. But he wouldn't say more. It would be too risky. From now on he'd be like a cloud going by, or like the skiff that washed up in a storm from Morattico. The one with no name.

That night, the light was off when Stick reached Hilda's porch.

Leaning against the doorway, he saw her in her rocker. "Offer you a beer?"

"I mostly drink port now." She held up a glass.

"I see that."

"Come sit." She took a sip.

As he dropped down into the rocker, the wicker creaked. Hilda passed him the glass. "Try it."

Held up against the front porch light, it was the color of blood. "Ain't much on wine," he said before taking a sip. Hilda dropped her head back against the chair and watched him drink through half-lowered lids. "Kinda sweet," he said, passing it back. "Nice little kick at the end."

Hilda chuckled briefly and shook her head. Her mother would've liked Stick in more ways than one.

"He's a good boy," she said, taking the glass from him. "From Virginia?"

"Charlottesville."

"What's he into?"

Streetlights quivered in the breeze outside. He wanted more port. "Father was an asshole and beat him up one night . . . " Hilda handed back the glass. "Boy's kinda fuzzy on it but says he hit him in the head with a glass, candle thing." Stick took a long sip. " . . . And the place caught fire or somethin'. So he ran to get his mother, but she was toasted. So he took off. Never went back."

"What d'you mean, toasted?"

"Drunk, I guess. Runs a whorehouse in Charlottesville. Said she was passed out next door . . . couldn't find her . . . so he runs back to where the fire was and the place was lit. Says his old man died in the fire, and a sheriff who came lookin' for him confirmed it, but says his momma's still alive." Stick took another sip of port. "This stuff's pretty good."

"You drank most of it."

Stick passed the glass and watched her mouth. The middle of her upper lip was still plump.

"Where'd you find him?"

"Floatin' in a river."

"Where?"

"Outside Lexington in August."

"What were you doin' there?"

"Tossin' my wife's ashes."

Hilda looked out towards the street. Bobbie's cat was on the picket fence. "Cat belong to someone?"

Finishing the glass, she reached down for a black bottle of port beside her chair on the floor. "Used to," she said, refilling the glass.

Stick watched the cat tiptoe across the top of the fence.

"What was her name?" Hilda watched the cat stare at them intently.

"Crystal-Ann."

Hilda passed him the port.

"What's the cat's name?" Stick waited for her to answer before he took it.

"Bobbie."

When the tabby jumped to the sidewalk, Hilda stood up and stretched. Her shoes were off. He noticed the hem of her dress climb up the back of her legs. They were still smooth with long, thin muscles.

"How old's the boy?" She lowered a long bamboo blind in front of their chairs.

"Says he's thirteen."

"When you leavin'?"

Stick drained the port and put it down. "You cut your hair."

"I did." Unbuttoning the front of her dress, she turned around.

Stick secured his feet against the porch floor as she slipped her legs over his knees and faced him. Her waist was small in his hands as she brought her head down and slipped her tongue gently under his.

CHAPTER TWENTY-EIGHT

Sheriff Weist put the phone down and went back to sleep. The sun would be up in an hour and, unless he got lucky, his wife expected him in church at nine o'clock sharp. Except for an accident on Route 7, it had been a quiet weekend. Under the front seat of the smashed truck, he'd found a Pennsylvania number in the dead man's wallet. It was always the same when you called. Like a one-way conversation with yourself until they started crying.

The boy had been spotted by a local patrol car outside Fredericksburg where he'd been standing by the side of the road. He and the man with him were thought to be hitchhikers. The officer had noticed his picture later at the station, but by then, the kid was long gone. He'd had a knapsack over his shoulder and appeared to be traveling east with a white man resembling the description of Stick Watson. He'd call Sheffield before church and let him know. Of course, his mother would want to know too. Even a whore had family. He was tired of chasing losers. His wife said he looked like shit most of the time and that half the town was after his job, which was fine with him. In five years he'd retire and head to Pensacola with or without her. In ten years he figured the price of an orchard acre would be more than the price of his cruiser. He'd seen it happen, like a virus, turning everything good about a place into everything bad. The more people there were, the more they wanted. A guy who called at three in the morning with a cat up his tree would slit your throat, once you got it down and if the price was right.

At noon the following morning Tangier was cool and overcast. Willie stood on the front porch of the shack and listened for Salty's boat. At a quarter a pot he figured fixing crab traps must be easy or they wouldn't let him do it. Stick said there were plenty of pots to go around and that was good because he was down to his last few dollars. Rebecca's letter was in his back pocket. He'd done the best he could telling her that he was all right without leaving too many clues. Maybe someday he'd tell her where he'd been, or go back and visit. It made his heart heavy to think that he'd spend the rest of his life running. He couldn't imagine such a thing. But given what he'd done, he might be looking over his shoulder for most of it. Hilda *was* probably one in a million like Stick had said. She'd told him to leave the letter with Salty at the end of the day and that she'd take care of it.

When the boat pulled up to the front of the shack, a dark-haired boy about his age stood on the bow wearing long rubber boots. It startled him at first.

"Mornin', Willie!" Salty shouted from behind the wheel.

"Mornin'," Willie managed, curious about the boy.

"Got you in the stern here!" Salty instructed, putting the boat in reverse. As the stern swung into the floating dock, Willie jumped on board. *"Auggie, take the wheel!"* Salty ordered, descending into the open hatch. Willie stood in the stern and watched the boy move nimbly aft along the port side of the boat. It alarmed him to see no one steering.

"Hey, Willie." The boy grinned, dropping into the cockpit and grabbing the wheel. As the wheel turned, the bow swung out into Mailboat Harbor. Where Salty and the boy were headed, he wasn't sure, but they seemed to have a plan. The night before, Hilda had said that he'd be fixing crab pots for the next few weeks because every year they needed a going over.

Increasing the boat's speed, the boy turned back to Willie.

"Salty wants to show you around first and we got some pots to pick up! Then we'll do some work!" he shouted over the engine. The boy was about his age, but he was much more confident. *"You wanna steer?"*

"No, thanks!" Willie wanted to, but he was too afraid.

"Nothin' to it once you get the hang of it!" The boat looked like the *May Jane*, but was wider and had more gear on it. Looking around, Willie could see it needed paint.

"Bilge pump's lookin' good! You meet Auggie?" Salty shouted, popping out through the hatch with a wet rag, spreading his feet apart for balance.

"Yes, sir, I did!" Willie stepped forward to join them.

"Name's Salty!" The old man lowered his voice, a twinkle in his eye. "Wife's the only one on this boat goes by that name."

Willie thought he might be serious about his wife until Auggie turned around and laughed. "Got a chart here," the old man said, slapping his hand on the cabin top. "Left some pots down off Sund Spit. Thought we'd pick 'em up and run up West Ridge on our way back. Give you the tour."

Leaning against the cabin, Willie stretched his neck towards the chart. There wasn't much land to look at and the water had numbers all over it. "What's all these numbers?" he asked, spotting Sund Spit on the southernmost tip of the island.

"Depth," Salty answered, leaning overboard and dipping his rag in the water.

"What's the deepest place?" Willie scanned the chart for a high number.

"The Hole," Auggie replied, turning the wheel south from East Point.

"How deep is it?" Willie's eyes were on Auggie.

"One hundred and seventy-four feet," Salty affirmed, wringing his rag over the railing.

"Don't see it nowhere." Willie slid his hands over the chart.

"Hole's in Maryland off Bloody Point. Show you 'nother time. Bay's twenty-one feet on average. Ain't far to fall when your number's up." He tied the rag around some rigging. "But we got more shore than the whole West Coast, Willie. And three hundred and fifty different kinds a fish."

Salty took in the horizon ahead. Willie had never seen so many cracks on one face before.

"Indians call this place 'Tschiswapeki.' Means somethin' like 'great shellfish bay.' Before we run 'em off." Off the port side, the shoreline passed. "We're just east a town right now. 'Main Ridge,' they call it. You're lookin' at Canton. First people on the island settled there, fishermen mostly. Not too good for farmin'. Did that south a town in a place called 'The Field.' "

"Not a lotta trees," Willie observed.

"Just a lotta bay . . . " Salty gestured towards a large boat off the stern in the distance. "Mail boat's in." Auggie and Willie spun around to see a large white vessel work its way into Mailboat Harbor behind them.

"Got my schoolbooks, Miss Riser says," Auggie announced. "Shoulda been here a month ago."

Salty looked at Auggie tenderly. "Long as you read 'em, son, don't matter when."

"What grade you in, Auggie?" Willie asked.

Auggie hesitated, as if he weren't sure what grade he was in.

"We're all together so I guess you could say I'm somewhere around the seventh. What grade are you in?"

Willie blushed, shifting his gaze to the bow. "I ain't in school right now." He tried to sound ambivalent. When Salty gave Auggie a fierce look, he knew it was time to change the subject.

"Well, today, I'm not either. Come on and steer for a while," he offered, backing away from the wheel. He sensed that Willie was afraid. "Nothin' to it," he said confidently. "Not much out there to run into except water."

"And the Lump Light," Salty added.

"What's that?" Willie felt unsure as he took the wheel.

"You'll know it when you see it," the old man answered, stepping through the hatchway below.

The morning sun had worked its way through the clouds and afforded them longer views. Rounding Sund Spit, Auggie pointed towards a distant lighthouse farther south in Kedges Straits.

"Solomons Lump Light," Auggie announced. "It's real big when you get close. We jumped off it last summer, my brother and me. Hurts your balls, if you land wrong!" Auggie winced, laughing, and Willie laughed with him until neither could stop. "About tore me up, man," Auggie bleated with tears in his eyes.

Salty appeared in the hatchway with a box of saltines and a jar of peanut butter. "What you boys doin' up here? Be pissin' all over my boat in a minute. You know where we're goin'?" Salty said half-seriously.

"Puttin' in at MacCrackin's dock is what you told me." Auggie nodded towards a dock up ahead stacked with crab pots.

Salty put the peanut butter and crackers down next to the chart. "Help yourself. Got your Swiss Army, Willie?"

"Yes, sir."

"Give me the wheel. You boys get somethin' to eat. Then we'll take the pots on."

As the boat headed north, shoreline grasses fired up in the emerging sunlight. Salty had read to his wife in *National Geographic* of mastodons, camels, and peccary once roaming the Chesapeake, and she'd laughed at him, saying it was trick photography and you couldn't trust a magazine run by the feds. She was funny that way, but in spite of her stubbornness, Salty had come to believe that, sometimes, the hardest thing to imagine was true.

For a while, they rode in silence, until the boat slowed and Salty looked wistful as West Ridge passed. "Buildin' an airport there one a these days, Aug. You'll get your books on time, then."

Standing between two stacks of jimmy pots, Willie watched the sky over Tangier from the stern and imagined airplanes gleaming overhead in the sunlight like some kind of magic trick. He wondered if airplanes could wreck a place. He wasn't so afraid of the water today. He'd learn to swim, maybe in the summer if they stayed long enough for the water to warm up. Maybe he'd learn to fly when he was older and visit other islands and other coasts. And after a while, the world would become a part of him somehow.

Salty had two men waiting when he pulled up to his slip by the gas dock. At first Willie was worried. One of the men looked at him funny when he tossed the stern line. He'd seen him once before, walking back from Hilda's. His name was Bob. Salty said he sold oil next to a cemetery, but Willie had been too distracted at the time to pay much attention. The other man's name was Dave. He was short and had a happy face.

"Dave here's an oysterman from Morattico where your skiff come from. Got here 'bout the same way, as I recall," he joked, watching Auggie tie the bow line off.

"It was blowin' that day," the man confirmed.

"Got questions about the storm of '33, Willie, he's the one. No doubt about it," Salty said, stepping off the boat.

Sixty wire jimmy pots were unloaded and placed against a stack of another hundred or so. They looked like cages. Willie figured there were so many pots to fix that he'd make enough money to buy some winter clothes and supplies, and if he were lucky, have something left for a fishing pole. After Bob and Dave left, Salty said he'd need the pots in the bay no later than mid-May.

"You come on over here, Willie." Salty gestured, dropping a broken pot down in front of the boys. "Auggie's an ace at this, but here's how it works." Auggie's face beamed. "When you look at a pot, you look at the inside first, that way you don't miss nothin'. Got a break anywhere from the inside out, your pot's for shit and won't hold 'em. Crabs come in, crabs go out."

Willie recognized the wire he'd seen around Matt Abel's old chicken coop before it fell down. "Just chicken wire, so when you find a break, you get a piece from your pail and close it up with three good twists. Can't be nothin' open nowhere. You see a break, you fix it. Crabs ain't stupid. If there's a way out, they're gonna find it and your job's to make sure that don't happen." Auggie showed him the bucket of wire.

"Just use my hands?" Willie took out a wire.

"Best way to do it," Salty answered. "Plus, you boys got a leg up 'cuz you can get in there and work it good. Nothin' like a big fat hand to slow things up."

Willie stared into the pot. "What makes 'em go in there?"

"Birds 'n' the bees!" Salty joked, rolling his hips provocatively from side to side. Willie and Auggie exchanged looks and burst out laughing. "You can laugh, boys, but the best way to a peeler's heart in the spring is to find her some dick. And this here's the way to do it!" When Willie remembered his momma's bowl of room keys, his laughter died in his throat. Salty pointed to a smaller upper section of the pot. "You take two or three large jimmies—"

"Males," Auggie interrupted for Willie's benefit.

"That's right . . . males . . . " the old man corrected himself, " . . . and you use 'em to attract the peelers—"

"Females," Auggie said.

"—who didn't molt the fall before."

"How come they didn't molt?" Willie had forgotten what Stick told him about molting.

"Didn't mate. No fuck, no luck!" Salty's eyes got big while the boys giggled. "So they're pretty worked up by May, and when the males float the word out . . . "

"Pheromones," Auggie explained.

"Farra—what?" Willie asked.

"Pheromones," Auggie repeated.

"That's it!" Salty confirmed, snapping his big, thick fingers. "Well, that's the fancy word for it. Bottom line is they wave that big ole thing and the girls come crawlin', sometimes twenty or thirty at a time, with only one thing on their minds."

"It's called 'doubling,' " Auggie clarified.

"What is?"

"When they mate," Auggie said patiently.

"Won't even nick your fingers. You can just pick 'em up without your gloves 'cuz they're useless," Salty added.

"And real red," said Auggie.

"And real red. You know your peelers, don't you, boy!"

"Been with you awhile, Salt."

Salty looked at the boy. He was eight when his parents split up, and his mother, at the end of her rope, had brought him down to Salty's boat. "You're gettin' there, boy." He winked, taking a small notebook and pencil stub out of his back pocket. "Quarter a pot and I'll trust you to be fair 'bout it. End a the day, put your totals here." He handed the notebook to Willie. "On Saturdays run it up to Hilda and she'll have your money 'cuz it's her pots you're fixin'."

"These all belong to Hilda?" Willie admired the pots.

"And the peelers that go with 'em," said Salty.

Hilda would have a ton of crabs, Willie thought.

"So, there it is." Salty put his hands back in his back pockets and examined the boat lines.

"You seen Stick?" Willie asked.

"Here an' there. Ain't too far to wander 'round here, Willie. You need somebody, chances are they hear 'bout it first."

He figured Stick was probably busy fixing Hilda's roof. Maybe it was the water all around, but he was beginning to ease up. His momma would have liked the rich air and the way everybody knew everyone, and she would've been impressed by the size of the lighthouse in Kedges Strait. But like old Moses would say, he needed to "take the rope and git t'work."

Willie watched closely as Auggie grabbed the wire pail and a busted-out peeler pot. He was confident and cheerful about things, and Willie hoped if he stuck around long enough, they could be friends. He'd never had any growing up. Kids didn't last long in The Bottom. They moved away, or else they got tough too soon and stopped being kids. By the time he was ten, he was hanging out in the Lucky Bean, or with an old black man.

"So plop on down and knock it out, boys." Salty clapped his hands and ambled away.

The first hour, Willie worked slowly and kept a close eye on Auggie. Closing the holes was much more difficult than he'd thought, but the hardest part was hanging on to the wire with your fingertips while you threaded it inside the pot.

"Ain't done more than two the whole hour," Willie complained as he dropped another wire.

Auggie smiled. He remembered how hard it had been when he started with Salty. The outside edges of his hands were bleeding at the end of the day.

"You bleedin' yet?"

"Kinda." Willie sighed deeply. His hands were full of tiny scratches.

Auggie pulled his arms out of a pot. "Tore me up bad the first couple a days. Here, I got somethin'," he said, walking over to a workbench against the wall and reaching into a drawer to find a small round tin container, which he threw to Willie. "Put that all over your hands. Works real good."

"'Rosebud Salve,'" Willie read the top of the tin.

"Put it on top of your hands for now, otherwise your fingers will be slippin' while you work," Auggie advised, walking away. "I gotta pee."

When he returned, Willie was greased up and hard at work on his third pot. Lowering himself down on his stool, Auggie resumed work on the pot he had left unfinished. As they worked, the sun crossed behind a line of trees in front of Hilda's house. Occasionally, Stick's hammer could be heard on the roof.

"That your uncle workin' up there?"

Salty was right about things getting around quick. "Yep," he answered, counting a third twist of the wire. He didn't like having to lie to Auggie, but maybe it wasn't such a big deal, given the circumstances. Maybe it was just a question.

"You from here?" Willie changed the subject.

"Yep." Auggie didn't look up.

The boys worked for another hour before sitting up and watching a long shaft of sunlight shear the rooftops above the streets behind them. Willie's back ached from bending over but his hands didn't hurt much.

"Stuff works," Auggie confirmed, checking his own hands.

"Seems to," Willie agreed, looking weary. He'd done five pots in three hours.

"You did real well for the first time." Auggie stood up, testing his knees. "We need better stools or somethin'."

"Think my leg's sleepin'." Willie stood up cautiously and tapped the dock with his right leg. "Can't feel nothin'!"

"Wanna Coke?" Auggie asked, watching him dance.

The soda machine at the gas dock had been filled the week before. The Coca-Cola would go first and then, by Thanksgiving, the orange Fanta. Just before Christmas, goose and duck hunters from the mainland would clean out the Dr Pepper before they pulled the plug. Auggie told Willie this as they sat on the dock edge, sipping from their bottles. "For a Coke," he said, "timing is everything."

Willie felt a comfortable familiarity with Auggie as they dangled their feet over the Chesapeake.

"You miss school?" Auggie asked.

"No, not really," he lied.

Auggie looked forward to the day when he was done with school and he could be an oysterman.

"You like it?" Willie asked pointedly.

"Sometimes. I like science, geography, stuff like that. "But . . . other stuff's a waste of time and Miss Riser's kinda like that ole Solomons Light." He cracked up and Willie laughed with him. The woman who'd taught him to read smelled of lavender and another one smelled of gin. His mother had told him that they owed her a favor. They taught him in the kitchen. A thin red-haired woman with low-cut silk dresses taught him American history. A tall half-breed named Dodee taught him math. He understood now that they were prostitutes like his momma. But that didn't matter anymore. What they'd taught him had made him hungry to learn more. Sometimes, they gave him reading assignments and homework.

"You got school tomorrow?"

"Yep. But I'll be down after. You be around?"

"Far as I know. Like to get them pots done and make some money. Rate I'm goin', may take a while," he said, standing up. "Thanks for the Coke. Pay you back tomorrow."

"No big deal." Auggie hopped to his feet. He moved well for someone so tall.

"How tall are you?" Willie handed him his empty Coke bottle.

"Five eleven."

"Your dad real tall?"

A last shot of sunlight bounced off the water into Auggie's face. He had a smooth tan complexion with tiny faint freckles below the bridge of his nose. When he heard the question he forced his eyes open and looked at Willie. His eyes were crystal blue. "He died."

Willie averted his eyes.

"I was nine. Boat went down off Cedar Island," Auggie said dispassionately, looking east out Mailboat Harbor. "Summer squall."

The water sparkled beyond East Point as the sun seeped into the bay behind West Ridge. Willie wanted to tell him about his own daddy.

"Not much of an oysterman," Auggie said sadly. "But he was real tall."

Stick had filled the stern of the skiff with so many groceries Willie had to sit in the bow for ballast. It had been a long day for them both, but they were glad to be together. Hilda had given Stick two small ribeyes and the last of her canned tomatoes. Salty had left a bag of charcoal with a grill that he'd fashioned from half a buoy. The skiff would have an outboard motor next week. It was pretty cold at night. There would be frost on the ground soon, and in a few days, Willie would turn fourteen.

After dinner, the boy was whipped.

"Get a bath, Willie, while I clean up." Stick was washing at the sink. His hands looked pretty beat-up.

"Want me to dry?" Willie asked halfheartedly.

"Want you to wash them cuts out. I got somethin' you can take afterwards. The Rosebud was smart. Salty have some?"

"Auggie knew where it was." Willie shuffled over to the sink.

"Used to have it on the rigs," Stick said, taking Willie's plate and glass with a sideways glance. He was getting older. He looked taller and a little more muscular now. "Salty's kid a nice boy?"

"He's all right." Willie tried not to sound too enthusiastic.

"Salty's crazy 'bout him." Stick put Willie's dishes into the sink and turned on the tap. "Got enough hot water for you in a minute so get yourself ready."

"You workin' tomorrow?" Willie looked around for his towel. His legs were sore.

"First thing. Weather looks good. Be another week before it's done."

"I got pots to fix in the mornin'," Willie boasted.

"That you do. Got a bunch, don't she?"

"Only did five today. Like to do better than that." Willie located the towel under his bed blanket.

Stick turned the faucet off and dropped a bar of soap into the warm water. "Day at a time, Willie. Get your bath."

Closing his eyes, Willie sank to the bottom of the tub. He imagined the sound of distant trains and the smell of his momma's hairbrush. He wouldn't tell Auggie much. Or then he'd make shit up, like Stick being his uncle and how they'd traveled together on a rail. Until he remembered more clearly what had happened the night of the fire. Rising suddenly to the surface, he opened his eyes and gasped for air. Someone had been standing behind him! Frozen in the tub with water dripping off his shoulders, he remembered how the Beautiful Lady had risen up over his head to protect him.

When Stick's shot of warm rum kicked in, he was gone. They'd talked a bit. Willie seemed out of sorts after his bath. Something was bothering him, but he was too giddy from the rum and too tired to make much sense. Stick sat at the table with the bell jar of hooch.

"Hands hurt?"

"Not really. That rum ain't so bad. You put somethin' in it?" he asked, lingering over the aftertaste.

"Honey." Stick leaned back in his chair and stretched his legs. "Warms you up, don't it?" The boy closed his eyes. His hands weren't hurting anymore. "Feelin' better?"

"Yep. Stuff makes you sleepy."

Stick took a sip from the jar. He needed to know what the sheriff was up to. Hilda was on the mainland for a few days buying books and other supplies, and he'd asked her to do it discreetly. He still needed more answers from Willie.

"Wanna talk?" Stick asked.

Willie sighed at the question. If he was going to remember what had happened, Stick would be the one to help him, but he was too tired and it was all too complicated. Every time he thought about his father, every time he conjured up his face, he started to sweat. It wasn't just being knocked around—he'd gotten used to that. But all his life he'd called Willie names. He'd never fought back. There was no point. Sometimes his momma had seen what was going on, and afterwards, in a drunken haze, she'd asked him to read from the Bible. One time, out of spite, he'd read a page from one of Matt Abel's copies of *Popular Mechanics* about fixing lawnmowers, and she hadn't even noticed. "Lovely," she'd said before passing out.

Willie had felt barely human sometimes. When he'd been beaten, "It was for your own good," his father would say. When he was spared, he was "lucky." On his seventh birthday his parents were so stoned, they tied a red balloon to the back of his chair, sat him down, and waited for Santa Claus.

By noon the following day Willie had fixed six pots with only one scratch to show for it. Salty had told him to keep his hands still and go slow until he figured out where the rips were, and then speed up. At the rate he was going he might be able to keep up with Auggie someday.

"Damn, Willie!" Stick exclaimed when he showed up. "Done all these today?"

Willie tried to suppress his grin. "Ain't so hard once you get the hang of it."

"Ready for a cheese sandwich?" Stick held up a brown paper bag.

Willie jumped up. "I'm starvin'."

"Been down to that sandy beach?"

"Not yet."

"I'll get us a Coke on the way. I brought you an extra sweater just in case."

"Hey, Stick?"

"What?"

"Can you spot me somethin' to pay Auggie back? He got me a Coke yesterday."

"Sure." Stick gave him two dollars. "Keep on with them pots and you'll be rollin'."

"Don't need so much," Willie said, stuffing the dollars in his jeans pocket.

Stick deposited a dime into the soda machine and opened the glass door. "Take what you're havin' so I can get mine."

Willie grabbed the end of a Coke bottle and pulled hard. He could hear the row of glass settle into place as he jerked one out of the hole.

Willie closed the door and Stick put in another dime. "That roof workin' out?"

"Doin' all right, I suppose. Grab me one too—you like it here, don't you?"

The question was simple enough. He just didn't know how to put it into words.

From the opposite dock, Bob Novack watched Stick and the boy step onto the beach. Something wasn't right and he could cut it with a knife. Ten years ago he and Stick had almost crossed in the bar. Stick was cocky when it came to women, and when it came to Hilda, he acted like the cat's meow. He'd seen her face the day Stick left and the day he showed up ten years later. It was a small island, after all. His brother said she'd been asking questions about the boy in Reedsville. She never left the island unless there was a good reason. He told his brother to keep his ear to the ground and to call him on his ship-to-shore radio if he heard anything. The telephone operator, Eunice Blanchard, was a nosey pain in the ass, so he'd have to watch his back. And Hilda could pack a punch. She controlled the price of a six-pack and set the price of blue crabs before the first pot went down. If you pissed her off, there was hell to pay.

Willie plopped down on a mound of soft white sand and took the two pimento cheese sandwiches Stick offered. He was glad he'd made so many. Fixing pots was hard work and it made him hungry. Chewing, he looked across the bay towards East Point. The Coke was cold and delicious. Auggie said in January the bottles had ice at the top. Maybe there'd be some left for New Year's! He'd never had a New Year's with his momma. It was too big a night for her to be home. It made him sad to remember. But he felt grateful to Stick and Hilda, and glad he was out of the reach of the sheriff. As he sipped his Coke, surrounded by the bay and sparkly white sand, he knew things could be worse.

"Pretty, ain't it?" Stick looked off to his left. "Snowy egret down there, see him?"

Willie stopped chewing when he saw it. Except for the osprey, he'd never seen a bird so big before. It was polished white and had long, glossy black legs.

"He's fishin'," Stick explained, reaching blindly down for the Coke between his legs. "See how he's got his head cocked?"

"What kinda fish they like?"

"Killifish. Might catch close to a hundred of 'em a day."

"Hundred for just one bird?" Willie marveled.

"What Salty says, plus some crabs 'n' frogs."

Willie grabbed his Coke bottle to dislodge the Wonderbread stuck to the roof of his mouth. "Ssat de nsst?"

Stick smiled. "The what?"

As the bottle tipped, bubbles rose up into his nose.

"Careful, boy!" Stick chuckled. "You'll be shootin' that shit out your ears in a minute!"

As bubbles of Coke sprayed from his nose onto his T-shirt, Willie coughed and laughed at the same time. Clutching his sides, Stick was undone. He'd laughed uncontrollably before when he was drunk. He was sober this time. It took a while to stop, but when they finally did, they dropped their heads back against the sand and stared up into the cloudless sky. Neither realized it at the time, but they'd made their own nest. And, for better or for worse, whatever plans needed making would be made with the other in mind.

Hilda was glad to be home. She'd bought birthday presents for Willie and a winter coat for Stick. Two years back a nor'easter had dropped three feet of snow on the island. The Chesapeake was funny that way.

When he asked about Willie, Hilda assured him that she'd mailed his

244 / Peter Skinner

letter without a return address and had sniffed around.

"A friend of mine runs the police department. But the town's a beehive, so I had to be careful. Nothing's in the paper and nothing's up at the inn—so I called D.K. Wells in Richmond."

"Who's he?" Stick sat down on a wooden chair and patted his lap for her to sit. She'd always had beautiful eyes.

Hilda leaned back against the sink; she was barefoot in a brown skirt and long gray sweater. They watched each other for a long time before she answered.

"I swear, you'll be the end of me."

Chapter Twenty-nine

At seventy-six years of age, D.K. Wells had been the Scarburgh family lawyer for quite some time. He was smooth and impeccably vague and you could hear it in his voice. He'd handled everything aboveboard and below. He knew what to grease and when to lay low. But, most important, he was connected. A missing boy was nothing special. Sadie Graves was offering one thousand dollars to anyone with information. The sheriff in Charlottesville had issued an All Points Bulletin asking for help. A cop in Winchester had missed him by ten minutes. Another outside Fredericksburg had ID'd him too late. After that, the trail went cold. He'd been gone since August and would turn fourteen on November 30. His father was dead and his mother ran a whorehouse. The lab work in Richmond had finally turned up with partial fingerprints. Maybe it would bear fruit or maybe it wouldn't. Either way, he'd call her back.

Hilda was a fair woman, but you didn't rock her boat. If the boy had acted in self-defense, she'd take care of him. And if he'd yanked her chain— she'd turn him in.

Sitting around waiting was not what she was good at. However it played out, it wouldn't be easy. At forty-six she knew better than to try and change a man, but after what he'd done to her over the kitchen sink, she'd miss him.

When they finished fixing pots, Auggie asked Willie to spend the night. Stick had told him to be careful. If Willie messed up, he'd be caught. Unless, of course, the lab work came up clean, as Hilda had explained. And if the boy was jerking him around, Stick would be charged with haboring a fugitive. It was just that simple.

Stick didn't give a shit about the law. The law went into the Bay of Mexico with Wink's arm. What mattered was the boy—the boy who fought back, the boy who'd survived the Kitchen and lost his pole.

Lying in her bed, Stick watched the curtains frame the moonlight and smelled her hair. Her legs were silky from bath oils. He was sure he was spent, but to his surprise she made him hard again. The day he'd left she'd wanted him to father a child, but he was too fucked up at the time. On the boat to Reedsville he'd never looked back, or called later to say he missed her. Staying would've been harder, because it was harder to be loved than it was to love back.

After dinner Auggie showed Willie the minerals that he kept in a shoebox under his bed. One was a shaft of black crystal that had belonged to his father. "It's mine now," he said, closing the lid.

Auggie's mother was in her room listening to a radio. All night he'd felt her watching him—not as if he'd done something wrong, but more as if she were looking for something. He wondered if being alone was as hard as being misunderstood. Lying in a sleeping bag on Auggie's bedroom floor, he thought again about the basket of keys in the hallway. His momma must have had one. Maybe she changed her name when she loved a stranger. Like he'd made up the story about Stick being his uncle. Until he'd run away he'd never known how much grown-ups had in common with children—and how much they made up.

Moses Henry leaned against his wooden chair and listened. With exams approaching, the students were quiet and it was easy to hear everything the professor was saying. When a word went by, he'd capture it, and when he had enough in his head, he'd string them all together until an idea sunk in. One way or the other, if he sat there long enough, he'd catch something. "Be like fishin'," he told Willie one day. "Patient man always git somethin'." It made sense to Moses that the oldest tree on earth was in the West. "Where duh sun go to," his momma was fond of saying. He could barely make out the slide over the students' heads. The curly gray-haired professor paused to remove his tweed coat.

"On this screen, ladies and gentlemen, is a Bristlecone pine from the White Mountains of California, nearly five thousand years old. Now you might reasonably think, given its age, that this Methuselah would be far taller than our own Rotunda here, but sometimes trees stop growing to avoid being knocked over in a big storm."

That seemed pretty smart to Moses, though he didn't know how he felt about trees and such. His momma had the biggest fringe tree in Keene, Virginia. When he was bad she'd cut a branch from behind their shack and use it on him. "Lord know'd you needed it!" she'd say later. "An' it good for duh bush."

As the lecture hall emptied, Moses straightened up in his chair and stared down. To some students he was a ghost, or just a nigger who rang the bell, or a curiosity, a page from history, a living relic. He could tell by the way they looked up at him who thought what. Some glanced at him shyly. Some looked at his hat. Some would nod. Every now and then, one would whisper hello, as if in deference. Moses could recognize the ones who wanted to say something without knowing how to say it. He'd felt that way himself.

When the seats were empty, he thought about Willie's fourteenth birthday. It had been little more than a semester, but he imagined the boy might be taller now. He'd be older in the eyes from all that running. Or maybe he'd be like the trees out West that stop growing so the storms can pass on by.

On the morning of November 30, Stick watched as sunlight pierced the front porch window before slipping sideways towards the boy's bed. By the time it hit his face, the bacon would be done and he'd wake up and be fourteen.

"Hey, Stick," Willie called out quietly. His head sunk in the pillow, he had one eye open.

Stick was pouring pancake batter on the skillet. As the puddles froze in place, he put the bowl down and looked over at the boy. He looked happy enough for a kid on the lam. And his hair was getting longer.

"Hungry?" He grabbed a spatula.

"I'm always hungry, Stick, you know that." Willie sat up suddenly, remembering what day it was.

"Jacks are done!" Stick put Willie's plate on the table.

Lowering his head down, away from the glare, Willie looked through the window. The surface of the water was glazed with sun. The year before it had rained in Charlottesville and his parents had forgotten his birthday. It wasn't the first time. He wished he could call his momma today, but he knew it was too risky. He was a fugitive, and he feared that maybe her heart had turned against him because of what she thought he'd done. He didn't want to think about that. Or maybe Stick or Hilda could call the barbershop and get a message to old Moses somehow.

"Ain't servin' you in bed, junior, let's do it!" Stick ordered, flipping his pancakes over and reaching for a plate. Willie shot out from under the sheets and dove towards the table. However things shook out, it was a bright sunlit morning and he didn't want to piss Stick off—especially on his birthday.

While they ate, Salty's boat passed with the sound of its gurgling engine, different from the other boats. Auggie would be down at the dock around noon, he'd said. His school was closed for the Thanksgiving holiday, and he was happy about that. Auggie's heart didn't seem to be into school the way it was into fixing pots, or tending to Salty's boat. Willie wanted to feel that way about something someday. Moses said things like that snuck up on you.

Hungover from the moonshine, Stick didn't talk much.

"Good bacon, Stick." His mouth half full.

Stick took a gulp of hot black coffee and looked across the table at the boy. "Guy in Reedsville makes it for the inn. Nice and thick, ain't it?" He pushed away from the table. "Hilda's cookin' somethin' special tonight for Thanksgiving, so you need to hose down before we go."

Realizing that Stick had forgotten his birthday, he tried not to show his disappointment. "What time'll you pick me up?"

"Ain't pickin' you up today," Stick said curtly.

Willie looked at him. He seemed a little more than just hungover. "How come you ain't pickin' me up?"

Stick took another sip of coffee and put the cup on the table. His head felt slightly better. There was no reason to worry the kid. Rising to his feet, Stick moved towards the door. "Come on."

As he walked out, Willie jumped up and followed. His eyes towards the dock, he saw it instantly, a skiff!

"Happy birthday, Willie!"

It was white like a birthday cake with light blue trim inboard. When he saw the motor, his breath came up short. He couldn't believe it, even if it was true. His momma was wrong about people. They weren't dirty and sinful deep down inside. If you treated them right, they were good—and not just good to people they knew, but good to people they didn't know from Adam.

Folding his arms across his chest, Stick leaned against the rail next to Willie and gave him time to catch his breath. It had been Hilda's idea. She always had skiffs around and Salty always had a good motor. "See the name?" Unfolding his arms, Stick pushed off the rail, and Willie followed him down the steps of the dock to get a closer look at the stern. "Salty put it on last night."

"Sir Swims Alot," Willie read aloud through tears turning quickly to laughter.

Stick watched the skiff looping through Mailboat Harbor. Salty would show him a thing or two before he let the boy loose, and by the time the last shingle went down, Willie would be strapped to a life preserver and on his own. It made him happy to imagine what the boy might be thinking. His birthdays must have been so fucked-up for so long. That was one thing they had in common. The roof would be done today and he'd winter over or head out. For a moment the air turned brisk and the Chesapeake pulled flat, dark clouds down into the horizon. Crystal-Ann would've liked Hilda. They would've laughed about the same things and, most especially, about him.

CHAPTER THIRTY

Stick sat in the bow on their way in. Using a streetlight as a marker, Willie steered just like Salty had taught him, approaching slowly from the side before putting the motor in reverse.

Hilda had cooked a goose for Thanksgiving and tied birthday balloons to a brass ceiling lamp over the dining room's largest round table. When Stick and Willie arrived, the inn was lit up like a great ship.

Salty and his wife, Peggy, Auggie, and Zach Parks were waiting on the porch. Peggy was a large woman with more wrinkles than her husband and hands that felt like sandpaper. "Pleased to meet you, Willie," she said enthusiastically, shaking his hand. "Heard some nice things 'bout you."

"Thank you, ma'am." Willie blushed, looking over at Auggie, who was sipping a Coke in his rocker. "Heard some nice things 'bout you too, Miss Crockett," he replied shyly. Everybody laughed.

"Nice like what, darlin'?" Peggy asked as her chuckles subsided.

Willie couldn't tell if they were laughing at him or laughing about what he'd said.

"Well . . . Salty says you kinda run the show," he stammered, looking to Auggie for help.

Peggy's head fell back over her shoulders before it careened forward in a

252 / Peter Skinner

deafening scream of hysterics. Salty bellowed and as the others joined in, Willie was reminded of the time he hit Matt Abel's backyard door with the apple. The feeling was not unlike that entirely—as if, without intending to, he'd made them all very happy.

When Stick brought the goose out, everybody clapped and whistled. Hilda had done it herself. It was bigger than the egret. "Where in the world did you get a bird like that, Hilda?" Peggy Crockett chortled, leaning forward under a red balloon.

"Shot him at Fester Poon's place this morning," she replied, watching Stick lower the tray to the table. "Eighteen pounds and enough feathers to make a good pillow!" Auggie and Willie sat side by side as Hilda stood before the goose with a large two-pronged fork and carving knife. Their eyes got bigger as she cut down into the breast.

"Fine-lookin' table for a fine young man." Zach raised a bottle of beer in the air and toasted Willie.

As other bottles were raised, Stick reappeared from the kitchen with a bowl of garlic mashed potatoes and hot corn pudding.

"Happy birthday, Willie!" everybody chimed in.

"Thanks! Sure looks good! And happy Thanksgivin', Miss Hilda," he remembered to say, looking first at Stick, then down at his plate.

"Got wine on the table, people, so don't be shy," Hilda announced, looking out at them with a warm smile. "And pass me your plates." By the time Stick returned with serving bowls of green beans, pickled beets, and cranberry sauce, Hilda had filled each plate, including his. "Gladys made the rolls," she said as Stick sat down. "And there's plenty of bird if you want more."

"Thank you, Miss Hilda," Willie said, mostly to himself. "And thank you, ma'am . . . " He didn't know exactly how to put it into words. " . . . for letting me use your boat."

Hilda smiled warmly at Willie. For the first time, she didn't think of him as a lost child or as someone who was in trouble. Stick was right about the boy. He was worth it.

"Not mine, sweetie. Belonged to a friend and he'd be glad about you having it—especially today." Hilda took the glass of red wine that Zach had poured her and raised it in the air. As she'd bled the bird over a fence that morning, a faint rainbow had appeared briefly above the ridge behind Fester Poon's barn. As it faded away, she'd thought about the boy and what she'd say to him that night. She'd never had a child of her own, but she'd been one. After her mother had died, Hilda had given up on Christmas and Thanksgiving, but, standing by the goose that she'd slain, the boy's presence felt almost fortuitous.

"So like they say, Willie . . . " She looked at him tenderly from across the table. "The heart would see no rainbow had the eye no tear."

The table hummed with quiet delight as dishes and plates moved in silent circles. When the inn closed for the season, occasions of this kind were infrequent. Except for a cousin or gentleman caller, folks stayed away. Many found Hilda imperial, irreverent, and sometimes reckless, but they admired her all the same. In addition to blue crabs, Tangier produced genuine people. People with more regard for life than for the reputations it manufactured.

According to Peggy, it had been a lousy year for crabs. "My man's puttin' in twice the time for half the take. And don't tell me it ain't 'bout somethin', 'cuz this is the third year now and it ain't lookin' any better."

"Skip Johnson says the grass beds are fine," Zach offered, pouring himself some more wine.

"Skip Johnson's a horse's ass," Peggy shot back. "He also said the swans were killin' the skimmers." Auggie and Willie exchanged looks, smiling under their napkins. "Problem is all these friggin' dams and crap they're puttin' in the bay. Ain't any swans doin' it! You know that, Zach, you see it every trip you make. Salt says they got fifty new places built out on Ingram Bay just this summer alone."

"More than fifty now, Peg. Saw a bunch more goin' up when we run the boy out," Zach said.

"Bob Novack wants an airport up on West Ridge. Called me 'bout it last week," Hilda added.

Peggy leaned forward in her chair and raised her voice. "So he can sell his fool oil to all them eggbeaters from Richmond is all that's about. He told Salty the same thing at the Christmas party two years ago—'bout how he's headed for the Keys when the last drop's gone. That's what's takin' the blues and all the grass. Excuse me for sayin' this in front of the chil'ren, but there's too many greedy-ass people out for themselves. That's all it is and all it ever will be . . . and what's bad for the goose is bad for the gander!" There was a collective sigh around the table.

"And let that be a lesson to you young 'ens!" she added, looking at the boys with a large finger in the air and fire in her eyes. "Ain't what you take from this world—it's what you leave behind when you go."

Moses would've understood exactly, Willie thought, even if she was a little worked up when she said it. Moses had told him more than once that it seemed like people wanted something for nothing all the time. He said the only way to hear a bell was to ring it.

As the cake candles were lit, Willie remembered his momma and Moses, Rebecca and the Lucky Bean and his lost fishing pole. He didn't make a wish or imagine a better place waiting for him now that he was fourteen—he didn't need to. Leaning his head forward, he saw that the candles were separate, but all lit by the same flame. Taking a huge breath, he managed to extinguish them to a round of applause.

When Auggie returned from the kitchen, he handed Willie a small box wrapped in brown paper. It surprised both of them when the moment came to open it, because they realized how quickly they'd become friends. "Thanks, Auggie." Willie admired the wrapping. "Sorry your momma was sick today."

"Awe, it's nothin' much." Auggie shrugged, glancing at Stick. After the kite string slipped off, Willie unwrapped the brown paper and lifted the top. Inside the box, nestled in torn clumps of soft white cotton, was a metal fishing lure shaped like a minnow, with a cockeyed head and three-pronged hooks on both the front and back ends.

"Man!"

"It's a 'Sonar,' Willie! It's adjustable so you can fish the bottom or the top. Got a whole new way a movin'. Says it finds 'em and catches 'em! It'll get you tons of stripes under Oyster Creek Bridge in the mornin'!"

Willie's eyes widened in amazement. "What kinda bait goes on it?" He lifted it out carefully to get a better look.

"It doesn't take bait." Auggie hoped Willie didn't feel stupid for asking the question. "They make these babies in Michigan!"

"Michigan?!" Salty barked.

"What it says on the paper there!" Auggie pointed to the bottom of the box.

"Don't need no worm?" Willie repeated dumbly.

"Fish won't be lookin' for a worm . . . it's just gonna wanna bite 'cuz it's got this AC/DC way of movin'," he elaborated.

"What the hell?!" Salty barked again.

Auggie looked annoyed. "AC gives you the action and DC gives you the depth," he explained.

When Peggy kicked Salty's leg under the table, he smiled first at Auggie, then at Willie. "Well, hot diggity! Be gettin' your limit now!" He clapped his hands twice.

Willie figured that with all the money he'd made fixing pots he'd be able to buy a pole by Christmas. "Stripes run good in December?" he asked.

Salty smiled at the boy. "Don't know 'bout Michigan, but 'round here they do," he said, winking at his wife.

Finding a small pamphlet on the lure under the cotton, Willie put his "Sonar" back in the box and closed the top. "Thanks again, Auggie," he said with a big smile.

Auggie wanted to ask Willie to spend the night, but he had school in the morning and it was getting late. "Nothin' much, man," he said, working up the nerve to ask for another slice of cake.

Hilda checked the table to see who needed coffee. "You boys ready for some more cake?" She sliced some more.

"Yes, ma'am," Auggie replied quickly.

"Thank you," Willie added.

When Hilda returned from the kitchen, she had a pot of coffee and a red paper shopping bag in her hand. "Willie?"

"Ma'am?" he answered, with cake in his mouth.

"Got something here for you." She placed the bag on the table next to her chair. "Why don't you come over here and open it up?" she said, circling the table with an offer of hot coffee.

Willie wiped his mouth with his napkin and stood up. He felt as if everyone knew what was going to happen before he did. As he reached into the bag, he saw a whale's mouth swallowing the bow of a boat. The book was *Moby Dick* by someone named Melville. Hilda said he was a little young for it, but that if he had problems to ask Miss Riser for help. Except for the Bible, the only books he'd ever read were from a box his momma had gotten from the St. Anne's School for Girls. She said most of them had come from an army man who'd taught the girls about exercise and posture and owed her a favor.

There was another book in Hilda's bag called *The Adventures of Huckleberry Finn* she said she'd read when she was fifteen years old. "Good books get even better with time," she told him.

"Aint' like people," Salty mumbled into his coffee cup.

Willie put the books back in the paper bag. It was hard to find the right words to thank Hilda. She was still a stranger and yet she made him feel completely at ease.

Awkwardly, he reached out to her and she hugged him. Her sweater was warm and soft. Briefly, the side of his head lay gently against her neck. She smelled like roses.

"All right, Willie. I got one more thing for you," Stick declared, standing up.

Willie was taken aback as he picked up his bag and returned to his chair.

"We all figured now that you're fourteen . . . " He lowered his voice. " . . . and now that you got your own skiff and a Sonar AC/DC . . . you might need this."

As he pulled the Shakespeare Wonderod out from under the table, Auggie let out an appreciative whistle and the others started clapping. They'd waited all night to see the boy's face.

"Got a Wondercast with Platyl line, Willie!" Auggie shouted enthusiastically, pointing to the reel.

Utterly transfixed by the shiny pole, Willie slowly rose out of his chair, then sat down again and covered his face with his hands. He didn't want to cry in front of Auggie, but he couldn't help it. His feelings were no longer exclusively about himself. His tears seemed perfectly natural to them, and most especially to Auggie. He'd wanted to cry sometimes just like Willie, but he could see that it frightened his mother, so he didn't. One by one they came to Willie and touched his shoulder or ruffled his hair. It had been one of those nights, and as they passed his chair, he looked up at them, clutching his pole, but could only shake his head with gratitude.

At the front gate there were no stars, but it would be warm enough to enjoy the walk home. After Auggie, Willie, and Stick had left, Peggy, Salty, and Zach gave the house a brief look before they separated. Tangier had always been a special place to live, but there was something about their time together that night that made them love it even more.

Willie rode back to the crab shack in Stick's boat. He was too tired to drive his new skiff and too happy to pay attention or focus on anything except the streetlights as they faded away. He didn't need stars or a moon or one more bite of Gladys's cake. He wished his momma could have been at the table. That would've been the only thing to make his birthday more perfect. It would have eased her mind to see him so happy and made her less anxious about not knowing where he was. As the empty shack drew near, he leaned forward over the bow and wondered if she would always feel him in her heart, wherever he was.

CHAPTER THIRTY-ONE

Sadie Graves heard the door again. Two o'clock in the afternoon was late for Moses to be knocking and some of the girls were still asleep. It had been a while since she'd seen him.

Moses had come every Sunday whether she was drunk or sober, and if she'd passed out, the girls had explained the situation. Standing at the door, Moses would shake his head, but he wasn't much surprised. He'd told Willie it didn't matter where a man lived or how much money he had in his pocket. "People," he'd explained, "are like melons. Even duh sweet ones got seeds."

Sadie squinted when the door opened. Her eyes were dark and hollow as if her face had shrunk. It startled him at first. She had one foot in this world and one foot in the next. Removing his hat and offering his bag of lemon drops, he could see that she'd become a child again. His momma said it happened just before the angel came to take you back.

"You sweet old thing, Moses Henry, with my Timberlake drops jess like always," she marveled, stifling a deep cough. "Not sure you'd be comin' today," she said.

Hearing the rasp in her chest, he furrowed his brows.

"Now, don't be lookin' like dat," she scolded him.

He could smell her rancid breath and got a good look at the bloodstained handkerchief. Moses looked down at his boots while she tucked it into her robe.

Sadie lowered her voice. "Ain't nothin' but a broken heart, 'n' you of all people know that."

"Yes'm," he spoke awkwardly, staring at the porch floor.

"Ain't no news 'bout nothin'," she said wearily, leaning up against the edge of the open door. "Been five whole months an' still nothin'. Like he ain't livin' and he ain't dead, jess . . . gone somewheres." Out on the front sidewalk, two boys about Willie's age threw her a sideways glance and giggled as they passed. Moses' eyes teared as he looked up at her. He didn't mind being old until the young ones started dying. It made his stomach turn to think of it.

Neither spoke for a moment as he came in. Climbing the stairs to her room, he heard the lemon drops rattle inside the tin. She fixed him tea with his favorite shortcakes and asked him how he was getting on. They talked about the small things for as long as she could muster, until the afternoon light crossed over her bed and out the open window. Dusting his coat of crumbs, she took his hand and thanked him for everything he'd done for her boy. "You was like a daddy to 'im, Moses," she said with some difficulty in the hallway outside her door, "a daddy with a bell."

After Moses had gone, Sadie drew a bath. Her arms screamed for the remaining batch of heroin under her bottom dresser drawer. She'd backed off the night before to have enough until Monday when Johnny-Joe Walker came down from D.C. The girls loved Johnny-Joe. He was a good-looking black man with the biggest dick in Arlington County. "It's made for lovin'," he'd say, pulling it out for the girls to fuss over. Johnny-Joe was proud of what nature had given him and Matt Abel didn't know what to think. As long as he paid cash, he didn't care too much. He didn't know about the smack. He figured the girls were just crazy for his cock.

Except for an odd night or two during the week, Sadie was too messed up to be of much use to Johnny-Joe. He needed women who could go the distance with some attitude to go with it. That was the deal.

As the tub filled, Sadie bit down on the rubber strap and pulled her head back. The spoon was full this time and the shot would be perfection—like lighting the Beautiful Lady and watching her eyes get big in the candlelight before the wax turned to liquid.

Dropping her syringe to the floor, she pushed down on the tourniquet until her body fluttered with warmth. Stepping carefully over the bathtub edge, she stood in the water.

Scratching at her arm absently, she stared at an elastic drip of water from the faucet. The door was locked. The girls would be at it soon enough and the keys would jingle as they passed along the hallway. She was used to the sounds. The keys changed hands, but the men were all the same.

Her head had become difficult to balance. Dropping to the water, she sat back and stretched her legs out. Something in the wallpaper reminded her of the skies over Chandeleur Sound outside Biloxi. Willie would've liked it there. They would have treated him right, like he was part of something instead of some poor boy living in a gum tree, keeping company with an old black man. Right before Moses knocked, she'd put another envelope in the cellar wall. It was all she had. She was bursting with smack and fresh out of luck.

Dropping her head, she heard her breath against the sides of the tub and forgot about the sheriff's visit. The boy would be all right. He was surrounded by water now. And light. That's where they'd find him. That's where he was. Staring down into the tub, his gentle face smiled up at her from the bow of a small boat. His hair was long with large brown curls at the end.

Underwater she heard his heart beat. It wasn't the bayou, or a tree, or a dirty street. It was an island—with crystal clear light and salty-sweet nights.

Breathing in, her body filled with warm seawater and he read to her.

"I heard a great voice, Momma . . ." She let go. " . . . and no more shall the sound of weeping be heard."

They found her in the morning floating in the tub with her eyes open and called Sheriff Sheffield. For most towns a dead prostitute was of small consequence, but in Charlottesville, this one was a different story. The body was bagged and taken to the morgue. The paperwork was easy: A prostitute leaves no trace, no legacy, and no forwarding address. No one was surprised she was dead. She'd died a long time ago. This was only her body, laced with smack, bloated and empty. "Witches of hellfire!" A Baptist preacher railed the following Sunday. "Appealing only to our weaknesses, to our wicked desires, and to our greed!" As the week went on, townspeople would hear the sanitized version, before they got to talking. No photographs were taken, no list of kin appeared in *The Daily Progress*. The countless men she'd fucked would run for cover, as if nothing had happened, as if the nights had been more imagined than real.

CHAPTER THIRTY-TWO

Hilda ran in from the rain when D.K. Wells finally called. His voice was always reassuring, even if the news was bad. "You doin' fine, Hilda?" Being her lawyer was tricky sometimes, but being a friend was more complicated.

"I am. Thank you," Hilda answered, holding the phone with her shoulder and removing a pair of work gloves. "Just taking up the leaves." She was slightly out of breath.

"Got a ton at home, but I've been backed up here for a while. The wife's on me—says I need to do some honest work for a change!" He chuckled softly. Hilda didn't laugh. "Hang on a minute, Hilda." He pulled the phone from his ear. She heard papers being shuffled and braced herself. The bad news would matter less to her than to Stick, but she'd become fond of Willie.

"So, what is it, D.K.?"

"Hang on. Just one more thing to sign and we're good to go, sorry." She could hear him whispering to his secretary, Joyce.

"You there?" he asked after a long pause. "Joyce says hi." Hilda's heart was pounding. "She told me you helped her cousin out last summer at the inn."

"I did. He ran out of gas outside Cod Harbor and had a bunch of kids with him," she remembered.

"Well, they certainly appreciate what you did," he replied as Hilda held her breath.

"They charging him, D.K.?" She stared at the wooden floor, tired of listening to him beat around the bush.

"Looks that way," he answered. "Gotta find him first, though."

When she heard it, it was as if for a moment she'd forgotten where she was.

"Public prosecutor's going before the grand jury for an indictment against the boy. Evidence includes an eyewitness and some prints from a plate, or somethin' like that. Lab in Richmond's workin' on a print from a piece a glass in the guy's head. Fire burned a lot of it, but it don't take much. Kid's in more than a little deep, Hilda. They posted a new warrant for his arrest yesterday," he informed her with some remorse.

Hilda dropped down into a chair and sighed. Stick had been wrong. He'd be back in a few hours and she wondered what would happen when she told him. "It was Willie's birthday yesterday," was all she could say.

He interrupted her thoughts. "There's something else, Hilda, and it isn't good."

Straightening her back against the chair, she listened to the rain. Her piles would be heavy and wet by now. Stick and Zach would be calling from the dock at Reedsville before heading back and she'd need to heat up the goose.

"His momma's dead."

CHAPTER THIRTY-THREE

As was their custom, Captain Snyder stood in front of his newsstand on the Corner and read the paper to Moses. He didn't know much about old Moses, but he knew about his relationship with Sadie. Whether they acknowledged it or not, almost everyone knew something about her. As he read, Moses shook his head, as if they were talking about someone else. Even in a white man's world, he figured, when it came to dying, people were the same. But the article didn't mention Willie or the many fine and unselfish things that she'd done in her life—like the money he delivered each year on her behalf to the university for a student's tuition. It left out the times she'd found a doctor for girls in trouble. And there was nothing about how pretty she'd been. As Moses listened to Captain Snyder, he kept quietly to himself. Maybe newspapers were meant for worse things, like wars and hurricanes and such. Maybe a person's life was too small to get right. Or then, maybe, he'd finally outlived the kinder world he once knew.

CHAPTER THIRTY-FOUR

Hilda sat in her rocker drinking a double pour of port from her coffee cup and listened to the rain. Willie was upstairs taking a hot shower. He'd wanted to try out his new pole, but when Auggie explained that fish don't like the rain, he took it in stride. Walking with him to the inn, Hilda had been quiet. Stick was still an hour away and she'd ask both of them to stay the night. The whole town knew what was going on—not that she gave a damn. People talked about a lot of things. The trick was to figure out what they meant.

She heard the rain on the porch roof. Willie was in her old bedroom, where she'd been as a child. It looked east into the harbor over a large purple rhododendron. People told her mother that rhododendrons didn't grow on Tangier. They said the soil had no acid in it, so she chopped up iron rebar and planted it around the roots. Hilda never listened to anybody, really. But out of respect for some of them, she pretended to every so often.

After dinner Willie had gone to bed. He was tired from the night before and excited about fishing the Oyster Creek Bridge with Auggie early in the morning. Hilda had given him an alarm clock and explained how it worked. He'd never had one. He said he used the sun, mostly, to know what time it was.

Stick was tired too, but after three beers and two glasses of port, he'd caught his second wind. Hilda could see that he was a drunk, but so was she. Except when it came to trusting each other, they were alike in many ways. She loved him in a way that she had never loved another man. She had her inn and he had his trains. Life could go on without him, but his touch was irresistible.

"I can tell you got somethin' on your mind tonight," he said as soon as they sat down in the rockers.

Hilda stared at the white picket fence and took a deep swig of port. Bobbie's cat was somewhere dry. "D.K. Wells called today. Said Willie is a potential suspect in his father's death," she said, fighting tears. "Got prints on somethin' . . . " Stick stopped rocking and looked at her as if he'd misunderstood. " . . . and someone who saw him run from the house."

"Don't mean he did it," Stick shot back. "No reason for the warrant 'cept they got no one else." He waited for the rest of it—there was always something else.

Hilda took a small sip and wondered if their voices were carrying up to the boy. It had been a while since he'd gone upstairs and she was sure he was asleep by now. She took a deep breath and exhaled slowly. "His momma's dead."

Stick looked into her eyes as if he were looking for something else and she knew him well enough to know what it was.

"Last night on his birthday. Overdosed. Found her this morning in a bathtub." As she shook her head, her lips curled in disgust.

"Fuck!" he said. Stick emptied his glass and stood up. He needed to walk somewhere. Willie had been so close to something good, until life stepped in and shit all over him. "Your man, D.K., did it quiet, right?" He touched the screen door lightly.

"What I'm paying him for."

"Still—there's no way to . . . track him down?"

"No," she said, trying to figure him out. He seemed more resolute than upset.

Stick nodded his head pensively. "Back in a minute," he said, opening the door and walking heavily down the steps.

The rain felt good. It always did—unless you were stuck in a coal car. Under the lights his breath steamed. He'd forgotten his coat, but he wouldn't be long. Somehow he'd explain the situation to the boy and then he'd tell him that his old lady was dead. Maybe it wouldn't surprise him entirely. Rain rinsed his face under the last streetlight. Past the cemetery, water gushed from the sides of his boots before he stopped. Six months ago he would've walked, but on Tangier there was only so far you could go.

When he shuffled in, she laughed. "Got wet?"

Standing there with puddles under his boots, he looked defeated. "It's rainin'."

By midnight the rain had stopped and they were still awake under the warm sheets, staring at the ceiling. "You need to tell him," she repeated.

"I suppose."

"He needs to get on with it, Stick." She turned her head towards him. "So do you." She was right. He was playing games in his head. "He doesn't belong to us."

A deep sadness washed over him. It was true, but at the same time, it wasn't the way he felt. "Ain't about that." He sat up, leaning against the headboard. "It's hard to walk away, that's all."

"From what?"

"Him an' me," he said, getting out of bed.

Ten minutes later it was raining and he smelled of rum. Zach had brought it back from Cuba, and it was strong.

"You drunk enough to tell me now?" she asked, as he slid into bed.

He didn't like the tone of her voice. "Don't have a drinkin' problem less I can't get a drink," he recited before kissing her on the cheek and settling in.

He was a mess, but he was the kind of man who didn't apologize for it. It was part of the deal. Moving closer, she put her head on his shoulder and listened to the rain.

"It's hard to walk away," he said in a voice she'd never heard.

CHAPTER THIRTY-FIVE

Sir Swims Alot was gone when Stick pulled up to the shack. He was too hungover and tired to track Willie down in Oyster Bay. He figured his headache would be gone and he could think straight by the time the boy was back for lunch. He'd spent most of his life running from something and he didn't want that for the boy. He needed to know one way or the other what had happened that night. Hilda had given him two days.

Lying on his bed, he closed his eyes and tried to sleep. The bulls would be all over the local tracks. They'd need to fix on a place before he figured out how to get there. Or not. Maybe Hilda was right. He'd say fuck it once and for all, the way Indians taught their babies to swim.

When Willie appeared at the door, he was startled to find Stick snoring in bed at midday. He was probably drunk again. He wanted to wake him up and tell him about his new pole and the big shad.

Auggie had gutted the fish in the skiff before they'd headed back. He'd lied to Auggie about how much fishing he'd done. He knew it was wrong, but, except for Moses, he'd never had a real friend.

Auggie wondered how Willie had learned to read without going to school but he didn't want to ask. He knew something bad had happened—he could see it in his eyes. As Auggie sliced the belly of the shad open, he figured he'd tell him someday. The last thing he wanted was to bust his balls. Willie was different. After two days, he could fix a pot in under three minutes. He knew about trees and trains and apples. He never complained, and he asked a lot of questions. Auggie's mother said he was anxious, like someone with a secret. Then, of course, there was the color of his skin. Mulatto meant he was half black and half white. He'd heard his mother telling Eunice Blanchard this on the phone after Auggie had punched an older boy at recess for calling Willie a pickaninny. If he'd learned anything from his father's rocks, it was that they all had a story. Where they came from explained how they looked, and if you didn't know that, you didn't know much. He didn't know how Willie had lived or what he'd done, but he liked him all the same. The night Willie had slept over he'd talked in his sleep, and though he couldn't make out the words, it sounded like he was in trouble, as if he'd been calling for help.

He was glad the shad bit Willie's lure first. They were hard to come by lately. Between the dams and the roads they'd gotten mired in the muck and couldn't reach the place they'd come from. He knew Willie had a home somewhere and when his fish hit the bottom of the skiff he promised himself that, someday, he'd help him get there.

Stick heard the refrigerator door close. The shack smelled of raw fish and gasoline.

"How'd it go out there?" He sounded sleepy.

"Good. Got me a shad." Willie tried with all his might to suppress his enthusiasm as he stood at the sink, washing his hands.

"A shad! Way ta go, Willie! That pole work out?"

Willie dried his hands. He sounded pretty good. Maybe he hadn't been so drunk after all. He hadn't had much at dinner. Maybe the roof had worn him out or the trip to Reedsville with Zach.

"Aw, man, Stick, it's the greatest pole that ever was! And that Sonar just makes 'em crazy—I was gettin' bites all morning like they was goin' nuts or somethin' and Auggie said he never saw nothin' like it. I almost died when the shad hit! Bent my pole in half and I thought, oh, sweet Jesus, hang on to that pole, man, and I just kept on him, you know, and Auggie kept sayin', 'Go slow,' and then he'd shout, 'Reel him in! Reel him in!' And all of a sudden he's floppin' 'round my feet and Auggie gives me a big ole wrench and I let him have it!"

"Ain't that somethin'." Stick half smiled, before his face became more serious.

"It's the first time I ever got one so big, Stick! It was like I always thought it would be 'cuz they really fight you like they mean it and you gotta hold on or otherwise after all that fightin', you'll just lose 'em."

"Good feelin', ain't it?"

"Let me show him to you!" Willie darted over to the fridge.

"Clean it all out?" Stick propped himself up.

"Auggie did it! I was too excited!" He opened the door. "Auggie said it was too early for the eggs."

When Stick saw the fish, he approached the table. It was an eighteen-inch female. "She's a monster, Willie," he agreed, admiring the fish. "How long it take to get her in?"

" 'Bout . . . don't know, really, seemed like forever. Kept bendin' my pole. Auggie said that line you got was real good."

"Well, she's a beauty, that's for sure! Wish we could do something special with it," Stick said as he remembered the boy's situation.

Willie was still too excited to pick up on the tone of Stick's voice. "Auggie said they got thirty thousand eggs in 'em sometimes before they find a place with fresh water in the spring to dump 'em."

"Used to get up to the Blue Ridge," Stick said, his eye on the fish. The greenish-blue luster of its back had faded but the sides were still streaked with silver. "We can cook it up tonight. Best get it back in the fridge, though." He moved to his bed and sat down. "Did you salt the water for the ride home?"

"Yeah, Auggie thought a that, too." As Willie wrapped the shad in newspaper before returning it to the fridge, he noticed Stick's knapsack was out and his dictionary wasn't on the chair.

"I split oak for the Wakefield plank in '49."

Willie closed the door of the fridge and plopped himself down in the empty chair next to Stick's bed.

"Pretty down there," Stick went on, mostly to himself. "Got a big ole swamp and everything. Worked some cypress and punched a few roads into Lake Drummond before a big fire broke out."

"What kinda fire?"

"Buncha maples and then all the dry stuff underneath."

"Thought a swamp was wet."

"They get dry sometimes and the roads don't help. Not much a anything they do down there's good for the swamp. Mostly just about the money, but, you know, 'bout the same wherever you go these days . . . " Stick trailed off, remembering what they needed to talk about.

Willie could tell he had something on his mind.

"Everybody's workin' an angle," Stick said, seeing that he finally had the boy's full attention.

"Why you lookin' at me like that?" Willie wiggled in his chair.

"We need to talk." He stood up and closed the front door.

When the latch caught, Willie's heart stopped. Whatever luck he'd had that day was about to run out. Stick leaned back against the door and folded his arms. "Hilda's man in Richmond says they got another warrant out . . . " He knitted his brow. " . . . an' this time it ain't about being a person of interest."

"What's it 'bout?" Willie's head was spinning as Stick's eyes pierced his.

"'Bout you bein' a suspect."

It took a moment. "Suspect?"

"'Bout you killin' your ole man."

Willie swallowed hard and shook his head, trying to collect himself. "But I didn't *do* nothin', Stick! They ain't right about that," he pleaded, looking up at him.

"Says they may have prints on a piece of glass."

Leaning forward in the chair, Willie folded his arms tightly together and stared at the floor.

"Says people saw you runnin'. One in particular said she'd testify she saw you runnin' out of the house when it was burnin'."

Willie looked at Stick in disbelief. "But I didn't—"

"I think you ain't been back 'cuz maybe you done it!" Stick interrupted, pointing a finger at the boy. He could see that he was losing it.

"But that ain't what happened!" Willie screamed, leaping up out of his chair.

Before Stick could reply, the mail boat's horn sounded from Oyster Creek. With Christmas on the way, the hold would be full. He didn't think much of Christmas, or of telling Willie about his momma. That could wait, but he needed to know about the fire. Hilda had already made up her mind and he was the boy's last chance. Banging his heel against the door, he strode over to the table and sat on it.

"We been down this road, Willie, an' I wanna believe you, son, but somethin' ain't right here with this whole thing, 'cuz somebody did it, and if it wasn't you, then who the hell was it?" Willie's expression hadn't changed, but tears streamed down his face. "Can't help you till I know. An' this would be the time."

Willie's chest heaved. A few tears sprinkled the floor as he wiped his face and collected himself. He didn't think Stick would believe him, but he'd try to explain it again. Whatever had happened, he had to put it right and not just with Stick. He couldn't live his life always looking around to see if someone was after him. He didn't want to be like his momma was, always rewriting the past.

Willie dried his face with his sleeve and took a final deep breath. He'd tell Stick everything he knew and it would be exactly how he remembered it, leaving nothing out. This time, he'd tell him about the hand that took the glass with the Beautiful Lady from his and sent it crashing against his father's face.

Chapter Thirty-six

Bob Novack stood on the dock and looked up at the bow of the mail boat as it pulled in. After his brother had put in a call to Charlottesville, everything had dropped quickly into place. He'd meet the sheriff and run him over to the shack. Once the boy was caught, the reward would come from Richmond and he and his brother would split it, however much it was. Like their parents before them, the Novack brothers were about supply and demand, at the best price, and in cash.

Auggie saw the badge under Sheriff Sheffield's jacket at the gas dock while he was buying a Coke. If Bob Novack was involved, it wasn't good. Moving under the gangplank, he loosened the line of his pole and dropped a lure over the edge of the dock, pretending to fish.

"Bob Novack?" the big man asked, stepping onto the dock and extending his hand.

"Be me." He shook his hand. "You ready?"

The big man looked around to see if anyone was listening before he spoke. "Like to see where we are first, Mr. Novack, before we move in," he said, leaning his head closer.

"Call me Bob, Sheriff. We can go to my office if you'd like. It's just up the street here."

"That'd be fine, Bob. Thank you." He lowered his voice even more. "Where's the boy?"

Bob Novack looked across towards Willie and Stick's shack and nodded with his head.

"Ten shacks out on the left. Skiff's out front and so's the one for the guy he's traveling with."

"Stick Watson?"

"Be him. Tall fella, dark hair, mid-fifties?"

"Be 'bout right," the sheriff confirmed. "Come on," he directed, taking Bob by the elbow, "let's get a move on."

Stick listened patiently as Willie told the same story, but this time adding in something about someone standing behind him with a hand on the glass candle. "Whose hand was it?" Stick crossed his arms again, and leaned his shoulder against the wall with a sour look.

"I don't know. I was in the bathtub and then it came to me like . . . " he stopped.

"Like what?" Stick asked, irritated.

Willie looked up at him with an utterly hopeless expression. "Like it was real."

"So who the fuck was it?"

"I don't know. I wish I did, but I don't," he pleaded.

"Wasn't your momma?"

"She ain't big like that."

"Wasn't that ole Negro?"

"Moses?" Willie's eyes softened as he thought about it.

"Well, shit, then . . . who was it, Willie?! 'Cuz they're sayin' it was *you!*" He pointed his finger at the boy again. "An' till you come up with someone, it's stayin' that way *till they fry your ass! Ain't gonna be the fella with the big hand!"*

When he heard the engine of Salty's boat, Stick slid off the table. "What's he doin' here?"

"Stick." Willie stood up. "I didn't do it," he barely whispered.

"That's what you keep tellin' me, boy," Stick said quickly, moving towards the window. "But I swear to God—"

The door burst open so fast it hit the wall, and when Auggie rushed in, pale and breathless, Stick knew immediately.

"Gotta go!" Auggie blurted out, frantically waving his arms like a madman. *"Sheriff's here, Willie! Grab your money and get on the boat!"*

CHAPTER THIRTY-SEVEN

From his window Moses listened to the last bell echo off the Rotunda roof and fade away. The wind was up today, carrying the sound quickly away and ridding the trees of their leaves once and for all. Winter would be hard this year; he could feel it in his bones. He didn't mind the cold so much as he minded the icy streets.

In winter the bell rang slow and the rope was tight, but the sound was sharper.

The clouds had told him that this would be his last December. He had bells to ring for a winter wedding, and he suspected a pregnant bride. He'd seen more than a man was meant to see. Even that "other place" his momma had told him of in the Bible, he'd had glimpses of when the sky was just so. He had no fear of what awaited him. He'd see his momma again and his daddy, he thought, as he smiled in contemplation. He might even get himself a new coat out of the deal.

Chapter Thirty-eight

From the hatch of Salty's boat, Willie watched Tangier disappear in the distance. He hadn't had time to think in the rush of leaving. Stick had thrown him his knapsack, and they were in the boat and away. As they hugged the docks on their way out, the mail boat passed through the port window. In a matter of minutes Sheriff Sheffield would know they'd run and be on their tail. Salty would be pissed when he found out that his boat was gone, but his flathead V8 would get them to Deep Creek on the western side of the Outer Banks in under an hour, and after that, they were on their own.

Stick lay on the hard bunk with his head against his knapsack. While the boy had been fishing, he'd packed their things. He'd spent the night with Hilda trying to make up his mind, but by morning he was no closer to a decision. It wasn't until he'd tied up his boots later that day that he knew he couldn't leave the boy. There was too much blood between them now.

Willie turned back from the open hatch. A bitter feeling came over him with the knowledge that they were running away again. Saying goodbye to Auggie would just about kill him. They'd never fish or fix pots or spend the night together again. He'd never get to ask Miss Riser questions about his books. Or smell Hilda's sweater.

"You sure 'bout this?" Willie asked, as the boat turned slightly.

Stick looked out to get his bearings. "Well . . . " He sat up. " . . . 'bout time we got outta there."

Willie was relieved to be with him, but afraid of what would happen. If they were after him, they'd be after Stick. "Ain't you gonna miss her?" he asked.

Stick stood up. For a fourteen-year-old boy, Willie had a way of getting to it. "Put the trap money in them books a yours. Be a load to carry."

"Where we goin'?" he asked tentatively.

"Auggie!" Stick yelled through the hatch.

"What?" he answered over the engine roar.

Stick checked a line of clouds over the hatch ladder. *"We all right?"*

The bay was flat. They'd need a ride down Route 316 to the dock at Cape Charles. He'd been that way a time or two, and with a little luck, it would still be dark.

"Thirty minutes!" Auggie shouted, steering south.

Sheriff Sheffield stood in the empty shack with his gun drawn and shook his head.

"Sonovabitch!" Bob Novack exclaimed, slamming his hand against the open door.

This would not sit well in Richmond. It had been too long a trip from Charlottesville to come up empty-handed. He could tell by some clothes and a knife on the floor that they'd left in a hurry. As he walked around, two other things got his attention: The knapsacks they'd been seen with were gone and the shack smelled of fish. He'd make some calls. It was a big bay and it would be dark in four hours. The mail boat needed to be searched before it left, whether they were on it or not.

For some time, Hilda stood at her bedroom window looking down onto the front yard. It had set her back when Eunice Blanchard called. She'd hoped Stick had turned a corner with the boy, but when she hung up she remembered that, in the morning, his eyes had looked small and far away. It wasn't the first time he'd left. But this time, he wouldn't be back. It would hurt for a while, but life would go on. She'd remember what she liked about him and how it felt when he touched her. That's what she'd miss the most.

The window was open and she felt the wind pick up. It would be dark in a few hours. She was low on firewood and in a year or so the roof would need more work. The Chesapeake was hard on things. Something familiar moved behind the gate. There were always reminders, she thought. For the holidays, she'd get a juniper off the back of Rusty Spiedel's farm and place a good-sized mackerel out for Bobbie Tyler's cat on her mother's finest china.

CHAPTER THIRTY-NINE

As the chop picked up, Auggie gripped the wheel and noticed a red metal roof off the port bow. The water would muddy up soon. He'd dropped liquor in a shack on Russell Island with Zach a year or so earlier. For the Outer Banks, it was a good place to put in—especially if you wanted to keep it quiet. Auggie knew that Salty would be upset, but by the time he'd chewed him out, Stick and Willie would be long gone. He wouldn't ask them where they were going. It would be one less thing to have to lie about. He didn't care if the sheriff grilled him. Life wasn't always about being straight.

As the boat slowed to a crawl, banks of marsh and spartina drew closer. Stick poked his head out of the hatch. The place Auggie had in mind was called Mink Creek. There'd be just enough water and the chart showed a launch. With a little luck they'd catch a ride south to the ferry, but the Outer Banks was flush with mischief and they'd need to move quickly. One false move and they were cooked.

Willie stared uneasily at his hands. Leaving felt like dying, he thought. He wasn't prepared to say goodbye to Auggie, and to all that he'd miss on Tangier: the open sky, the water's reflection over his bed in the morning, the wind against his face, and the way that nothing else mattered when he steered his skiff through the bay towards Oyster Creek. Strapping on his knapsack to climb the ladder, his eyes filled with sadness. He'd never caught a big fish. He'd never had a friend his age, except for Rebecca, but that hadn't lasted. Or maybe it had, if friendship didn't die when you left someone behind. Moses had said friendship was better than gold, " 'cuz you could take it to heaven." Clearing the hatch and looking out towards a disappearing Chesapeake, he hoped he had a lot of living to do before he found out.

When the Mink Road launch appeared dead ahead, Auggie cut the engine and swung the stern around. The tide was up enough to keep the propeller from hitting, but hearing Salty's instructions in his head, he raced aft for a pike pole to guide the stern. Standing anxiously under the cabin top, Stick and Willie watched the boy's progress as the water turned to glass. Well into the creek, surrounded by thick marsh, the boat backed easily towards shore, where they'd say their goodbyes and jump. When Auggie got home, there'd be hell to pay for what he'd done. If his story had holes, they'd work on his mother until he talked. He'd never been in the business of lying, but for Willie and Stick, he might have to start. Saying goodbye would be tough, but he'd manage. He'd build a boat and mend his own pots and someday, like his father had said, he'd understand that a life worth working for was a life worth living.

As Willie gave him one last look, Auggie leaned against the pole and held the stern, waiting for him to jump. He wouldn't let go long enough to put his arms around him or do anything stupid like that. On an island people came and went. That's just the way it was.

"I'll always remember what you done, Aug," Willie struggled.

"It's nothing. I'm not goin' anywhere. And hang on to your pole this time," Auggie's voice cracked.

Willie held his fishing pole tightly. Auggie had grabbed it off the porch as he'd dashed towards the waiting boat.

"Got your Sonar?" Stick put his hand on his back.

"I got it." Willie saw the launch and bent his knees, preparing to jump.

The sooner they got it over with, the better, Auggie thought. After checking the end of his pole through the murky water, he smiled at Willie, who was standing on the stern. "Next time I see you, you'll be flyin' an airplane!"

"And you'll be a great waterman." Willie grinned.

"Come on, Willie—this boat's gotta git," Stick ordered.

When Willie's boots hit the launch, a small wave slapped against the stern. Stepping back, he made room for Stick.

"Auggie?" Stick prepared to jump at the transom as Auggie strained at the pole.

"Sir?"

"Let the pole loose and say goodbye proper. You done a fine thing helpin' us out."

"It's nothing, Stick. Just wish—"

"I put some gas money down below," Stick interjected. Pulling the pole off the launch, Auggie dropped it on the deck and faced Stick. "You better have a story for the sheriff," Stick warned. "And it better be good."

"Don't worry 'bout me. I'll be fine." Auggie felt the bow swing.

"Well . . . " Stick adjusted his knapsack. " . . . I got your story, Auggie."

"Sir?" Auggie was confused.

Stick spoke calmly. "You tell him I put a knife to your throat and *made* you do it."

"Naw, Stick, I can't say that about you . . . "

"And when you tried to turn around . . . " Leaning back, Stick lowered his right shoulder and made a fist. " . . . I knocked your lights out."

Stick's punch sent Auggie flying backwards against the gunnels and a split second later his body dropped to the deck.

"*Stick?!*" Willie screamed in shock, racing towards the boat. "*What'd you do that for? You outta your head?!"*

With his hands, Stick gently examined Auggie's face to make sure he was all right. It'd felt about right when he connected. He'd be awake in a minute or so. Most important, his right eye would close before he got back to Tangier.

As the boat shifted away from the launch, Willie peered down at Auggie. *"Why'd you hit 'im like that?!"*

When Stick landed, the water was knee deep. He'd explain once the boy calmed down. Drifting away, the boat would nudge the marsh until he woke up. There was plenty of light to get back and the wind would drop at sunset. Auggie had gone the distance. No matter how pissed Salty would be about him having taken his boat, Stick knew the old man would be proud of what he'd done. He wouldn't show it at first, he figured. But when things died down, he'd pack a jar of peanut butter with saltines and show the kid his secret spot for blues three miles north of Tangier on the leeward side of Fishbone Island.

Sheriff Sheffield stood at Hilda's open gate and whistled. She'd given him a room downstairs for the night and let him use the phone. At this point, there wasn't much he didn't know about Stick and the boy. He'd had plenty of time to ask around. Salty's boat may have gone west to the mainland, a shorter distance east to the Outer Banks, or north into Maryland. The time it returned would tell him more about the distance than about the direction. For that he'd need the young captain and his mother. He had cops spread out everywhere. The older guy was pretty sharp, but all things wind down, he reminded himself, and Stick Watson's day would come. It always did.

It was getting dark. Off the gas dock the sheriff saw a light-blue workboat pulling into Salty's slip.

"Be the one," Hilda said from an upstairs window.

He'd go down and work the boy some. He'd go easy at first, but either way it wouldn't take long. After forty-plus years he'd finally figured it out. Cops were like the people they chased.

CHAPTER FORTY

Moses Henry didn't let dying get in the way of Christmas. He was down to ninety pounds, but it was just enough to get the job done. On Christmas Eve, as he had done unfailingly for fifty-three years, he peeled off his coat and rang with all his might. He was tired and he tasted blood from time to time, but these things didn't much cross his mind. He'd lived a good while longer than most, but he was ready whenever the Lord saw fit to take him. He'd told Sadie he'd been ready ever since the boy left. He'd stopped dreaming—as if the inside of his mind had gone dark. He'd told her about his three wives, his thirty-seven grandchildren, and how, the day Monticello had changed hands, he was sold to Colonel Peter Carr. On their last visit, he'd kissed her gently on the cheek, and in the morning she was dead.

As the rope fell away, Moses listened to the snowflakes. His momma said being alive was all the truth you needed and Moses considered himself lucky when it came to the life that he had had. As he shuffled home just after midnight, a few frosted hats tipped kindly as he passed.

CHAPTER FORTY-ONE

Oscar Black's five-ton Lokie needed oil every morning. The Great Dismal Swamp chewed up a lot of things and a thirty-six-inch-gauge Plymouth locomotive was just one of them. January had been cold and he was up to his ears in work. For a locomotive there was none better, but after twenty years on eight miles of track, it was just a matter of time before he'd break it down for parts, or park it at his sawmill on U.S. Highway 158. It took patience and grit to work the swamp and Oscar had done the best he could. Unlike most Maroons he'd stayed and made a way of it. His grandfather, Osman Black, had paid for his freedom twice. "Keep yo' head 'bove water an' you be all right," he'd repeated to Oscar over and over until he died. For thousands of Negroes the swamp was a window to the world. But it took guts. They found dry spots for corn, and hogs, and fowl beside shacks made of juniper poles with sawdust floors and chimneys daubed with mud. They fought yellow flies, mosquitoes, and snakes. And they died swamp deaths, their bodies deep in soil or faceup in pocosin. The swamps of Virginia and North Carolina were littered with their bones, like shells on a beach, as one life ended and another began.

When the Lokie fired up, Oscar laughed. A stack of bald cypress would make it back to the yard by lunch. Hiring another man had been a good move. The extra time at home made his wife, Ethel, happy and the Blacks had done pretty well. Most Maroons were too busy making a living to have much fun. In the swamp, it was more about hanging on than letting go.

When the train pulled out, a startled flock of blackbirds jettisoned sideways from a stand of inkberry and disappeared. As the locomotive gathered speed, dirty black smoke erupted from the stack. Lifting his nose into the air, Oscar inhaled. He enjoyed winter most of all—the moist, flat air, the stillness, and the long views. But he especially loved the dances.

For a fat man Oscar Black could cut a rug. At a recent juke joint contest outside Sunbury, Ethel had hung on for dear life as he'd carried them to victory and won a bottle of pink champagne. While the crowd roared, his body moved as bodies were meant to, and Ethel loved him for it. On the drive home, Oscar gave her a sheepish grin and winked. "Nothin' to it, baby. Jus' clownin' 'round."

Stick had heard about the storm during lunch. By four o'clock, heavy snowflakes had collected on the Black Lumber Company roof, followed by a hollow silence. With a system drifting south through the Chesapeake, it would reach the swamp soon. Snow was rare in Camden and Pasquotank County, but when it fell, time stood still.

When the last shingle cleared, he'd close the big sliding doors and lock up for the night. On Monday the workers would be back. It had been a long week and he was ready for a drink. Oscar had given him some work gloves for the yard, but they only got in the way. Being cold was better than wearing mitts, and on Saturday nights, being drunk was better than being sober.

The house would be hard to find in the snow. The swamp was full of ditches, bogs, and estuaries. The flashlight might help, but his sack was heavy with bourbon and potatoes, and a jar of Ethel's apple butter. Upstream from a landing, he stopped midway across a steel roller bridge and shined a beam of snowy light into the canal. Extinguishing each flake, the water appeared lifeless and dark, as if it were connected to another world. As he reached into his sack for the bourbon, snowflakes tickled his cheeks. It wasn't far now. He'd need a better coat and a new pair of boots. After a month at the mill there was money for clothes and a drive to Sunbury for liquor. On his off-hours he'd fix the house and keep things quiet. That was the deal.

Rounding a line of juniper, he saw a lantern in the kitchen window against updrafts of swirling snow, and smelled smoke from the chimney. Finding Oscar Black again had been a kind of miracle. Crystal-Ann would have hated the swamp. It was a dark place. But he'd had no choice. There was plenty of firewood and he'd fish the canal, and keep his eye out for black bears.

At the window, Willie waved. Leaving Tangier had been hard for both of them. He'd settled in for the time being and was at peace with things, but the boy needed a real home. Life was hard enough.

Stick crouched down and scooped up a handful of fluffy, dry snow. Bounding out the front door, Willie ran towards him in the snow-lit night, before dropping to his knees and forming his arsenal. Within a half minute, their volleys were flying, neither one showing any mercy. As snowballs buffeted Willie's face and chest, he shot back in the general direction from which he'd been hit, until, empty-handed and spent, he charged. Crashing to the ground, they tumbled over in each other's arms, misty waves of snow enveloping them until they rolled against a large maple trunk and stopped. Disentangling from each other, both were wet with snow, and as they rose, Willie shivered from the snow under his pants and shirt.

"Goin' to show you somethin'," Stick said, taking a few steps, then lying down on his back on a clean patch of snow and moving his legs apart and his arms up and down.

"Huh?" Willie scrunched his face. He thought Stick had lost his mind, until he saw the impression. It looked like an angel. "Look at that!" he said, amazed.

Stick laughed and took a sip from his bottle. "My ole man taught me that." Out of breath, he squinted at what he'd made.

Willie didn't think Stick belived in angels, but what mattered most was the part about his daddy. Willie felt the snow sticking to his hair. "You miss him sometimes?"

Putting the bottle away, Stick lifted the sack up over his shoulder. It was a stupid thing to do, speaking about his father like that, especially after all the boy had been through. "Come on, man." He placed his hand on Willie's shoulder, turning him towards the house. "You got spuds to peel."

By the time Willie had fallen asleep in his room above the kitchen stove, Stick was too drunk to make much sense even to himself. He and Willie had cleaned and painted the place until it felt more like a house. The Blacks were putting their necks on the line and he was grateful. If they lay low for a while, they might be able to shake the sheriff, but he wasn't sure. He'd kept the news about Willie's momma to himself. It wouldn't do the boy any good to know.

In 1952, Oscar Black had bought the two-story frame house from Demarcus Cooke, owner of the Dismal Swamp General Store, in exchange for two loads of cypress. Built for a canal supervisor in 1935, it had been empty since the winter of 1950. Like most structures in the swamp, it was missing a foundation and had fed some termites over the years, but the floor and ceiling beams were essentially solid and the land was dry. Stick had made it clear to Oscar that he would spend his weekends fixing up the house, mending what he could, and burning for heat what he couldn't. As both he and Willie worked throughout the winter, coffee cans filled with hinges, rusty nails, and screws collected in the downstairs hallway, with various-sized piles of discarded lumber outside. In March, after the windows were fixed, they pointed the brick.

In the spring, one hundred thousand acres flushed with life as red maple, tupelo, sweet gum, and tulip trees leafed and budded around the rejuvenated house. Beyond a spreading sweet pepperbush, yellow-green warblers flitted about from tree to tree looking for bugs. Some birds were brilliant with flecks of red and black; others were mottled and brown. They'd arrived the night before on the heels of departing robins, blackbirds, and swans.

Staring through the back screen door into a cascade of warm sunlight, Willie listened to the whistles, tweets, and caws. Stick would take him fishing on Sunday, and the week after they'd string out a garden and go to work. He was tired of hiding. Stepping outside, he remembered what Moses had said about his apartment door: "Git me where I gots to go."

He'd keep an eye out for dwarf trillium. Oscar said it bloomed for two weeks in March and drinking its leaves in hot water was good defense against selfishness and "certain personal desires," as Oscar had described them. Willie had an idea what some of them might be. A compress of pine needles on the temple was good for easing guilt and the smoke from dried fireweed assuaged a person's anger. Oscar talked like Sister Mo sometimes. He said the swamp gave you everything you needed, if you only knew where to look for it.

On weekdays Willie fished the ditch alone for speckles, yellow perch, and flyer sunfish. The bullheads were good for eating, but when he saw what they looked like, he prayed he'd never catch one again. Stick had found him lighter lures that gave the crappies and sunfish a run for their money, but he missed the skiff and the smell of an open bay. His first week in the swamp he'd cried into his dirty pillow. Despite its improvements, the house still gave him the creeps, and the trees were shadowy with the ghosts of runaway slaves. The air outside smelled rank and dead. Stick said the swamp was like a tea bag and everything that ran through it turned brown. He said its water made the moonshine look like bourbon. He'd warned him about the cottonmouths. The full-grown snakes were mostly dark. The younger ones had yellow on the tips of their tails and something between their eyes and nose that detected heat. He said non-poisonous snakes had round eyes and poisonous snakes had eyes like a cat.

Gutting his first sunfish, Willie saw that the swamp was more alive than dead, as great blue herons and kingfishers soared above ditches littered with stinkpots. Oak toads and water dogs hid within the embankments of orchids, yellow jasmine, and cinnamon ferns. One day, with the fruits of pawpaw, black gum, and wild grapes dangling overhead, Willie chewed on a stem of smartweed as an otter family drifted feet-first and upside down before him, waving with their paws as they passed, heading home.

One morning a red fox approached him on the steel roller bridge while he was fishing. When his pole moved, it skittered away in the direction from which it had come. Oscar said it was a good sign when you saw a fox, but only if it ran the other way. When a juvenile barred owl fell to the ground beside the outhouse, he did his business and backed quietly away. As bats swooped down almost touching his head along a ditch edge at sunset, he tried with all his might to sit still. When skunks and possums pilfered the compost of eggshells and peach pits he gathered up the mess and piled it back again with shovelfuls of dirt. The swamp was anything but dead. He'd learned to take it in as if it were a part of him somehow, as if it would not do him harm.

As the summer heat swelled, days came and went indiscriminately until the bass stopped biting and a mound of sweet corn was piled on the kitchen floor. One afternoon a bobcat crossed the old railroad bed half a mile south. It had been an active summer, Oscar said. Bobcats meant redemption, minks gave you luck, and yellow-bellied turtles made a fine soup.

In the chimney, Willie found a tiny nest at the bottom of the flue. Holding it up in his big rough hand, Oscar cocked his head to one side and chuckled.

"What kinda bird is it?" Willie asked quietly.

"Hummin'bird, man. Them's horse hairs, see dat." He lowered it down for the boy to get a better look. "Ain't dat sweet?"

"How they do that?"

Oscar liked Willie's inquisitive nature. He'd heard the boy was a reader.

"Pull 'em off a fence post where dey rubs. Be duh mane or be duh tail— dem smart little fellas, you know?" He dropped the nest gently back into Willie's hand. "Ain't nothin' wrong wit' bein' small, Willie!" he declared. "Sometimes ain't nothin' but good!"

Stick never explained how he'd come to know Oscar. "We go back," was all he'd said.

Willie was used to his evasiveness. Like when he'd ask him about being in the army. He'd pick up a name or a place when Stick called out in his sleep or in a drunken stupor. One night, he shook his head from side to side wildly and whispered the name of a bank. Another time, he called out for a man named Wilkens.

"*Leave it, man, fuck!*" he'd shouted, his body writhing in sweat.

In the morning Willie knew better than to ask questions. That's how it worked. Answers came in their own good time, and you didn't get them any faster by asking. Willie saw the good in Stick, but there were times, when his drinking got bad, when he didn't seem to give a shit. He was like his momma that way. The bad stuff about people could fool you, he had come to learn. And sometimes, the hardest part was remembering the good.

CHAPTER FORTY-TWO

By late winter, Sheriff Sheffield was stumped. Stick had called Hilda on her birthday from a phone at the mill. Her voice was clipped and remote and he knew at once she was pissed. Auggie was fine, but Peggy Crockett had died in June after asking Salty to feed her to the killifish. The blues were still down. She drew things out before giving him what he really needed to know. According to D.K. Wells, the boy's trail had gone cold.

She didn't bother asking him where he was calling from. Eunice Blanchard was on the line.

"You good?" he asked uncomfortably.

"Right as rain, Stick," she said flatly, before hanging up.

Spring and summer turned to fall. On a Sunday two weeks before Christmas the rains came. Stick thought the paint was a waste of money, but Oscar insisted. He said a house with no paint was like a snake with no skin—and it helped with the termites. It had taken a season to finish, but when it was done, they were proud to look upon it. Oscar had been right.

Seated on a large maple stump inside a patched-up woodshed, Stick and Willie split a cup of Ethel's apple cider and stared out into the rain. At fifteen, Willie had learned to play a fish and his gardening and carpentry skills had improved considerably. Maybe it was time to move on. He needed schooling and friends his own age. They talked about it sometimes. Tangier was ancient history. They weren't out of the woods entirely, but when you got right down to it, things were looking up if they'd survived this long.

"Ain't as good as the Pettits', is it?" Stick passed him the cider cup.

He liked Stick when he was sober. He took a sip and offered it back.

"Keep it." Stick knocked his boots together to loosen the mud.

"Ain't as sweet," Willie agreed, staring into the cloudy liquid. "Figure they done their applin' by now?" He imagined an empty bunkhouse.

"More a less . . . " Stick looked up at the sky over their house. "Depends."

"On what?"

"Frost, mostly." He felt a chill in the air. "Heatin' some gumbo inside." He rose from the stump and stepped out into the rain. "Come on an' tell me 'bout that big fish you've been readin' about."

Willie drained his cider and ran into the house. He was happy to explain *Moby Dick* to someone. Reading was a private thing, but this had been a long, hard book filled with lots of new words. Sometimes he used Stick's dictionary to figure them out. Some parts he'd read over and over again until things made sense. The story had passages like his momma's Bible and sometimes he could feel the words before he understood them in his head. He hadn't read that many books, but what he had read made him wonder if most stories, except for the names and the places, were pretty much the same. While the rice simmered, Willie sat near the kitchen stove describing Ishmael's arrival on a cold and gloomy December night at the Spouter Inn in New Bedford, Massachusetts. He described his yearning for adventure and a heavily tattooed Polynesian harpooner named Queequeg. There were a lot of things that Willie didn't know about Stick. But it didn't matter so much anymore because, like Ishmael and Queequeg, they were in the same boat.

In the morning Stick loaded cypress logs onto trucks with Oscar's new forklift. The clutch was tight, but it handled well, and when a cold rain kicked in, he appreciated the way it kept him dry. Oscar was pretty sharp and, even with the cypress half-gone, the Chesapeake construction business was booming, not to mention what had happened to the paulownia market. Oscar had planted ten acres of it off Lake Drummond after the war. They'd said he was nuts to plant a tree that grew on the side of a road, but returning soldiers had told him that the Japanese used it to make sandals and a broker in Norfolk said they paid cash. Oscar still remembered his first pair of leather shoes and how proud they'd made him feel. And the tree grew quick.

Stick liked the way Oscar wrapped his head around something and stuck with it. Most men were all talk. But like his dancing, when Oscar made a move, it was usually a good one. They'd spilled some blood together and dodged a bullet or two; he wasn't proud of that. But they'd stayed free of most of the bullshit and done all right. During a botched bank robbery in Portland, Maine, a shot had been fired and, in the brief exchange, Oscar had been grazed by the bullet. In the confusion that followed, an innocent man was killed entering the bank on his way to work. Neither Stick nor Oscar had pulled the trigger—one of their partners had—but they'd been along for the ride, which was just as bad.

Stick had bandaged Oscar and tossed him on a train to Massachusetts. "Get back and start somethin'," he told him. "And don't breathe a word of this shit or I'll cut your throat."

Ten years later on a Saturday night he heard about the swamp mill from a drummer named Zeebo Finch out of Merigold, Mississippi. He'd played a juke joint near the Dismal called the Spunkey Monkey with Sonny Boy Williamson. When Stick mentioned Oscar's name, Zeebo's eyes lit up like the skies on the Fourth of July.

"Dat big nigger wid duh mill?!" he squealed. *"Yo' Mista Black kin shake 'iz money make-ah!"*

As Willie rode in the back of Oscar's Lokie late in December, a thousand flashes of white lifted off a frosted field in the Green Sea east of Route 17.

"Snow geese!" Oscar shouted, pointing over the engine. *"Don' like snow!"* he added, shaking his head, lowering his hand to the throttle. Screaming down the Great Dismal tracks, holding onto Oscar's enormous arm, Willie watched the cold, glittering sky and understood that he'd come to the right place after all. Every place had something good about it, he realized, and it didn't matter what you called it.

Stick had loaded the last truck with pine and hemlock by sundown.

"Buy you dinner?" Oscar offered, watching him drop from his seat onto the ground.

"Sold," Stick moaned, stretching his legs and letting his head fall back against his shoulders.

"Coulda waited on some a dem loads till Friday, man." Oscar shook his head and grinned.

"Well . . . " Stick straightened up. "I figured we'd be on our way to Mexico by then."

Oscar slapped him on the back. "Shit, man, can't lose you now'z I found you!"

Stick gave Oscar a hard look. He liked the situation with the boy. But he was a long way from settling down. "Appreciate the meal, Oscar," he said, hiding the forklift key under the seat.

"Got it comin', Stick. I been meanin' to ask, but ain't had duh time," Oscar replied, heading towards the office. "Let me tell duh wife."

"Need to wash up and then get the boy," Stick called back.

Ethel Black had hounded Oscar about the boy. She wanted him in school and in church, but Oscar knew Stick well enough to know that Ethel was going to lose on both counts. And then there was Oscar. He didn't care much for school, and less for church.

"Ain't nothin' dat boy ain't gittin' from dem books—an' don't git me goin' on Beulah Baptist, 'cuz we been down dat road. God ain't talkin' if you ain't listenin'—an' most of dem people too damn busy preachin' t' hear what he got to say. Take duh God right outta livin', duh way I feel 'bout it!"

Jimmy C.'s turn-of-the-century sharecropper's shack was in a field of cotton two miles down a gravel road off Route 158. A hand-painted sign nailed to a fence post spelled out the rules:

NO BEER BOTTLES NO DROOPY JEANS
$3 AT DOOR COLD BEER MUSIC

As Willie read the sign, he felt excited. Finally, he was out in the world and free to look around.

Oscar looked up at a slender moon slicing through coal-colored clouds. "Be quiet t'night, but Lord have mercy, Willie, come Thursday, duh C Spot gets t' cookin'!"

"That the name?" Willie asked, admiring a deep red '48 Buick convertible with Florida plates parked next to Oscar's truck.

"Yeah, or 'Duh Spot,'" he said, taking in the car as well. "Heard me some tunes here, man. Had Po Man Sprat, Esby Shank, and Pinetop Perkins. One Christmas when I'ze a little thing, Pinetop paid a visit wid a cousin dat live nearby somewhere, and dis was somethin' . . . some girl cut him in d' arm duh night befo'—so he was on duh piana dat night with one hand and, *man-oh-man,* he shook duh joint! When duh sun come up, dey was carryin' people outta here!" Oscar smiled nostalgically and shook his head as he looked the place over. "Spot be fallin' down, but duh music don't quit."

While they stood in the windy driveway, white smoke shot over their heads into a nearby stand of pines. The building had more patches than windows.

"Kind of a dump, ain't it?" Willie observed, catching the smell of burning wood.

Stick and Oscar laughed as they headed towards the steps. Rusted metal panels of old roof, shards of ripped tar paper, and tattered sheets of plywood covered exterior walls from top to bottom. Off to one side a torn screen door hung four feet above ground with nothing below. Under a covered porch at the top of five sagging planks, there was a doorway next to a propped-up truck seat.

"I got no money," Willie whispered, climbing the stairs behind Stick.

"Be all right." Stick heard the faint twang of an electric guitar.

"Night's on me, Willie!" Oscar assured him, reaching the top step. "Only one thing . . . " He turned to the boy with a hard look. "Whatever you do . . . " Meeting his eyes, Willie swallowed hard as the door swung open, flooding their faces with light. " . . . don't git duh shrimp!"

When Jimmy C. saw Oscar, he cracked a smile and slid around from behind the bar. He was taller than Oscar, skinny, wore a bright orange shirt with tiny blue stars, and had a gold tooth. "O-man," Jimmy purred, slipping his long fingers into Oscar's hand.

"Jimmy." He nodded at Stick, but didn't shake his hand.

"Stick," Stick replied, noticing three scraggly men at the end of the bar. "And this here's Willie."

Willie straightened up. "Nice ta meet ya, sir."

"Call me Jimmy. Ain't seen you 'round befo'."

"Told Willie 'bout dem steaks a yours, J.C.," Oscar interrupted, changing the subject. "Stick here's my new man."

Jimmy sized up Stick. Ethel had filled him in one night when she'd called for Oscar, but after so many years in a juke joint, he could smell a situation. Oscar and Stick had something between them and the boy was another story—or at least a wrinkle in this one.

"Plop down, Willie," he said, nodding towards a row of picnic tables off the main room. "Outta shrimp, but we'll get some steaks on the grill. How 'bout a Cheerwine?"

"Don't drink, sir." Willie blushed.

Jimmy flashed his gold tooth at Oscar. The boy wasn't from Carolina. "Not a wine, Sugar Ray," he chuckled. "Looks like wine, but tastes like cherry!"

"Oh." Willie bit his lip, looking down. "Never had it."

"'Bout time you did, then. You boys come get yo'self a drink."

Willie sat at an older cedar picnic table and watched Oscar and Stick talking to the three men at the bar. The one-room shack was lit by kerosene lamps on the walls, with a bandstand, a long bar to the side, and a side room with three picnic tables. Dangling from the rafters were strands of colored Christmas lights above a floor littered with sawdust. From behind the bar Jimmy C. reappeared through an outside door in a cloud of barbeque smoke.

"What you boys want?" He opened an old fridge, casting himself in an eerie blue light.

Willie's mouth watered when he bit into his steak and Oscar moaned with appreciation as he chewed. *"Damn, J.C.!"* he shouted across the bar. *"You duh grill man!"*

As the three men at the bar hunkered down over their drinks, Jimmy C. picked up a thin red electric guitar and leaned back against the sink. Willie had never heard an electric guitar before. The clarity of it startled him at first. He stopped chewing momentarily and watched Jimmy's fingers. Depending on how they moved, the guitar responded with soft waves or edgy twangs, and when his hand came down on all the strings at once, the notes all washed together.

"Talk to me, Jimmy!" Oscar cheered, reaching for his bourbon and sitting back on the bench to listen. "Boy kin play, dis one," he muttered over the chords.

Jimmy C. had jammed with so many musicians the notes flowed like falling water, running naturally where they liked for as long as he wanted. Watching his chin drop onto his chest as he played, Willie thought about Moses and how when he rang his bell, it all looked so easy. Stick's eyes glazed over as he listened. Crystal-Ann would be feeling it about now. She'd want to dance, but he'd say no, and on her way to the dance floor solo, she'd take her shoes off and let her hair down.

Stick took it all in as he chewed. Willie's face was flush with good food and music. Maybe it was time to get him drunk or find him a woman. He'd made it with a waitress from Florida when he was fifteen.

When Stick went for drinks, Oscar slid down the bench next to Willie. He was glad the boy had come. Kids grew up quick in the swamp, and at Jimmy C.'s they grew up quicker. Once Stick said it was all right, he'd give him a pair of gloves and put him to work at the mill, or find him a job somewhere else. His kids were grown and his wife wanted the boy over for a visit. He'd kept things quiet until now, but the boy wasn't a prisoner. It wasn't right to keep him from the world. He'd tried to explain that to Stick. Living was like dancing, he told him, and once it gets going, the whole thing's got a mind of its own. Listening to Jimmy's guitar under the Christmas lights, Oscar felt a sadness wash over him. The boy's smarts would help him, but running wouldn't change the color of his skin.

"Stick tell you what happened?" Willie said frankly.

"'Bout the fire?" Oscar replied, watching Jimmy C. give something to

Stick.

Willie nodded.

"He did."

Leaning back against the bar, Stick put a harmonica to his lips and blew. A warm hum slipped between the notes quickly.

"Heavens to Betsy," Oscar whispered. Stick's harmonica followed Jimmy C.'s guitar in perfect harmony.

"Didn't know dat!" Willie gushed.

"Full a tricks!" Oscar shouted, as the three men at the bar leaned towards Stick to listen.

After a while, one of the men left his stool to join Oscar and Willie. His skin was jet black.

"Boys be jammin', Eli!" Oscar shouted as the man sat down. "Willie Graves, Elijah Franklin," he introduced them. When Elijah leaned out to shake Willie's hand, Willie did the same.

"Sweet sound for a white boy," he said, letting go of Willie's hand.

Oscar giggled. "You tell 'em, peanut man! Sweet like dem Spanish nuts you got!" Willie thought Oscar had offended Elijah, until the man's face lit up.

"AinSpanishyoudummassniggr," he slurred. *"Virginia nuts what I got!"* He screamed at the top of his lungs.

When the music stopped, Stick and Jimmy C. laughed and shook their heads. "Nice Hohner," Stick mumbled, with an empty glass.

"Good playin', man," Jimmy replied casually, pouring himself a drink. "Want some?"

"That rum?"

Jimmy filled half of Stick's glass with a thin brown liquid. Stick smiled as he took a whiff. "Plenty more where dat from!" Jimmy toasted, clinking his glass against Stick's. *"Music in duh mouth an hooch on duh house!"* he announced joyously.

The two men at the bar had worked their way north from Macon, Georgia, on peanut farms. They were skinny and worn out from years of hard work. It was their first winter in the Carolinas.

"Sparky Lamb," one said.

"Abel Jackson," said his friend.

Neither had much to say until it came to peanuts.

"Eli run a smooth operation down dere," Abel explained, after a hearty sip of hooch. "An' dat new combine beat duh rain fo' sho."

"Ain't jus duh rain wid dem nuts," Sparky added. "Also be duh cleanin' and duh shellin', too. Man says to me down in Macon, 'Be no time 'fo 'dey got sometin' dat look at duh nut an' see if it be dry . . . an' if it be wet, dey blow it on dis rubber road a some kind till it be dry.' Man told me ain't more den two men need to be 'round duh whole time do dem nuts." Sparky shook his head. "'Fo' long be no mo' a me workin' . . . 'cuz pretty soon I'ze jess be in duh way. But how dey gonna pull dem nuts widdout breakin' dem shells?" he protested.

"What I hear, dem tings can pull duh hair from a monkey's ass!" Abel declared, canvassing the men at the bar.

By the time Sparky and Abel were done with their hooch the shack was upside down.

"Dat woman was four hundred pounds ta duh day, an' I said, Miss Hattie, I said with ma last breath, or what*ever* yo' name is, *Good God, woman! Get off me 'fo' my balls turn ta grits!*"

Though he'd never been with a woman, Willie laughed just the same. It was good to let loose, even with strangers. He'd give anything to be there on a Thursday night. Oscar said sixteen would get you in, but you couldn't touch the sauce.

As things slowed down, Willie popped the question. "Hey, Jimmy? Can

I come on a Thursday sometime?"

The shack got quiet when they heard the question. Except for Stick and Willie, everyone knew the rules and it didn't matter who was asking.

Jimmy C. looked the boy over closely. He liked his spunk. He had a good head on his shoulders, but he was still short of sixteen. "How old are you, Willie?"

Willie looked at him straight-on. "Sixteen."

"Bullshit!"

"In a year."

The men watched Jimmy C.'s expression carefully.

"Want a job?" Jimmy poured himself some hooch.

Oscar's mouth dropped open.

"Sir?"

"Want a job?" he repeated.

Willie glanced at Stick. "Kinda job are we talkin' 'bout?"

"Doorman."

"Doorman?" Stick nearly choked on his hooch.

Oscar giggled nervously, glancing at Jimmy. It didn't add up.

"Simple, man." Jimmy turned to Oscar. "You remember dat fight last summer?"

"Nothin' like it, man. Dem boys was off duh planet. Big, ta boot!"

"Big, ta boot?! Shit, man—bigger den ma Buick, both of 'em! An' what happened, O-man?"

Oscar swallowed hard and put his glass down. "Kicked duh ever-lovin' shit outta each other."

"An' why dey do dat?"

"Nobody big 'nough to stop 'em. We just sat 'round an' watched." Oscar shook his head.

"Wish dey had, man." Jimmy smacked his palm with his fist. "Hate dat

314 / Peter Skinner

shit! Hookers an' drunks! Tired dat shit! Git me some smart young man ain't *nobody* gonna fuck wid! Can't fight 'im—jus' be out front lookin' sharp's all! Be ma eyes on duh outside. Watch duh wheels an' be ma man!"

"Yo' right, J.C.! Like dey home when dey see duh boy," Sparky agreed, popping off his stool.

A gust of wind knocked against the front door. "Law come an' he ain't inside—ain't doin' nothin' but sayin' hi an' sayin' bye," Jimmy clarified, watching Stick.

Stick took a long sip of hooch and let it move around inside his head before he spoke. Willie's eyes were as bright as the Christmas lights. He liked Jimmy enough to think about it. The boy would probably be safe, but it was still a swamp.

"What kinda hours we talkin' 'bout?" Stick asked.

Heavy with rain, strands of Spanish moss dangled over the road to Route 158. Oscar called it "tree hair" and said it was full of snakes, spiders, and bats. Yellow-throated warblers made their nests in it, he explained, along with owls, egrets, and mockingbirds. Maroons mixed it with mud to caulk their cabins, burned it, slept on it, and used it for mulch. His uncle dried tree hair for saddle blankets, bridles, and broken fishing nets. For months it cured on wires behind the Black family compound. They called it a moss yard.

Along Route 158, porches flickered with lanterns, leaving Willie with a sense of calm. Working Jimmy C's door would earn him a certain place in the world, or at least in the swamp. It surprised him how quickly his life was changing. Maybe that's the way it worked. Maybe things just snuck up on you like Moses said. On the final stretch of dirt road to Stick and Willie's house, a hard rain bore down upon them until it was difficult to see. But at times, through the wipers, the headlights stood still long enough to recognize something familiar—before it passed beyond the taillights into silver sheets of rain.

CHAPTER FORTY-THREE

At the three o'clock ring the ends of Moses' fingers went numb. Captain Snyder had read to him the night before, but he'd been too tuckered out to follow much of what he was saying. The boy was old news and he'd been out of the paper for a long time. Their time together on this earth was over, but he knew in his heart that Willie was alive somewhere. It'd been a hard week for Moses and his bones ached. The Lloyd brothers closed their barbershop at lunch and paid a visit in their white barber coats and matching mustaches. They smelled of Old Spice and brought a box of red lollipops. Dr. Inge sent medicine from his drugstore to improve the circulation in his hands, and his landlord stacked white oak by the back door. But it was only a matter of time now. Many had never known a day without him, but a man could ring a bell for only so long, they figured.

"Ain't never had no enemy at dis university," he'd told Willie one day. "No, sir. If dere's finer men in duh world, I ain't seen 'em an' I ain't spectin' to."

"You like them lectures?" Willie asked.

"In duh Cabell Hall?"

"Ones you go to."

"Learn more from dem lectures den a colored man gets outta readin' and writin'," he insisted. "Be good to know duh world, Willie. Make you sit up an' listen stead a goin' off at duh mouth 'bout nothin'."

On the occasional afternoon, Moses had taken Willie with him to visit a group of students behind 45 West Grange. They were a wild but tender sort for whom he had a certain affection. Moses, in turn, reminded them of the larger world—beyond the prejudice and inheritance that had soured their faces. Lying in the grass, drinking beer, listening to an old black man, they forgot all of that.

"Hey, Moses!" one beefy boy with a guitar blurted out. "Sing me a song, man. Something pretty." Moses reached down and broke off a thick blade of grass. Placing it between his thumbs, he lifted his hands up to his mouth and closed his eyes. Like most slaves, his momma had learned to blow weeds working fields at Monticello. "Ever' grass make a differen' soun'," she'd whispered to him, molding his tiny hands around a piece, " 'cuz ever' one be different."

Despite their protests Moses would not drink. "Bell's all I need, sirs," he would say more than once.

Willie wished his momma had felt that way about something. But always in the morning her eyes were vacant, as if whatever chance she'd had of finding it had been lost forever.

In one hundred and two years Moses had slept with three women. Their names were Pearl, Nora, and Gwendolyn. They'd borne children, worked jobs, and attended to his family as most black women do. They were of similar height and complexion with stable hearts and simple minds, for which he was most grateful. And he had no doubt they were all in Heaven.

"Take some work bein' wid a girl," he confessed, walking Willie to a streetcar one day.

"Stronger den us," Moses said, stopping to reach inside his overcoat.

Feeling something in his hand, his face flushed as he opened his fingers. "But . . . dey smells good!"

Three small hairpins rested in his palm. He was so old it was hard for Willie to imagine him with a woman. On the other hand, he figured living so long didn't prevent a man from wanting one—or from missing them when they were gone.

CHAPTER FORTY-FOUR

In April fiddleheads swelled off the back steps and the swamp hummed with mischief. Stick had wanted Willie to work with Elijah planting peanuts. The owner was a fair man and he'd be less visible than he would working for Jimmy C. But the new combines had sent Abel and Sparky packing and dashed whatever hopes he'd had for the boy.

It had been a while since he'd hopped a train and the world was changing every day. A good ride would be harder to come by. As he watched the trucks pass at lunchtime, his need to go was sometimes greater than his need to stay. But they'd traveled too far together to get restless now. And if they weren't careful, their luck could change in a heartbeat.

For a buck an hour on Thursday nights, Willie watched for trouble on the Spot's front porch. By June he knew most of the names. In July he spotted a cop car with its lights out halfway down the road—the same night a drunk from Suffolk gave him two dollars to watch his Studebaker. With the door wide open he'd heard Big Joe Spears on piano, Bill Hurley on drums, and Nellie Jones on guitar. People did a lot of crazy things, he began to understand more clearly, and for all kinds of reasons. On most nights Stick kept an eye out from the bar, until he was too drunk to care. There were hookers and farmers and gamblers and priests, and a one-eyed midget named Angel. A night at Jimmy C.'s left him wired and dizzy with the sounds of saxophones, snare drums, and bottleneck guitars. Riding home in the front seat of Oscar's truck, thinking about all he'd seen was sometimes overwhelming.

"You see that man with one eye?!" he gasped, rolling down the window.

"Angel? Hard to miss him, man." Oscar chuckled.

"Thought he'd never stop screamin'! Seemed pretty nuts 'bout somethin'." Willie shook his head.

Turning the wheel, Oscar watched Stick's limp body through the rearview mirror as it lurched to one side of the bed. He was drinking more now and showing up late on Friday mornings. He'd seen it in Maine all those years ago. When he drank, he ran, and when he was sober, he worked. "Little man screams," Oscar replied, sounding tired.

By the end of August, Willie was working Wednesdays through Saturdays at Jimmy C.'s. Most times after work, someone from the mill dropped him off on their way home or Jimmy C. found him a ride back. In the boy's presence, no fights broke out and business was up.

"Got a way wid duh clientele," Jimmy C. told him one night, casing out the cars. "Dolly Ames says she's waitin' on you to grow some 'fo' she makes her move."

"Miss Ames's real sweet. Give me fifty cents comin' in," Willie said proudly.

"Don't be messin' wid no hooker, boy. Save it fo' a rainy day," Jimmy joked. "Who's drivin' dat El Dorado?"

"Never seen him before. Plates from New York. Fat man next to the Galvin brothers," Willie said, pointing through the open door.

"Well, keep an eye out, Willie," Jimmy instructed, turning on his heels and skipping down the steps.

When J.C. was gone, Willie wiped a line of sweat off his forehead. His momma had been a whore, but Miss Ames smelled so good, he sometimes thought about her in his bed at night, or early in the morning when he was still half-asleep. Soon he'd be sixteen. Stick said sixteen was old for a dog. He said the first time with a woman was something special, and that once you gave it up, you never got it back.

At age sixteen, Dorthula Ames had arrived in the swamp from Kingston, Jamaica. It had been a hard journey, with several winters in Nova Scotia and a lifetime of heartache along the way. Like most Maroons she'd lived by her wits and her faith. She'd loved men for money and prayed for understanding. But she was only human. On Dolly's first birthday, Dorthula Ames left with a white Baptist minister bound for Alabama and never returned. She believed in destiny. She liked to drink. And she was six months pregnant.

Dolly never met her brother. A cousin said he was dead, but feeling his presence from time to time, she chose to believe otherwise. He would be tall, she imagined, with a gentle face and smart-looking eyes. She searched for him in other men, but kept a wall around her heart. Like most prostitutes, she had her eye on the horizon.

Climbing the steps slowly that first night, she smelled of lilacs and Camel cigarettes. When the boy looked up, she smiled as if they'd met before. It confused him at first.

"Well, lookee here . . . " she purred in a sultry voice, lifting one hip in the air, " . . . got dem eyes dat make a big girl dream, baby."

Dropping his head, Willie was wholly unsuccessful in suppressing his gratified expression.

"Name's Dolly," she said confidently, reaching into her purse.

Willie raised his eyebrows. "I'll keep an eye on that car a yours, ma'am," he assured her, nodding towards her car, changing the subject.

"You workin' here?" Dolly watched his eyes scan the parking lot.

"Yes, ma'am."

By his shyness she figured he couldn't be any older than thirteen or fourteen.

"What's your name, sugar?"

"Willie."

His eyes were smart. "Willie what?"

"Graves."

"Where you from?"

Staring at her car, he wanted to stop, but could not help himself. "Up north," he answered.

Closing her purse, she looked him over one more time before heading in. "Well, Willie Graves from up north . . ." handing him two warm quarters, " . . . I got the Lincoln, but you got my heart!"

He caught his breath. The job was to watch cars, not fall in love with women twice his age. Swamp hooch was illegal, everybody knew that, but so were the ladies. Watching J.C.'s Buick pull in, he remembered their conversation from the night before. Some people were sweet and some were poison, but they had one thing in common, he'd explained. "Spot don' run on love, Willie G. 'Round here, money talks an' shit walks."

Stick watched the man at J.C.'s picnic table finish his second steak. His fingers were as fat as his money clip. And the gun in his pants made him look like he had a hard-on. He said he brokered peanuts up and down the East Coast, but his eyes told another story. Brokers were nothing but pimps with cheap suits and big cars. They didn't smell like French cologne and they didn't leave tips.

Around midnight the sound of J.C.'s guitar drifted through the parking lot. His songs were mostly about trains and mules and fast women, and every now and then some of the tunes made the boy think about what he'd been through. Stick joined in on the mouth harp when he wasn't too drunk, and Arvo Galvin worked his washboard. But most reliably, it was the beat-up Fender that bled the porch of darkness and sponged the sky with morning light.

Willie'd had a long night. When Dolly left, he badly wanted to stop her. She was stoned and smelled like liquor, like his momma those mornings when he'd find her at the kitchen table passed out on her Bible. He felt sad seeing her drive away in the fat man's car.

As he rode home in the back of a pickup truck, soft curtains of morning light passed through the Spanish moss overhead. He was beat. There were six dollars in his pocket, but his hair felt sticky. Maybe at the end of the day, life was more bullshit than magic.

At noon the next day Stick came home for lunch and found the vegetable garden full of weeds and the boy asleep in his bed. His face looked haggard against the pillow, pocked by mosquito bites. Working Jimmy's porch would teach him a thing or two. There was a price for everything, but pimps and whores were not the same as peanuts. Opening his eyes, Willie was surprised to see Stick at the foot of his bed, shaking his head.

"Still got your shoes on. What time you get in last night?" The room was stuffy with the windows closed.

" 'Bout six o'clock, I guess. What time'd you leave?"

"Midnight. You were droolin' over Dolly," Stick joked, opening a window. "Hungry?"

Willie stretched his arms out until his hands hit the wall. He was outgrowing his bed.

"Starvin'! They ran outta steaks so I didn't get much."

"You're right 'bout that. Nothin' 'cept hookers an' booze."

From the kitchen table Willie could see the garden was a mess. He'd spent most of his August days sleeping and reading.

"You done with that book?" Stick asked, handing him a pimento cheese sandwich and a glass of milk.

"*Moby Dick?* Yeah."

"Whatcha readin' now?"

"Twain."

"Never heard a that."

"Ain't the book's name," he said before draining his glass of milk. Stick could see he'd need another sandwich. "It's the guy's name who done it." He stared at his empty plate.

Stick reheated a pot of coffee and watched him finish his second sandwich. Stick's hands were shaking under the table. "Gotta run to Chesapeake this afternoon. Wanna come?" he asked casually.

Stick was hungover. Willie could hear it in his voice. "No, thanks," Willie answered, sounding disappointed. "Been late on them weeds all month—I'd better do that before we lose somethin'."

Stick poured himself another cup of coffee. "Corn looks good. Want some java?"

"No, thanks. Gives me the runs," Willie confessed, leaning back in his chair and smiling.

Stick smiled. "Make a shitty hoe boy."

Willie looked up brightly. "Where do you shit when you hop?"

"Depends."

"On what?"

"On the rig."

"What's the difference?"

Gulping the last of his coffee, he half-smiled at the boy. He was persistent. "Can't believe you wanna talk about shittin'. Well, there's more places than you think . . . lots a places . . . boxcar roof, off the side of a flatcar, through the pocket on a hopper, in a bucket on a gondola, and real quick on a reefer."

"What's a reefer?"

"Forgot already?"

Willie pressed his knuckle into his palm, unable to remember.

"Refrigerator car. Need some juice and a good coat for one a them," Stick said, standing up to leave.

On his hands and knees in the garden, he thought about leaving the swamp and catching out with Stick. He'd be sixteen soon and his fear of the fire had been put out long ago. His arms were covered with bites. As he moved the tips of his fingers together, the soil felt moist and smelled more alive than it had a week earlier. Sitting back on the heels of his boots, he recognized the look of a cloud passing over a maple stand off in the distance. The bottom was dark and the top was white. He'd thought of Moses lately, especially riding home in the early morning when his mind was all atwitter. "Bring duh new way when you sees it," his voice echoed in his head.

Holding tight to a branch of the Lucky Bean in his dreams that night, he watched his mother passing below towards the distant ice stacks at the top of Garrett Street. She didn't walk so much as float. At the top of the hill, she turned deliberately back in his direction. There was no regret in her smile or malice in her expression, and as she walked away, he understood how beautiful she'd become again, and how much he would miss that part of her.

The next morning at the table, as they ate breakfast together, Willie's dejected expression caught Stick's attention.

"My momma's dead," the boy said flatly.

Stick wasn't sure how he'd found out. Maybe someone at the Spot, or maybe he'd been at it in his sleep again.

"How you know that?" Stick tried to sound surprised.

"Had a dream."

Stick rested his elbows on the edge of the kitchen table and leaned forward. He'd never been much on dreams until he met Crystal-Ann. She'd said reading the paper was a waste of time, but dreams would set you straight.

Willie stared at Stick with a dazed look, tears cascading down his cheeks.

"Yeah, well . . . " Stick started feebly.

"Ain't no big surprise, but . . . just wish I was . . . " Willie choked, letting his head fall. "I know I never spoke 'bout her much . . . " he sputtered, covering his face with his hands. Stick got up from his chair and moved around the table. When his hand touched the boy's shoulder, Willie jumped up from his chair. They'd never embraced before, but after everything they'd experienced together, it was time. As the boy sobbed against his chest, Stick remembered crouching on the banks of the Maury with her ashes.

"Shh . . . " Stick whispered, rocking back and forth. He should've told the boy himself. Maybe it would've been easier on him. Or maybe it would've made no difference at all.

"They told me a while back," he admitted, holding him tightly, his eyes closed. Willie's arms froze. "But I . . . " As a gray squirrel raced across the roof, he waited for Stick to say something, but all he felt was a teardrop on his head.

CHAPTER FORTY-FIVE

On Wednesday night pink moths swirled around the front door light and Dolly's car was still there. Willie'd had a bad feeling about the fat man, especially after Jimmy C. had told him to keep an eye out. He didn't broker goobers, everybody knew that. Ethel had said it was no place for a boy. The Spot was a juke joint and when things went south, they got there fast.

In October business was down and Dolly's car disappeared. When he asked about it, Jimmy C. flashed his gold tooth and handed him a Coke.

"Man come and take it," was all he said.

"Where'd he take it?"

"No clue." Jimmy C. shrugged, walking away.

For Willie, the Spot wasn't just license plates and howdy-do's. It taught him other things—like when to ask and when to tell. And how to smell the bullshit.

On the night of his sixteenth birthday the place was dead. Ethel Black had given Oscar a stack of books from the library and a cherry pie to take to the Spot.

At nine o'clock Jimmy C. told him to come inside and warm up.

"Night ain't over, J.C." Willie shook with cold. "Don't need to trouble

328 / Peter Skinner

with me."

Jimmy C. gave the boy his best smile. He wouldn't tell him right away. Money was tight, but he could always sell hooch. Still, more calls were coming in and the voices were just as mean. After all these years, it was a miracle they hadn't torched the place yet. The Klan was like a still, hidden away and dripping with poison.

Willie sat at the bar with a paper birthday hat in front of him. He wouldn't embarrass himself by putting it on, but he thanked J.C. for getting it and told him he appreciated the gesture. As his swamp family gathered around him, Oscar was the first to speak.

"Now I don' know 'bout dem Galvin boys, but take a whole lot to get Elijah Franklin out middle duh week."

"Hooch an' pussy's all!" Arvo Galvin blurted out unceremoniously.

When the laughter died down, Oscar glanced nervously at the front door and giggled.

"To this boy, Willie, here on his birthday." He raised his glass of hooch. " 'Cuz truth is, this good little fella, well . . . he ain't no 'little fella' no mo'." Oscar smiled tenderly. "He's been on dat porch and wid all duh buildin' an' paintin' an' duh gardnin' 'n' all. An' all dat readin'! He done read a *ton* a books, people! All kinds a books, you know . . . And now he be more like a *man* den a boy!" Oscar took a quick sip of hooch.

Willie blushed and fiddled with his paper hat.

"So, we ah . . . " Oscar glanced at the door again. " . . . we ahh . . . got together and talked 'bout it an' figured a man don't need no cake an' cookies!"

The Galvin brothers and J.C. chuckled.

" 'Cept Elijah, dat is!" Oscar paused. "So we all pitched in . . . to make dis . . . a special kinda day, you know."

Willie gave Stick a questioning look.

"Willie?" Stick slid off his stool and handed him a glass of hooch. "Tonight, son, you're gettin' drunk!"

"Happy birthday!" "Amen!" "Hallelujah!" "Woohoo!" "Sweet Jesus!" The men shouted in a chorus.

As they stomped their feet and danced about, Willie's first sip of hooch made him grab his throat and yell. But when the front door opened and J.C.'s guitar started up, the shack grew still. Willie tried to make sense of what he saw. If her car was gone, then she was gone. But there she was—all sweet and pretty, standing with one hip in the air.

"Been lookin' for the birthday boy," she cooed from under the Christmas lights.

His forehead was hot and it was hard to swallow.

"Well, don't play hard ta git wid me. Dance with Dolly, baby." Swaying her hips, she opened her arms to him. "I'm duh lady in duh pie."

Because they'd gone to all the trouble of finding Dolly for his birthday and because the hooch made him feel so loose, Willie was up for a dance. He'd forgotten he'd never danced before except with his momma. He'd dreamed about Dolly long enough. They'd been in moonlit cars together and tangled in each other's arms along sun-drenched ditches. But he'd make it look like it was no big deal.

Marinated in the dangling lights, their skin turned the same color, and she was the first to notice. It surprised him how much he'd grown since the summer. Or was she just small? Her hand fit perfectly in his. Under her coat their bodies moved seamlessly together. His momma had shown him some steps, but this was the real thing, he figured. Maybe every hooker danced the same.

When Stick's harmonica joined in, Dolly tossed her coat to the men and backed away.

"Got a sweet face." She let go of his hand and combed his brown curls of hair with her fingers. "An' you dance real nice."

"My momma showed me some."

"Your momma?"

"Pretty much all I know 'bout dancing." He wondered if she was making fun of him.

Dolly's face moved closer to his. "Where you get dem eyes?" she asked, as the men watched.

"My momma."

"Yo' daddy white?"

"Yes, ma'am."

Her hips stopped swaying as she gave him a look of mild scorn. "Baby, when we dance—I ain't no 'ma'am'!"

"Sorry."

As she pulled his body to hers, she gave him a sultry smile. "Ain't nothin' t' be sorry 'bout. First time I saw you . . . you remember?" Her hair smelled of jasmine. "Was like we knew 'bout each other." His warm face against her neck, she was nothing like his momma. When the music stopped, they kept on dancing.

"Ain't time fo' duh pie yet, Miss Dollie!" Jimmy C. hollered, leaning his guitar against the back wall. *"Get you a drink 'fo' duh boys go home!"*

Willie's next three glasses were diluted with Cheerwine, but by the time the music had stopped and the shack had emptied out, he was shitfaced. He remembered the delicate touch of her tongue in his mouth when they kissed through the car window before she drove away. He remembered Stick pounding on the outside of Oscar's truck door as the stars flew upside down overhead. She'd slept next to him, he thought, tossing in his bed. He'd heard her moaning in the night and calling someone's name, and in the morning, he still smelled like jasmine.

Stick hadn't planned on Dolly following him home in her shiny new Oldsmobile—it just worked out that way. One way or the other, she said they'd all paid her for the night and a deal was a deal. Standing by the fire, she was a fine-looking woman and it had been a while. Black women were easy, Stick thought in a drunken haze, watching the back of the dress slide over her ass. They could love and forgive a man all at the same time.

In the morning the fire was out and a model wooden sailboat was on the kitchen table. It had rained all night. By the time he found Stick on the couch, his head was pounding. "Stick," he whispered, pushing against his shoulder with his fingers. Stick's eyes opened—and closed just as quickly. "It's ten o'clock," Willie insisted, pushing with more determination. Opening his eyes again, Stick rubbed them with one hand, and focused on the empty fireplace. His feet were cold. "Late for work, man, come on!"

Willie had fixed scrambled eggs and toast and a new pot of coffee. When Stick saw the boat, his eyes lit up. "Elijah's boat! Thought I left it."

Willie's head hurt so much he didn't remember Elijah handing him a boat.

"Carved it outta old cypress. Said it sails real good, if you got some wind."

Stick raced through his breakfast and was out the door before Willie could say another word.

"*Find an ant hill!*" Stick shouted to him from the end of the yard.

CHAPTER FORTY-SIX

While the sailboat bobbed, maple seeds helicoptered down onto the water below. As Willie prodded the bow with a long stick, the hull heeled slightly in the breeze as the stern drifted away. The boat had no name. He wanted to write something on it, but all he had in the house was a carpenter's pencil.

He thought about Auggie. Soon there'd be pots to mend and hulls to paint. There were no model boats or fancy Russian novels in Salty Crockett's world. A passing cloud turned the water deep brown and his boat stopped. Falling back against the ground, he stared into the darkening sky and remembered how, near Oyster Creek, golden flames of grass had reflected off the *May Jane* as the cedar tops glowed. You didn't need much to get on in life. When a blue crab found deep winter water only the tips of its eyes showed, and a small opening for air.

On a bank near the ditch with his boat, Willie saw a stream of black ants that led to a colony nearby. As he held his palm an inch above the mound, hundreds of ants flipped over to protect it. Their spray tasted bitter when he licked it off his hand and he felt the pounding in his head lessen as he walked home. Stick had said ant piss was a poor man's aspirin. When it came to ants, Stick was pretty sharp, but when it came to liquor, he had a lot to learn.

That night in the kitchen Willie heard that Dolly had a new pimp. "What's a pimp?" he asked, looking away.

"Pimp's like a . . . manager," Stick explained thoughtfully. "Keeps her safe and finds the work."

He thought about Matt Abel and his momma's house. "What's he get out of it?"

"Piece of the action," Stick grinned.

Willie made a sour face.

"What she charges," he explained.

"Ain't her money, then?"

"Not all of it, no. Most likely less than half."

"That stinks! She's the one doin' the trick!"

"How you know 'bout tricks?!"

Willie tried to remember. It had been a while. "Jimmy, I guess. Or Dolly mighta said somethin' about it. I don't know."

"Jimmy was her pimp . . . " Stick stretched his arms out. " . . . but he sold her to the fat man's brother."

"Sold her?" Willie's mouth dropped open.

Stick pushed his chair back from the kitchen table. "How it works, son. Like buyin' cattle."

Dolly's hands had been no bigger than his.

"Got her a new car and a place in the Bronx." Stick handed the boy a scrap of paper.

"New York?" Willie read aloud, trying to decipher her handwriting.

"Said you can see Yankee Stadium from her bathroom and the Empire State from her roof."

"The one with King Kong?"

"Yes, sir. Wants us to come see her sometime. Told her we don't get 'round much these days . . . on account a your situation."

"You *told* her?!"

"I did."

"On my birthday?"

"Last night."

He liked the idea that Dolly knew. She was running too. He could see it in her eyes.

"Think she'll tell?"

Stick smiled tenderly. The boy had had a big night.

"There's one thing you can trust in this world, son."

"What's that?" Willie sounded tired.

"A hooker." He winked, standing up.

Sadie Graves was buried next to her parents behind the First Ebenezer Baptist Church in Happy Jack, Louisiana. A week earlier Matt Abel had stood alone on the West Main Street Bridge and watched the train pull out with her coffin. No one else had shown up to say goodbye. As the roof of her boxcar passed underneath him, a long line of empty coal cars followed. It would never be the same. The girls were restless. It took charm and a strong personality to run a whorehouse and some balls to keep it safe. When he first saw her all those years ago, after only five minutes, he knew he'd struck gold. His three-story clapboard was empty and the town had a permanent hard-on. "Money don't grow on trees, honey," she'd said, " 'less you own the forest."

She'd been right about a lot of things, in particular the money—but the boy was a different story. Looking down at the empty tracks, he thought about Willie. If he was dead, none of it mattered. But if he wasn't, he'd be back someday, because the only way to start over was from the beginning.

CHAPTER FORTY-SEVEN

On a warm day in May, Moses reached for a wasp's nest with the end of his broom as a strong smell of pollen hung in the air. His lungs were tight and his legs trembled, but you didn't fool with the landlord, and according to his momma, the sting of a wasp brought on envy and hate. Barely touching the hive, his broom only bent at the ends. He would need his hoe from the shed by the back fence and a kitchen stool. Passing under a locust through pools of shade, he stopped to remember something. The boy's envelope was by his bed and Mr. Matt would collect it the next time he was up this way.

When his bell had faded earlier in the hour, there had been no clouds to speak of. But as he retrieved the hoe and stool from the shed, he looked up at islands of long, dusty drifts, their wispy edges rimmed with a sudden and intense light. He smiled to himself as he stood on the stool, raising the hoe with his frail arms. As the hive bounced off the ground, a swarm of wasps beat up against his legs. Stepping down carefully, he was not afraid. He'd lived too long for that. The insects tickled his skinny legs, causing him to dance a little at first, before the first sting and then the next. And then dozens. Lowering himself to the ground, he did not wish to harm them for he knew that they wished no harm to him. They were not spiteful. His head on the ground, he stared resolutely into the sky, and saw it at first abstractly before the clarity and substance of its meaning set in: a low and gilded cloud, just as his momma had said. As his eyes closed, the stings intensified, a strange and voluptuous calm enveloped him. After so many years of waiting, it was time: Here behind the barbershop on a quiet afternoon, his journey would begin. It wasn't what you took with you that mattered, he thought, before releasing the hoe and taking his final unfettered breath—but what you left behind.

CHAPTER FORTY-EIGHT

Looking out his office window, Oscar smiled to himself. After three weeks of stripping pine, and the fire at Jimmy C.'s, Stick had finally sobered up.

Oscar's Lokie was full from stem to stern and the builders were screaming for more. Stick knew the houses would piss Salty off, but the truth was, when it came to commerce, somebody always got screwed.

"Stick!" Oscar shouted over an idling forklift.

Straddling a long pine, Stick wiped his brow. His back was sore. The men had gone to lunch and Oscar was gesturing from his office window. His pants were filthy with bark and grime and the insides of his fingers stuck together.

The men gathered quietly around a long picnic table tucked against the building and ate their lunch. Someone had fresh corn bread and another man had fried chicken. *The Virginian-Pilot* was calling for rain, but the air was stagnant and still.

"Nothin' on duh fire?" Oscar asked, nibbling on peanuts.

Stick opened to the last page.

"Ain't much dey goin' say 'bout dat," Moss Motley replied sarcastically, balling up his brown paper bag. "Dey all know who done it."

Ten years earlier the Motleys had bought a cotton field west of the swamp from a white man in Richmond. When they turned a buck, the barn was torched.

"Be blamin' Jimmy's geetar, I 'magine. Get dat ole fire chief and sheriff on it and it be real special."

"Be dem Christmas lights," another man interjected.

Oscar scanned the men's faces. Except for Stick they'd been with him awhile. But Stick was a white man.

"Well, I'll be," Stick muttered to himself from behind the newspaper as the lunch broke up.

"What you got?" Oscar dusted peanuts off his lap.

"Bell man's dead."

"Who duh bell man?"

"Willie's friend, Moses."

"Moses?"

"Henry," Stick said, spreading the paper out on the table.

"Moses Henry," Oscar repeated absently.

Placing his elbows on the table, Stick ran his hands through his hair and considered the article.

"Never said nothin' to you 'bout Moses?"

"Not dat I remember." Oscar slid closer to the paper to have a look.

"'Hundred and two . . . Rang the University of Virginia bell for fifty-three years,'" Stick read. "Was special to Willie . . . Shit!" He frowned and stood up.

The photograph of Moses Henry with his hand on a big bell made him look small.

"'. . . kept the people moving' . . . '" Oscar read aloud. "Born befo' duh War, Stick damn! Dats a lotta bells, man!"

Oscar folded up the page carefully and handed it to Stick. "He gonna take it hard?"

Stick stuffed the article into the back pocket of his pants. The boy's world was slowly coming apart.

"Maybe," he muttered, walking away.

Willie put down the Russian novel and finished his peanut butter sandwich. He smelled rain and the skeeters had turned it up a notch. In the swamp they hung around until Christmas. He was tired of scratching. His arms and legs were covered in bites most of the time. Stick told him to drink some hooch. "They hate that shit," he'd said one night. "Makes your blood sour."

Returning to the garden, he laid out his flat of cherry tomatoes for transplanting. In the real world he'd be in school right now, side by side with boys his own age, or with a pretty blond girl with glasses. Rebecca would be ten by now and Auggie would be counting the days until summer. Raindrops hit the metal roof of the house. Oscar said Ethel was busting his balls about Willie not being in school. "Won't give it up," he'd complained one day during a visit. Ethel's mother had been a high school teacher in Scotland County near the South Carolina border. She said it wasn't natural for a boy to be by himself all day, whether he wanted to or not. Willie didn't think much about what he wanted anymore. When Stick was gone, most of what was missing he found in his garden or got from his books. He read about anarchy, patricide, and God. He remembered stories like he remembered orchards, or a boat ride from Reedsville to Tangier. Moses said Willie's head took photographs of things. Like the pink camellia bush in front of St. Peter's Episcopal on Route 158 or the taciturn face of Peter Kalganov in *The Brothers Karamazov.*

At the four o'clock whistle the men were paid. Walking home in the rain, Stick counted his cash and thought about Jimmy. Most fires in the swamp didn't start on their own. If they'd fingered the Spot, it wouldn't be the last time. The

Klan was like a shark—one strike, and it couldn't let go.

"Got my last tomata in the ground," the boy shouted triumphantly when he saw Stick, who smiled approvingly at a long row of newly transplanted tomatoes. Willie must've been at it most of the day, he figured. His knees and hands were covered in mud.

"You're a mess, boy, but you got one fine-lookin' garden!"

"See this, Stick?" Willie beamed, pointing to a new chicken-wire fence. "Taller 'an you are! When I finish this off, them deer be outta business!"

Stick admired it. The news would hit him hard. "It's a fortress, Willie. Them Maroons got nothin' on you. Now come in outta the rain an' I'll cook these chops up for us."

"Dang, you got chops?!" Willie wiped a streak of mud off his forehead.

"Ethel run it over from her brother's shop. Good inch, too—just the way you like 'em. And strawberries." Stick held up the bag.

"This time a year?!"

Stick laughed at his stupefied expression. "Place called Florida, man," he said, walking towards the house. "Gators, girls, an' berries."

The boy fell off his chair when he told him, like he'd been punched in the face. Seeing that was the worst of all. He'd rather be stripping pine logs for the rest of his life than telling a kid the truth. Crystal-Ann said he was afraid of it sometimes, and that's why he drank so hard.

Willie would hurt for a while, but in time he'd be stringing up crappies and asking for books again. He didn't completely understand what the old man had meant to the boy—they must've just clicked, he thought.

"I wanna say 'bye, Stick," Willie moaned, curled up on the floor next to his chair. "One thing 'bout my momma leaving was wrong . . . never said goodbye the way I should."

Stick resisted the urge to pick him up.

"An' I can live with that, but . . . Moses . . . I gotta go," he choked, his body trembling as he sobbed. "Got two days."

"For what?"

"The funeral."

Stick felt his jaw tighten. "Funeral's in Charlottesville, Willie. Don't think that's gonna happen."

Willie stopped crying. "Why not?"

When Stick left the house, he was pissed. The boy was so messed up he hadn't heard a word he'd said. He'd laid it out as best he could. "In a church full of niggers there's always a sheriff outside somewhere and just a glance will tip him off. Black or white, they'll run you down till you're dead or till somebody beats them to it." On the back steps his jar of hooch was half full. He'd finish it all and hit the road for a fuck. Maybe that's what the boy needed. Or maybe Moses was like Crystal-Ann and you only go the distance for the ones who don't hurt you.

It was late and being drunk was a good enough excuse. He'd knocked on her door once, but she'd been out dancing with her sister. People called her Sally.

In the meager light she remembered. He was a good man, Oscar had said. His clothes were dripping wet, but his eyes were clear.

"You're Oscar's man." She took his hand and led him inside.

Her hand was small like Dolly's, but not as soft or as smooth. When she touched him, he felt tired and cheap, until the pink bedroom light hit her shoulders.

Standing naked by the open window, he smoked a joint and watched a large magnolia out front dripping with rain. The drops sounded like fingers tapping against a tabletop. It had been a while since he'd been stoned. He didn't know if it was her or the reefer, but his dick was still hard.

"Close the window an' lay with me," she called from under the sheets. He was a strange man—tender and rough at the same time.

Stick put the joint in his mouth and closed the window as the magnolia flushed with headlights.

"Muss be my sista," Sally said, hearing the truck and reaching out for him. "Forget dat, honey." She pushed back the sheets and sat up. "Jess come here let me show you somethin'."

Walking home, the sound of tree frogs careened through the distant woods. He didn't give a shit about the cypress. He needed a shower. Women turned your world around. It was simple stuff, really—the way they smelled, or the way you forgot everything when they hiked up their skirts.

Approaching the house, Stick realized the boy would be asleep. He was wrong to have left him alone, but he was old enough to make up his own mind. Charlottesville would string him up. Maybe that's what he wanted. Maybe, after all the running and sitting around thinking about what was right and what was wrong, all he wanted was to make his own choice. Like Oscar fucking Sally's sister in his truck.

An hour before sunrise Willie stood uneasily on the tracks and waited. The paperboy had said a hopper would be by any minute, but the minute had turned into an hour and the sun would be up soon. He could have hitchhiked to Suffolk by now. He had two days, and if the bulls wanted him after that, they could have him. Standing on a rail, he heard a rooster in the distance. He'd miss something about every place he'd seen, but he'd reached a point where standing still was harder than going back.

The tracks were dead. Stick had taught him how to listen with his feet for oncoming trains. Hopping in the open was stupid, unless you were in the middle of Kansas, or needed a good night's sleep in a local jail. He'd said the law was harder than the cold sometimes. He had fifty dollars in his sack and a thick slice of cheddar cheese. With four hundred miles to the Albemarle County line, he wouldn't look back until he saw the old man's box.

When a Norfolk and Western finally appeared, Willie heard a voice behind him from a wall of kudzu.

"Forgot your pole."

As the sound of the train consumed them, he focused on the passing cars and looked for an open door into a boxcar, sliding in on his knees.

When Willie stood up, Stick was on board with him, facedown and out of breath.

"Saw you 'round four o'clock walkin' the line," he said, rolling over and sitting up.

"But how'd you find me?"

"Followed the tracks."

Willie squeezed his pole and leaned back against the boxcar wall. He could smell the booze, but it didn't matter.

"Thanks for comin', Stick."

The boxcar in Suffolk had a Mexican girl named Dizzy and her man. She'd switch in Richmond and catch out for El Paso. If you dodged the bulls in Roanoke, the trip to Charlottesville was butter, but they'd need to ditch in Belmont and take side streets to the church. Stick knew Charlottesville. He'd seen it working apples on Carter Mountain. The university was one thing, but most of the town was a fucking country club.

"Know what I like 'bout Charlottesville?" Stick confessed to Willie, his eye on one of the men at the other end of the boxcar. "Full a smart people," he said, as the train entered a tunnel.

Before the sun came up he'd given the boy some money. Except for the occasional fuck or a decent bottle, Stick was pretty tight. Sister Mo said money was just another color.

At a stop north of Petersburg, a group of men slipped through a crack in the door and lay down on the opposite side of the car. The Mexican girl and her husband had ditched at Fort Lee, just south of Petersburg.

"What happened to Jimmy C.?" Willie asked, curled up against his sack, watching as the men settled in.

"Split," Stick answered, leaning back against his pack, noticing one of the men.

"Where'd he go to?"

" 'Nother county, I s'pose." Stick closed his eyes. His head hurt.

"Will he be runnin' long?" The boy sounded sleepy.

"Long as it takes," he mumbled over the rattle of the tracks.

As the boxcar rocked, Stick was finding it hard to drift off. He didn't like their chances. They'd find the church and blend in as best they could, but the rest of it was a crap shoot. If the boy loved Moses so much, he'd do him one last favor. After that, the road was wide open. Crystal-Ann had said the trees in Seattle were big and the clouds were pretty.

"What the hell's this?" Hook's brother said, holding up the dictionary he'd pulled from Stick's knapsack. Hook didn't give a shit, rifling through the bottom and finding cash rolled up in an empty can of Beech Nut. He'd split it with his men. Back in Florida all those years ago, Stick was pretty sharp, but he could see from his face that he'd lost his edge.

"You awake, asshole?!" Hook shouted.

Opening his eyes, Stick recognized him. They were broke coming up from Florida and he'd been a prick for the whole ride.

Hook threw the knapsack against Stick's chest. "That's right! Like old times, maestro—'cept this time . . . you're fresh outta luck!"

"That you, Hook?" Stick mumbled as he stood, bending his legs for balance. He counted seven men. He'd have to play his cards right.

"In the flesh, Stick!" Hook brandished a bowie knife, stepping forward. Willie's eyes popped open as the blade entered Stick's neck.

"Remember me now?" Hook shouted, pulling the knife out as Stick fell to his knees.

As the tunnel swallowed them, Willie screamed. Unless he found Rebecca's knife they'd kill him too. It was all he had. As he stood up in the blackness, a sudden rush of wind from the open door knocked him back against the wall. Fumbling in his knapsack for the pocketknife, he resisted the urge to scream again. Stick had looked bad. Blood had been gushing from his neck.

When the train cleared the tunnel and light flooded in, Willie saw that Hook and the men were preparing to jump. There was a trail of blood on the floor, but Stick was gone. His hands trembling, Willie swallowed hard, and held his knife straight out in front of him as the train slowed for a switching station, and some of the men jumped. It was hard to breathe. Stick had to be somewhere back in the tunnel.

When the last man jumped, Hook wiped his bowie knife clean with a handkerchief and smiled at Willie. He'd been a kid once.

When the train finally stopped, Willie sat in shock, frozen against the back wall of the empty boxcar, his knife against his chest. Until he remembered the tunnel. Grabbing the knapsacks, he scrambled frantically to the door on his knees, and looked out to see if the coast was clear. He'd have to be fast about it. There was blood all over the floor; the knife had gone in deep. Throwing the knapsacks to the ground below, he took a deep breath and jumped.

Flying over blackened crossties, he finally saw the tunnel before coming to a stop. The darkness frightened him initially, until he realized that Stick was inside. Moving cautiously, he passed through the opening and felt a chill in the air, watching his arms turn gray in the dwindling light. He'd stop the bleeding and patch him up somehow. After everything that Stick had done for him, old Moses would understand. The dead were gone, but Stick was still living.

When he dropped the sacks, his shoes felt lighter as the sounds of his footsteps echoed off the walls. As the darkness intensified, a faded light appeared at the end of the tunnel. Stepping slowly forward, he smelled cat pee, until he saw something and stopped. A body lay twisted up against the wall fifty yards away. Even from a distance he could tell there was nothing left of it. He owed Stick his life. He owed him his freedom and his way with boats and gardening, and apples, and he appreciated his quiet and patience and all the places they'd seen together. Willie heard footsteps behind him at the tunnel opening, but there was no time to look. Moving forward, it was easier to see now—blood against the wall where the body had hit. He saw a shoulder. Stepping up to it, his mind went blank as it had under the bridge when he'd taken the river in and finally let go. As he crouched down, the smell hit him, before he noticed and gasped. The dead deer's eyes were open.

At the tunnel opening, the switchman could barely make him out. This one looked more like a boy. When the men had run, he'd called the bulls. The last man out was holding a knife, but except for all the blood, that was it. He wasn't a cop. For forty-seven minutes the light would stay red, until the sheriff came. Then the C&O would scream eastbound to the coast.

CHAPTER FORTY-NINE

Joe Hall watched him in the rearview mirror of his patrol car. He wouldn't take gum and he wouldn't say much, except that a man had cut his friend and tossed him off the train. He looked wild, but he hadn't run when they'd found him.

"How far we goin', sir?" Willie asked finally, watching the large brick factories pass.

"Another ten minutes, son. Then we can sort it all out." The sheriff gauged the boy's expression. He was older than the pictures and his skin looked more Negro than Caucasian.

He'd never been in a police car. It was shiny like Matt Abel's, but the windows were up and the doors were locked. As they drove past sidewalks full of people, he leaned against the back seat. Garden dirt still packed his fingernails and his hair smelled of smoke. Stick said a train could fill your pores with iron. He said you could smell a hopper from ten feet away—like the breath of a coal man or the hands of a crabber. Willie watched the sheriff's hands on the steering wheel. They were puffy and red, like the overripe peaches Rebecca's father turned into jam.

As the buildings got bigger, he grew tired. If Stick had survived the fall, where was he now? And how long could he make it with that gash in his neck?

Turning onto Monument Avenue, Joe Hall looked in the rearview mirror one last time. The boy looked like a caged animal. "How about a shower and something to eat?" he suggested.

At the next corner, a nicely dressed couple held their young daughter's hand. Blond and pretty, with shiny black shoes and a frilly blue dress, she looked suspiciously into the back seat of the police cruiser. When their eyes met, he saw his younger self in her expression and pressed back against the seat.

In the shower his shoulders finally relaxed under the hot water. He hadn't touched his food because it reminded him of the deer. Stick was like an injured cat, and unless he'd found a doctor he might just crawl under a porch and die.

The bed in his cell was hard, but he was too tired to care. Staring at a triangle of deep blue sky hanging sideways through a window on the back wall, he listened to a cacophony of voices, toilets flushing, and the chatter of a dispatch radio.

When his eyes opened, the cell was dark. One way or the other he'd answer for what he'd done. Curling up and turning his body towards the wall, a deep, sinking loneliness enveloped him. Stick was dead, maybe, and the men who did it were long gone. He would never see Moses or his momma again.

At midnight Sheriff Hall slid the small hatch open and looked inside. He'd broken some rules and let him sleep—the answers would come soon enough. People who run don't forget why they're running.

CHAPTER FIFTY

In the morning, Willie heard footsteps outside his cell and stopped pacing. The sun had been up for hours and so had he. When the door opened, a big black deputy smiled and handed him a tray of food. His nametag said "D.J. Bickers."

"Hungry yet?" he asked gently.

When he saw the steaming scrambled eggs with bacon and toast his eyes teared. "I could eat, thank you."

Closing the door with the back of his foot, the deputy admired the boy for making his bed. "Well, then, here, man, take your time," he said, holding the tray out. "Sheriff will be waitin' when you're done."

From behind his desk Joe Hall counted ten phone messages. Most could wait, except for Sheriff Sheffield. He'd put the most into finding the boy and deserved a call. The Florida number was Weist, the happy sonovabitch.

The kid seemed healthy enough, but after so many years of running, he looked a whole lot older than sixteen. He'd miss the funeral that he'd spoken of, that was for sure. The *Dispatch* called for a big crowd. It seemed that one way or another, most of Charlottesville had known old Moses Henry.

Joe Hall's desk was a mess, but he knew exactly what he was up against.

He had a lot to tell the boy and just as many questions. "I'm waiting," he called, leaning back in his chair when Deputy Bickers knocked with Willie.

When he saw his pole leaning up against the wall he felt a longing, almost a relief, until the deputy pointed to a chair and shut the door. The sheriff looked younger with his hat off. "Have a seat, Willie. They get you something to eat?"

"Yes, sir." Stick's bag was next to the pole. He'd left it outside the tunnel when the sheriff picked him up.

"Did you sleep all right?"

"Yes, sir, I did."

"Good," the sheriff answered, calmly pushing his chair back and parking the heels of his boots on the top of the desk. "It's been a long road for you, son, and I, ah . . . " He rifled through desk papers with an exhausted look. " . . . wanna make this easy on all of us."

Willie watched him cautiously. He seemed to mean it, but still—it wouldn't change his situation.

"So." He folded his hands over his large stomach and leaned back. "What the hell happened?"

A tram passed by the open window. He tried to stay calm, but thinking about the fire made his hands sweat.

"How many men we talkin' 'bout?"

Willie felt immediate relief when he heard the question. There were eight men and the Mexican woman. "Eight."

Scrutinizing the boy, he could see that he'd need some help remembering.

"Plus a woman," Willie added.

"Coffee?"

"No, thanks."

"What did the woman look like?"

"'Bout twenty, maybe. Round face—big belly like she was pregnant or somethin'. Had a guy with her named Antonio, 'bout the same age, but his skin was darker and his accent was different. They ditched early near Petersburg."

"Early?"

"Said they were gonna ditch in Richmond."

"Something happen?"

"Not somethin' I remember, 'cept . . . " He gazed out the window. " . . . maybe they knew somethin' was up."

He'd heard the kid had a sharp head on his shoulders. "Where were they headed?"

"El Paso. You gonna stop 'em?" Willie asked.

"They're not who I'm after, Willie."

Willie looked at the floor. It was swirling gray linoleum like in his momma's kitchen.

Dropping his boots from the desk and sliding forward, the sheriff pushed a button at the bottom of his phone.

"Jenny, get me two Cokes, please, would you? A Coke okay?" He raised a brow.

"Yes, sir," Willie whispered, his eye on Stick's sack.

"And a PayDay, would you please?"

Willie took in all the paperwork on the sheriff's desk. If he had to spill the beans, maybe this was the place. It was as good as any other.

"Stick and the guy had somethin' between 'em," Willie blurted suddenly.

Taking up his notepad and pen, the sheriff played it cool. The Coca-Cola had worked. The boy would give him what he needed, and when the questioning was over, he'd get him a sandwich. When Jenny left, they sipped their Cokes and listened to the traffic outside.

"So, in Suffolk you and your friend, Stick, met up with the Mexican girl and her man on their way to El Paso."

Willie nodded.

"They get off and after Petersburg, seven boys jump on."

"Yep." Willie nodded, staring through his bottle. The linoleum floor had some pink in it.

"So, where were they going?"

Willie thought a second.

"Here, I guess."

"How do you know that?" the sheriff pressed.

"Well, they were pretty calm 'bout it all—like they knew the place."

"What place?"

"Well, not the place so much, but more where the train was goin'."

The sheriff looked puzzled.

"You can tell when they're hoppin' to a place they never been. It's different, 'cuz you gotta find a place to jump or a place to set up somewhere." Willie remembered their faces when he woke up. "They looked real sure of themselves, Sheriff. Plus, their sacks were light." Jotting all this down, Hall nodded. "They were all white, but one guy was kinda pale, maybe forty and tall and not as skinny as Stick—but pretty close. He had some kinda hat on like those French people wear."

"Beret?" The sheriff glanced up.

"Flat like a pancake. 'Nother guy was short with a fat face and maybe ten years younger. He had overalls."

"What color?"

"Blue. With a pipe sticking out of a pocket."

The sheriff clicked his pen. "A pipe?"

"Brown with busted edges like he'd dropped it a buncha times."

Shaking his head, he scanned his notes. He had a hard time getting two people to agree on the color of a car.

When their Cokes were done, he passed his notes to the deputy, who had remained stationed in the hallway. If the men were local, he'd find them, and if they'd run, it sounded like they'd be back. Blood from the boxcar was in the lab and a pipe had been found in a ditch. If Willie was right about where the knife went in, they'd find his body in a day or so. He couldn't have made it too far before bleeding to death, there was no way around it.

When the sheriff read his statement back to him, Stick's situation seemed even more hopeless than Willie had initially thought. A bowie knife is at least nine inches. That would be enough to cut arteries easily. There'd been a lot of blood on the floor of the car and along the walls of the tunnel. The only remaining question was where to find him. Beyond the opening of the tunnel, a trail of blood veered off the tracks and up into a line of paradise trees at the top of a ditch.

At the bottom of the first page of the sheriff's report, Willie saw Stick's social security number and date of birth. The year looked about right, nothing special, until he saw the date.

"You all right, Willie?" Sheriff Hall asked, taking a pistol from his drawer.

Willie leaned over the report, checking it again to make sure. His face was dumbstruck.

"I get something wrong?"

"Date of Birth," Willie stammered, his eyes pleading. "I never asked him."

"'Bout . . . his date of birth?" the sheriff struggled, trying to understand.

Tears racing down his cheeks, Willie shook his head in disbelief. How could he have been so selfish? How could he have cared so little not to think of it in the first place?

As his eyes shifted to his pole in the corner, he remembered the candles at Hilda's table and how when he blew them out, they'd all held their breath. "His birthday was yesterday," he finally said.

The uneaten sandwich in his lap, Willie shut his eyes and listened to the muffled traffic through the window. He'd never seen the jail in Charlottesville, not even from the Lucky Bean. The funeral would be over by now, and Sheriff Sheffield was on his way. He was surprised they'd let him sleep so much. Stick had been right all along. If he'd stayed in the swamp, everything would've been fine. He'd warned him a thousand times to keep his head down. He'd told him from the start to keep his mouth shut or the whole thing would turn to shit.

When he returned, Joe Hall took the car keys from behind his desk. The boy's face was hard and he hadn't touched his sandwich.

"Well?" he said, adjusting his revolver belt and waiting for the boy to stand up.

"We takin' my stuff?" Willie asked miserably.

"Stick's also, if you want it." He figured the kid was smart enough to have figured it out by now.

Willie felt disoriented. He didn't know what the sheriff had in mind, but at this point, he was too tired to think about it. Too much had happened. He looked over at Stick's knapsack. Maybe he could take the dictionary. It would give him something to read.

The sheriff examined the boy closely as he shuffled towards the pole and knapsack in the corner. "Don't know, do you?"

"Know what?"

Falling back in his chair, he exhaled audibly and gave Willie a weary smile. "You're a free man, Willie."

"I just remembered something . . . 'bout that man and the way he pulled the knife out," Willie suddenly realized, not registering what the sheriff had told him.

The sheriff listened patiently.

"Wasn't a ring I saw," he said, dazed.

"No?"

"Was the handle."

"I'm not sure I understand what you're saying, son." The sheriff furrowed his brow.

"The man was missin' a finger," he replied, looking pleased, "the pointer finger on his right hand!"

People must have taken to the boy. What he was saying would help. "Willie, did you hear what I said?"

" 'Bout what?"

"About you."

When he saw the sheriff's expression, he remembered what he'd said earlier, but it didn't make sense. "No, sir. I don't understand what you're sayin'."

"You're free to go."

He heard voices in the hall.

"Your name was cleared a while back—since last summer sometime, I think it was. We got word, but you made yourself pretty scarce."

Willie's eyes dropped to take in the floor. The lava was gone.

"You okay?"

Willie couldn't get his mind off Stick curled up and bleeding in the bushes. "What about the prints an' all?" he asked, faintly.

On his desk Joe Hall located a manila file marked "GRAVES." "Here," he said, offering it to the boy.

Willie saw a faded photocopy of his picture in the file. He looked like a little boy.

"Next page," the sheriff directed.

Stamped across the top of the next page were two words: "CASE

CLOSED."

The sheriff saw Willie's face take on some life. "Grand jury ruled there was insufficient evidence for an indictment, son. Could've hit his head on the counter, or it could've been some glass object that hit 'im, we don't know—fact is . . . got no evidence one way or the other to prove it."

"But what about the prints?" Willie was stupefied.

"Fire messed 'em up. Most of 'em, that is. Got a few off dishes in the kitchen, but Matt Abel cleared you for that. Said whatever dishes were done in that house was done by you."

"But what about the witness?"

"A half-drunk hooker staring out a window one house down. Didn't know what day it was. Willie, the bottom line is . . . "

Willie closed the file and looked up. Joe Hall had gentle brown eyes and a kind face.

" . . . Mopsey Graves was an asshole and nobody's gonna miss him."

CHAPTER FIFTY-ONE

The boxcar was empty. Watching the eyelets of his fishing pole bounce against the floor, he pressed his thumb against the corner of the dictionary and watched as embankments of blurry red clay raced by outside the open door. The air was sweet with something blooming. Oscar would call it lilacs, or Dolly's cheap perfume. He'd never entirely understand what had happened. But it might come with time.

On the flat tracks past Gum Springs, he swung outside and grabbed the ladder to the roof. Stick was right about the wind. As he crouched down, it was hard to concentrate, and it was hard to hold on. But eventually, after several miles, soft rolling mountains stretched from left to right in the distance, bathed in a sultry, blue light.

When dust from a Keswick gravel pit blasted his face, he tucked his head between his legs and waited for the train to stop. Standing up, he recognized the town's spires and gentle contours. A town was as much a feeling as a place, he thought, seeing the ice stacks.

After he jumped, it all went quickly enough. The streets were quiet and he knew the way. Everything was smaller than he'd remembered. At the top of

Garrett Street, he looked down at long last into The Bottom and caught his breath. The shutters to Matt Abel's house were closed but the gate was wide open.

As he dropped the knapsacks at the front door, his shoulders ached. The doorbell was broken. His fishing pole in one hand, he knocked. He was tired suddenly, as tired as he'd ever been. The place was dead and so was his momma. Watching a car pass, he thought he heard footsteps, before the door opened wide.

Matt Abel stood inside the hallway in his bathrobe wearing a sensational grin.

"Catch anything?" he inquired happily.

The hallway still smelled of cigars and liquor. When he saw the red dish, he remembered where he was.

Halfway down the hall Matt Abel called back, "Park your stuff, Willie. Got Hoko Chocolate on the back porch." He looked at the boy in utter astonishment. "Been a while, goddammit!" He disappeared behind a corner.

Willie dropped his sacks and pole against the wall of the back porch. As he crossed to the rail, tiny flecks of green paint stuck to his boot soles. The bottle pile was gone and the outhouse had fallen over.

Matt Abel appeared through the broken screen door with two glasses of chocolate milk and an envelope in the pocket of his robe.

"Been meanin' to fix this thing." He kicked at the door. Willie jumped when it slammed against the wall. "My kingdom for a hinge," the old man protested, stepping through.

Taking the glass, Willie's fingernails were dirty and worn. "Mmm," he murmured, after a sip. It was a whole lot better than hooch.

"Taste good, don't it?" Matt Abel took a swig.

Sitting down together on two rickety cane chairs, each one looked at the other.

"Got chocolate on your lip," Matt Abel said.

"You too," Willie replied.

When a car honked in the distance, the old man sat up, his face more serious. "Put your momma on a train, Willie. Did what I could, but . . . well, you know how she was," he said, looking down at his slippers. "Figured she'd want to be with her momma and daddy. Always said she missed the water," he added sadly. Glancing at the boy, he turned his attention to the backyard. "You need to call a lawyer . . . I've got his number upstairs. And you're supposed to check the cellar."

Willie noticed his legs. They were skinny and white. But his voice was still strong.

Leaning forward in his chair, Matt Abel looked briefly towards the property next door.

"Your momma bought me out a long time ago," he began, staring up into the midday sky. "Just wasn't in me—the business side, that is. I was just a handyman with a big house."

"You were more than that, Mr. Matt," the boy acknowledged, turning to face him.

"Well . . . I was always there, Willie." His eyes met the boy's with deep affection. "Always," he nodded, looking back down at his slippers. "But the place is yours now, son."

Willie stared at the old man.

"Need to call that man and check the cellar. House needs work, but there you are. A year after your momma died, the girls took off for Richmond. Took about a month until it was wrapped up—'cept for Carla."

"The Swedish lady?"

He was surprised Willie remembered.

"She was stinkin' drunk one night and your momma tossed her out. I offered to do it, but she gave me that look a hers and we all knew better. She called a cab and threw her clothes out the window. Said Carla was acting like a whore and not a lady. " 'Magine that?"

"She go to Richmond?"

"Nope, never made it." He finished his chocolate and wiped his mouth with the top of his hand.

"Where is she?"

Matt Abel put his glass down.

"Your momma found her in the front yard the next day and apologized. Said she had no right to treat her like that. Helped pick up her clothes and brought her back into the house."

"You said they all left."

"They did." He watched a bird fly by.

Willie figured he'd forgotten to tell him a part of the story.

"Carla's there." He pointed over the rail toward a flat grave by the fence under an oak, where the mound of empty bottles used to be.

"Stopped drinkin' the night she came back. Musta been what killed her," the old man joked.

Willie stood up and walked to the rail to get a better look.

"Oh, yeah," he remembered, reaching into the pocket of his robe. "Then there's this."

Willie took the envelope.

"Told me to come get it. Said one of the barber boys helped him write it. Found it where he said it was. And I wanna tell you . . . " He paused, shaking his head. "I never seen so many folks in one church before . . . and not just black people, Willie. Everybody! Mayor Tibbs, Judge Preston, Jumpin' Joe Smith, the sheriff with all his deputies, the president of the university, and that ole Civil War colonel who's outta his mind . . . And, get this!" he went on, looking mystified. "There were speakers outside for all the students in the streets—musta been a thousand! Never seen anything like it in all my days!"

Taking the envelope, Willie walked to the end of the porch so his tears wouldn't show. He was exhausted and spent, but this time it wasn't from running. The Lucky Bean was there waiting for him, beyond the charred foundation of the house.

"Was me, Willie."

His eyes on the tree, the boy stopped momentarily.

"I know," he said, moving down the steps.

Standing where the kitchen had been, white clover and bloodroot danced around his boots, as if in the end, living was the only thing that mattered. After two years in a swamp, the richness of the place took his breath away. If a house that harbored so many bad memories had to burn, so be it. Like the Lucky Bean, his momma would always be rooted in what she was. And so would he.

Looking up into the black gum, his eyes traced the larger branches that he'd climbed so often, to see if they'd changed, or broken off. Lifting the envelope from his back pocket, he lowered himself to the ground. He'd never thought to write Moses a letter for the captain to read aloud. Except to say that he was still alive and that he loved him, he'd said what he needed. Unfolding a single page of paper, he read the penciled script:

> *See Prof. Lilly bout sittin ma chair for learnin.*
> *Wid grate afection,*
> *Mr. Moses Henry*

Leaning back against the tree, he took a deep breath. Moses had shown him where he sat at the back of Cabell Hall. He'd said the hardest thing about an education was learning how to listen.

Standing up, he put the envelope in his pocket and began to climb. On the second branch he noticed green flowers at the base of new leaves and felt the rough, furrowed ridges of the trunk against his hands. Thirty feet higher, his sadness lifted. If Stick was dead, a part of him would be dead as well. But if trains were like rivers, he'd be on his way by now.

Grabbing hold of a large branch, he slid down against the trunk until he was able to sit comfortably. Looking out finally, he saw the city stretched out before him like a kind of miracle. It surprised him at first to see how the pockets of trees had given way to roads and houses, robbing the view of a certain softness he'd remembered. The Midway School was gone. Steel cranes rose up from Vinegar Hill like alien invaders slicing into the ground. Scanning farther beyond, he saw the farms and baseball fields on Pantops before the treetops over Lee Park exploded in a sudden burst of sun. The trolley cars were gone, replaced by buses, cars, and Pepsi trucks. But still, he thought, as a flock of purple martins touched down on Carter Mountain, it was the place that he belonged to and the place he'd missed the most.

On a late Sunday afternoon, Willie Graves looked out over the fractured roof of his new inheritance, past the burgeoning streets and billowing ice stacks into a rack of golden clouds moving ever closer towards the falling sun. Stick was out there somewhere—licking his wounds and waiting for the next train out. A hot shot whistled east of Preston Avenue as the two o'clock bell sounded from the university grounds. Moses had been right. When it came to the human heart, it was one thing to hear, but quite another to listen to its call. And as the bell drifted out over Albemarle County, he felt the wisdom of everyone he'd ever loved and the countless souls that he would meet along the way.

Notes

1. Psalm 119:77 *The Open Bible, New King James Version,* Thomas Nelson Publishers, 1983.

2. *The American Experience: Riding the Rails,* a film by Michael Uys and Lexy Lovell, 1997.

3. Stick's refrain from "Hoboes' Lullaby" by Bob 'Guitar Whitey' Symmonds.

4. *Webster's New World Dictionary, Second College Edition,* The World Publishing Company, 1976.

ABOUT THE AUTHOR

Peter Skinner is the author of *White Buffalo*, also published by Birch Brook Press. He is the father of three children and a stepson. He and his wife live in Virginia.